# A Haunting in
# MATTAPOISETT

*Richard Rezendes*

# CONTENTS

*A house on Route 6, 66 6th Street was built in the late 1960s, a two-story Cape Codder. It has a finished basement and a shed in the back and the house is on a two-acre lot. The town has a variety of hauntings that lead to this home. Which its homeowners will find out in this story, starting when the town real estate office, Arthur's Realtors, sold the house to a couple, three kids, a dog, and a cat.*

# ONE

## THE CHANGS

The Chang family is a Chinese American family and Lori is a fifteen-year-old, Bobby Chang is thirteen, and Xavier is ten. Tai Chang, their father, is forty-six years old and the mother Lynn Chang is forty-two. The dog is about four and it's a golden retriever and the cat Chee Chee is a kitten. Tai and Lynn were driving around looking for a house and one morning they stopped at Cerilli's Bakery/Restaurant for breakfast. They picked up a newspaper looking for homes and they called a number on a payphone outside the restaurant.

"Arthur's Realtors, Ruthy speaking."

"Hi this is Tai Chang, me and my wife Lynn are looking for a house. We have three kids, a dog, and a cat."

"Yes Mr. Chang I have what you're looking for. Drive down Route 6 and look for 66 6th Street, the house is right on Route 6, and I will meet you there at 2:00 p.m.," said Ruthy the realtor.

At 2:00 p.m. the couple was there and met the realtor. It was June 20, 1979.

"Are you Ruthy?"

"Yes you made it."

"I am Tai Chang and she's my wife, Lynn."

"Pleased to meet you. Please come in. This is the porch and this door leads to the kitchen; you have a brand-new refrigerator and electric stove. The next room is the dining room on the right with two windows. On the left is the living room with a corner fireplace and three windows.

The fireplace is real, you burn natural wood. The door at the bottom of the stairs is the front door going outside. The bathroom here on the right is your full bath. Down the hall we have two bedrooms on each side with plenty of closet space.

"Let's go upstairs. Straight ahead is a restroom with a toilet and sink. You have two bedrooms up here. The one on the left has two windows, closet, and attic storage; check it out you can put plenty of stuff in here. The room on the right is the master bedroom and you have three windows here and a big walk-in closet and another attic storage space and you have a small shoe closet on the other side.

"Come downstairs and I'll show you the basement. Down here is a built-up family room. You have washer and dryer hook ups and under the stairs you have wood storage and another real wood fireplace. You have a door that goes outside and on to the right you have hookups for a deep freezer and a stove and refrigerator. You also have a small restroom here with a sink, toilet, and walk-in shower.

"Come out to the backyard. You have a cement slab to put a picnic table on and a flower bed from the house to the end of the yard and a walkway leading out into the woods. You have a lot of tall trees here with plenty of shade on a warm day like today. On the right side of the yard you have a double shed. Up the ramp in here is a work shed with a work bench. Come outside, over here you have a walk-in shed for tools, and your lawnmower goes in here. Back here used to be an old farm years ago and now it's a big open field with vegetable beds. All the paths leading out in the woods are still part of your property.

"Let's go back inside, it's thundering. Here is the front yard by the way," said Ruthy.

"We like it very much and we want it," said Tai.

"Let's go inside and do the paperwork. The house and the land sells for $250,000," said Ruthy.

"That's a little over our budget. I was thinking $130,000, we have three kids," said Tai.

"Done, if you pay up front $65,000 down and the rest in six months," said Ruthy.

"It's a done deal!" said Tai.

Then the family started moving in—they had a lot of shit. A

twenty-two-wheeler pulled up, backing over the front lawn to start moving in through the living room. First comes a piano, then couches, then a TV, then a couple of recliners, tables, and lamps, then a stereo in the living room and a big center table, then comes the dining room set: a hutch, a table and six chairs, a Chinese china set. In the porch there was another recliner, a small table with two chairs, and a TV.

Then a twin bed set in the first-floor left side bedroom where the young girl will sleep, Xavier. Bureau, table, and lamp. The same furniture in the left bedroom for the boy, Bobby, age thirteen, plus he has three basketballs, two footballs, two soccer balls, five baseballs, twenty golf balls and a set of golf clubs, tennis rackets, a dozen tennis balls, and a bowling ball. He likes sports. The kids filled their closets with clothes. The boy also likes music and he has two guitars, a drum set, a keyboard, a trumpet, and two horns and a stereo in his room. All kinds of shit packed to the ceiling! Then the girl Lori Chang, age fifteen, slept upstairs and she had a full size bed, a double bureau loaded with clothes, her bras and undies hanging out of the drawers, two nightstands, two lamps, and posters of men on all the walls. And a small couch and chair in her room. The master bedroom had a queen bed, two nightstands, two lamps and two chairs, a stereo, and a small piano.

Then the truck backed up to the backyard in the pouring rain and got stuck in the mud. The kids, Tai and Lynn, had to carry the sit-down lawnmower to the shed, then carried rakes, shovels, boots, and all kinds of tools to put in the shed. While the shed was being filled the movers brought in a deep freezer, a stove, a refrigerator, a washer, and dryer. Then the kids set up a doghouse in the backyard, then a pool table complete with balls and sticks, a ping pong table, and another TV and a work sink to hook up.

It took the Changs three days to move all the shit they had. The last thing to unload was a snow blower. Then the truck had to be towed out of the mud.

Lynn was upstairs in the master bedroom and a black shadow moved from one side of the room to another. She didn't think anything of it, and she looked out the window and fast clouds were moving over the sun because a storm was on the way.

Lori Chang was in her room hanging clothes in her closet and the room darkened briefly then the sun came back out. A face that looked like the devil appeared in her bureau mirror, but she didn't see it. Then she went in the bathroom then she went downstairs to play music with her brother in his room.

Tai was in the living room playing the piano when suddenly he heard what sounded like wings flapping in the fireplace. He got up and he closed the glass doors on the fireplace. The next day he was installing air conditioners in the windows and he heard a hissing sound. Later he was raking the dirt driveway and he heard a sound like popcorn popping. He stopped then he continued.

Bobby was playing his guitar and recording on his tape deck and he heard a voice calling, *get out*! He continued playing and recording his music and he thought nothing of it. He stopped briefly then he continued playing.

Xavier Chang was playing outside with the dog Roxbury and she heard a growling noise and it was pretty loud and she ran in the house crying. "Mommy, Mommy, Mommy, there's a bear or something growling outside."

Tai and Lynn went looking for the animal and found nothing. The dog didn't even bark!

The cat in the house was acting strange in the new home, hiding all the time, coming out only at mealtime. She's only a kitten; the kids are calling and always looking for the cat. Xavier keeps calling for her. "Here Chee Chee, here Chee Chee. Here Chee Chee." But she's nowhere to be found. Sometimes when you move from one home to another animals act strange.

Tai was downstairs hooking up the washer and dryer and stove and refrigerator and deep freezer and he heard a baby crying in the cellar. He stopped to check around the basement and he found nothing.

He said to his wife, "Lynn, did you hear that? It sounds like a baby crying."

"No, I don't hear anything!"

"I think I may be hearing things because I'm very tired from trying to get things organized in this house."

Later Tai went upstairs to take a nap. He heard thunder but the sun was out, then he heard it again and he got up and he looked out the window and he saw dark clouds coming. He closed the window and he went and lay down for a while.

Lynn was making soup and breaking up a chicken and throwing vegetables in a big pot to make chicken soup. She saw a dark shadow briefly that caught her eye then a bright flash of lightning and a loud *bang*! "Lori, Bobby, and Xavier, close all the windows. A thunderstorm is coming."

Then she went to the kitchen to finish cooking the soup and she saw a black spot on the kitchen floor. When she went over to get a better look it was gone. "That's strange!" she said to herself, and the tea kettle went off and she moved the kettle off the burner and she turned it off.

Then she fed the kids dinner. "Come on kids it's dinner time!" She put the soup in dishes and gave it to her kids in soup bowls and she put warm bread just coming out of the oven on the tables for the kids to cut up and eat. Then she fed the cat and the dog outside. Then she saw a huge raccoon running across the yard out into the woods and the dog was barking at it, scaring it away. She gave the dog her food in the doghouse. Then she went in the house. It was still raining with flashes of lightning.

Tai came down from his nap and he grabbed a bowl of soup to eat with the kids. He said, "Lynn you left the burner on," and he shut it off.

"Oh my God, I thought I shut that off earlier!" Then she grabbed a bowl of soup and the family ate together. Then Lynn went to pour some tea and the burner was on again. And she turned it off. Then she brought the tea kettle and cups to the table and sat down to finish dinner and drinking tea.

Her hair stood straight up in the air and the three kids screamed, "Ahhhhhhhhhhhhhhhhh!!!!!!!!!!!!"

"Lynn don't be scared, it's from the lightning storm outside. Sometimes when there's lightning the electricity from the lightning will make your hair go straight up like a Christmas tree! I can feel it too," said Tai.

"I hope it doesn't hit me!" said Lynn.

"No, it's just the electricity from the storm. Lightning acts funny sometimes," said Tai. The kids laughed. Then *bang*! The loudest crack of thunder. "Lynn, I think it likes you," Tai joked.

Tai is a book author and Lynn is a nurse's aide and she goes to work in Wareham while Tai works from home. He has an Apple computer and typewriters and printing machines he works with in the basement.

Nighttime: The kids had their showers and then Tai and Lynn had theirs then everyone was in bed. It was still raining hard outside.

Around 3:00 a.m. everyone was sleeping, and a big black mass appeared in the master bedroom where Tai and Lynn sleep and Lynn could feel something like gravity pulling her. It was the big black mass drawing energy from her and she woke up out of a sound sleep and the black mass disappeared when she woke up. She didn't see it and she got up to go to the bathroom and then she put the air conditioner on and she walked around the room and she went back to bed. Tai woke up briefly and he lay down and went back to sleep.

Xavier woke up to go to the bathroom at 4:00 a.m. and she heard an animal growling and she screamed! "Ahhhhhhhhhhhhhhh!" Lynn woke up hearing her scream. "Mommy, Mommy! I hear that bear outside again!"

"Go back to bed Xavier and Daddy will go out and find it."

Tai got up and he grabbed his shotgun and he went out in the back-yard looking for the growling animal and nothing was out there. "Don't worry Xavier, if something is out there the dog will get it or she'll start barking."

"I heard it nearby Daddy."

"Whatever you heard it's gone now; it may be a passing raccoon." Then everyone went back to bed.

The next day Lynn went to work, and the kids were in summer camp and Tai was at home mowing the lawn. He heard a loud roar coming from the woods when he put the riding lawnmower away. He went in the house and he grabbed his shotgun and he went out in the woods looking for what sounded like a bear. He saw a raccoon running in the woods, but that growling noise was not a raccoon. He looked all around his property looking for a possible bear because it sounded like the roaring of a bear! He walked around the shed and he cocked his gun and he saw nothing. He went in the upper shed to look around and he saw nothing.

Then he started trimming the bushes and watering the flowers then he heard the growls again. He had his dog Roxbury walking beside him; she didn't even bark, which is unusual. He went to the shed to get his gun and went back out in the woods with the dog this time and he saw nothing. Then he grabbed a tall ladder and he went up on the roof to find out where the growl was coming from and he found nothing. The dog was looking out at the woods and she started barking. Tai came down from the roof and he put the ladder away and he grabbed his shotgun and he went back out in the woods to the end of his property and the dog Roxbury was with him.

"What's out there Roxbury?"

The dog looked at Tai and then straight ahead! Tai and the dog walked all the way to the water and then back to the house and he saw nothing. The only animals were a red-tailed hawk and a couple of seagulls. After finishing up in the yard he went in the house through the finished basement. He called Arthur's Realtors.

"Hi, this is Tai Chang calling from 66 6th Street, the new people who bought the house. I have been hearing loud growls coming from the woods. My daughter has heard them too and I know it's coming from the woods in back of my house!"

"What kind of growls?" asked the realtor.

"It sounds like a bear or a wild animal or a wolf maybe!" said Tai.

"That's strange! We have raccoons, coyotes, and bobcats, but I never heard of a bear in Mattapoisett. We will check it out," said the realtor.

"Thanks a lot," said Tai.

Around 4:00 p.m. the kids came home from summer camp and they went for a journey in the woods and the branches on the trees started moving in all kinds of directions, like if they were walking. But the kids kept walking through the woods and came up to a blueberry patch and started picking the blueberries and came home with a bunch of them. The kids never noticed that the woods on their property were haunted.

"Look at all these blueberries, we'll bring them home so Mom can make some pies!" said Lori.

"Ah! That's cool!" said Bobby.

"Look here! Raspberries too! And rhubarb!" said Xavier.

The kids brought a bunch of blueberries home. "Mommy, Mommy, we have blueberries, raspberries, and rhubarb we found in the woods!" said Xavier.

"Oh my goodness, where did you find all that!?"

"Out in the woods Mom!" said Lori.

"Can you make pies with these Mommy?" asked Xavier.

"Sure, go out and fill this bowl and I'll make some pies. Let me wash these and go out and get some more just make sure you don't go in someone else's yard."

"Okay Mom," said Lori.

Then the kids went out to fill the bowl with blueberries, raspberries, and rhubarb and brought them home. A big black mass of shadow appeared in the woods behind them, watching the kids leave and the branches on the trees started moving again like hands trying to grab, but the three Chang children didn't notice. The black mass vanished, and the rotating tree branches stopped when the kids exited the woods and they brought lots of berries in the house, washing them, and Lynn fixed supper and then made some pies. Blueberry, raspberry, and rhubarb. Lynn cooked a roast. Mashed potatoes with peas and carrots for dinner, and the pies for dessert. Tai sat down to eat and the kids told them about their day.

"Daddy we found all kinds of berries in the woods, blueberries, raspberries, and rhubarb, and Mommy's making some pies," said Xavier.

Lynn sat down to eat and Tai was chopping up the roast and feeding the kids. Then Lynn was serving the potatoes and vegetables.

"Children listen to me. Don't go out in the woods unless we go together. There is something out there! It's some animal roaring out there. I don't know what it is because I can't find it, it sounds like either a bear or a wolf. I heard it earlier today when I was cutting the lawn and watering the flowers."

"Daddy, it's the same growls I heard last night!"

"I heard the same thing Xavier."

Later, after the pies were made, Tai and Lynn had a bowling league to go to while Lori was babysitting the kids. Fairhaven Bowling Lanes. Tai and Lynn got their bowling balls out of their locker, ready for bowling, and while they were bowling with their team Tai was telling them about the growls.

"It's something growling out in the woods out in back of my house. I don't know if it's a bear or a wolf. My little daughter heard it too. She thought it was coming from inside the house."

"You never heard about the Greenman haunting the woods in Mattapoisett?" said one of his teammates.

"No, we do not believe in that stuff!" said Tai and Lynn.

"The Greenman is a male possessed by the devil and if you come in contact with him it will make your life miserable. Some people see it and some people don't and if you challenge it, it can kill you. Some people see shadows, and some see the green ghost! If you see it, don't make eye contact because if you do it will come after you!" said the teammate.

Tai and Lynn laughed.

"If you don't believe me you will see!" said the teammate.

Tai bowled six strikes in a row for a 248 game and he bowled a 600 series for the night and their team won. After bowling they went to the snack bar and then had a drink together before leaving the bowling alley.

The kids had their showers and went to bed. Lori saw a bright green flash of lightning outside and there was no thunder. She looked out the window and it was dark. Roxbury was outside, then she went in the dog-house. Tai and Lynn came home from bowling a little late.

"Mom and Dad, did you see the green lightning; it lit the sky so bright! But there was no thunder?" said Lori.

Lynn put her hand over her mouth because she was shocked at what Lori saw. She pulled all the shades down and later everyone was in bed. 3:00 a.m., Bobby woke hearing something moving in his room. He woke up hearing the wind blowing outside and he got up and he saw the tree branches blowing in the wind. Roxbury started barking for a minute then the wind stopped, and she went back into the doghouse. Bobby was looking out of the window then he closed the shade then he went back to bed. He heard something moving in the room again like someone moving something heavy. He got up and he turned on a lamp and the cat ran out of the room.

He called, "Come Chee Chee, come Chee Chee." The cat ran back into Bobby's bedroom and she jumped up on his bed. Bobby turned the light off and he went to bed. The cat slept at the foot of his bed. Then he felt the bed move, then he heard a thump and Chee Chee went *meow!* He woke up and he turned the light on the lamp and the wind was blowing hard again outside at 4:30 a.m. in the morning. The cat was still at the foot of Bobby's bed and he looked under the bed then it started thundering pretty loud outside the cat ran out of the room to go hide somewhere, the cat is scared of thunder. Then Bobby went back to sleep.

Lynn got the kids up about 7:30 a.m. in the morning for breakfast. Bobby had Cocoa Puffs cereal, Xavier had Fruit Loops, Lori had a bowl of cornflakes, and Lynn had Cheerios. There was orange juice chocolate milk, and Lynn had coffee. Then the kids went to summer camp and Lynn went to work.

It was pouring rain and Tai was sleeping. He had a dream that a tornado hit the house and he got sucked out into the funnel holding part of the roof, flying through the sky going around the tornado like a merry-go-round, flying higher and higher. Then he heard the loudest bang of thunder, waking him out of a sound sleep, and he fell out of bed screaming! "Help!!!!!!!!!!!!!!!!!!!!!!!!!!!!!!!!!!!!!!!!!!!!!!!!!!!!!"

In reality he saw a bright flash of lightning followed by another loud *bang!* Then it was over. Tai was crawling on the floor trying to get his senses realizing it's only a dream. He said to himself, "It's only a dream! This is the second time I had this dream."

He sat on the floor thinking back when the family moved from West Chester, Pennsylvania where a tornado blew the roof off of his house, they'd put on a new one. He and his family were away on a camping vacation; they had just left the house in the morning instead of the next day. Before that high winds blew all the windows out of that same house. Tai was the only one home that day and he ran to the basement to safety.

Back in the present, he got up and he got dressed and he went downstairs to make breakfast. He had scrambled eggs, toast, bacon, pancakes, sausage, orange juice, and coffee. Then he heard a *thump* followed by another loud *thump!* Then he saw the fireplace doors wide open and he saw what looked like dark gray and black smoke coming out of the fireplace while he was washing the dishes.

"What the hell is going on here?!" He went and closed the glass doors on the fireplace, and he opened the windows and the front door and the smoke went out and disappeared! It is not what he thinks it is; the smoke was a ghost passing through! He called a chimney cleaning crew to come and clean the fireplaces. The house smelled like smoke. Then the Rex Chimney cleaning crew came.

"You need your fireplaces cleaned. How many do you have?" said the cleaning crew.

"I have two: this one in the living room and one in the basement."

"My name is Eddy Edwards and this is Joel Monteiro."

"Pleased to meet you, my name is Tai Chang."

"Did you hear we had a tornado warning earlier this morning about 8:30 a.m.? A waterspout went right up the Cape Cod Canal?"

"Oh my God, I didn't hear the news yet today, but I had a dream last night that I was in one; it was one of the worst nightmares I ever had. It was during a thunderstorm that knocked me out of bed! In my forty-eight years of life I never had a dream like last night," said Tai.

"Well we will start from the roof and will empty all the ash boxes."

"Eddy, do you think the wind from last night caused all this? I heard *thump, thump* and the fireplace doors popped open and there was black soot everywhere, and the house filled up with smoke and I had to open all the windows and doors to get it all out?" said Tai.

"Absolutely!" said the workers. The workers spent a couple of hours cleaning the fireplaces. Tai was downstairs printing pages on his computer and typewriters. "Mr. Chang, your fireplaces are immaculate! We found no soot or ash, all the boxes are clean, no smell of smoke. These fireplaces are very clean! It's sixty-two dollars and you're all set," said the chimney cleaning crew and then they left.

Tai put a piece of wood through the handles on the fireplaces' glass doors to keep them shut. Later in the day he was working downstairs and his computer was turning on and off and he lost all his documents. A few minutes later everything came back. He checked all the cables connecting to his computer and some of them were loose, so he tightened them and he was printing copies off the computer. Then he heard a scratching sound in the house, and he went to investigate and he found nothing. He put his ear against a wall, and he heard nothing. Then he finished getting printed copies off his computer and a black rolling mass moved across the basement ceiling. Then he could smell something like a dead animal, and he got up and opened the outside door to get the smell out of the house and the black mass went up the basement fireplace and the smell went away. He opened windows then the smell of flowers came in the house because the garden is nearby. He never saw that black mass that came in for a visit. Then he went looking for the dead animal he could smell earlier inside and outside the house and he found nothing! Then he went back to the computer to finish what he was doing. After finishing all the prints, a voice came over his computer speakers, *get out!*

He laughed and he shut the computer off and he went upstairs. Then the kids came home from summer camp and his wife came home after that.

She cooked dinner and Tai took the kids to the beach for a while because it was a hot day. The dog was barking up a storm for a while looking up in the air because a black mass was flying over the doghouse. Lynn looked out the window and she saw nothing. The cat jumped up on the counter where she was cooking and she put the cat down and fed her, then she fed the dog.

Later Tai and the three kids came home from the beach. Lynn said, "Tai, how was your day today?"

"It was a strange day for me. I don't believe in haunted houses, but some strange things happened to me today! First I was making my breakfast and when I finished eating I heard a thumping noise and a suction of wind. Then the fireplace doors popped open and dark gray smoke came out and I had to open all the doors and windows to let it out and I called the chimney cleaning company. To clean the fireplaces cost sixty-two dollars and they told me the fireplaces were very clean and the ash boxes were empty. Then my computers kept going on and off, then I smelled a bad odor and I searched the house for a dead animal and found nothing. The bad smell went away and when I aired out the basement; the smell of fresh flowers drove it away."

"Tai, that's very chilling, maybe something is haunting us," said Lynn.

"Daddy, I heard that thumping noise in my room last night," said Xavier.

"It doesn't appear to be a scary situation, but I have been hearing some strange things around this house. We had a tornado warning during the night; that explains why something went through the fireplace, but everything is okay."

"I heard about that when I was going to work this morning. A waterspout did some damage in Cape Cod!" said Lynn. Then Lynn put dinner on the table.

The phone rang and Tai answered then the phone went dead, and he hung up. Lynn cooked a ham dinner. Later the kids sat down to watch

TV and Tai went for a walk in the woods and he didn't see anything strange. The hauntings went away for a few days, but it will be back stronger later on.

Saturday morning Tai and Lynn went to Cerilli's restaurant up the street to meet people for breakfast while the kids were home watching TV and playing videogames. Two more Chinese couples were there talking about the ghosts in Mattapoisett.

"Good morning, Mindi and Tua Chi and Mel and Linda Wechee," said Tai and Lynn Chang. Tai and Lynn were talking about the strange happenings at their house.

"Mr. and Mrs. Chang, welcome to Mattapoisett. You haven't seen nothing yet. You have a nice house but it's been vacant for at least five years, nobody has lived there. I don't know the reason why that house has been vacant so long but we have a lot of strange history in this town.

"It's a beautiful town; there's lots of nice places here. We have some nice beaches, Ned's Point Light House, the Mattapoisett Inn hotel across from Shipyard Park and the town beach. Harbour Beach is not far from where you live, and neither is Oxford Creamery, one of the best seafood places to eat. There are a lot of private areas, but it's a quiet town. However, there are many hauntings here.

"There's a story about a UFO that landed here sometime between the late 1920s and the 1930s and a mysterious Greenman appeared here and he has haunted Mattapoisett since then. Other people say it was witchcraft bringing the spirit from the dead, while some say it was the devil rising from hell under Cape Cod. The Greenman has been spotted at Ned's Point, Harbour Beach, and some private woods and wetlands not far where you live! The Greenman has been known to have power over you and if you see it, keep your distance and run as fast as you can and get away because if it catches you, whatever happened to it will happen to you. A lot of bad things have happened from this so-called Greenman. It's an evil spirit, mostly visible late at night," said Tua, one of their friends at Cerilli's.

"My daughter saw a flash of green lightning the other night while we were at our bowling league in Fairhaven. Someone on our bowling league was telling us the story about the Greenman," said Lynn.

"That green flash is the Greenman trying to make contact with you.

Keep your shades and curtains closed. As long as you don't make eye contact you will be okay," said Tua.

"Can this Greenman kill you?" asked Lynn.

"I don't know much about it but I did hear if you challenge it, it can attack you by burning you as it goes through you or inside your soul. The burning sensation is not known to be worse than a jellyfish sting because it's known to be coming from the sea. The Greenman is not the biggest threat in Mattapoisett; it's devil witchcraft that was practiced here in the 1600s. There are spirits here that are not at rest and attack certain areas. If your house is haunted you're more likely to be haunted by these spirits as well as the Greenman. If the Greenman shows up you will not miss it; it stands about ten feet high and gives off a bright vision. Sometimes it's very dull when he's not active, but when he's bright you better run for your life the other way!" said Tua.

"Tua, have you ever seen anything of these strange sights here?" said Tai.

"The only thing I saw the five years I have been living here was a big black moving shadow crossing Route 6 at the Salty Seahorse. Right outside this restaurant on the left-hand side, you'll see it on your way home. I was coming home from the bowling alley at 1:00 a.m. when I saw it in the headlights."

"Tua, what did it look like?" asked Lynn.

"It looked like a black rolling fog running across the street. I think I drove through it!"

"Mindi, did you see it?" asked Lynn.

"Yes I did!"

"Mel and Linda, have you seen anything haunting here in Mattapoisett?" asked Lynn.

"No, just Mel when he's naked," said Linda.

After Tai and Lynn went home after breakfast, Lynn cleaned up the house and the kids were outside playing with the dog then they went to pick more blueberries in the woods. The cat was on the windowsill looking out at the kids playing. Tai was outside cutting the lawn and Lori brought a big bowl of blueberries for Mom to make more pies.

"Xavier and Bobby, come in for lunch."

The Chang family sat down for a bowl of soup and some blueberry pie and then they went to the beach for the day. The kids were playing in the water and Tai and Lynn were lying in the sun. A lady came over to them and she said, "Excuse me. I'm sorry to bother you but you people are in great danger!"

Lynn looked at her and she said, "Miss, I think you're talking to the wrong person."

"I'm Maria Cooper. I am here to inform you that an evil entity is coming for you and your family I don't mean to scare you but I am here to protect you."

"Excuse me miss, but we're trying to enjoy a nice day at the beach with our kids so why don't you get lost!" said Tai.

As the woman walked away she disappeared into thin air while Tai and Lynn watched in shock! Lynn went over to the lifeguard and she asked, "Do you know that girl talking to us?"

"What girl?!"

"The girl in the black bathing suit," said Lynn.

"There's no girl here with a black bathing suit," said the lifeguard.

"Never mind."

Then Lynn went back to her husband and she said, "Did you see that girl Tai? It appeared that she disappeared while walking away!"

"Yes, I did. I thought it was strange, maybe it was a ghost!" Tai laughed.

Lynn said to this girl lying next to her at the beach, "Did you see that girl in the black bathing suit talking to us?"

"No, but I did see you talking to yourself," the girl said.

Later Tai, Lynn, and the kids left the beach and they went to Oxford Creamery for dinner and to get ice cream after before going home before dark. They fed the dog and cat and Bobby was playing music in his room then the girls were playing games and Tai and Lynn were playing cards. Later everyone had some blueberry pie and milk before going to bed. The next day they got up to go to church. Then later they had a cookout in the backyard, eating hamburgers and hotdogs, and family and friends came over. The next day was Monday and Lynn went to work and the kids went to summer camp. Tai was home working on his books and the hauntings stayed away for a while.

August 1979 Hurricane David brought strange creatures up the coasts. The storm blew out some windows and knocked a tree down in the yard.

Tai cut the tree up in tiny pieces to use for firewood this coming winter and stored the wood in back of the lower shed. Then he boarded up the windows until they could get replaced. A few days after the storm passed new windows were installed. Lynn was working and the kids were still going to summer camp. The storm dumped jelly fish on the lawn and fish landing in the trees and dead birds in the yard one morning when he noticed after the kids left for summer camp and Lynn going to work as the hauntings are returning.

The dog Roxbury stayed in her doghouse, barking up a storm. Tai came out of the house one morning and he saw fish hanging from the trees and birds everywhere eating the fish. Jellyfish lay in the grass and birds were eating them and the jellyfish were stinging the birds, leaving them dead in the yard. Tai could not believe what he was seeing. Portuguese man o' war were moving across the lawn like injured animals and some were hanging from trees like dripping paint as the birds were eating them. Then bats arrived and giant vultures joined the feast before being stung by the jelly-fish and landing dead in the Changs' yard at 66 6th Street.

Tai didn't know what to do! Not much later, thousands of seagulls arrived to come eat the fish the storm blew in and get stung to death by the jellyfish. Some fish and jellies landed on his roof. The dog was barking for hours! Tai called the police.

"Mattapoisett police department, Officer Truesdale speaking."

"Hi, this is Tai Chang calling from 66 6th Street. Something strange is happening at my house. There are fish, jellyfish, and thousands of birds in my yard. I have never seen anything like this! Some are hanging from the trees and landing on my house!"

"I know; there have been a few complaints here in town. It was caused by the storm. Call Mahoney's Hardware to come and burn them and the animal rescue crew will remove them. The birds will do a pretty good job getting rid of the fish. Just stay away from them until they come," said the police.

The environmental team arrived with blowtorches to burn the jelly-fish and the dead fish and birds laying in the yard. The fire department hosed down the fish, birds, and jellies off the roof. By the time they came, the seagulls had polished up most of the mess.

A few minutes later Roxbury stepped on a live jellyfish. *Yelp! Yelp!*

*Yelp! Yelp! Yelp!* As the dog was screeching, she lay near dead in front of her doghouse being stung by a Portuguese man o' war!

The kids came home from summer camp. Lori said, "What's going here?"

Tai said, "Go in the house, we were attacked by a sudden storm."

Then at that minute Roxbury was stung by the jellyfish. The kids started screaming and crying! Xavier watched Roxbury get tortured and lit up by the big jellyfish! Bobby saw it too and they cried hysterically! Tai cried as he saw the dog die as well. Lynn came home early and she saw fire trucks at the house and men going around with blowtorches burning dead birds and jellyfish while workers were raking the mess into wheelbarrows and hauling them away in a dump truck. Then the yard was watered down before dark and the dead dog was removed. The firemen hosed down the house and the mess was removed.

"Lynn, I believe that we might be haunted because I never heard of sea creatures invading our yard. The police said the remnants from Hurricane David uprooted fish and jellyfish from the ocean and dumped them into neighborhoods. This has happened before in Mattapoisett but not like this. Poor Roxbury was killed by a stinging jellyfish!"

The family cried and mourned over this dog! Tai said to the kids, "This is not a haunting, it's a problem all over town. An unusual rainstorm spun up a waterspout sucking fish out of the ocean near Ned's Point, dumping fish in neighborhoods. We live near Ned's Point; that is why we got the worst of the dumping. I picked up quite a few fish that we will be having for dinner tonight out in the yard. Tomorrow we will go to the Fairhaven dog pound and get another dog. You do realize that Roxbury was a sick dog and she wasn't going to last too much longer. It's too bad it happened this way, but we will get over it! Our house is not haunted. It's a new home; we've been here for a couple of months; it's going to take time to get used to. You will hear noises because we live in a quiet town not the city anymore. Let's have some nice fried fish Hurricane David left us. After dinner do not go outside in case there's more jellyfish lying around because you may get stung; that's how Roxbury was killed," said Tai.

The night went okay with no hauntings. The fish was delicious! The next day it was a late August cloudy rainy day and Tai got up at 6:00 a.m.

to patch all the burn marks, digging up parts of the lawn with a rake and putting new seed down in the rain. Then he went inside to have breakfast with Lynn and the kids before Lynn went to work and the kids went off to summer camp on the Cape. Tai went back outside to finish fixing up the yard. Then he went downstairs and worked on his computer, then the doorbell rang, *ching chong chang!* Tai went to the door.

"Hey bud, do you remember me? Roy Chung. Tua Chi's friend from Cerilli's!"

"Yes, I do! Come on in. Can I get you a cup of coffee?" asked Tai.

While having coffee Tai was telling Roy about the strange happenings in the house. "You know Roy, I don't believe in haunted houses, but since we moved in some strange shit has been happening. Check this out on my computer. Mega storm dumps fish from the ocean into Fairhaven and Mattapoisett neighborhoods!"

"I saw that on the news, it was a freak tornado or waterspout. It was the second one we had in the last week or so," said Roy.

"That's not all. I heard growls from a wild animal and when I went to investigate, bringing my gun into the woods, I never found the animal; I guess it knew I was coming. The thing that really freaked me out—I was at the beach last weekend with my wife and kids and this lady came over, telling us that we were in great danger and an evil spirit was coming. I told her to get lost and she turned around and she walked away. Suddenly she disappeared in thin air right in front of our faces. She was a pretty thin girl, Portuguese or Italian with a black bathing suit, and her eyes looked black. My wife Lynn asked questions if anybody had seen her on the beach and we were told there was no girl on the beach with a black bathing suit on. She identified herself as Maria Cooper. I checked her out on the computer, and she was listed as the Mattapoisett beach ghost! Then one day it was the day the waterspout went up the Cape Cod Canal—I guess it was last week. I was making breakfast and I heard *thump, thump!* Then the living room fireplace doors popped open and strange dark soot came out filling the house up with smoke! I had to open all the windows and doors to let it all out and call the fireplace cleaning crew to clean my fireplaces. And they told me it was clean, no smoke or soot. I thought that was strange. Other than that I heard a few strange noises, but that was it!"

"Tai, let me tell you about the Mattapoisett Beach ghost," said Roy.

"Hold that thought I got to go for a pee!" Tai went to the bathroom and Roy was sitting near the computer. A voice came to him. *"Get out!!!!!!!!!!!"*

When Tai came back out Roy said, "Did you just hear that?"

"Hear what!"

"A voice came from your computer telling me to get out!"

"I heard that a few times, it always says that."

"Tai, it might mean something. Getting back to the beach ghost. Her name is Maria Cooper and she was killed on the beach by a mysterious force back in the 1700s known to be the Greenman. The Greenman is a story of trees coming alive from the swamps. Strange bacteria from the swamps and the saltwater forms energy from storms at sea washing fish or live small animals or insects into tree roots, making them come alive. The Greenman is visible just before or after a big storm. There are so many legends about the Greenman; some are good and some are evil. The Mattapoisett beach ghost comes to people at the beach warning people that danger is coming and she's there for protection from the Greenman," said Roy.

"I told that Maria to get lost, and she walked away and she somehow disappeared."

"That could be a problem Tai because you told her to leave."

Roy kept telling Tai about ghost stories in Mattapoisett. Later the kids came home from summer camp and Tai took them to get another dog at the dog pound. Lynn came home to get dinner ready and there was no electricity and the power was out.

Fairhaven Dog Pound. Tai walked in with the kids and there were no dogs, just cats.

"Can I help you?" asked the animal shelter manager.

"Yes, we're looking for a dog, but you only have cats here!" said Tai.

"We only have one dog left if you don't mind adopting a Shih Tzu-bulldog mix."

"Can we see it?" asked Tai.

"Here she is. Her name is Susu, an easy name to remember. S-u-s-u," spelled the manager.

"It's a cutie Daddy, let's get it!" said Xavier.

Tai got the dog and he signed the papers. "This dog is classified as a miniature bulldog/ Shih Tzu/ a bull shitter," said the manager.

Tai took the dog home and the kids had fun playing with her. Lori and Bobby got a good laugh over the strange dog. They brought the dog in the house and fed it and the kids were playing with the dog and it was chasing the cat all over the house. The dog was a good fit for the kids but it does not appear that it likes cats. The cat was hissing at the dog. And the dog had to go in the doghouse. When the dog was chasing the cat it gave the cat a pretty good bite!

"Bobby, take the dog out to the doghouse, she's getting a little too rough with Chee Chee," said Tai. Bobby chained the dog outside and she kept barking and it wouldn't stop! After dinner Bobby had to go get the dog to be with the kids. Later Lori took the dog for a walk.

"What did you get Tai, a baby bulldog?" asked Lynn.

"It's a Shih Tzu-bulldog mix, a bull shitter," said Tai.

Lynn got a good laugh and she said, "It's a cute little thing and she loves the kids!"

Lynn had to close the cat in their bedroom so the dog didn't tear it apart. Bobby put a doggy bed in his room for Susu. Bedtime. Bobby played with the dog and he put her in the doggy bed and he went to bed. The dog laid quietly late at night

Lynn woke up and she looked at the alarm clock and the time was 3:02 a.m. She got up to go to the bathroom, but she left the door open and the cat ran out and ran down the stairs into Xavier's bedroom and hid under her bed. Later that night Bobby heard *thump thump meow!!!* Susu attacked Chee Chee, biting her head off, and there was blood everywhere in front of the fireplace in the living room. The dog was standing over her. Lynn heard the cat screeching and she went downstairs, turning on a lamp, and she saw her cat decapitated lying in a pool of blood.

At the same time Bobby was calling the dog. "Come Susu, come Susu, come Susu."

She screamed hysterically, "Ahhhhhhhhhhhhhhhhhh!!"

Xavier got up and she saw the dead cat and she was screaming and crying hysterically. Then Bobby got up and he saw what happened and Susu came to him waggling her tail, her tongue hanging out with blood still dripping out of her mouth. Then Lori and Tai came downstairs. Lori threw up while Tai grabbed the dog and tied her up outside as she was barking up a storm! Tai went to the shed and he grabbed his shotgun and he cocked it twice and blasted two shots to Susu's head and the dog was blown into pieces! It was body parts and fur everywhere! Then Tai picked up the pieces and he threw them into the woods and he hosed down the blood at five o'clock in the morning. He buried the cat in the backyard behind the shed and he put a cross on the burial site. Lynn was up all night cleaning up the cat's blood and Lori's puke!

The Mattapoisett Beach ghost warned Tai and Lynn that they were in danger and by telling her to get lost now the bad things are starting to happen. The kids and parents couldn't sleep for the rest of the night and had sleepless nights for the next three days.

"Kids, we got a bad dog! That's why the shelter had one dog, because nobody wanted it. Who would want a bull shitter for a dog; it had the devil in it, this dog? She killed our favorite cat! Chee Chee was only a kitten. I will get you another cat or two cats, but not a dog and a cat so this doesn't happen again! Uncle Ben Tua has a brown and white cat Lacy he wants to give away. I will talk to him tomorrow. We're going to get another cat or dog, not one of each. Whatever you want either a cat or dog. So kids make your choice! You want a cat or dog?" asked Tai.

The next day Uncle Ben Tua brought them a cat.

September 1979. The kids were in school and Tai was on a business trip. He flew in a 747 out of Boston to Germany for a national book convention because he's a book publisher. He's away for two weeks, until the middle of September. Lori is a sophomore at Old Rochester Regional High School. Bobby is in the eighth grade at the middle school and Xavier is in the fifth grade at St. Anthony's Catholic School in Mattapoisett.

One day Lynn was home all by herself dusting furniture in the living room when suddenly a jet-black mass formed, rolling across the ceiling. It was as black as the ace of spades and she saw hands and faces forming in the black mass and arms trying to grab her. She opened the windows and the front door trying to push what she thought was smoke but it would not leave. Then a devilish looking head formed and she found herself pinned to the couch and she couldn't move or scream for help, watching these hands and arms trying to grab her, and faces appeared, making strange noises! Then a mean looking devilish creature with red eyes, horns, and sharp teeth was blowing cold air on her and it made the loudest growl, worse than a bear. It opened its mouth, threatening to eat her, until she was ready to have a heart attack watching in shock. She couldn't move or speak as the black mass was working itself into her soul!

The doorbell rang. *Ching chong chang!* The black mass quickly disappeared! Lynn quickly answered the door on the porch. "Hi Lynn, it's Ruthy the realtor. I have a couple of things to go over with you."

"Before you say another word, I have a bone to pick with you! I have a demon in my house! I'm not signing any more papers and I'm out of here and I want my money back! We have nothing more to say!"

"What do you mean a demon?" asked Ruthy.

"Come in and see for yourself! I was dusting and moving furniture when I heard a noise in the fireplace then the room filled up what looked like black ink dripping on a piece of paper and it got bigger. I thought it was smoke coming from the fireplace so I opened the doors and windows trying to get the smoke out of the house and it would not leave and it got thicker until it pinned me to the couch. I couldn't move, and hands and arms came out of this black thing, then I saw a face that looked like the devil trying to grab me. Then the face looked like a mean animal with red eyes and horns and a mouth like a great white shark and it growled at me and it was trying to eat me until you rang the doorbell. I was able to get up and answer the door and this black thing vanished!" said Lynn.

"Where did you see this?" asked Ruthy.

"I saw it right here on the ceiling and it came down trying to get me. I couldn't scream, move, or do anything and it felt like it went through me!"

"Okay Lynn I will call Father Finn from St. Anthony's church to bless the house and whatever you saw will go away!"

"Ruthy, you do what you got to do because I'm out of here!" said Lynn.

Later the kids came home from school and Lynn was sitting outside. Bobby and Lori came home first, and Lynn said, "We're not staying here anymore we have a demon in our house. An evil ghost was trying to kill me this morning; this house is evil and we have to get out of here!" Lynn told the kids what happened to her that morning and related the message to Xavier when she came home.

Lynn called her friend Tua from the bowling league and told him what happened and he was shocked and he said, "The Greenman creature may have found you."

Lynn said, "Go in the house and get what you need because we're staying at the Mattapoisett Inn until we find another place to live."

The next night she went to her bowling league and told her teammates what happened. The following weekend a group of people from the bowling league helped move everything out of the house and put it in storage. Lynn hired a lawyer to go after Arthur's Realtors while they stayed with Tua's family in Marion.

Tai knows nothing about what happened because he was away in Germany.


*'Flashback,'*

*While flying before landing in Germany, Tai was sleeping when suddenly he heard a voice from the Mattapoisett beach ghost on the plane, about 3:00 a.m.*

"Tai this is Maria Cooper warning you, a demon is going after Lynn and then your kids, pervading them with evil. When you get home it's going to get you!" *Then a gray fog flew over him and the vision vanished.*

*Tai got up looking around in the plane and the flight attendant said, "Sir you need to be seated and seatbelt fastened because we're getting ready to land." The time of his vision was when Lynn was being overtaken by the evil spirit in their home.*


Lynn's and Tai's friends moved everything out of the house and shed to put in storage then Lynn's lawyer came to the house and Lynn let him in when the house was emptied. The lawyer was in the basement and he heard a voice coming from a fireplace, *get out!!* Then he went outside and he saw branches moving on the trees out in the woods and there was no wind. Then he saw a black round mass that had yellow eyes rolling across the yard. He jumped back to get out of its way. Then he saw something black moving in the woods and the branches were still moving in different directions as the lawyer was outside taking pictures.

He said, "Lynn, you better leave, there is something evil going on here." Then the lawyer went back in the house as it was getting dark. He had a flashlight with him and he searched the basement. Then he went upstairs looking around in the rooms, then he went up to the master bedroom looking around, and the door slammed shut in the spare room. He quickly ran downstairs. Then he clearly heard a voice in the living room. *Get out!!!!!!!!!!!!!!!!!!!!!!!!!!!!!!!* Loud and clear!

The lawyer went out the front door and he left. He heard what sounded like someone throwing something at him, but it missed. He got in his car and he left. Lynn and her three kids went to stay with the Tua family in Marion, Massachusetts. 3:00 a.m. the burglar alarm and fire alarms were going off, alerting the police and fire department to the house at 66 6th Street. The police came, then fire trucks arrived, and no one was home! The Mattapoisett police checked all the doors and they were locked so they had to force open a window to get in the house and reset the alarm. And they let the fire department in the house and the house was full of smoke, but they couldn't smell smoke, then this rotten smell of death came upon them! The stink was unbelievable!

The firemen said to the police, "Something is dead in here!" The firemen reset the fire alarms and the police were searching the house. The police were upstairs and the firemen were in the basement. The firemen found nothing wrong with the house but the fog in the house is strange. The police shined the flashlight in the fireplace and heard something growling and a voice, *Get out!!!* The police and firemen got spooked and ran out of the house. The police wrote up a report at the police station. There's no fire but something was dead in the fireplace, an animal in the chimney.

One officer said, "I clearly heard a voice in the living room at that house telling me to get out. We found smoke in the house but it smelled like something dead."

Another cop said, "That house has been haunted for years. I hope you took the batteries out of the smoke detectors in case they go off again!"

The other officers said, "No!"

Sure enough an hour later they went off again. The same officers with guns drawn went to the house to silence the smoke detectors and the house alarm. The voice was heard once again, *get out!!!* The police and firemen left. The next day the fire department and Rex Chimney cleaning crew came to get the trapped dead animal stuck in the chimney at 66 6th Street and found nothing.

Things were going well at the book expo in Germany and Tai flew home early. He called his wife when he got to Boston and the phone was disconnected. "You got to be kidding!" he said to himself.

He called again and again! The same thing, no answer. Then he drove home to Mattapoisett. When he got to the house he went in with his house keys and the house was empty. "What the fuck!" he said to himself and he walked through the house and he heard *get out!* Then he heard it again, *get out!!* Then he left the house and he drove to Tua Chi's house in Marion.

He rang the doorbell. Tua answered. "Tai! I'm glad to see you back! We had an emergency! Lynn was chased out of your house by a demon! She's in the other room." Lynn was surprised by his early arrival and she jumped into his arms!

"What's the matter Lynn? What happened?" said Tai.

"I was attacked by a demon in our home last week. After the kids went to school, I was moving and dusting furniture when I saw a big black cloud covering the ceiling making strange noises. I thought it was smoke coming from the fireplace so I opened the windows and doors to let it out and the black cloud started spinning me around until I landed in the couch and I couldn't move or scream for help. Then I saw hands, arms, and faces trying to grab me then I saw a head with horns, red eyes, and a mouth like a shark open wide and trying to bite me. It growled at me and it was so loud, louder than a bear, and the cloud was as ugly as the devil! I thought it was it! I'm going to die here. It felt like the spirit was taking me over, then the doorbell rang.

"It was Ruthy the realtor and the demon released me and disappeared! I told her about it but she didn't believe me. I told her I want my money back and she said to stay and she will get a priest to bless the house, but the fear was so terrifying I wanted to get out of that house as soon as possible. Tua and his bowling buddies moved all the furniture and put it in storage and he fixed up his basement for us to live in for a while. I hired a lawyer, Michael Bloomberg. He went to the property and he saw some hauntings and was told to get out of the house. He saw black ghosts and tree branches moving in the woods," said Lynn.

"Where are the kids?"

"They're at school," she said.

When the kids came home to Tua's house they came to hug Daddy and Tai came home with a cat. The next day Tai went to the house with a couple of pans to pick blueberries. "Lynn, you stay here, I'm going to pick some more blueberries and raspberries so you can make more pies for the kids.

The next day the kids were off to school and Mindi and Lynn went out for breakfast and Tai went back to the house with a shotgun and he went through the house to make sure everything was out. He got a good look at the ceiling in the living room, visualizing what happened to his wife while holding the shotgun, but everything was normal.

Later Tai put the gun in the car and he grabbed a chainsaw and the big cooking pans to fill up with blueberries, raspberries, rhubarb, and summer squash. He loaded his car with vegetables he found on his property. Then he started picking the blueberries and he filled one big pot and brought it to his car. Then he found some marijuana growing on his property and he picked all that and loaded his car, then he started picking and filling the second cooking pot and the tree branches started moving strangely and he was slicing brush. That didn't work so he went to the car to get his chainsaw to cut his way through to get to the rest of the blueberries and raspberries and fill the bucket.

Then he heard cracking sounds and two big branches came down and grabbed Tai right by the waist, squeezing him to death, until he grabbed his chainsaw and cut the branches grabbing him! He stood up and cut the other branch loose then he grabbed his blueberries and chainsaw and he was outta there!! He went to Tua's house with the blueberries, raspberries, and rhubarb and he put the buckets in the kitchen and hung the chainsaw in Tua's garage.

He said to his wife, "Lynn, you're right there's something wrong where we were living. I was cutting brush with a chainsaw to get to more blueberries to pick and I heard a crackling noise. It was the tree branches moving and two big branches came alive and grabbed me right by the waist, squeezing me until I cut the branches with the chainsaw. It was the scariest day of my life; I could not believe it! The tree came alive like the one on *The Wizard of Oz* throwing apples at the lion. It looked like two hands coming from the tree, grabbing me with a tight grip. We need to contact the realtor to get us another house or apartment until the kids get out of school," said Tai.

"I want to get out of here and move back to Pennsylvania," said Lynn. She was baking pies.

"I don't think that's a good idea because if whatever is haunting us follows us there then we're in trouble. Find something here and if the hauntings continue then we go back to Pennsylvania," said Tai Chang.

A short time after the Tai Chang haunting a cop was called to the wooded area in back of 66 6th Street. Neighbors were complaining of a loud chainsaw; it was the same spot where Tai was cutting vines and attacked. The cop was flashing his flashlight looking around and he saw the branches moving in the trees and he flashed his light on the moving branches. Finally he was grabbed by the waist the way Tai was attacked! The branches grabbed the cop with a tight grip but all he had on him was a gun. He fired one shot in the air and a big loose branch flew off another tree and struck the cop in the chest, going through his heart and killing him!

The cop was pinned to the ground standing up with two branches around his waist and another branch driven right through his heart and the blood dripping out of him standing between the branches, dead! The attack happened shortly before 8:00 p.m. At 9:00 p.m., no report had come back to the police station. 10:00 p.m. no report, 11:00 p.m. no report.

"Headquarters to Car #8, Officer Jennings over." No response.

"He must have gone home because that was his last call for the night and he goes home in his police car," another officer said at the police station.

His car was parked on a dirt road not far from where he was attacked. He lives by himself and nobody checked up on him during the night.

Back at Tua's house Lori was in bed and she saw a mist rolling around the ceiling and she woke up screaming. "Ahhhhhhhhhhhhhhhhhh!!!! Lynn went running to her room and she saw Lori screaming, "Mom there's a presence in here! I saw a fog on the ceiling coming down on me!" Lori was hysterical!

Tua came downstairs and he went in her room, shining a flashlight on the ceiling, and he said, "There's nothing here! You may have had a bad dream because my house is not haunted."

"It's not a dream Tua, I saw something!"

"Why don't you sleep in the living room? I will get you some blankets and sheets and fix you up a bed on the couch," said Lynn.

Tua had a pit group in the basement apartment he fixed up to make a comfortable bed for Lori. Tua shut her bedroom door. Bobby had a bad dream that the Greenman attacked Daddy and he woke up screaming. Xavier had a bad dream that she saw the Greenman and she woke up screaming.

# Two

## THE GREENMAN

A couple was going for an early morning walk down the dirt road between 66 6th Street and the next-door neighbor and they saw a police car parked on the side of the dirt road. They saw the policeman's dead body standing up full of blood with tree branches driven through him! The lady screamed! "Ahhhhhhhhhhhhhhhhhhhhhhhhh!!!!!!!!!!!!!!!!!!!!!!!!!!!!!!!!!!!!"

The man got a good look at him; the dead policeman even had twigs driven through his eyes and a big branch driven through his chest pinning him to the ground upright!

The couple ran out of the woods back home and called police. The police arrived at the scene and saw Officer Jennings' dead body, victim to the trees.

"Oh my good God, how could this happen!?" one officer said.

Another officer said, "How can a tree overcome a body like this? We had some wind yesterday but nothing enough to overcome a body like this unless he fell into the branches. It looks like he was pinned up by two branches going through his waist but the one driven through his chest remains a mystery!"

A third cop radioed back to the station. "Headquarters, Officer Reynolds speaking."

"Hi, this is Officer Baker here with Officer Ricci and Officer Coffee. Officer Jennings has been killed in a strange way. He somehow got caught in some brush and two tree branches were driven through his waist and back and another branch was driven through his chest in an upright position and there's blood everywhere!" Officer Baker cried.

Several police cars arrived and a rescue team arrived at the body. It wasn't anything like this had happened before. The fire department arrived to cut branches away to get to him and cut the branches away that struck him. "Maybe the Greenman did something to him because the house up there on the right is haunted," one cop said to another.

Another cop said, "Maybe he was spooked by some animal and ended up like this, because his death is very strange."

"What's the Greenman?" said the first cop.

"The Greenman is an evil spirit summoned by witchcraft back in the 1700s and he has haunted Mattapoisett for more than three hundred years," said the second cop. The first cop walked away.

The strange death was on the news. Back in Marion the Chang family was watching the evening news. "Good evening, we have breaking news on Channel 6 in New Bedford. A Mattapoisett policeman was found dead in the Mattapoisett wetlands from being wrapped up and stabbed by tree branches in a way that can't be described! Officer John Jennings went to a call around 7:30 p.m. to investigate complaints from a noisy chainsaw near the end of his shift and he never returned. The body was found by a couple going for their daily morning walk who called police. The police can't describe how he was killed or if someone did this.

"A hurricane is coming up the coast, so expect tropical storm winds by tomorrow evening.

"The Patriots lost to the Philadelphia Eagles 34-0. More news after these messages."

"I was just there before that policeman was killed, that could have been me if I didn't have my chainsaw to cut the branches after I was attacked! I saw the branches moving in a strange way and heard noises before I was attacked. I was told that the trees come alive and attack people when the legendary Greenman is active according to the book of black magic. I saw this before in back of our house. I thought it was unusual but I didn't think anything of it.

"I never believed in hauntings until I moved in at that house. I heard noises, I saw smoke, and I saw and heard unusual things and growls from an animal but I could never find where it was coming from. However when I was attacked by moving tree branches I found out for myself that there is evil out there! I had a suspicion when me, Lynn, and the kids were at the beach and this lady came over and she told us that we were in danger and I told her to get lost. When she left she disappeared right in front of my eyes! That freaked me and Lynn out...but when I was attacked by the tree branches—no I'm a believer!" Tai was telling Tua and reporters at Tua's house.

The next day was a partly cloudy day because a hurricane was coming and a man at Harbour Beach was out in the water untying boats to take them out of the water. It was low tide and he had to walk out to untie boats, raise anchors, and bring the boats in. A shark bit him, grabbed him by the waist, and chomped him in half! The shark ate his legs and his ass and the rest of the body washed up on Harbour Beach. Then a truck pulled up to load the boats out of the water, but more were out there and it was getting dark and the storm was on its way and it started raining.

He moved the remaining boats and loaded them up on the truck, but there was one far out so he went out in a rubber raft to get the last boat and a shark knocked the raft over and ate the man. Parts of his body washed up on one side of the beach and the other half of the body washed up on the other. The hurricane went out to sea and it was gone.

The next day it was a beautiful day and the same couple that saw the dead cop was walking down to Harbour Beach and a police car was parked down there but the officer did not know about the shark attacks. The couple walked down to the beach.

The woman started screaming! "Ahhhhhhhhhhhhhhhhhh!! Another body!" They waved the cop over. The lady said, "There's a dead body in the water!"

The policeman came over and he saw the dead body chopped in half. "Oh my god. He was probably attacked by a great white." Then he radioed back to headquarters and more police and a rescue team arrived at the beach. The police wrote up the report and the couple left the area. Another cop saw another body at the other end of the beach.

"Hey fellas, we have another dead body over here!" one cop said to another. Other policemen searched the beach for more bodies. Then they closed the beach and led out a truck with boats loaded on it. Then rescue boats went out looking for more bodies but it was only those two.

"I believe these bodies were attacked by great white sharks. They swim in here once in a while during low tide looking for dead fish and these goddamn fishermen are feeding the fuckin things. There have been shark attacks in Harbour Beach before. The boats come in and dump their waste, feeding the sharks. Seals and sea turtles come in here occasionally inviting sharks! This beach has been closed several times because of shark warnings," one cop was telling the others.

Signs were put up: "No swimming, beware of sharks." The town of Mattapoisett was making the news again with TV, radio, and newspapers reading: "Sharks Kill Two Fishermen at Harbour Beach in Mattapoisett." An iron gate was placed at the entrance so people can't drive in there. Coast Guard boats were searching the shorelines looking for sharks and none were found. Teenagers visited the beach late at night with their drinking parties, but found gates at the entrance, forcing them to go somewhere else.

This young couple decided to walk at Harbour Beach at three o'clock in the morning. It was a clear brisk night and they were sitting on the beach drinking from a canteen when suddenly the water had a green glow to it, then a green swamp ghost came out of the water and it was on top of them in seconds! The couple was pinned down on the sand by the Greenman ghost and they couldn't move or scream for help. The ghost's spirit got inside of them and stayed with them, pinned down in one spot until dawn when the spirit let go and disappeared. Then the couple ran off the beach with no explanation and went home. The boy called his friends and told them what happened. The girl went home and she went to bed. Her parents were away. The boy had snuck out in the middle of the night to meet his girlfriend. He got home around six thirty in the morning before his parents got up. He went to bed.

8:00 a.m. his father woke him up. "Come on Kevin, get up, get breakfast, feed the horses, and you're going to help me fix the tractor today." The horses started whinnying like crazy when Kevin, the boy, was feeding them, as the Greenman spirit in the boy was affecting the horses. Then he went in the house to eat breakfast and energy feeding off the boy's body got into the mother as she felt static electricity all around her.

She said, "Kevin where did you go last night? You were not home after 11:00 p.m. when we went to bed."

"We went horseback riding and then we took a long walk to Harbour Beach." The energy went back into Kevin when he went to go out and help his father. The mother kept looking around the house because she could sense something watching her! The father was working on a broken-down tractor when suddenly it felt like something was going inside of him. First he got a chill then a sudden headache almost knocking him over and he was getting dizzy. Kevin was next to him feeding the Greenman spirit into the father. Now he had it.

"Kevin, where the hell were you last night after midnight?"

"Out riding horses, and me and my girlfriend went for a walk to Harbour Beach."

"Kevin, go in the house and get me a couple of aspirin then get my toolbox in the garage." Then the father could feel like he was not alone and he heard a voice, *You're next! You're next!* Then a hissing sound. Then it stopped when Kevin, his son, returned and the spirit went back to him. The father was walking around in circles going around the tractor.

"Dad, what are you doing?"

"I heard someone calling, 'you're next' a couple of times and it was not you, but I clearly heard the voices, then it started hissing like an angry cat."

"Wow, that's strange, maybe it's a ghost! Me and Sheila saw something green at the beach last night. A glow that we couldn't understand came over us and we couldn't move then it released us and we got out of there. I wasn't thinking that it was a ghost. I thought it was algae coming out of the water; either way, it was scary. It didn't hurt us but we didn't wait to find out," said Kevin.

"Okay, let's start working on this tractor so I can get it going." Kevin and his father worked on the tractor all day and finally they got it going. Kevin's father was changing belts and putting new sparkplugs in and fixing the grading blades and putting air in the tires and kerosene in the tank and working on the engine.

Kevin was bathing the horses, wiping them down, and feeding them with hay. Then he was taking care of the animals on the farm where they live. The animals were making all kinds of noises while Kevin was with them, then he took one of his horses for a ride. The animals quieted down when he left.

Kevin's mother was in the house doing housework then she went downstairs with a load of laundry. She put the laundry in the washing machine then she went upstairs to finish her housework. Later she went downstairs to put her clothes in the dryer and she found the washing machine door open and the wet clothes spread all over the cellar floor and scattered everywhere! Thrown up on a table and workbench, hanging on nails. And on top of clean clothes!

"What the hell happened here!" she said to herself. Then she picked up the scattered clothing like fifty-two pick up and put some back in the washing machine and some in the dryer and she sat down to read a book until the washer and dryer were done. No strange things happened this time! She took the clothes out of the dryer and she put the rest of the wash in the dryer then she folded the dry clothes then she heard a faint growling from an animal. It drew her attention and she closed all the cellar windows.

When the rest of the clothes finished drying she folded them and took the clothes upstairs and they were done. Then she went into the kitchen to start cooking and Kevin was taking a nap. When the strange happenings with the washing machine were going on was when Kevin came in for his nap. The kid is being haunted by the Greenman trapping him and his girlfriend on the beach.

Earlier, Kevin's girlfriend, Sheila was home by herself; she would be until her parents came home on Monday. Back at 6:30 a.m. she got home, took a shower, had some cereal, then she went to bed. Around 1:00 p.m. a football game on TV came on all by itself and it was full blast!

She woke up out of a sound sleep and she turned the TV off. She looked at the alarm clock and the time was 1:02 p.m. Then she went back to bed. An hour later the TV came on very loud again, waking her up! She got up and she shut the TV off again then she pulled the plug. Then she went back to bed. Then she woke up and she looked at the alarm clock and the time was 4:20 p.m. Then she got up and she got dressed and she boiled a couple of hotdogs and she opened up a can of baked beans and she put them in the microwave oven and she had franks and beans for dinner, a simple meal for a seventeen year old.

While she was eating she felt someone breathing down her back and she looked back and nobody was there! Then she heard water gurgling. Then she put the dishes in the sink then she got a glass of orange juice and right after she finished the glass slipped out of her hands and broke on the floor. She got a broom and dustpan to pick up the glass and wiped the floor.

Then she heard the toilet flush. She said, "Who's here!" Then she got a big kitchen knife and she ran to the bathroom—no one in there! Then she went in to make the bed and the bed sheets, pillows, and blankets were on the floor and the bed was stripped. She held the knife and she opened the closet door swishing the clothes around and no one was there! Then she called the police.

"Police."

"Hi, this is Sheila Watson and I live at 83 Lane Street not far from Harbour Beach. Someone is in my house but I can't find him or her."

"Okay, get out of the house and wait for me in the street and we will be there in a couple of minutes. Stay in front of the house," said the police.

The police came and Sheila let him in and the cop searched the house. "There's nobody here!" said the cop.

She told the police what has been happening in the house. The policeman said, "It could be the Earth's magnetic field, caused by sun's radiation, causing static electricity that moves things. It sounds like a ghost in the house moving things. But this happens once in a while around this time of the year when summer is going into the fall season or the beginning of winter and spring. The Earth's magnetic field can do some strange things but it will be over in a few days," said the policeman, then he left. The cop is not going to tell her a ghost is in the house; Sheila has the Greenman spirit in her and it's haunting the house.

Sheila went back in the house and the strange noises continued, then she went to her boyfriend's house and she met him in the barn in his father's yard. And she told him what happened in her house. The two of them are not quite sure if they are haunted.

"My dad heard some strange things outside when he was working on the tractor. He told me he heard someone that was not me calling, 'you're next' twice, then he heard a hissing sound like a cat or wild animal and he said he felt something going inside of him, something he could not explain. I saw him walking around the tractor and I asked 'Dad what are you doing? and he told me what was going on and he sent me in the house to get him a couple of aspirin. Later I went to take care of the animals in the barn and they were all acting up and when I left they quieted down.

"Mom was doing laundry and she found it all over the cellar floor when she went to put it in the dryer and she felt like she was not alone and she heard strange noises. Sheila I don't know if the green glow at the beach was a ghost but now I wonder if it was," said Kevin, her boyfriend.

"Me too!" she said.

Nighttime, it was a Saturday night and Kevin went to Sheila's house to watch movies on TV and love it up on the couch, drinking Kool-Aid and eating popcorn. During the evening they heard noises and things moving around. Kevin got up to check it out and it was nothing. Sheila set up a camera to see if there was any paranormal activity in the house. Kevin went home at 11:00 p.m. because he's got to go to church in the morning.

When Sheila went to bed she put a chair under the doorknob in case something came in for a visit and she had a baseball bat beside her bed. The camera in the living room was rolling for the night. Sheila's parents came home at 1:00 a.m. Her father said to her mother, "I think someone is spying on us. What kind of trick is Sheila up to now, or Kevin!" he joked.

Sheila woke and she heard them. "Hi, Mom and Dad. I set up a camera because we might have a ghost in the house; here's the police report on the table. Me and Kevin heard some strange noises in this house over the weekend. Friday night we went for a walk to Harbour Beach and we saw a green fog coming off the water and somehow it knocked us down and we had to get out of there! When I got home and went to bed it was a quiet night, but during the day strange things started." Sheila was telling her parents about what happened in the house. Then she went to bed and slept through the night.

Her parents left the camera on for the rest of the night. Nothing happened. The night was quiet at Kevin's home too. The next day Kevin and his parents went to church and then invited Sheila over for a cookout at Kevin's parents' home and watched football games on TV. The next day they went to school; they were both seniors at Old Rochester Regional High School.

During lunch Kevin told his friends about his strange weekend.

"You never heard the story about the Greenman hauntings in Mattapoisett?" said one of his friends.

"The Greenman, I never heard of him Erica."

"The Greenman is a ghost, a very dangerous ghost! In the 1700s a big storm washed a big boat ashore during a hurricane and all the trees were washed away and fish were washed into the roots of the trees that were damaged, and dead bodies from the storm and strange algae from the ocean. It leveled the Mattapoisett coastline. When the storm was over the trees came alive like animals and chased people and killing them," said Erica.

Then the bell rang and it's time to go back to class. Kevin and Sheila were in the same history class and the teacher was talking about the Greenman ghost. "Good morning class. My name is Arthur Arch, a substitute history teacher. Today we're going to talk about the Greenman ghost in Mattapoisett. Back in the late 1700s a big sea storm started in Ireland, pulling away a dangerous flesh-eating algae from the green fields and pulling trees out to sea.

"Then the storm struck the U.K., drawing marsh and sea growth into the sea crossing the Atlantic Ocean and ended up hitting the Massachusetts coastline striking Cape Cod and the islands. All the algae settled here in Mattapoisett and Marion. The dangerous algae got into the trees along with sea life and humans from sunken ships. Humans and animals were washed into the algae, which ate the dead flesh as it rotted away. The dead washed into the roots of the trees from under the ground, deformed by this dangerous green algae from the sea. When animals and birds feed off of this algae and rot away and the sea washes away the decayed humans and animals, the spirits from the dead become alive from this dangerous algae. It makes the ground move and trees come alive through the spirit of the Greenman.

"Make no mistake; the Greenman has several folk tales about it. Some are good and some are evil. The one in Mattapoisett is evil. Sometimes it's active here in Mattapoisett and they're times you may never see it, but if you do he will appear as a green glowing fog giving you a warning to keep your distance and it will trap you if you don't get out in time. Then it appears as a tall man ghost with a straw face and it's covered in tree leaves and it will come after you and get in your soul. It will not hurt you but it will knock you down and has an odor of death! If it's in your soul it will make you do evil things, or spirits from it will interfere with your life. The Greenman of Mattapoisett is an evil spirit. The legend of the Greenman is spiritual, good or evil. Any questions?" asked the teacher.

"Hi Mr. Arch, my name is Kevin and that's my girlfriend Sheila sitting at the end desk. We were at Harbour Beach last Friday evening and we saw the green fog and it got bright and overcame me and her and we felt like it went inside of us and it knocked us out and held us down and we couldn't move until daybreak. Since then we have been experiencing some strange happenings."

"My advice Kevin and Sheila will need to go see a priest to get the spirit out of you because if you don't the spirit will get stronger and you will have to get an exorcism from a Catholic priest."

"Mr. Arch, can this Greenman kill you?" asked Sheila.

"Only if you provoke it, challenge it, or invade his territory. You may hear a voice telling you to get out. You can go there the next day in the same spot and you're okay if the Greenman is not active. But I don't think it's a good idea after challenging the creature. If you see the glow or the Greenman ghost just back away and don't turn your back because he will chase you and overtake your soul. Keep your distance until it disappears!"

"Mr. Arch, is the Greenman the devil?" asked another classmate.

"Not exactly, but it is an evil spirit!"

Later after school Kevin and Sheila got a ride from the high school to St. Anthony's church in downtown Mattapoisett and saw a priest. The couple told the priest what happened and the priest threw holy water on them and said prayers and a pre-exorcism to get the Greenman spirit out of them!

"Father Frank, is the Greenman a devil?" asked Sheila.

"He is a demon. Any ghost that makes an appearance to you is evil, always remember that. Here is a bottle of holy water, one for you and one for Kevin. Keep it in your room and the Greenman and other evil spirits will not bother you anymore! However stay away from Ouija boards or ghost boxes or any games to bring spirits in, because if you do it will come back stronger and may hurt you or even kill you. Understand?" said Father Frank.

"Yes sir," said Kevin. Then Erica drove them home. What does she do, she starts talking about the Greenman ghost again! "Erica, let's not talk about it anymore!" said Kevin.

"We just had an exorcism at the church, so let's change the subject?" asked Sheila.

Erica drove them home and now Kevin and Sheila are clean and so are their parents. Next the Greenman evil spirit got into Erica, with things slowly happening to her because of it. The next day Erica had a headache all day at school. Wednesday she had a stuffy, runny nose all day at school. Thursday she had an earache all day at school. Friday she had a stomachache, the shits, and peeing all day.

"Erica, if you're sick why don't you go home!" said her math teacher. When she left school she threw up in the parking lot then she drove home. It was raining that day and the rain washed her vomit down a sewer drain.

The next day was the homecoming football game between Old Rochester Regional High School and Wareham High School and Erica was dressed up for a chance to be the homecoming queen. She was with the cheerleaders and the dance team and the band was playing. Kevin was a wide receiver on the ORR football team. The national anthem was playing and Erica's panties fell down and she was embarrassed. Her mother yelled, "Erica tie your slip!"

The game started and Wareham ran the kickoff back 86 yards, went for the two-point conversion, and it was 8-0 Wareham. Old Rochester went three and out and kicked to Wareham and they ran down the field running and passing first downs until they scored another touchdown at the end of the first quarter and made the kick for a 15 to 0 lead.

Erica kept yelling, "Put Kevin in!" Kevin came into the game to start the second quarter and the quarterback kept throwing to Kevin and getting first downs but the Wareham defense tightened up and Old Rochester only managed to get a field goal, 15-3. Then Wareham ran the kickoff back for another touchdown and the point after and it was 22 to 3. Then before halftime the ORR quarterback threw a long pass to Kevin wide open but never turned around to get the ball and Wareham picked it up and ran 90 yards for a touchdown and the conversion for a 30 to 3 half-time lead, ruining Old Rochester's homecoming game. Then the band was playing on the field then the cheerleaders came out then the dance team came out to dance while the band was playing, then the homecoming queen was announced.

"Ladies and gentlemen, the homecoming queen is Erica Eagle Eddy!!!" Erica was so excited being the queen of Old Rochester Regional High School.

Then the second half started. The sky was cloudy and a green color because a thunderstorm was developing but there was no rain happening yet, and the second half was underway. Old Rochester got a long run to start the second half. Four plays into the second half a pass was thrown deep to Kevin in the end zone and he caught it for a touchdown he kicked the pat and the score was 30 to 10 Wareham. Then Old Rochester kicked a squib kick on the kickoff and recovered the ball. The next play was a drop back draw play and the ORR running back ran 60 yards for a touchdown straight up the middle and the crowd was going crazy. Kevin booted the extra point and Old Rochester was getting back in the game with two quick touchdowns and trailing 30 to 17.

On the next kickoff, Wareham got the ball at the 10 yard line and ran it back for a touchdown and a bunch of boos from the Old Rochester side but a penalty flag brought the play back from a block in the back and the penalty placed the ball half the distance to the goal line. Wareham put the ball in play and the quarterback fumbled and Old Rochester recovered and ran it in for the score and the Old Rochester crowd went nuts!

Kevin booted the point after good now it's 30 to 24 Wareham. Then on the kickoff Wareham called for a fair catch then with four seconds left in the third quarter Wareham went for a run and shoot pass and ORR picked it off at the 36 yard line and ran it back 64 yards for a touchdown! The ORR crowd was going insane and very loud. A bad snap on the pass attempt by Kevin hit the left goalpost and caromed through, giving Old Rochester the lead 31 to 30 scoring four quick touchdowns and 28 points in the third quarter. Then Wareham got the ball at the 28-yard line and worked it up the field for six minutes and attempted a field goal to get the lead back quieting the Rochester crowd. Then ORR blocked the field goal, scooped the ball up, and ran it back for a touchdown. Then after a penalty trying for two points the ball was brought back five yards and Kevin buried the extra point. Now Old Rochester has a 38-30 lead, playing an incredible second half!

Then Wareham got the ball and kept passing downfield and scored on the last play of the game and they went for two for the tie. The quarterback got the ball from under center and he fumbled the snap and the play was dead and Old Rochester won the game 38-36. The team poured out on the field to celebrate the victory, sending the homecoming crowd home happy, but not before a bench clearing riot after the game as both teams were exchanging punches.

The refs screwed and Erica ran to her car and got out of there. Coaches and school officials tried to break up the brawl then the police came and the rain came down as well. It was a brawl in the pouring rain thunder and lightning.

Later Erica went home to eat supper then she took a ride to Ned's Point to meet some of her friends from school, leaving the Greenman ghost with Mom and Dad until she returns. About 7:00 p.m. Erica's mom was boiling water in a glass tea kettle and she was taking dishes out of the dishwasher and putting them away. Suddenly the glass tea kettle broke into pieces and the hot water went everywhere, putting out the pilot on the gas stove. She shut the gas off and cleaned up the mess.

Then Erica's dad was reading the newspaper while the TV was on and something hit the newspaper and knocked it out of his hands and the TV shut off all by itself. The events with Erica's mom and dad all happened at the same time. When the glass tea kettle broke she screamed. When the newspaper got knocked out of his hands he said, "Come on Gloria stop playing around!" Then the TV shut off. He thought that was strange, then he heard screaming and he ran out in the kitchen to help his wife.

"I had this glass teapot for thirty years and I just put the water on to boil and it broke."

"Something strange is happening here, someone whacked the newspaper out of my hands. I thought it was you then the TV shut off all by itself!" he said.

"We've been living here for thirty-three years and we never had anything paranormal happen here," said Erica's mom.

Erica was at the Ned's Point lighthouse hanging with her friends and it was raining and her friends didn't stay there for long because of the bad weather. She was all alone looking at the water then she saw a bright green flash. It stopped raining and she got out of her car. It was about 11:00 p.m. when she saw a glow toward the woods and she went to investigate and she saw the Greenman ghost. It was a man with a straw face with no eyes nose or mouth and its body was covered with green leaves, as were its arms and legs. It was just standing there!

Erica got closer to it, walking toward the ghost. Before she could get any closer a head looking like a wolf or wild dog with sharp fanged teeth charged out of the Greenman ghost, opened its mouth wide, and growled at her very loudly, chasing her back to her car. The ghost was growling louder as it was right on top of her, knocking her to the ground and the wolf-looking creature kept growling and it looked like it was going to eat her as she screamed at the top of her lungs! "Ahhhhhhhhhhhhhhh!!!!!!!!!!!"

Then a cop pulled in, putting on his flashing lights and drove over to the screaming girl. The ghost vision disappeared quickly when the police car drove in then a second police car arrived.

The cop said, "Miss, are you alright!"

"I just saw a ghost and it was chasing me back to my car. It was a Greenman with a head of a wolf!" Erica cried.

"Miss, you need to leave, the park closes at 10:00 p.m. and it's 11:20 p.m.," said the cop.

Then the cop helped her to her car and she drove out of Ned's Point and went home. The first cop took the report she was haunted by a green ghost in Ned's Point. The second cop laughed! The policemen checked the area, flashing their flashlights, and they saw a dog running in the woods, running away from the light beams and it disappeared.

"Yep, she saw a ghost alright, a German shepherd retriever mix!" one cop said to the other. They searched the woods then drove around and out of Ned's Point but found no ghost!

Erica saw a deer with red eyes crossing in front of her while driving home and she almost hit it! And she screamed, "Ahhhhhhh!!!!!!!!!" slamming on her brakes. Then she drove home without any more ghostly experiences!

She got home just after 11:30 p.m. and her parents were watching TV. "Hi Dad and Mom, I saw a ghost at Ned's Point. It was the Greenman we were studying in history class last week and it had a wolf that came out of it that charged after me trying to eat me. Finally the police came to rescue me and the ghost disappeared! Had the police not come there on time it would have killed me!" Erica cried.

"It serves you right! You don't go out alone at night, I told you that before. Now go upstairs for your shower and go to bed. We have to get up and go to church in the morning!" said her mother.

The father said, "I hope she didn't bring something home with her because a lot of these young kids are practicing witchcraft. It's inviting to high school kids, mostly girls. I heard about the Greenman ghost and if she's practicing witchcraft with her friends and bring in any spirits that we don't want, we are going to have a problem with that! The Greenman ghost is a marsh mixing with salt water and when sea life or insects get into it and get washed into tree roots it becomes alive and acts as an evil spirit. This type of ghost has several weapons to work with. Otherwise it's a hard thing to understand what the Greenman really is!

"Since I have been watching this college football game on TV I have been hearing strange noises, like an animal growling outside, knockings, or a baby crying, or just noises like tapping and cracking sounds," he said.

"I have been hearing the same noises, I wonder if it has something to do with the teapot breaking and the dishwasher not working."

"I don't know Cindy but it's after midnight and we better get to bed if we're going to get up and go to church in the morning," said the father.

3:03 a.m. everyone was sleeping in the house and a mysterious fog developed in the living room and a black mass of a man looking like the devil roamed through the living room, kitchen, and dining room for about an hour then dissipated! While it was going on the father woke up and he was pinned to the bed and he heard a soft voice calling, *Evelyn-Evelyn-Evelyn-Evelyn!* Then it stopped and released him!

The fog and the demon ghost exited the home. He got up and he grabbed his gun and he searched the house and nothing was there. Erica is practicing witchcraft and she's playing with more than the Greenman. The father was freaking out. He stayed up for a couple of hours before he went back to bed and the noises stopped. He left the lights on.

The mother woke up before 5:00 a.m. and she got up to go to the bathroom and she saw her shadow as she went one way and another shadow going the other way briefly, then it went away. They got up around 7:30 a.m.

"Something strange is going on here Cindy. I woke up around 3:00 a.m. and I couldn't get out of bed and heard strange noises. Finally I was able to get out of bed and checked the house but I found nothing."

"Jim, I saw a shadow moving along the wall when I got up to go to the bathroom and it didn't look like me going by; it was going the other way, then it went away!" said Cindy. Cindy and Jim are Erica's parents.

Then Erica got up, had breakfast, and then she went to church with her parents. During the mass Erica let out a loud roar like an animal then she passed out in the church! A black fog came out of her mouth before she passed out and it floated above the people; it was as black as the ace of spades! Then it dropped down into empty seats and disappeared before reaching the altar! Everyone in the church started screaming and running out of the church. The priest started saying some prayers. Erica's parents were hysterical, screaming, and her mother was crying. When the priest finished saying prayers Erica came out of it. The priest came over to her and he said, "Erica are you okay?!"

She said, "I'm okay."

"Do you realize what happened to you?!" asked the priest.

"I felt a little dizzy but that was about all!"

"You don't remember what just happened to you?!" asked the priest.

"No, what happened? Where did everybody go?" she asked.

"During the mass, a strange growl came out of your mouth when you tried to cough, and a black fog mass formed coming out of your mouth and floated over the people. You released an evil spirit that was in you. We have to do an exorcism as soon as possible to make sure it's gone. The good news is coming to church released what you had inside of you. But it might not be gone! By doing an exorcism we can get rid of what's inside of you!" said the priest.

Erica was shocked! She said, "That's strange because I don't remember anything!" The priest, Erica, and her parents went to the back of the church to the priest's room to do the exorcism.

The cop who rescued Erica last night at Ned's Point was at the church and he contracted the evil spirit because he was in the way before it disappeared!

"Mr. and Mrs. Eddy and Erica. My name is Father Frank the head priest here at St. Anthony's church here in Mattapoisett. Before we do this exorcism I need to ask Erica some questions. First of all, how did you get this evil spirit in you? Are you practicing witchcraft?"

"Father we have been studying the Greenman ghost in history class the past week at school. Then Saturday night I went for a ride to Ned's Point to watch the lightning over the water and I was there for a while with my friends and when they left I stayed to watch the storm. When the storm was over I saw a green glow turn into a man and I went closer to get a better look and he looked like a man covered in leaves with no face features; his face looked like a wicker basket. I called hello! Then the head of a dog or wolf meaner than a junkyard dog came out of this man and came after me! The mean dog opened its mouth wide trying to eat me and it knocked me down! The police came over to help. I was able to get to my car and drive away. Then on the way home I almost hit a deer with red eyes! I told my parents what happened," said Erica.

"Erica, have you ever used spiritual boards to call or challenge spirits at any time during your life?" asked the priest.

"I used an Ouija board in a school project at the high school," she said.

"How long ago?"

"Last week Father."

"Okay. Do yourself a favor. Find another way to do school projects, don't use an Ouija board, because you just opened up the spirit world and hundreds of them can affect your life and pass on to others like dominos! It can make your life miserable! Good thing you're a Catholic and you go to church.

"The Greenman ghost is an evil spirit; any time you see a ghost or forms and shapes, they're evil. The Greenman is known to be a ghost in view in hauntings. Some believe it's a creature from outer space, others believe it's protecting its territory, others believe it's a vision of good others say the visions are bad.

"One day I saw the Greenman ghost myself driving through Hollywood Beach and the next day I bowled a 300 game and a 711 series at Fairhaven Bowling Lanes. At that time I didn't know if it was good or evil. But in your case you invited the Greenman ghost and others it had with it! The black mass that came out of your mouth was from something else and we need to get rid of it. So let's all join hands and say prayers and begin this exorcism!" said the priest.

The exorcism went smoothly. "Good news, the black formation you coughed out of your mouth went somewhere else and you're clear from evil spirits. I am going to give you a bottle of holy water and your mom and dad will get one as well, and I want you to sprinkle some in every room of your house, your car, and Erica, take some to school with you. Stay away from Ouija boards, ghost boxes, and calling cards. Do not do any witchcraft because if you do the evil spirits will come back," said the priest.

# THREE

## BILLY WILKINS' FAMILY HAUNTINGS

Six years later a Mattapoisett police officer and his family brought the house at 66 6th Street in Mattapoisett. He was a devoted Catholic at St. Anthony's church. He's the cop who contacted Erica Eddy's ghost when he rescued her at Ned's Point in the late fall of 1979.

And when the evil in Erica was released in the church he knew when the black formation vanished with no warning because he was in the wrong place at the wrong time. When he was in church that day the black formation went right through him and he yelled, "Fire, everyone get out of the church." He never knew what happened because he didn't wait long enough to find out!

He was a new cop at the time then he went in the army for a while right after that day in church. Then after six years in the army he returned to the Mattapoisett Police Department. His name is Billy Wilkins with a wife, Becky, and twin sons Bobby and Ben, twenty-three years old, who were both in the army, and a daughter Brenda in the Air Force.

He and Becky met with Ruthy Smith from Arthur's Realtors at 66, 6th Street. 'Round and round, here we go again! The three others were away in the military.

"You must be Ruthy Smith from Arthur's Realtors," said Billy.

"That I am! Welcome to 66 6th Street. Please come in."

"Ruthy, this is my wife Becky, and I have twin sons, Bobby and Ben, both twenty-three years old and in the army, stationed at Fort Bragg, Indiana and my daughter Brenda, twenty-seven, in the Air Force and stationed at Cape Canaveral, Florida."

"Pleased to meet you both. This house is a Cape Codder with a finished basement, and you have two fireplaces. You are going to love this house and with the cold weather coming you have plenty to keep warm. This is the porch and next is the kitchen with a refrigerator and stove already in place, the stove is electric. And you have a double sink and dishwasher.

"The next room on the right is the dining room and on the left is the living room with a corner fireplace, and the front door going out, and a closet to hang your coats at the bottom of the stairs. You have two bedrooms and a small bath upstairs we will see later. Next is the bathroom on the right: tub, shower, toilet and sink and linen closet. This door goes down to the cellar and we will see that last. Here we have two bedrooms, one on each side with a closet in each room. You have a lot of closet space in this house you will see later. The bedroom on the left is bigger than the one on the right.

"Let's go upstairs and see the rooms up there. Here we have a small bath, sink, and toilet. The bedroom on the left has two windows, a closet, and attic storage space that goes from one side of the room to the end of the house. The next room here is the master bedroom with three windows, a walk-in closet, and a small closet to put shoes in or bedclothes. Here is another attic storage area from one side of the house to the other and you have a new roof put on.

"Come on downstairs and see the finished basement. Down here you have another fireplace and washer and dryer hook ups and you have a place for a deep freezer. Here you have a small bath with a sink, toilet, and stand up shower. This door leads outside and you have a long picnic table and a doghouse. On the right here is a walk-in shed and the bottom half is the barn and you own all this land up to two acres all the way to the water. You even have your own private beach. And you have berry bushes in the woods and plenty of wood to cut up for the fireplaces. Parking for up to four cars, two on each side.

"The house and the land go for $200,000. The mortgage is $25,000 down and $1,000 a month. You have a steal here because the property goes for a lot more than that!" said Ruthy.

"Let's talk inside," said Billy and Becky Wilkins.

The couple signed the lease and trucks came to move them in. They had three bedrooms set up for their kids. The first-floor left bedroom had a double bed, the one on the right had a twin bed, and upstairs the master bedroom had a king size waterbed, and the smaller bedroom had a queen bed. It was November 2, 1985 when everything was moved in. The couple had a washer, dryer, and a kitchen area in the finished basement. Electric stove, refrigerator, and deep freezer, and pit group couches in front of the fireplace in the finished basement. And a TV in the kitchen area. Upstairs they had a dining room set: table and six chairs and a hutch. The living room had couches, recliners, rocking chairs, and a TV. The porch had a table, two chairs, and a TV.

Billy works for the Mattapoisett Police Department during the night, 11:00 p.m. to 7:00 a.m. Becky is a hairdresser and she works from 9:00 a.m. until 5:00 p.m. Billy has Mondays and Tuesdays off with the police department and Becky works in Fairhaven at Sally's Hair Salon Tuesday through Saturday and she has Sundays and Mondays off.

One night, Billy went to work and while riding through Ned's Point in his police car he saw a bright green glow that looked like a glowing statue, but no face or figure, just a green fog near the lighthouse. He put on the flashing lights, driving through, and the green glow disappeared. He looked at the clock in the police car and the time was 3:02 a.m. Then he drove out of Ned's Point and he saw a deer with red eyes in the middle of the road and he put the police lights back on and honked then the deer ran off!

Later he was driving by the town beach and he saw a lady in a black bathing suit walking along the beach then she faded out and disappeared. Billy drove into the beach to check her out; it was an unusual mild night in early November. He got out of his car and walked along the beach shining a flashlight, looking for the lady, but she was long gone.

Then he drove to Mattapoisett Harbour and he parked his car there until the end of his shift. He just saw three ghosts but he doesn't realize it; he doesn't believe in ghosts. The green glow is the ghost of the Greenman, the red-eyed deer is another, and Maria Cooper the beach ghost is the third one!

While Billy was at work Becky was at home sleeping. Then around 3:00 a.m. Becky woke up to a scratching sound. She turned on the lamp, got up out of bed, and looked in the walk-in closet and nothing was there. She put a rocking chair up against the attic storage door fearing something might come out of there. She went to the bathroom then she checked the other bedroom—no animal in there—and she shut the door. Then she went to bed. An hour later she woke up to a flapping sound and she turned on the lamp and the flapping sound stopped. The flapping sounded like it was in the walk-in closet. She opened the closet door and turned on the light, moving the clothes around, and there was nothing.

"We have bats! What the fuck!" she said to herself. Then she closed the closet door, leaving the light on, and she put a heavy duffel bag against the closet door then she went back to bed. A big black shadow moved across the room in the dark but she didn't see it. Then it vanished! An hour later she woke up again hearing *thump thump*! She turned the lamp on and it stopped! She got up at 5:00 a.m. after searching the house for the animal making noises.

Then Billy came home and Becky hugged him and told him, "We have an animal somewhere in the house. I heard scratching, a bird flapping, and a thumping noise. Either there's a big bird or we might have bats."

Billy went upstairs to check out the animal noises, checking the closets and the attic storage, and he tapped on the wood and he heard the scratching too. "I heard scratching too. We might have a raccoon or a crow living in the eaves between the walls but they will not break through; they're just trying to stay warm or get out of the rain. All animals do that. Later I'll check to see if any nests are anywhere near the house and check the gutters because sometimes birds make nests there and they can be noisy during the night," said Billy.

"How was your first night in your new job?" said Becky.

"It was very interesting. Captain Walker said that I saw three ghosts during the night: my first stop at Ned's beach I saw a green fog trying to form a figure. I was told that I saw the Greenman ghost. Then I saw a girl walking on the beach in a bikini at fifty-three degrees. I thought that was unusual. The captain said I saw the Mattapoisett Beach ghost. Then I saw a deer with red eyes; the captain said it was another ghost. I don't believe in ghosts. I heard a lot of ghost stories in Mattapoisett in the police department. I think it's a big joke! They have too much time on their hands, telling ghost stories instead of being real cops!

"About six years ago before I went in the army, I was working the 11:00 p.m. to 7:00 a.m. shift then, and I got a call to chase kids out of

Ned's Point at 11:00 p.m. My first assignment of the night, and I saw a girl laying on the ground crying. When I drove up to her with my police lights on she told me she was attacked by the Greenman ghost and I told her to get out, the park was closed. The next day I was in church and someone told me that I was covered in a black mist as black as the ace of spades. I saw like if someone was smoking but I never saw a black mist. On that day and all six years being in the army I have never experienced a ghost! There's no such thing, give me a fuckin break! Have a good day at work I have to get some sleep," said Billy.

He kissed his wife and gave her a big hug then he went upstairs to bed and his wife drove off to work. Billy got undressed and he looked at the alarm clock and the time was 8:18 a.m. He felt a cold draft under the bed blowing on his feet. He looked under the bed and there was nothing! He closed the shades on the windows and he made sure the windows were closed tightly. A ghostly figure was standing in the yard near the shed but he didn't see it and he went to bed and he fell asleep.

2:00 p.m. he woke up to the loudest growl! *Rooooaaar!!!!!* Then he heard loud scratching sounds! Then it stopped. He got up and he got dressed and it was clear the growl was in his bedroom!

He said to himself, "That's not a bird or a raccoon, it's something else!!!!!!!!!!!" Then he grabbed his gun, loading it up with bullets, and he searched every room in and out area of the house and he found nothing!

"What the fuck was that!!!!!!!!!!!!!!"

He checked the walk-in closet, the storage area, and he was banging on walls and he heard nothing, saw nothing. He checked under the bed and he searched every room and closet space in the house from top to bottom and there was nothing. Then he went up on the roof, looking for clues on where this growl was coming from. He cleaned the gutters out. Then he checked the yard and he went in the shed and the barn in the back, gun at the ready. He saw nothing! "Is it my imagination or was I dreaming!" he said to himself.

Before it got dark he grabbed a beer out of the refrigerator in the basement and he went outside and he sat at the picnic table drinking his beer. The wind outside started picking up and he saw the branches moving strangely on the trees in the woods, then it stopped, then started again. Then the wind was blowing stronger and the tree branches were not moving all of a sudden. He didn't think anything of it, then he went back in the house to get dinner ready until his wife got home.

Becky got home and she gave Billy a hug and kiss and she said, "How was your day today?"

"I woke up at 2:00 p.m. and I heard the loudest growl, like some wild animal. It sounded like it was right in our bedroom. I got up and I searched everywhere in this house from top to bottom. I even went up on the roof to check to see if some animal got in the house and I cleaned out all the gutters and nothing! The growl I heard was not a raccoon or a crow. It sounded worse than a mean bear; I can't describe it! I don't believe in ghosts! I think I was dreaming while I was awake because if it was some animal I would have found it!" said Billy.

The couple sat down to have dinner about 7:00 p.m. Becky said, "Those are the same noises I heard last night; the growling, birds flapping, and the scratching noises in the walk-in closet."

"I'll write it off and see if it happens again. We might have some animal living in the walls somewhere, but that growl sounded like it was right on top of me, and it's so funny that I can't track it down," said Billy.

8:30 p.m. Billy and Becky got a good fire going in the fireplace and they sat down and watched TV in front of a warm fire. Billy fell asleep and Becky got up to pour herself a glass of wine. The fire formed a face that looked like the devil: a head with two blue eyes, and a bluish orange flame looking like a nose, and two fiery rotating horns in back of the fiery head, and pointy flaming ears, and bluish lips burning in the flames! Becky was watching it and she kept feeding the fire with kindling wood and a couple of logs. Then *pop pop*! The wood was making strange popping sounds, then its fire burned normally. Becky never noticed the vision of the devil in the fireplace. It would have scared the shit out of her!

Billy woke up and he looked at his watch and the time was 10:02 p.m. Becky fell asleep in front of the warm evil fire. It made the face of the devil again as it died down. Then Billy went in for his shower and he put on his police uniform and he went to work. The fire in the fireplace was going out. Becky closed the glass doors on the fireplace to smother the fire for good. She gave Billy a hug and kiss and then she went to bed. Billy went to work at the police station and wound up telling the officers about the loud growl he heard that afternoon, and they were telling ghost stories again until 2:00 a.m.

Becky woke up to a sound. *Chit chit chit chit chit!!!!!!!!* She woke up and she turned on the lamp and the noise stopped. She looked at the alarm clock and the time was 3:02 a.m. She got up to go to the bathroom and she closed the bedroom door then she checked the house for the noise's source. She made sure all the doors were locked. Then she went back to bed and she slept with the light on. One hour later a big black rolling mass moved from one side of the room to the other and hands and arms were coming out of it and it looked like it was trying to grab her, but Becky slept through it!

She woke up minutes after it disappeared and she looked around the room, then she lay down and she went back to sleep. She does not know what's at stake in this house. Becky slept through the night and Billy had an easy night; he comes home and Becky is off to work. He got something to eat and he heard a hissing sound. He checked the boiler in the basement and the bathrooms, and he checked the house to make sure nothing was leaking then he went to bed.

Around 4:00 p.m. he got up, got dressed, and he went outside to the barn. He grabbed his chainsaw and he went out to cut up wood to store for the fireplace, stacking it in back of the shed. He saw one tree branch moving slowly along the ground and he cut it off the tree to get at more dead wood lying around. Then he went in the house before dark, bringing some wood inside to get a fire going later. The couple heard noises, but they didn't see any ghostly figures.

Then Thanksgiving was near and the rest of the family came to visit. The daughter Brenda arrived on Saturday with her kids, two girls named Donna, seven years old, and Debbie, five years old, and her husband Jack Daniels. The twin boys, Bobby and Ben arrived the next day. Brenda, Jack, and the kids came in from Florida. Their plane landed at Logan Airport in Boston and they rented a car to drive to Mattapoisett. They arrived shortly after 4:00 p.m. the Saturday before Thanksgiving. As soon as they pulled in the driveway a black rolling head moved across the ground with yellow eyes, then a black cat walked in front of the car.

Donna and Debbie said, "Mommy, Daddy, what's that!?"

"What's what?" asked Brenda.

"I saw a head with yellow eyes go round and round on the ground," said Donna.

"I saw it too; it was a big black ball head rolling on the ground with yellow eyes in it!" said Debbie.

"I see a black cat with yellow eyes in front of the car," said Brenda.

"No Mommy, it's a big head!" said Debbie.

"Oh my goodness, I only see a cat outside," said Brenda.

"I didn't see anything!" said Jack.

Then the daughter, husband, and kids were greeted going in the house. Becky said, "Well hello Brenda, Jack, Donna and Debbie, welcome. Please come in. Welcome to our new home in Mattapoisett." Then Becky and Billy helped them unload the car and put things in their rooms.

"Debbie, you will be sleeping in this room on the right, put your things in here. Donna, you will be sleeping in this room on the left. Brenda and Jack follow me upstairs; you will be sleeping in this room on the left side. Put things away and come down for drinks and we will have dinner in a little while. We will be having pot roast, mashed potatoes, and mixed vegetables for dinner with white wine and Italian bread and blueberry pie for dessert. Then after dinner Billy will light the fireplace," said Becky.

Billy started the cooking and Becky finished and brought the dinner out, talking about the family health and the kids. The kids told Billy and Becky about what they saw outside.

"A big round head with yellow eyes, that's strange," said Becky.

"It could be a bald eagle chasing an animal because they have them here in Mattapoisett. They're mostly seen in Marion. It's a big eagle with a white head and a yellow beak. When they land they roll on the ground to smother their catch," said Billy.

"I saw a black cat with yellow eyes in front of our car when we pulled in here," said Brenda.

"No Papa! It was a big black head with yellow eyes rolling inside of it!" said Debbie.

"Whatever you saw we will see what's out in the yard tomorrow; it's dark out there now.

Later the kids were going to bed and Becky, Brenda, and Jack sat in front of a nice cozy fire on the cold Saturday night, and Billy went in to work early at the police station after getting a nice fire going. Brenda and Jack were drinking bourbon and Coke and Becky were drinking white Russians.

11:02 p.m. the lights went out; only the fireplace was lit.

"Oh my God! We just lost our power," said Becky.

Then the power came back a minute later and it was thundering and lightning outside and raining hard. Billy was riding through the parking lot of St. Anthony's church in his police car and he saw this strange black mass racing across the parking lot. The black mass had no legs or arms—it just looked like something running at a high rate of speed—then it vanished! Billy said to himself, "What the hell was that!"

He called back to the police station to describe what it was. "Car #12 to headquarters, over."

"Go ahead, Car #12."

"I just saw something running across the parking lot at St. Anthony's church that I can't describe. It looked like a black bag running through the parking lot then it vanished! It looked like something running with no feet or hands. It could be a dog or some animal trapped inside a black bag, but it vanished right in front of me!" said Billy.

"You saw a ghost. Headquarters over. Stay there and I'll send someone."

A second police car arrived and the vision was not seen again.

"I saw it right there, running toward the woods, then it disappeared," Billy said to the other cop.

The two policemen went to where the ghost vision was, armed with flashlights, and they found nothing. Then he went home early.

The next afternoon, Bobby and Ben arrived. And they slept in the basement; one slept on the pit group and the other on a couch pulled out to a bed. Bobby and Ben flew into Logan from Indiana and rented a car and drove to 66 6th Street in Mattapoisett. Billy greeted them while Becky was out shopping with Brenda. The two girls watched TV and played some games.

"Bobby, Ben, welcome. How was your trip?" asked Billy.

"I thought we were not going to make it because of a tornado warning in Indiana. But it passed and we were able to get our flight," said Bobby.

"The flight was kind of bumpy because of a lot of turbulence leaving Indiana. Do you get tornadoes here?" asked Ben.

"Not really. Massachusetts gets some during the summer months but I never heard of one here. But we do get hurricanes," said Billy.

The two men set up downstairs. Billy put up a divider to make a bedroom in the basement before he showed them around in the house.

"You have a bathroom at the far-right end of the cellar and you have a sink, toilet, and stand up shower. Here is the kitchen with stove, refrigerator, a deep freezer, and a table with six chairs. A washer, dryer and this door goes outside. We have two acres of land and here you have a fireplace," said Billy.

"Can you use the fireplace?" asked Ben.

"Sure you can use it any time. I have plenty of chopped up wood and kindling in back of the shed," said Billy.

Then he showed Bobby and Ben the rest of the house. Then Becky and Brenda came home to greet her brothers and the girls came out to hug them. Then something pushed Brenda in the kitchen and she asked, "Jack did you push me?!"

"No Brenda, I was in the dining room."

"I was just wondering because I felt someone pushing me."

Brenda helped Becky do the cooking and Bobby and Ben helped Billy in the dining room, pulling out the dining room table and putting in an extra middle piece to make it bigger. Then Billy put more chairs around the table to seat eight. Franks, beans, and brown bread were served for dinner and blueberry pie and vanilla ice cream were served for dessert. After dinner, the kids played games with their toys and the adults played cards and watched TV in front of a warm fire.

The hauntings are about to begin at two minutes after every hour starting with the father, mother, the kids, and down to the grandchildren. All eight will experience something from the oldest to the youngest.

Billy was driving out of the police station and he saw the deer with red eyes looking at him and the car stalled out. He looked at the clock in the car and the time was 11:02 p.m. He tried starting the car and it wouldn't start. The deer with the red eyes was still looking at Billy face to face. Then the car started a minute later. When he got the car started the deer vanished. Then he drove to his post. Sunday night is his last night because he has Mondays and Tuesdays off.

12:02 a.m. *Thump, thump!!!!!* It was pretty loud, waking Becky out of a sound sleep. She kept hearing the thumping as it got softer and softer. Then it stopped. She looked at the alarm clock and the time was 12:03 a.m. She got up and walked around the house, checking on the girls downstairs, and they were fast asleep. Then she went to bed.

Brenda woke up just before 1:00 a.m. to go to the bathroom. Then when she was getting into bed she looked at the digital alarm clock and the time was 1:02 a.m. and a mysterious force pushed her again.

She screamed! "Ahhhhhhhhhhhhhhhhhh!!!!!!!!!!" She put the light on and she felt like she was ready to be thrown or pushed again and the force did not stop until a minute later! She kept screaming, waking Becky up, and she ran to her room.

"Brenda, are you alright! What's wrong?"

"Something is here in this room pushing me; it's not Jack he's downstairs watching TV," said Brenda.

"I heard a thumping noise earlier tonight. I can't figure out what it was. I checked on you to see if you fell out of bed, the kids too. Jack was passed out on the couch. Unless Bobby and Ben are making noise downstairs, but I found nothing wrong in the house. "

Jack came upstairs with a bottle of beer in his hands and he said, "What's going on up here!?"

"Something pushed me. It's the second time this happened to me. There must be a ghost here," said Brenda.

"You must have had a nightmare, there's no such thing as ghosts!" said Jack.

"It was not a nightmare! I felt something and this force would not let me get in bed. I felt like I was going to be picked up and thrown. I had to grab a bedpost to avoid being pushed or thrown across the room or something like that," said Brenda.

"Let me finish watching this movie downstairs and I'll be up in a few minutes. Just go back to bed," said Jack.

Jack was watching TV and the fire was going out in the fireplace and he looked at his watch and the time was 2:02 a.m. While drinking his beer the fire erupted in the fireplace, making a face that looked like the

RICHARD REZENDES

devil! He heard a popping noise and a faint noise, *get out!* Then a face appeared with red eyes, curling horns, pointy ears, and an ugly flame. Then it disappeared a minute later followed by a hissing sound then the fire went out completely! Jack watched and was surprised by it, but stayed there finishing his beer. The movie was over at 2:35 a.m. He closed the glass doors on the fireplace and he went upstairs to bed.

Bobby woke up to something pushing him in bed, waking him up, and he looked at a clock in the basement and the time was 3:02 a.m. The bedclothes were moving and he checked to see what it was. There was nothing and the movement stopped a minute later. Bobby got up to go to the bathroom then he went back to bed.

Ben woke up hearing a voice, *get out!!!!* He looked at the clock and the time was 4:02 a.m. He got up to go to the bathroom and he felt something blowing in his ears. He said, "Boy, that's strange; maybe it's quite windy outside!" talking to himself. Then he went back to sleep.

One hour later Donna woke up to something slapping her right across the face, good and hard. She also woke up screaming! "Ahhhhhhhhhhhhhhhh!!!!!!!!!!!!"

Debby woke up hearing Donna scream. The time was 5:02 a.m.

Brenda and Becky heard the screams and they came running downstairs. "What's wrong down here!?" asked Brenda.

"Someone punched me in the face!" Donna cried. Brenda looked at her face and head and there were no marks.

"You must have had a bad dream!"

"No Momma, something hit me really hard in my face."

"Come up and sleep with me and Dad. Something weird is going on in this house. I don't believe in ghosts but strange things are happening. To me, you, and now Donna. Just to be safe you might get a priest to come bless this house, just in case there is some kind of haunting here. I have heard of haunted houses but I never believed the devil can come in and take over; that's nonsense! I did hear stories of people who died in houses and spirits doing strange things to get answers, but I don't see it like being a devil...ghost—it's all fake! But I was pushed twice, the thumping noise—you heard the ghost stories Dad was telling—and now Donna getting slapped in the face by a mysterious force. I'm now a believer; something is in this house that shouldn't be here!" said Brenda.

A few minutes later when the house started getting quiet, Debbie felt something grabbing her and moving the bed covers and she screamed at the top of her lungs! "Ahhhhhhhhhh!!!!!!!!!!!!"

Brenda got up. She looked at the alarm clock and the time was 6:02 a.m. Then she heard her daughter screaming and she ran downstairs like a bat outta hell!!

Debbie was screaming. "Mommy, Mommy, Mommy! Something is grabbing me in my bed, is it a rat!!!!!!!!" Brenda put the light on in her room and she searched the bed and nothing was there!

"Look under the bed Mommy!" Brenda looked under the bed and nothing was there. She pulled the bedclothes off the bed and found nothing. Now both girls are sleeping with Mommy and Daddy for the rest of the night.

Billy left the police station after his 11:00 p.m. to 7:00 a.m. shift. On his way home he looked at the clock in his car and the time was 7:02 a.m. His car stalled in the middle of the road and a black cat jumped up on the hood looking at him; the black cat had yellow eyes. He beeped the horn and the cat jumped off his car and ran away. Then he tried starting his car at 7:03 a.m. and it started and he drove the short distance home.

He got in the house from the porch and he shut the door and the door opened again. He shut the door again tightly and locked it. Then he went upstairs to bed.

Becky said, "How was your evening?"

"It was like Halloween instead of Thanksgiving. At the beginning of my shift I'd just pulled out of the police station and I saw a deer with red eyes, as red as Rudolph the Red-Nosed Reindeer, and my car stalled and it was looking at me. When I beeped the horn the red-eyed deer scrammed, then my police car was able to start. Then coming home, my car stalled—it was two minutes after 7:00 a.m. when I was leaving the police station. I tried starting my car and it wouldn't start, then a black cat with yellow eyes jumped up on the hood, looking at me. When I beeped the horn the cat scrammed and my car started and I drove home.

"When I got in the house and closed the porch door, it reopened by itself! I shut the door tightly and made sure it was locked. When you get up check it!" said Billy.

"Some strange shit has been happening here—ouch!!!!!!!!!!!!!!!!!!

Something is biting my leg! It's my right leg!!!" said Becky. The time of her pain was 8:02 a.m. She got up to walk it off and the pain went away a minute later.

"You better go to the town ER in case you have a blood clot!" said Billy.

Becky went to the town ER to check her leg out. She got X-rays and she was fine then she came home.

Jack woke up coughing his brains out. The time was 9:02 a.m. The coughing was nonstop until a minute later, when it broke off all at once.

Brenda got up with a banging headache and the time was 10:02 a.m. She got up and took a couple of Advil and the headache stopped a minute later.

She and Jack got up and had breakfast with Becky when she got back from the ER.

Bobby got up to take a shower and he looked at the clock in the basement and the time was 11:02 a.m. When he got in the basement shower the water looked like blood and he let it run for a while. Once the water was clean he waited a few minutes then he took a shower.

Ben was making up the beds and getting fresh clothes when suddenly he saw a flash of lightning. Then came a loud crack of thunder and pouring rain. He looked at the clock on the basement wall and the time was 12:02 p.m.

Donna was watching cartoons on TV and the TV shut off all by itself!

Brenda was at the stove cooking and she looked at the time and it was 1:02 p.m.

Donna yelled, "Mommy the TV shut off!"

Brenda went to check the TV and it came back on a minute later.

"Don't worry Donna, strange things are going on in this house. Lunch will be ready soon."

After lunch Bobby and Ben were outside, sitting at the picnic table talking about football games, and Debbie and Donna were playing in the leaves. Until Debbie saw a black thing running and she said, "There's a big rat running in the leaves!" Then the two girls ran in the house.

Debbie saw the movement in the leaves at 2:02 p.m. It was her turn.

Ben and Bobby were kicking the leaves around looking for the big rat Debbie saw outside. She said, "Mommy, Mommy, I saw a big black rat running through the leaves and it scared me."

"You did! Don't worry about it, they will run away from you. Rats are more afraid of you than you are of them. They will not bother you," said Brenda.

Billy was taking a shower just before 3:00 p.m. and the shower shut off all by itself because it was 3:02 p.m., his turn to be haunted. He started sudsing up and the shower came back on with cold water. He jumped back then he turned the nozzle too hot to get a hot shower. He thought it was odd for the shower to turn off and on by itself.

Becky had just finished baking a cake and warming up the tea kettle. Water was leaking out of the boiling kettle so she shut it off and moved it out of the way. She looked at the digital clock on the stove and the time was 4:02 p.m. She took the cake out of the oven and put it on the counter. Then it jumped off the plate three times, settling back down on it after the third landing!

She screamed! "Ahhhhhhhhhhhh!!!!!!!!!!!!!!!"

All the action stopped a minute later! Brenda and Billy went to her and Billy said, "What's the matter Becky!"

"Something strange is going on in this house. I just finished baking a cake and I took it out of the oven and put it on the platter and it leaped up and down about three times. It looked like the cake was coming alive before it finally stopped!"

An hour later Jack and Billy were outside chopping wood for the fireplace and Jack saw a black shadow brush by him. He heard, *Woooooof!!!!!!!!* He looked at his watch and the time was 5:02 p.m. He said, "Billy did you just see that!"

"No, what?"

"I just saw a black mass I can't describe and it made a 'wooo' noise or something like that! I don't believe in ghosts but it was strange. Last night before I went to bed I also noticed a weird looking face in the fire in the fireplace! I couldn't describe it!" said Jack.

"I've been experiencing some strange things myself. I was taking a shower earlier and the water went off all by itself then it came back on. This morning coming home my car shut off and a black cat with yellow eyes jumped on my car, looking at me! And last night at the beginning of my shift the same thing happened but it was a deer with red eyes. I beeped the horn and the deer ran off, then my car started and the rest of the evening went normal until I came home.

"I don't believe in ghosts either, but now I'm beginning to wonder because so many strange things are happening to me and my family lately. They seem to happen at two minutes after the hour," pondered Billy.

Billy and Jack finished cutting wood and brought some in for the fireplaces. Later everyone was eating dinner. An hour before, Brenda started cutting the jumping cake and it broke into pieces. The time on the stove clock was 6:02 p.m. The cake fell everywhere on the countertop in pieces! She said, "The jumping cake broke into pieces; I can't put frosting on it!"

When Brenda put the cake together on the platter and put it on the table she and Becky told their stories and everyone laughed! The twins had a couple of girls come to visit them in the basement. Bobby lit the fireplace there and the four of them sat in front of the fire, toasting marshmallows, and drinking shots and beers.

Bobby was wearing a Colts hat and the hat flew off his head then he heard a popping sound in the fireplace. He looked at his watch and the time was 7:02 p.m. He thought one of the girls knocked his hat off and he went over to pick it up. Nobody was paying attention to Bobby's haunting; he didn't recognize it himself after a few shots. An hour later Ben was feeding the fire and suddenly a couple of hands were coming out of the fire and a strange face appeared that looked devilish.

The girls started screaming, then the fire was normal; the time of the haunting for Ben was at 8:02 p.m. One of the girls said, "What was that in the fireplace?"

"I don't know Jody, but it scared the fuckin shit out of me!" said Ben.

"It looked like some kind of demon!" said the other girl.

"Yeah, it did! I never saw a fire act like that before but Mom and Dad said some strange things have been happening in this house. We're not ghost believers but what I just saw was pretty scary! The fire tried to burn me with arm-like flames coming out of each side. Whoever wants to feed the fire next, be my guest! I have never seen anything like this!" said Ben Wilkins.

Bobby never noticed the scary looking fire, but the girls did and that was the end of the marshmallow toasting for the rest of the night. Nobody was going near the fireplace! The roaring fire was going for two hours. Slowly, it died down until it blew out during the night.

Donna was watching the fire in the fireplace still lit in the dining room and she was sitting close to it when suddenly a strong gust of wind blew the fire out. The hot wind blew Donna's hair straight up in the air and she screamed, "Ahhhhhh!!!!!!!" The time of her haunting was 9:02 p.m.

Brenda saw it and she said, "Donna get away from the fireplace, you're sitting too close! It's very windy outside!"

Brenda closed the glass doors and the fire settled, back to normal. At 9:32 p.m. Ben was screwing one of the girls in the basement bathroom shower.

Then Brenda got her little girls ready for bed. "I want to sleep with you Mommy! I don't want to sleep down here!" said Donna.

"Okay!"

"Mommy I want to sleep with you too, I don't want to see a rat in my bed!"

"Debbie you can sleep with Grandma. Look, Daddy's putting up a Christmas tree in here!" "Ahhhhhhh nice!!!!!!!!!"

Debbie was so excited and she sat and watched the blinking lights on the tree. Then around 10:00 p.m. the branches were moving on the tree as Debbie was smiling and touching the moving tree branches. Then a ghostly looking wolf with sharp fang teeth came out of the tree opening its mouth wide in a vicious loud growl. It went back in the Christmas tree as Debbie watched in shock. The time of the haunting was 10:02 p.m. She screamed hysterically!

"Ahhhhhhhhhhhhhhhh!!!!!!!!!!!" And she ran out of the master bedroom screaming! "Mommy, Mommy! There's a monster in the Christmas tree! It was a monster with red eyes, horns, and sharp teeth and it was trying to eat me and roared like a bear!" Poor Debbie was petrified!

"Go in bed with Donna and I'll check the Christmas tree," said Brenda. She went in the master bedroom and the tree was perfectly normal, the lighting was beautiful! Brenda walked around the tree, looking inside the branches and an ornament fell off onto the floor. She picked it up and she hung it back on the tree then she went to bed to keep the kids quiet.

10:32 p.m. Bobby was in the basement shower fucking the other girl. Then she jumped in bed with Ben after they were through. The first girl jumped in the sack with Bobby. Billy came down to a quiet basement after it was quite noisy earlier that night. Ben was fucking the girl in his bed after she was done with Bobby, and Bobby was screwing the other one in his bed, then it got quiet.

When Billy got to the bottom of the stairs he looked at the clock on the wall and the time was 11:02 p.m. and he saw Ben in bed with a girl. He said, "Hey fellas, you can't be bringing in girls to sleep with, we have kids here. You girls will have to leave."

One girl was dressed and the other with Ben was butt naked! She got dressed in a hurry and the girls left! "You boys are bad boys; you can't be sleeping with girls when we have kids in the house!" said Billy.

He laughed then he went upstairs and sat down in the living room with Becky and Jack Daniels, who was drinking Jack Daniels whisky. They sat in front of a warm fire talking about ghost stories.

When Billy was downstairs and saw the girl in bed with Ben, a mist left him and went first into the girl with Ben, then the other girl as they were leaving. No one saw the mist. The hauntings are going away for a while until the family leaves after Thanksgiving.

Brenda came downstairs to join Jack, Billy, and Becky for a few drinks and snacks after the two girls were asleep upstairs. Brenda said, "Dad, you and Mom may need to talk to a priest because there's a lot of strange things going on in this house. You need to do that tomorrow before someone gets hurt. I never believed in ghosts but something is going on here that I don't understand!

"Debbie said she saw a wolf like monster coming out of the Christmas tree upstairs and she has been seeing big rats. She said something growled at her like a mad dog and that the monster was trying to eat her! I have been pushed and pinched and held down.

"I have never experienced anything like this living in Florida and neither have my kids. If these strange things keep happening we're going to go to a hotel because Thanksgiving is three days away and my kids can't be going through these strange happenings here. I never knew Mattapoisett had happenings of the unknown; this is crazy," finished Brenda.

"We have been hearing strange noises too. It's almost midnight, too late to call a priest tonight, but I will call in the morning," said Becky.

"I don't believe in ghosts either but I have also heard strange noises, scratching...feel that I'm not alone, and it's not someone in our family watching. But when my car stalls and creatures—deer or cats—with colorful eyes jump on my car looking me in the eyes it's a sign of some kind of warning. I have seen things that maybe I shouldn't have with the police department. But I never had these strange things happen to me until we moved into this house. The police officers told me that I saw all the Mattapoisett ghosts! I laughed at them but I'm beginning to wonder if something is going on. What is it?!" said Billy.

"Last night, the fire in the fireplace formed into a strange looking face, almost like the devil. It only lasted a minute or two then it burned normally. Then I saw a black shadow that didn't match mine; I thought that was strange!" said Jack.

The four of them kept telling ghost stories until 3:00 a.m. not noticing any hauntings; it all stopped at after twenty-four hours. The next day Becky called the church.

"Good morning. St. Anthony's church, Father Frank speaking."

"Hi, I am Becky Wilkins calling from 66 6th Street. I fear that I have something evil in my house and I need help. Me, my husband—our visiting kids and grandchildren...we've been hearing and seeing strange things in this house since they got here!"

"Okay, I will come by about 4:00 p.m. and do a blessing and throw holy water in every room," said the priest. Becky and Billy had time off from work in support of their family visiting for Thanksgiving. It was Tuesday afternoon and the house was quiet with no hauntings. Billy was working in the yard blowing and packing leaves. Jack was splitting more wood and the boys were helping their father in the yard. Brenda and Becky were cleaning up the house and the two girls were playing with their toys and stuffed animals. 4:02 p.m. the bell rang and Becky answered the door in the living room.

"Hi there! My name is Father Frank."

"Becky Wilkins, please come in Father." The priest came in to bless the house, throwing holy water in every room and downstairs in the basement.

"Mrs. Wilkins, you do have activity in this house and it's coming from the boiler room. Where is your boiler located?"

"The boiler room is here. It's a gas light boiler and water heater, Father." The priest threw holy water and incense in the boiler room area and he placed a cross on a wall and he said some prayers. And he said, "We need to bless the shed, your cars, and the yard, and the evil spirits will go away. I have a glowing statue of the Blessed Virgin Mary. Place it in your bedroom, it will protect you from evil spirits during the night."

"Father, is there such a thing as ghosts?"

"Yes, some are evil and some can be friendly! If you see a ghost it's usually evil! The landlord never told you that this house is haunted. She's a jerk because it's not the first time I have been here. No one has lived in this house for the last six years!" said the priest.

"Father, my name is Ben Wilkins. I was with my brother Bobby and a couple of girls who were over last night, toasting marshmallows in the basement fireplace, and the fire made a formation that definitely looked demonic! The flames formed like a demon, burning in the fireplace, and flaming arms came out trying to grab me! It was the scariest thing I'd ever seen. My brother and the two girls with us never noticed what I saw. I never was so scared in my life—what I saw in this fireplace! Then I heard a loud popping sound and I got out of the way in a hurry!"

Everyone including the kids had their stories to tell the priest. The priest said, "You should be okay now, but if the hauntings come back, call me and we'll do a series of exorcisms to get rid of the demonic entities," said the priest.

"Father, after the blessings, the holy water, the statues, and the prayers, could the evil spirits get worse?" asked Brenda.

"Yes, but you would know it by now, because as soon as I threw the holy water and said prayers the evil spirits would be acting up. My prayers and my presence have caused no trouble. We went through the house and all the property and nothing strange happened. You should be alright," said Father Frank.

Then he left. There were no hauntings for the rest of the week. The girls were too scared to sleep in their rooms so they slept with their mother and Jack slept in Donna's room.

The next day was Tuesday and Brenda and Becky went shopping to get ready for the Thanksgiving holiday. Bill, Jack, and the two girls went bowling. The boys went to the mall. Bobby and Ben met the two girls they had over the other night at the Dartmouth Mall and they went out to eat, went to the movies, and shopped around until the boys came home at suppertime. After dinner, the girls came over to see them and had another party in the basement, but no fireplace and no sex, just drinks and snacks. Billy brought in some wood and he said, "Boys, behave, no nookie in here tonight!"

"Yes Dad," they said. The visiting girls laughed.

The next day was the day before Thanksgiving and Becky and Brenda were doing the cooking. The two girls, Donna and Debbie, were playing with their toys and watching TV. Billy, Jack, and the boys were partying all day into the evening.

Billy set up the Christmas tree and Becky and Brenda started decorating it. The next day was Thanksgiving Day and it was cold and windy. The fireplace was going in the living room and the Christmas tree was lit. Then at 2:02 p.m. dinner was served. Turkey, stuffing, mashed potatoes, squash, sweet marshmallow potatoes, turnip, string beans, carrots, corn, broccoli, and turkey soup were served and white and red wine and apple pie, squash pie, and pumpkin pie were served for dessert. Coffee for the adults and hot chocolate for the kids.

After dinner Billy, Jack, Bobby, and Ben watched football games on TV and Becky, Brenda, and the two girls went out to play in the snow.

The next day the family spent the day packing. Jack, Brenda, and the kids left on Saturday. The two boys and Billy spent the day watching college football games on TV. Becky was cooking and cleaning up the house.

The next day they went to church and later Bobby and Ben left to go home, at the time the army station in Indiana. The twin boys left later on Sunday afternoon in a monsoon of a rainstorm. They got their flight out of Boston to Indiana just before the rest of the flights were cancelled.

Christmas time the boys came back over for Christmas and New Year's, then went back to Indiana. Billy and Becky lived alone in the house.

Six months later it was June 3, 1986. Billy got a promotion with the Mattapoisett Police Department. Working Tuesday through Sunday 3:00 p.m. until 11:00 p.m., he didn't have to work the graveyard shift anymore. Becky was still nine to five at the hairdresser in Fairhaven.

One day Billy was outside, cutting a path through the woods to the beach and blueberry and raspberry bushes using a chainsaw. The new path invited the Mattapoisett ghosts back in. This part of the woods had not been cut down in years. It was getting attention now because Billy was making his yard a lot bigger and putting in picnic tables and tents because he planned to run a kids' camp on his property that summer.

The next day after all that work he'd done a nasty thunderstorm came through to ruin his idea! He finished the campsite before he went to work on Sunday afternoon at the police station.

Becky was putting tablecloths down on all eight of the picnic tables when the wind started picking up. Then she saw a green fog rolling in the woods, going against the wind out toward the beach. It disappeared as she watched. Then she heard thunder because the sky was darkening and went in the house, locked the door, and closed all the windows. Billy was working an office detail at the police station and he was watching the weather report on TV.

"Good afternoon. The National Weather Service has issued a severe thunderstorm warning for southeastern Massachusetts and Cape Cod. Doppler radar has reported a line of bow echo thunderstorms moving through Bristol County with straight line winds, hail, and cloud to ground lightning. An isolated tornado can't be ruled out. At 4:10 p.m. the storm is located over Dartmouth. The storm will strike Plymouth County within the next ten minutes. Please take cover immediately!"

Bill called Becky to warn her of the coming storm and the power went out. A microburst struck parts of Mattapoisett with 100 mile per hour straight line winds that tore through Billy's campsite and smashed everything he made. Lightning struck a couple of trees to add to the damage. The downburst just hit that area in Billy's backyard!

There was no electricity in the house when Billy got home.

"We had a bad storm. Thunder and lightning and strong winds knocked the power out, we have no lights," said Becky.

"I know, I tried calling you when we lost power at the police station. Just go back to bed and I'll check out the damage in the morning."

Billy got up the next morning to see all the work he'd done over the weekend unrecognizable! It looked like a tornado struck. The microburst knocked down several trees and smashed all eight picnic tables and the camp area was a total mess. Billy was sad. He said to Becky, "I'll have plenty of wood for the fireplaces next winter!" Billy hired a tree moving company to clean up the mess after crying all day. Then he spent the week cleaning up a little at a time until the yard was cleaned up.

Another thunderstorm with high winds did more damage on his property and it was a repeated routine. Windows in the house got broken and had to be replaced.

One early evening Billy was at work driving around in Ned's Point in his police car at about 9:00 p.m., dusk. Suddenly he saw the Greenman ghost walking toward the woods. He drove around to get a better look and he put on his police lights and the vision disappeared! He got out, shining his flashlight in the woods, and he saw a deer and it ran off! He continued shining his flashlight and he saw nothing. Then he drove away.

At the end of his shift he was talking to a police officer, telling him what he saw. "Officer Davies, I saw your favorite friend driving through Ned's Point. The Greenman ghost! I don't believe in ghosts but what I saw I can't describe. I saw what looked like a man in a glowing green flame covered with leaves and I couldn't see his face. Then I went to investigate and it was gone. I saw a deer but that was about it. I believe someone is flashing a movie camera on the trees to make it look like it was a monster. I didn't see anyone in the park, but someone may have been flashing something from the lighthouse because the light flashing was green!" said Billy.

"Billy, you saw what you saw! You saw the Greenman ghost!" said Officer Davies. Then Billy laughed and he went home.

The next day was Monday, Billy's day off. He and Becky went to the town beach and it was a beautiful day. There weren't many people on the beach at 4:00 p.m. This girl came over to Billy and Becky sitting on the beach drinking lemonade, and she said, "Good afternoon. My name is Maria Cooper, the town drifter."

"Pleased to meet you. My name is Billy Wilkins and this is my wife Becky."

"Pleased to meet you Maria," said Becky.

"I'm here to warn you that something is going to happen to you in your home and it's very evil!" said the Mattapoisett beach ghost. Then she walked away and vanished!

Billy started looking around on the beach, but neither he nor Becky saw the girl again. Becky went up to the lifeguard and she said, "Excuse me miss, did you see that girl in the black bathing suit?"

"No, there was no girl in a black bathing suit today."

"That's strange because the girl was just here saying bad things to me and my husband, telling us evil is going to get us in our home."

"Maybe she was a ghost!" said the female lifeguard.

"If you see her, tell her to leave because she was not speaking nicely to us. Thank you."

"I will!" said the lifeguard.

Later Billy and Becky went swimming and then lay on their blanket to dry off. Then they went home and had supper. Later in the evening they went bowling. Then bedtime. Becky woke up at 1:30 a.m. and she heard a big *bang!* sounding like the house was falling down.

Becky woke Billy up. "Someone is in the house!"

Billy got up and he grabbed his gun and he went looking all over the house and there were no signs of an intruder. He checked all the doors and they were all locked and the windows were closed. Then he saw lightning followed by a *boom!* He said, "There's your big bang Becky, it's thundering pretty good out there. The house is secure, no one broke in."

Billy couldn't sleep for ages, but just before 3:00 a.m. he fell asleep. 3:02 a.m. the bed covers flew off the bed and Billy was picked up and thrown across the room by a mysterious force! He bounced off of walls and the ceiling. It dropped him on the floor and threw him back in his bed. Becky saw what was happening and she was screaming!

Then a black mass formed when she turned on the lamp. Hands and arms were trying to grab her—it was an ugly demonic ghost going for its attack! Billy and Becky were pinned to the bed then the black mass was over them. The hands started grabbing them and the stench of death was unbearable!

Becky started saying prayers and the Blessed Mary statue started glowing, broke in half, and flew off the bureau and struck Becky on the head. Then the bedroom door closed and locked. Then the demonic ghost hands started scratching Billy on his back and legs. Becky was bitten on the neck and again on her foot and her hair was being pulled and the ghost was saying *get out!!!!!!!!!!* Then Billy was able to get to his gun and he fired a shot at the door! The door opened and the black mass of demonic ghost flew out!

Billy said, "Let's get out of here!!!!!!!!!!!!!!!!!!!!" He put on every light, grabbing the clothes needed to go to a motel. He and Becky were able to get out of the house in the way they were in the pouring rain, thunder, and lightning. Becky was in her PJs and slippers while Billy was in his underwear and slippers, and he grabbed a pair of shorts and a T-shirt to put on.

He drove down the street to a motel and there was a sign, "Closed, we're full." Then they went to the Mattapoisett Inn to spend the rest of the night. The injuries, scratching, and bite marks went away as soon as Billy and Becky got out of that house. Billy and Becky got to the Mattapoisett Inn at 3:30 a.m. and Billy said to the lady at the desk, "We have an emergency! Do you have a room available; we were chased out of our house by a ghost."

"A ghost! On my god! I have a room on the third floor, Room #302. It's $119.00 for the night and I will give you a twelve-noon checkout," said the lady at the desk.

"Could we get two nights?" asked Billy.

"Sure, it's $238.00," and they went to bed about 4:00 a.m.

Around noon they got up and went to the inn restaurant and had brunch. Officer Davies was there eating.

Billy went over to him and he said, "Hey buddy! You are right, there are such things as ghosts! When I got home last night my wife heard a loud noise in the house and when I went to investigate I found nothing. Meanwhile I couldn't sleep until almost 3:00 a.m. Suddenly the bedclothes were pulled off the bed then I felt something grabbing my legs. Next thing I knew I was being thrown up against the walls and hitting the ceiling, then dropped on the floor before the force threw me back in my bed. Then I saw a black cloud with writhing hands and arms and faces hovering over us, pinning us to the bed where we couldn't move until this thing started attacking us. I was grabbed and scratched and I felt something biting the cheeks of my ass! My wife was grabbed, scratched, and bitten, and the bedroom door closed by itself and locked while this ghost was attacking us! Then I was able to get my gun and I started firing at the locked door. It opened up by itself and the black cloud flew out— it stunk like death—and we were able to get out of there! We stayed here last night. As soon as we got out of that house the scratching and bite marks went away.

"I've known you for the last thirteen years and I never believed your ghost stories but I'm a believer now. The other day we met a lady at the beach and she told us 'something evil is going to happen in your home' and then as she turned to walk away she vanished. Becky reported her to the lifeguard and the lifeguard said she didn't see anyone. It was a lady in a black bikini bathing suit. The same lady I saw walking along the beach last November in the middle of the night when I was working the 11:00 p.m. to 7:00 a.m. shift," said Billy.

"It's the Mattapoisett Beach ghost! Her name is Maria Cooper. She was murdered on the beach by a witch," said Officer Davies.

Billy laughed and he walked away. He told hotel officials about what happened then he called Brenda in Florida and his two, sons Bobby and Ben.

"We're not going to your house again, you're going to have to visit us in Indiana," said Ben on the phone.

Billy and Becky stayed two nights at the Mattapoisett Inn and Arthur's Realtors had to get them a place to stay and give them their money back.

"Good afternoon, Arthur's Realtors, Ruthy Smith speaking."

"Hi, this is Billy Wilkins calling from 66 6th Street. I have bad news: our house is haunted. My wife and I were attacked by a poltergeist, a black ghost with arms and hands grabbing, scratching, and biting and throwing us around in the house. There were faces and my wife got bit and we have scratch and bite marks all over us! We need to get out of there in a hurry before we get killed!"

"Billy, where are you right now?"

"We're at the Mattapoisett Inn."

"Okay, stay there for about a month until we find you another home and we will cover the room; tell them at the desk to keep you there and have them contact Arthur's Realtors. Do not go back to that house. Our movers will move all your stuff out and put it in storage until your next home is ready. We have a condo available in Fairhaven next month, you can look at it later," said Ruthy Smith.

Billy and Becky stayed at the Mattapoisett Inn for a month. Ruthy Smith went to the house with a priest to bless the home and a moving company came to move everything out of the home and the Mattapoisett police were there to make sure everything was going as planned. The realtor gave Billy his money back to avoid a lawsuit. The priest was there doing blessings and throwing holy water. Billy and Becky came to get some clothes and other needs from the house while the priest was there. The priest was saying prayers to St. Michael the archangel to get rid of the devil. The house was dark and cloudy going in, and then brightened when the priest finished.

Billy and Becky got what they needed and went back to the Mattapoisett Inn. The next day they went to breakfast to meet friends at Curilli's restaurant for a breakfast/lunch gathering. Billy and Becky were talking to their friends about the hauntings in that house while having breakfast at Curilli's.

"Billy, my name is Archie Antilli. I come to Curilli's quite often and I overheard you talking about the hauntings at 66 6th Street. I don't mean to interrupt you but that house was built over an Indian slaughter graveyard where witchcraft and devil worship was practiced. Nobody built on that land until that house in the early 1970s. Witches called all the Mattapoisett ghosts to do sacrifices on that land. That house has been vacant since 1979 when the demonic marsh poltergeist chased them out. Everyone who lived in that house was chased out by poltergeists and evil spirits. Ghosts such as the Greenman, Maria Cooper the beach ghost, the marsh poltergeist cloud with hands, arms, and heads from the dead seeking revenge!

"Mattapoisett is a beautiful bedroom community town but it has a lot of history of demonic ghosts and there are several of them! Get out of that house and you two have a good day," said Archie Antilli.

Later Billy went to work at the police station, telling them what happened about the hauntings.

"Billy, we have been telling you for years. There is such a thing as ghosts!" said the police.

# FOUR

## HAUNTINGS IN MATTAPOISETT

One day a town meeting was held, a short time after Billy and Becky moved out of that house. It was held at Old Rochester Regional High School gym.

"Good evening and welcome to tonight's meeting for the town of Mattapoisett. My name is Captain Walker from the Mattapoisett Police Department. The reason for this meeting is because we have a serious ghost problem here in Mattapoisett, it has been a problem for years. For this first time in forty years the Greenman ghost has been quite active and several sightings have been seen lately.

"For years, bad things have been happening from the Greenman ghost. Not only sightings but attacks, and poltergeists have been visiting Mattapoisett lately. Reports of ground movement and tree branches grabbing people. People are dying here, including one of our police officers, John J. Jennings, who was attacked by tree branches moving from some kind of a force that we cannot understand!

"We have been getting shark attacks here, people are dying, and if we continue to have these problems the beauty here is going to vanish eventually and it has to stop. We have a lot of small businesses here and it's a tourist town during the summer and I want to keep it that way.

"I don't want the town of Mattapoisett to get a bad name. Whoever or whatever is bringing this evil in, it has to go! We never had reports of poltergeists here until now. Somebody is doing something here that's not good. The hauntings have been happening here for years in Mattapoisett—but now poltergeists! We have a problem.

"The towns of Mattapoisett, Marion, and Rochester were built on top of Indian slaughter graveyards and there have been hauntings here since the 1600s, but the poltergeists lately—something has to be done about it, things are getting bad! We have some people to share their stories. Let's bring Officer William Wilkins to the stage," said Captain Walker.

"Good evening ladies and gentlemen. I have been a Mattapoisett police officer since March of 1978 just after the great blizzard. Before I went in the army I was working the 11:00 p.m. to 7:00 a.m. shift on a detail in Ned's Point when I rescued a screaming girl claiming she was chased by the Greenman. I searched the area and found nothing so I left.

"In late November 1985, I saw it again, roughly the same place too! When leaving Ned's Point I saw a deer in the road with red eyes. Then I saw a girl wearing a black bikini walking along the town beach in the middle of the night. I thought that was strange. When I pulled into the beach area the girl was gone! When I finished my shift I reported all incidents to headquarters. They told me that I met all the Mattapoisett ghosts! I laughed at them because I didn't believe in ghosts.

"There's also the house I bought last fall at 66 6th Street. Me and my wife Becky are sophisticated professionals with three kids and do not believe in ghosts. I heard noises and saw shadows in the house but was too tired to worry about them. I'm not going to jump if I hear a noise or see a shadow. I have a house and a lot of property to take care of, not to mention an eight-hour overnight shift at the police station. My kids heard and saw strange things in that house. I saw the tree branches move but I didn't think much of it. I heard voices telling me to get out but I didn't pay attention to it; it's my house and I'm not going to be bullied! Many people told me about the ghosts here in Mattapoisett, but it went in one ear and out the other. I refused to believe, but one week ago all that changed.

"I saw the full Greenman vision walking into the woods and I told Officer Davies that I saw his favorite ghost. I still thought it was fake. I did not believe him. That night my wife woke up to a loud bang in the house and I checked the house and I didn't find anything. Then I couldn't sleep that night for ages, but as soon as I did, around 3:00 a.m. in the morning, the bed sheets flew off the bed! An invisible force pulled me out of bed by my feet and threw me up against the walls, tossing me up on the ceiling and dropping me to the floor. Then it picked me up and threw me back on the bed so I hit the headboard with my head. Then I saw a black cloud hover over our bed with hands grabbing, arms slapping, and faces full of teeth that bit my wife Becky in the legs and feet. I was punched and scratched and kicked by this black ghost while my wife was attacked!

"No blood, but the scars were there and if we hadn't got out in time maybe there would have been blood or we may have been killed! It shut the bedroom door and locked it so we couldn't get out. I was able to get my nine-millimeter gun and blast a hole in the door so it opened and the black mist ghost left the room. We got out of there as fast as we could! As soon as we got out of that house the scratching marks and the bite marks went away but the stress remains. We're currently staying at the Mattapoisett Inn. I'm a believer now!" said Billy Wilkins.

"Thank you Mr. Wilkins. Next we have Mr. Archie Antilli," said Captain Walker.

"Good evening, I will be as short as possible. I have been studying the Mattapoisett ghosts for the last ten years. I'm a history professor at Southeastern Mass University. The black mist ghost has been around in southeastern Massachusetts since the witchcraft days from the 1600s. Witches of Salem and the mist settled in Bridgewater, Massachusetts.

"Mr. William Wilkins experienced the worst ghost. Someone must have put a curse on Mr. and Mrs. Wilkins for them to be attacked by this force. This black mist fog was formed by sacrifices by the devil in the Bridgewater Triangle, a force too complicated to describe. The Bridgewater Triangle area is East and West Bridgewater, Abington, Whitman, Brockton, Freetown, parts of Fall River and Rehoboth, and some other towns in Plymouth County. All Indian burial grounds. Also, there are giant snakes, Bigfoot creatures, malformed birds called thunderbirds, and other deformed creatures in the Hockomock Swamp River corrupted by witchcraft practices.

"These areas are haunted and expanding into Cape Cod. The outside areas also possessed—you guessed it—right here in Mattapoisett, Marion, and Rochester. It's too complicated to go through complete detail, there is too much to this very strong poltergeist! The black cloud mist is the result of demonic practices in the Bridgewater Triangle. It feeds off the dead, manifesting as a tangled batch of hands, arms, and faces with teeth; giant snakes; monkey or Bigfoot formations; orbs of light; ball lightning; and sometimes even like a UFO, and it can change colors.

"This poltergeist can kill you! If you see it you have to stand your ground like approaching a bear. Do not turn your back; if you do and show fear it will get you. When it attacks you start throwing punches and fight back! Back away and fight it off and don't show fear and you can beat this thing. Throw something at it and say prayers while you are fighting it off. The Wilkins fired a gun to scare it off. That's how they survived. It pulled them out of bed, but they fought back even when they heard, 'Get out.' It left after the gunshot. The towns of Abington, Whitman, Freetown, and Rehoboth are those most haunted by this black mist because those are the places where most of the dead were sacrificed.

"The Greenman is another bad ghost and it will kill you. A Mattapoisett police officer was killed by it in 1979. Most of the time the Greenman appears as a green glow or mist and sometimes appears in a human shape. If it comes, back off and keep your distance. If you challenge it, it will come after you and make your life miserable! It's not an aggressive ghost. it appears as a warning. Just get away from it and leave the area where it shows its vision. The ghost looks like a man covered in leaves and his face looks like straw. You can't see its eyes, mouth, or ears, and this ghost is most active before or after a storm. Some people said good things happen to them after viewing the Greenman ghost. The Greenman was created from beings trapped during a huge storm and killed. People and animals died together and deformed into prophecy creatures from being caught in sea algae from the great storm washing people, sea life, land, farm animals, and birds into it. Further, it got sucked into tree roots to make trees come alive like in *The Wizard of Oz*. The old Indians believe it comes from the sea. The Greenman ghost is an Indian spirit from the devil. It's evil, but if you keep your distance it's not aggressive.

"The deer with the red eyes is another ghost seen in Mattapoisett, Marion, and Rochester. It's another evil spirit that will put a spell on you while staring at you. Do not make eye contact if you see it, because it's deadly and it has been known to cause fatal accidents! If you see this deer while driving just drive by it, through it, or take another turn. It's not an aggressive ghost unless you make eye contact.

"Maria Cooper, the Mattapoisett Beach ghost, is another. She's a friendly ghost, a victim from the red-eyed deer. She hangs at the beach; she's there year-round and she appears to warn people that evil interferes. If she comes to you, she will give you a warning that something evil is going happen. Then she'll disappear into thin air. If you get a warning from Maria Cooper, she will tell you what it is. You may want to see a priest. Otherwise she's seen walking on the beach usually around 3:00 a.m., the time she was killed.

"The invisible ghost is another one. It's an evil spirit that you can't see and it makes noises and may pass through shadows. Most of its shadows are invisible and it can move things, even pick you up and throw you. It can kill you, but most of the time it's an aggravating ghost that makes you notice things and plays with your head. It can punch you, knock you down, kick you. It can bite you and sometimes follows the black mist; that's what happened to Mr. And Mrs. Wilkins.

"One day I was at a football game at Bridgewater State and something bit me in the right ear and it drew blood! It was not a bird or some animal or insect. I was by myself and this mysterious force gave me a pretty good bite and I had to get medical attention. Sorry I took so long; we have a lot of ghosts here in Mattapoisett.

"Before I leave I want to warn you that Ruthy Smith from Arthur's Realtors was a witch and she practiced in Bridgewater before she became a realtor about ten years ago. Being on the police force I have a right to pass that information to you. Thank you," said Archie Antilli.

"Thank you for coming to tonight's town meeting. If you need to ask questions the floor is open," concluded Captain Walker.

# FIVE

## THE IT FAMILY HAUNTINGS

The house at 66 6th Street is ready for the next family to move in. A doctor, his wife, and three kids move into the house with their dog. Dr. Raymond It; his wife, Mary It; teenage daughters Michelle It, thirteen years old, and Marsha It, fourteen years old; their son Doug It, sixteen years old; and their bulldog Bryant. Former realtor Ruthy Smith was fired from Arthur's Realtors after the town meeting of 1986.

Six years after the Wilkins family lived there in 1985 the It family moved in the house in July of 1991. Dr. It and Mary met with the new realtor at the house.

"You must be Mr. Eric Drome."

"Yes sir. My name is Eric Drome from Arthur's Realtors."

"My name is Dr. Raymond It, and she's my wife, Mary It. We come from Montpelier, Vermont, and we're looking for property near the beach, instead of living in the mountains and being snowed in all the time. We have two teenage girls, a boy, and a dog."

"Nice to meet you Doctor, and your wife Mary. Come in and I'll show you this lovely Cape Codder. Let me show you the house."

Round and round, here we go again. The realtor showed the couple the house the same way Ruthy did and later the parents showed the kids and they loved the house. The realtor came back the next day to make arrangements for the sale.

"The house and the property cost $200,000. It's $25,000 down and a twenty-year fixed mortgage. The house is in great shape and the going price is $350,000 but the higher your income the cheaper the house will be by signing this contract. If you don't sign for twenty years then you pay the higher mortgage," said Eric Drome.

It was a done deal without a struggle and the family started moving in.

The truck came, "Burlington Movers in All of Vermont," with all their furniture. The kids brought the doghouse out to the backyard, set it up, and tied up Bryant the bulldog outside. It was a hot day in the nineties when the movers were moving the Its into 66 6th Street. The doctor was on vacation for the rest of the month of July 1991. He, his wife, and their three teenage kids started setting up the furniture and putting clothes away and organizing the house. Black shadows moved around in the house but they were not paying attention. The Its were not told they were moving into a haunted house.

"Girls, you will be sleeping downstairs in these rooms near the bathroom. Doug, you'll be sleeping upstairs in the room across from us," said Dr. It.

After dinner, the doctor took the kids for a ride around town. Doug said, "Dad, it's spooky here, maybe there're ghosts here."

"Oh my goodness Doug, don't say that!"

"It's really nice here Dad, it's bright, not like the ghost town where we used to live!" said Michelle.

"Yeah Dad, Mattapoisett is a hell of a lot nicer place than Montpelier. It was boring where we used to live," said Marsha.

Later they got home. The kids were outside playing Frisbee with each other and Bryant the dog joined in until it got dark. The dog started barking, looking up in the trees, and there was a big raccoon in one. Lightning started flashing and the raccoon jumped down from the tree and ran into the woods. The kids untied the dog and brought him in the basement for the night. The dog lay in its doggy bed during the night and he stayed in his doghouse outside during the day, tied to a long chain.

"Come on Bryant, let's go in the house, it's lightning out here!" said Marsha. Later the kids went in for their showers and went to bed.

Nighttime, Dr. It and Mary were sleeping. Then around 3:00 a.m. Mary woke up and she saw a big man in the doorway of her bedroom. She was not totally awake yet. She screamed, "Ahhhhhhh!!!!!!!!!!!" Then she turned on the lamp and nothing was there!

She woke her husband. "Ray, wake up, someone's in the house!" Dr. It got up and he searched the house and every closet.

"Is there something wrong, Dad?" asked Doug.

"No, Mom thought she saw something, but nothing's here." All the doors in the house were locked and he shut all the windows because it was raining outside.

"Mary you must have had a dream, there's nobody here!"

"I was beginning to wake up. Maybe it was a dream because when I turned on the lamp nothing was there. I was really tired; I was probably imagining things!" she said.

An hour later, Dr. It woke up to a loud bang in the house. He grabbed his shotgun and he cocked the gun a few times then went through the house. It was still all thunder and lightning outside but the crash did not sound like thunder. He found nothing then he went back to bed, putting the gun beside the bed in case something went wrong.

An hour later Doug woke up to a pinch on his ear. He quickly got up, turned on the lamp, and he found a clothespin lying on the bed. He picked it up and he threw it on the bureau, then he got up to check the room and under the bed covers and he found a second clothespin. He grabbed it and tossed it on the bureau. Then he went back to bed.

Mary hung clothes outside earlier today. Mary did see a ghost and the happenings are already starting out of the gate with this family.

The two girls went to the town beach for the day swimming and laying in the sun and Mary It was home doing laundry and cooking. Michelle and Marsha were lying on a blanket on the beach and three boys came over talking to them for a few minutes. They went swimming together then the girls went back to their blanket to lie in the sun. Then this lady in a black bathing suit came over to talk to them.

"Good afternoon girls, my name is Maria Cooper the town beach drifter." Then she vanished!

Marsha said to Michelle, "Did you see that lady in the black bathing suit talking to us then she disappeared?!"

"Yes, I did, maybe she's a ghost!" Marsha laughed.

Then she reappeared in the same spot she vanished and she repeated her identity. "Good afternoon girls, my name is Maria Cooper the town beach drifter."

"Hi there. My name is Michelle and she's my sister Marsha. How do you do?"

"Hi, I'm here at the beach every day. I am here to tell you; you girls are in great danger. There's a poltergeist coming for you from the wind. You must be prepared!" The lady in the black bathing suit walked away a few feet then vanished!

"Am I seeing what I think I'm seeing? That lady doesn't make sense! She disappeared again!" said Marsha.

Michelle went to the lifeguard and she said, "Excuse me lifeguard, did you see that lady talking to us?"

"What lady?"

"The lady in the black bathing suit. She told me and my sister a poltergeist was coming to get us in the wind," said Michelle.

"No, I didn't see the lady."

"That's strange! The lady was standing right in front here," said Michelle.

"I wasn't paying attention," said the lifeguard.

Then Michelle walked away and went back to her blanket. The lifeguard cannot tell people that a ghost owns the beach and has it under her protection. Later the girls left the beach, drinking out of their water bottles, and went home telling their mother what they saw.

"Girls, some older ladies go to the beach looking for drugs. They will say crazy things to get your attention. Just ignore them," said Mary.

"Mom, she vanished right in front of our eyes. The lifeguard was right behind where we were lying and she didn't see her!" exclaimed Michelle.

"She's a drifter looking for a quick fix and if you ignore her she runs away," said Mary.

"Mom, she disappeared in front of our eyes; she might be a ghost!" said Marsha.

Mary laughed. Later Doug came home in a 1977 Thunderbird two-seater he bought for five thousand dollars, a yellow car. He and his dad spent the day out looking for cars for the sixteen-year-old. He took the girls for a ride one at a time.

Bedtime. Dr. It had a dream that Doug cracked up his car, hitting a pole, and he went through the windshield and he was lying in the street dead! He woke up quick! He sat up on the bed and he looked at the alarm clock and the time was 3:02 a.m. He got up and he looked in Doug's room and he was fast asleep. He went to the bathroom then he went back to bed.

One hour later, Michelle heard a voice, *get out!* waking her up from a sound sleep. She got up and she walked around the house in the kitchen and the living room, turning lights on and off. She didn't hear the voice again and she went back to bed.

An hour later Marsha woke up to a beeping noise in her room then her alarm clock went off. That scared her, and she shut it off and she went back to bed.

One hour later their dog Bryant saw something in the basement, a ghostly dark figure, the same thing Mary saw last night, thinking it was only a dream. Bryant barked and barked all night until someone came downstairs to quiet him. The girls heard the dog barking in the cellar and they woke up to see what the dog was barking at. Bryant was barking at a wall in the basement where he saw the ghost. Michelle and Marsha went over to feel the wall where Bryant saw the ghost and there was nothing. The girls put lights on in the basement and Bryant stopped barking. Then the girls went back upstairs to bed. Bryant growled, looking at the wall where the ghost was. Then he stopped.

The next morning Doug brought the dog outside and tied him up. Dr. It and Mary got up and the doctor said, "Mary, I had the worst nightmare of my life last night. I had a dream Doug crashed his car and he was killed!"

"Oh my God! You need to say some prayers after having that dream. I had a dream that I was a muffler and I woke up exhausted!" said Mary. The doctor got a good laugh at her dream.

After breakfast Doug went for a ride in his car; he drives kind of fast. He stopped at his friend's house to show off his Thunderbird. Later he came home for lunch then the family went to the beach for the day. The kids, the doctor, and Mary played volleyball on the beach then went in swimming. Later they got ice cream at Oxford Creamery. Then later they had a cookout in the backyard. Dr. It was cooking hotdogs, hamburgers, and chicken on the grill. The doctor has one more week of vacation before he goes back to work.


Later they went to a show at Shipyard Park and a band was playing in the gazebo. The name of the band was The Ghost Busters. Then a musician came on to do a few tricks, then a comedian. Then a storm came with thunder and lightning, ending the show. Then everyone went home. Nighttime. The ghosts are active but no one is paying attention.

Doug went outside to get Bryant and bring the dog in the house from the storm. He saw a faint green fog in the woods then he went in the house with the dog and lightning was flashing. The green fog was the Greenman ghost. Doug thought nothing of it. Doug left lights on for the dog. The night was quiet.

The next day everyone went to church then it was another day at the beach. Doug and the two girls were playing in the water and Dr. It and Mary were sitting up on the beach and this lady in a black bathing suit came over to them and she said, "Good afternoon."

"Excuse me but I have to go to the bathroom, I'll be right back," said Mary, and she got up and the lady left, walking away, then vanished! It was the Mattapoisett beach ghost. Dr. It laid down when the lady left before she vanished. Dr. It never noticed her disappearing. The lady never returned. Mary came back and she said, "Who's that lady, she was acting kind of strange. Maybe it's the same girl Michelle and Marsha met the other day?"

"I don't know, she came over and she said good afternoon and she walked away. She looked like she was crying or rundown; she looked like she needed a doctor!" After the beach, the It family went to a flea market in New Bedford and Michelle bought a strange looking doll. It looked like vaguely humanoid, half human and half animal. Marsha bought a hairdressing kit. Doug bought a bowling ball. Dr. It bought an emergency hurricane alert weather kit. And Mary bought a hairdryer and some clothes. Then they went home.

Later the doctor went out to cut the lawn and Mary was cooking supper. A black mass-like bird flew over her head while she was cooking in the kitchen but she did not see it. She did feel a strong gust of wind blowing her hair straight up in the air. She shut the window in the kitchen and she saw the tree branches moving slowly like on a rotating robot. She didn't think much about looking out the window and she went back to cooking. The phone rang and she heard cracking sounds in the phone's receiver. She hung up and she continued cooking dinner, roasting a chicken in the oven.

The following week the kids were doing what kids do while the parents were at a bowling league in Fairhaven. Doug was out showing off his car to his friends, but the two girls were up to something else. They were playing with an Ouija board, calling in spirits, bringing the African ghost of Ebenezer into their house. They set up lit candles in the basement while playing with the game. This ghost had followed the family from Vermont and it met with all the dead spirits in Mattapoisett. Now Michelle and Marsha and a couple of girlfriends just invited the big black beast into their house!

They don't take the hauntings seriously playing this game but they'll soon find out! Even worse, the doll Michelle bought at the flea market is possessed and is in Mary's bedroom. Buying the doll and calling in the big Ebenezer—they are making a huge mistake! Ebenezer is a demon leader from the Bennington Triangle tribe from Vermont and has now been invited to Mattapoisett. He may not be welcome here because he has stronger demonic powers than the local ghosts. This will be a serious problem for the It family. The demonic black mass with the hands, arms, faces, and animal heads that attacks is the deadliest demonic spirit in Mattapoisett, but Ebenezer is the next thing to the devil and he looks it. Perhaps the ghosts here will push him out, but not before this family is in a shitload of trouble.

Michelle and Marsha are no strangers to playing with an Ouija board because they played the game before in Vermont when they were living there. Their parents do not know this, or that they're playing now.

They kept calling, "Ebenezer, Ebenezer, Ebenezer!!!!!!!!!!!!!!!!!!!!!" Then a black fog formed and they kept praising Ebenezer and then it growled like a wolf and the four girls playing the game yelled, "Stop!!!!!!!!!!!!!!!!!!!" They blew out the candles and closed the game and broke up the ring. Then the girls went upstairs to watch TV after hiding the game.

Ebenezer appeared outside and Bryant saw it and he was barking up a storm! Ebenezer looked like a jet-black mishmash of man, animal, and demon with horns, red eyes, and sharp teeth. He roared at the dog and Bryant charged after Ebenezer, biting at the ghost, and it disappeared! Bryant continued barking until Michelle went outside to get him and brought him in the house. The dog didn't want to stay in the basement so he ran upstairs to stay with the girls.

While the girls were playing with the Ouija board, Doug was at Ned's Point hanging with his friends. Some kids were smoking pot and drinking a few beers. The friends offered some to Doug and he said, "No thanks, if my father finds out I was drinking he'd take my car away."

One boy said, "Doug, you're in danger man."

"What do you mean by that?" he asked.

"I know you just moved here from Vermont and I am not trying to separate you from our group because we like you being with us. But I feel energy from you that is not good. Maybe a ghost might be haunting you. I don't know but I feel negative energy like loss of power coming from you. I'm sorry to tell you this, my name is Mike Haven."

"Pleased to meet you. My name is Doug It."

The boy laughed at his name. "Doug It!!!!!!!!!!!!!!!!!!!!!!!!!" Then the boy Mike introduced his friends to him and he became friends with the group. Later he went home. He got there just after his parents came home from their Tuesday night bowling league.

Dr. It had a bowling pin he brought home from his league. Doug said, "Wow Dad, nice bowling pin!"

"Thanks Doug. I bowled my first ever 200 game, 213, and the bowling alley gave me a pin."

"Cool, congratulations Dad. Take me bowling someday!"

"I will Doug."

Bedtime. Around 3:00 a.m. the Ebenezer ghost was checking out Doug's car then it vanished; no one saw it. A few minutes later Doug felt something pushing his head in his pillow and he woke up in a hurry. He turned on the lamp and Bryant jumped up on his bed and he played with the dog. Doug let Bryant sleep at the foot of his bed. Doug thought the dog was playing with him, forcing his head into the pillow, but it was something else, the invisible ghost. Doug felt safe with the dog in his room.

The rest of the week Dr. It and Mary took the kids riding through Mattapoisett, stopping at restaurants, going for ice cream, going to the beach, before he returns to work next week. The dog would not stay out at night anymore; he did not want to sleep in the basement. He started barking and growling until the kids let Bryant stay with them. The dog hung with the girls during the day and he slept with Doug every night. The doctor and Mary thought it was strange the way Bryant was acting. The kids felt safe with the dog in the house because Ebenezer is afraid of Bryant since he stood his ground like a roaring bear when the ghost made its appearance. But it's only temporary; trouble will come later.

Every once in a while Bryant would start growling when he felt the presence of any ghost threatening. Doug took the dog out in the morning and chained him up to his doghouse. Soon he had some trophies, killing snakes, raccoons, opossums, squirrels, rabbits, foxes, coyotes, and rats. Bryant is showing the ghosts that he's not playing around!

Doug laughed hysterically when he saw all the dead animals Bryant killed. Now he has an appetite from the wild. The doctor and Doug had to remove the dead animals Bryant killed and throw them in the woods. The next day Bryant had more trophies to discard. The dog was covered in blood from killing all these animals and Bryant was hosed down to get all the blood off of him. The next day Bryant killed some more animals, including a deer, and he was covered in blood again and Doug had to hose the blood off of him again and remove the dead animals. Why feed him, he's eating all the dead animals outside! He was big and fat after all the animals he killed and ate. The deer was torn open and Bryant ate the inside of it. This problem was so bad Doug had to move Bryant and his doghouse to the front yard to stop these attacks and brought Bryant in the house before it got dark. The plan worked. Bryant wouldn't leave Doug's side and he slept at the foot of his bed every night.

Dr. It is back to work. Today's Thursday and vacation is over. It was the first Thursday in August of 1991. He works at Toby Hospital in Wareham, from 7:00 a.m. to 3:00 p.m. Thursday through Monday. He has Tuesdays and Wednesdays off. Mary It is a housewife while Dr. Raymond It is at work.

Doug took the two girls to the beach until dinnertime. Just after the doctor got home he looked at the sky, and storm clouds were rolling in and thunder was heard. The clouds looked like the face of the devil! The formation looked like a face with horns and pointy ears with black dark clouds in the middle.

"Doug, come look at this! It looks like the devil is coming."

"I saw it Dad! We better get in the house, there's lightning!"

"Ray, Doug, get the dog in the house, a bad storm is coming," said Mary.

Dinnertime, the news was on. "Good evening, this is the Channel 6

News. The National Weather Service has issued a tornado warning for Bristol and Plymouth counties until 8:00 p.m."

"Everyone get down in the basement and stay away from windows!" said Mary. Then they watched the news on a TV in the basement, saying that an enormous storm was coming and it could be a monster! The storm brought strong winds, hail, thunder, and lightning. Bryant was barking up a storm because he's afraid of the real storm. The storm lasted three hours.

Then the kids got ready for bed and the dog went upstairs with Doug. The doctor had paperwork to do.

The next day was Friday and the doctor went to work and Mary was home alone. The girls went out with their friends for the day and Doug met a girl on the beach and later went to Oxford Creamery for some ice cream. Doug got a job there and he would start on Monday. Then he took the girl for a ride in his yellow 1977 Thunderbird convertible with the top down, driving kind of fast on Route 6. Then they went to bowl a few games. The girls went with a group of girlfriends—including the two that played the Ouija board game with them—to a summer play in New Bedford.

Mary was home with the ghosts. She was downstairs washing clothes in the washing machine and she could feel someone standing over her. She felt electricity going through her all over her body and through her hair. She felt like someone was running their hands through it. She quickly stopped what she was doing and she jumped back out of the way and the friction stopped. She looked around and she saw nothing. She went upstairs to get more clothes to put in the washing machine. When the first wash was done, she took the clothes out, ready to hang on the line outside. Then she put the second load in to wash. She felt someone standing over her again and she quickly looked behind her and there was nothing. She looked at the clock on the wall in the basement and the time was 11:02 a.m. Then she hung the first load of clothes on the clothes-line outside. Then when the second load finished she hung them on the line. Then she saw a big dark ghostly figure standing in the backyard behind the shed. *Ebenezer.*

She said, "Hey buddy, you're on our property. What are you doing here!?" The man was still there and Mary picked up a big stick and she went after him. The dark ghostly figure ran in back of the shed out of sight, then he vanished! Mary turned Bryant loose and the dog ran after him! She went behind the shed and he was gone! Mary left Bryant off the leash and she went in the house and she called police. The time was 12:02 p.m. when she saw the ghostly figure.

"Mattapoisett Police. Officer Archie Antilli speaking."

"Hi, this is Mary it from 66 6th Street on Route 6. I saw a big dark figure on my property near my shed. Please come and take him away!"

"Okay Mary, stay in the house until I get there!" said the cop.

The police came and he and Mary went out in the yard looking for the man as Bryant followed. There was nothing!

The policeman said, "There's nobody on your property. Just leave the dog loose because if it comes back the dog will let you know by barking at him. Keep the dog at your side when you leave the house," said the policeman, then he left.

Mary was in the house, sitting at the table in front of the air conditioner eating a sandwich. Suddenly she noticed the closed door going out to the porch vibrating like it's ready to bust open! Mary looked at her watch and the time was 1:02 p.m. The vibrating stopped a minute later. She opened the door and closed it and nothing.

Mary went outside to check the mail and a car was going down Route 6 like a bat out of hell. The police were chasing the speeding car, she had to get out of the way in a hurry to avoid being hit! The time was 2:02 p.m.

Then Mary was sitting in the dining room reading a newspaper, cooling off in front of the air conditioner. She looked at her watch and the time was 3:02 p.m., then she heard a crash downstairs in the basement. She got up and she ran downstairs to check it out and she found nothing. She went outside looking for where the crash came from and Bryant was following her. And there was nothing. She walked around the house and checked inside the house and she found nothing.

Then she went outside just before 4:00 p.m. to bring in the clothes on the line and she got tangled in the bed sheets as it felt like something was grabbing her. She was spinning in the bed sheets—the time was 4:02 p.m.—and the grabbing and spinning stopped a minute later. She was able to bring the dry clothes in the house. Then the doctor came home from work.

"How was your day today?" asked Mary.

"It was good but I have to go back in tonight for the 11:00 p.m. to 7:00 a.m. shift. I'll have the day off tomorrow and we can go to dinner tomorrow night with Sharon and Greg. They want to go to Mike's Steakhouse in Fairhaven. How was your day?" asked Dr. It.

"A lot of strange things've been happening here this afternoon. This morning I felt like someone was in the basement standing over me while I was washing clothes but I found no one. Then I saw a big dark ghostly figure standing outside near the shed and I asked him what he was doing and he just stood there, ignoring me. So I sent Bryant to go after him and he ran off, so I called police and they couldn't find him. Then the door going out to the porch was vibrating until it was ready to break, then a car almost ran me over going to get the mail. Then I heard a big crash in the basement. Then I was bringing in the laundry on the clothesline and I got tangled in the sheets and I was spinning like a top! It was scary," said Mary.

"Raymond, did you just grab me by the ass!?" said Mary.

"No, why?"

"Something grabbed me by the ass!"

"Maybe it was a ghost!" Dr. It laughed. The time was 5:02 p.m. when Mary's pants stuck to her ass!

Now it's Dr. It's turn to be haunted at two minutes after every hour for the next six hours. 6:02 p.m. Dr. It noticed it was getting dark in the house and the sun was shining brightly outside. Then it brightened up a minute later. Then he was eating dinner and drinking a beer when suddenly the lights went very dim and he looked at his watch and the time was 7:02 p.m. Then the lights in the house got brighter a minute later. Then he went in for a nap in the living room because he had to go back to work that night. Mary was putting laundry away and the girls were watching TV in the basement. Doug came home from his date and he warmed up dinner for himself. Dr. It felt ringing in his ears and the time was 8:02 p.m. The ringing went away a minute later.

Then he was woken to a voice, *Ebenezer, Ebenezer, Ebenezer!!!* at 9:02 p.m. He thought he was hearing things and he went back to sleep. Then he felt something pushing him, waking him up again, and Bryant was jumping up on the couch to greet him. He can still feel the jabs, but he's thinking the dog is pushing the couch.

He looked at his watch and the time was 10:02 p.m. Then he got up and he went to work. When he got to Toby Hospital he saw a black shadow of darkness move from one side of the wall to the other. He looked at his watch and the time was 11:02 p.m. He was starting his shift and his hauntings were over.

Mary is home with the kids and it was a quiet night. The doctor came home just before 8:00 a.m. and he went to bed. Doug got up, slapped five with his Dad, and he took Bryant outside and tied him up with his chain near his doghouse. He said, "Dad, I got a job at Oxford Creamery and I start Monday."

"Congratulations Doug, now we can get free ice cream!" Dad laughed.

Later he went to bed to get some sleep from working overnight. Later Doug went to the beach with his girlfriend. Mary took the girls to the mall and the movies. Dr. Ray It spent the day sleeping in the quiet house.

Doug said to his new girlfriend, "Let's do something tonight?"

"I can't, I'm going camping with my parents later."

Doug tried to change her mind but it didn't work. They were at Harbour Beach and nobody else was there, so Doug and the girl went way out in the water because it was low tide. While they were getting busy in the water, Doug heard a soft voice saying, *enjoy it, this is your last piece of ass!* Then he heard a hissing sound then it stopped. He looked around and he saw nothing.

He said, "Did you hear that Robin!?"

"No, I didn't!"

"It sounds like someone is here whispering in my ears. I heard a hissing noise like a snake but I don't see anything! Were you whispering in my ears?" said Doug.

"No I was facing you the whole time!" said the girl.

"That's strange, I guess I'm hearing things! I'll be seventeen on August 19, I guess I'm starting to get old," Doug joked, then he finished what he was doing. "Robin I just blew a big load between your legs!!!!!!!!!!!!!!!!! We have to do this again in my bed next time! When my parents are not home," Doug laughed.

The girl was laughing when they got through. The couple stayed out in the water and went at it again then started swimming to shore because the tide was coming in. They heard something else splashing around and they saw two big fish surrounding them and fins popping out of the water and *splash, splash!!!!!!!*

They started screaming, "Sharks!!!!!!!" They swam out of the water as fast as they could because three sharks were stalking them. When Robin and Doug were kicking while swimming the sharks swam away and they made it to safety! They got out of the water as fast as they could!

Doug said, "Let me put a blanket down and sit on the beach for a while."

"No! Let's get out of here! I am never coming to this beach again! We almost got eaten by sharks!" said Robin.

Doug took the girl home. While riding in his car, Doug said, "At least we got off a couple of times before the sharks came!"

Robin laughed. Then she said, "If I had known that there were sharks at Harbour Beach this sex wouldn't have happened!"

Doug laughed and he said, "You have fun going camping and I will see you next weekend." Then Doug hugged and kissed her goodbye. Then he went home to have dinner with his sisters.

Then the parents went out to meet friends at Mike's Steakhouse. "You kids behave while we're out, and I don't want any strangers in the house. We should be home by 10:00 p.m.," said Mary.

Doug took the sisters for a ride in his car, Michelle first then Marsha. Then he went to Ned's Point to meet his friends. Before he left he said to his sisters, "Do you like my car?"

"Yeah I do, it's cool," said Michelle.

"I want to go for another ride tomorrow Doug," said Marsha.

Then off he goes to Ned's Point driving kind of fast. The two girls that used the Ouija board with Michelle and Marsha came over to call more spirits.

Doug was with his friends at Ned's Point drinking a couple of beers and a joint was being passed around. Doug was getting a blowjob in his car. The girl was one of the friends from Ned's Point. A policeman drove through and everyone hid the beer and the joints until the cop left. Then it was party time again. One boy said to Doug, "Did you finish before the cop came!?"

"Yes I did!" He laughed. The girl laughed. Doug took the girl for a ride then went back to Ned's Point, back to the hangout.

Dr. It and Mary had dinner at Mike's Steakhouse. They had prime rib, baked potatoes and sour cream, a full salad, and martinis with a group of friends. "Doctor, do you have a ghost in your house?"

"Not that I know of, but I have been experiencing some strange happenings. I don't believe in ghosts but I don't pay attention to that stuff. I have very busy days at the hospital, so I don't pay attention to nonsense like that. Why do you ask, Sharon?"

"Because your house was haunted. You live at 66 6th Street on Route 6. That house has been vacant for the last five or six years."

"I didn't know that and I was never told that my house was haunted by the realtor. But my wife saw a dark ghostly figure in the yard and she got tangled in the clothes she hung on the line and felt something standing over her, she told me. I never saw anything but I did hear noises. I did see a thunderhead cloud that looked like the face of the devil and my son Doug saw it too and my girls were spooked. My dog Bryant barked a lot and killed a bunch of small animals and I thought that was strange. I thought I saw some shadows but it's mostly strange noises. I'm not threatened by it," said Dr. It.

"Doc, Is Ruthy Smith your realtor?" asked Greg.

"No, it's Eric Drome."

"That name doesn't sound familiar. But Ruthy Smith was a witch from the Bridgewater Triangle and she put a curse on the first couple that lived there. Back in the 1970s, the Chang family. She had an evil conflict against Asians and provoked evil spirits to drive them out! She was a devil worshipper," said Greg, a doctor and Mary's friend.

"Be careful going home tonight. I know you don't live far but be careful anyway!"

"Sharon, what are you telling me?" asked Mary.

"I fear that something is not right between you and Ray. Be careful when you leave here!" said Sharon.

"Well, it's time to leave. We have to get home to our kids because I have to work tomorrow," said Dr. It.

"Don't leave yet, there's a bad accident on Route 6 heading toward Mattapoisett. Can you hear all the police cars? Let's go to the bar and have a drink or two; we haven't seen each other in over a year!" said Greg.

"Oh what the hell, let's go!" said the doctor, and they went to the bar with Greg and Sharon for drinks.

"Dr. Allen, how are you doing? Can you do me a favor and go in at 7:00 a.m. tomorrow morning and I'll work the 3:00 p.m. to 11:00 p.m. shift for you?"

"Sure, anything for you Dr. It."

"Thank you so much buddy. This is my wife Mary, and my friends Greg and Sharon Haven," said the doctor.

"Pleased to meet you," they said. The five of them were drinking martinis at the bar.

After dinner is when the accident on Route 6 happened. Doug left Ned's Point just before 10:00 p.m. and he'd been drinking and smoking pot with his friends. Now alone, driving his car home on Route 6, he was driving a little fast when suddenly he saw a deer with red eyes! He swerved to avoid hitting the deer and he lost control of his car and hit a telephone pole. He went right through the windshield, smashing his head in the road, dead instantly! His brains were splattered everywhere and body parts were lying in the road! Police found the Thunderbird laying upside down on Route 6 on fire just feet from his house!

Officer Billy Wilkins (the same one who used to live at 66 6th Street) was just driving along on Route 6 and he heard a big *bang!* He saw a car flying down the road and then a fire! He raced to the scene and he saw the dead body in the road. Doug It's head was smashed and his brains were popping out of his cracked skull. His broken bones were everywhere! Officer Billy Wilkins threw up and he started crying. Then he called headquarters then several police cars arrived and closed Route 6.

Meanwhile, Dr. It was driving home from Mike's Steakhouse in Fairhaven, but was caught in parking lot traffic at 10:40 p.m. While he was trapped in traffic the police identified the dead body. Officer Wilkins parked a police car in the yard at 66 6th Street until the parents came home.

The girls and their friends never knew what happened. The visiting girls left by 9:30 p.m., before their mom and dad came home. They called many spirits leading to Doug It's death! Michelle and Marsha were still in the cellar playing cards until after 11:00 p.m. Then the accident was cleared at 11:09 p.m. The girls fell asleep in the basement on a couch. Then Dr. It arrived at home just before 11:30 p.m. And found a police car in the yard with the lights flashing.

"Good evening Officer, did you find a lot of speeders tonight resting in my driveway!" Dr. It joked.

"Yes sir, do you have a boy by the name of Doug It?"

"Yes I do Officer, what happened?"

"My name is Officer William Wilkins. I'm sorry to tell you that he was killed in an auto accident a little over an hour ago! He hit a telephone pole and his body went through the windshield! He was killed instantly! I am very sorry!"

Dr. It cried, "Oh no, oh no, my son, oh no!!!!!!!!!!!!!!!!!" Mary passed out! Then they woke up the girls downstairs and told them what happened and they cried.

Two days later was the wake, a closed casket affair. Then the funeral at St. Anthony's church, and the song "Amazing Grace" was playing. The wake and funeral were packed with people because Doug and the It family are well liked in Mattapoisett. There were a lot of policemen from the town, doctors and nurses, lawyers, and friends of the It family at the wake and funeral. Greg and Sharon from dinner that fateful Saturday night were there. Then everyone went to the cemetery site for the burial and the reception was held at Mike's Steakhouse.

After Doug It's burial, the priest went to the house to bless every room, saying prayers. The priest has no idea about the ghost of Ebenezer or any ghosts brought in from Vermont. He prayed for all evil in Mattapoisett to leave this house. Then an exorcism was performed the next day, exiling all the evil in Mattapoisett. Now what the priest doesn't know: Ebenezer is going to get his turn. He'd already started, turning the deer with red eyes to kill Doug It!

Next Hurricane Bob was on its way. The two girls and their friends blamed each other for calling spirits. Michelle said, "Ebenezer killed our brother. We never should have ever called on him. We need to get rid of the Ouija board; we have to burn it before the priest does the exorcism tomorrow. If Mom and Dad find out we were calling spirits from Vermont, they'll put us into a nuthouse. Dad's not going to work and Mom will be home. Let's go for a walk in the woods and put this game in a bag! We have to get rid of it!"

Marsha bagged the Ouija board after Michelle broke it in half. While the priest was talking with their mom and dad, Michelle diverted their attention until Marsha got back. The two girls called the spirits that arrived to take the Ouija board and burn it.

After the exorcism there were no more hauntings until Hurricane Bob arrived. Police were driving around, evacuating people a few days before the hurricane. Dr. It was boarding up the windows and preparing for the hurricane. Mary was watching the storm on the computer. Days before it hit the news came on the weather channel.

"Good afternoon, Hurricane Bob's track takes the storm directly into Providence, Rhode Island with winds over 120 miles per hour and up into the Worcester area. It should spare Cape Cod and the islands the brunt of the storm, but don't let your guard down in Cape Cod or southeastern New England; you will still see winds gusting to hurricane strength and a tornado can't be ruled out. But Rhode Island, Connecticut, and the Worcester area, you'd better buckle down because you're going to get the worst of Hurricane Bob. Expect sustained winds of 120 miles per hour with gusts as high as 150. Expect a major category four or five hurricane with tornadoes, thunderstorms, and twenty to thirty inches of rain and destructive winds. All of the New England states that live near the ocean are asked to evacuate at this time. Keep away from the water and get to higher ground because Bob is an unpredictable storm and could change directions. Please take this storm seriously because for whoever's in the path of this storm, it's going to be really bad! This is the weather channel."

Dr. It did not take Hurricane Bob seriously and he, Mary, and the kids stayed put. The news said sixty mile per hour winds and the eye might pass over. The storm changed direction and went straight up the Cape Cod Canal!!!!!!!!!!!!!!!!!!!!!!!!!!

# SIX

## THE GHOST OF EBENEZER

*August 18, 1991*

The night before the arrival of Hurricane Bob, Mary went outside to bring Bryant in the house. Though late, the sun was out. She saw the dark ghostly figure from before close by, standing near the house. She screamed! "Ahhhhhhhh!!!!!!!!!!!!" Then she turned Bryant loose and the dog ran after him and the man disappeared!

Bryant was barking and growling. Mary ran in the house hysterical. "Ray, I saw the dark figure again outside the house! It was near the dog-house standing by Michelle's bedroom window!" she cried.

The doctor went out with his shotgun following Bryant, looking for the black ghostly figure, and found nothing! Then he called the police. The police came and went through his property with big guns, along with the doctor Bryant. The stranger was gone! The wind was picking up.

The cop said, "How come you didn't evacuate?"

"Because the weather report said the storm wasn't going to be as bad, so we stayed. I boarded up all the windows and we're going to hunker down and ride it out!"

"Please be careful Doctor. We will be keeping tabs until we find this dark ghostly figure roaming on your property," said the policeman, then he left.

Bedtime! Bryant would not sleep downstairs; he slept in Doug's room on his bed. The kids went to their rooms and Mary and the doctor slept in their bed. Mary said, "I think we should all sleep in the basement in case the wind gets bad!"

"Not a good idea. Suppose the basement gets flooded, we're screwed!" said the doctor. Everyone was able to take their showers and go to bed before the hurricane struck.

The storm didn't arrive until after 11:00 a.m., everyone had breakfast before Bob came. 11:02 a.m. the wind picked up, 12:02 p.m. it was raining really hard and the wind was getting stronger. The two girls and their parents just got through lunch. Then at 1:02 p.m. it was thundering. Then at 2:02 p.m. the power went out and the house went dark because all the windows were all boarded up. Dr. It went in the cellar to get the hurricane lamps, and everyone gathered in the living room as the wind was getting even stronger!

"Mary, Michelle, and Marsha, you need to stay along this wall to protect yourselves against the wind. It's blowing a lot harder than sixty miles an hour and the basement is flooded already! Move the furniture and hide behind it! Put the pillows over your head to protect yourself and say your prayers! I'm going upstairs to get Bryant."

At 2:59 p.m. the wind, the rain, and the hail were pounding the house so bad something was ready to give way! 3:01 p.m., the doctor found Bryant hiding under his bed crying and he grabbed the dog. Suddenly the roof blew off and the doctor and Bryant went with it. The time was 3:02 p.m. when a 180 mile per hour wind gust blew the fuckin roof right off the house and Dr. It and Bryant got sucked up into the vortex! A hurricane blew the roof off the house and Dr. It and his dog Bryant went up like rockets!

The kids and Mary heard a loud *bang!* and they saw part of the upper floor gone and felt the strong wind and rain in the house. They heard Dad scream and Bryant went *yelp, yelp!!* And it was over and the sun came out at 4:02 p.m. when the eye of Hurricane Bob passed over. The rain, thunder and lightning, and the wind stopped. Mary and the kids went upstairs looking for Dad and the dog.

When the doctor and Bryant were sucked up into the hurricane vortex, he saw the apparition of the dark ghostly figure Mary was seeing at the house. The vision looked like the devil! The ghost of Ebenezer! The doctor was spinning and rising high into the vortex, and finally he was hit by flying debris that killed him! Part of the roof and whatever Ebenezer could throw at him! Bryant was torn apart from the strong winds and being hit by debris.

Mary said, "Michelle, Marsha, stay here while I look for Dad and Bryant." Mary went upstairs only to see the roof totally blown off and everything absolute soaked! They were gone, and she screamed and cried hysterically.

5:02 p.m. the second half of the storm was coming as she was moving things around, trying to find her husband and the dog before she gave up! Then she saw dark ghostly figure standing over what was Doug's bedroom and the wind, rain, thunder, and lightning picked up! It was the devilish ghost of Ebenezer standing there! Mary screamed holy, bloody, blue murder!!!! "Ahhhhhhhhhhhhhhhhhhhh!!!!!!!!!!!!!!!!" Then a tree came flying like a missile, striking Mary, and she was killed instantly!

The two girls were left to fend for themselves! Now face to face with Ebenezer, the girls were holding on to things for dear life because the winds were worse than before. The girls heard a loud growling roar and it was not the wind! Then the Ebenezer appeared, yanking Michelle away from the wall, breaking her grip, as she and Marsha screamed hysterically.

Michelle slipped away and she was blown away in the storm, carried for miles before it dumped her into a pile of broken trees in the deep forest!

Meanwhile Marsha was left and furniture and debris were piling around her. Ebenezer was choking her with his ghostly hands and he said, *"You called me, what do you want from me? Now I am stuck here with the unwanted dead and you're coming with me!"* Then a piece of wood flew at Marsha's head at high speed to finish her off with the help of the Ebenezer ghost! Then the ghost of Ebenezer vanished and Marsha's dead body was trapped under piling furniture! Then the storm was gone and the sky cleared.

The other two girls who helped call the mean Ebenezer on Michelle and Marsha's Ouija board evacuated before Hurricane Bob struck. Good thing, because the house they were living in was leveled. The home on the Mattapoisett-Fairhaven border was smashed into a million pieces! The next day, August 20, 1991, several homes were destroyed and there was no electricity in town. Bob destroyed a lot of property and there were a couple of tornadoes that went through; it'll take months to get back to normal. The town of Mattapoisett was closed off to the public except for the people who live there.

The police and fire departments and the National Guard went through town searching for the dead and the injured. Officer Billy Wilkins (yep, the one who used to live at 66 6th Street again!) was checking out the damage. The ghost of Ebenezer's black shadow followed him to the property. He sensed someone was behind him and he looked in back of him and he saw nothing! The shadow had disappeared!

He went in the damaged house to look for bodies and he found Marsha It dead, lying between broken furniture with her head smashed in. He choked up. He radioed to other policemen looking for bodies. He went upstairs and parts of the rooms were still intact, but the roof was gone and no more bodies were found there! The rest of the family's bodies were never found but feared dead! President Bush's helicopters were flying over the damage from Hurricane Bob.

The Mattapoisett Inn was protected from the brunt of the damage because falling trees were resting up against the hotel, sparing it. A trucking crew came in to remove the damaged trees. All homes hit by tornadoes were knocked down and destroyed by bulldozers. The house at 66 6th Street was (unfortunately) repairable.

The Longhorn family arrived to go to their house, including Kim and Karen, the girls who called the ghost of Ebenezer from Michelle and Marsha's Ouija board. The police had the street blocked off. The cop said, "I'm sorry, but nobody can go through here. A tornado spawned by Hurricane Bob destroyed the area; every house on this street was wrecked!"

"Officer, we live at 156 Jean Street," said the girls' mother.

"You need to go to the Mattapoisett Inn; they will give you instructions. Nobody will be coming down this street anytime soon," the policeman said.

"Oh, my God!" the mother cried. About fifteen or twenty people were killed in Mattapoisett by Hurricane Bob. Workers were moving the wreckage from the Longhorns' damaged house and all that was left was a cement slab.

Just before 9:00 p.m. the working crew saw a big dark figure—bigger than usual! One worker said, "Excuse me sir, you're not supposed to be here, you must leave!"

The dark ghostly figure just stood there and the police drove by, putting their headlights on it, and the ghost of Ebenezer vanished! Workers and the police went searching for the ghost and it was gone! They went crazy looking for him and never found him again! Later, Ebenezer appeared where the Longhorn family once stood.

That evening the news was heard. "Good evening, this is the 11:00 p.m. news on WLNE Channel 6 New Bedford, Providence. Hurricane Bob left a trail of destruction on Rhode Island, Southeastern Massachusetts, Cape Cod, and the islands with 147 mile per hour winds with gusts over 180, leaving thirty-six people dead. Twenty-two bodies were recovered in Mattapoisett where a couple of tornadoes touched down, destroying several homes. A tornado leveled nine homes on Jean Street, also in Mattapoisett. Mattapoisett got the worst tornado damage overall. Several homes and businesses were destroyed.

"At least two people were found dead in Rhode Island: one on Block Island and the other in Tiverton. There were millions of dollars in damage, and millions were left without power. The storm is not over yet; it's hitting the Maine coastline at this time and moving up to Canada. It will be a week or two before anything gets back to normal. Michelle Stone reporting on Channel 6 News."

During Hurricane Bob's clean up the ghost of Ebenezer made its appearance in some places after all the bodies and dead animals were recovered. Dr. It's body was found in Rochester in a wooded area behind a house, and his dog Bryant was never found. Large animals may have eaten him. Mary It's body was found in Marion in a wooded forest, covered with trees. Michelle It's body was found in a tree in Freetown. Marsha's body was found in the home at 66 6th Street by police; her head was smashed in. And of course, Doug It was killed in an auto crash a few weeks ago. The whole family was killed from the storm with the help from the ghost of Ebenezer!

Firemen and the National Guard troops were moving damaged debris from the storm and the ghost sightings caught them by surprise during clean up at night for about two weeks.

One such incident: A report of a man, standing in a damaged area ready to be cleaned. Floodlights shined on this man and he looked like the devil! "Hey buddy, what the hell are you doing here? This area is under construction, you have to leave!" a National Guardsman said.

The black, devilish-looking figure just stood there! The Guardsman told him three times to leave and he just stood there! The Guardsman pulled out his gun and he walked up to the man still standing there and he cocked his gun, and Ebenezer charged at the guard and growled at him! The guard fired a shot and the ghost vanished in front of his eyes and he was gone! He was shocked and he radioed to other guards from his walkie-talkie.

"Joey to Sergeant Jake, over."

"This is Sergeant Jake, come in please."

"Sergeant, I just shot a ghost believe it or not! I saw a big dark figure standing in a construction zone and I said to him, 'What the hell are you doing here, this area is under construction,' and he just stood there! I told him to leave three times and he wouldn't move so I loaded my gun and I went after him. He lunged at me and roared like a bear and his breath had the smell of death! So I shot him right in the stomach and he vanished in front of my eyes!"

"Joey, are you on drugs!?"

"No Sir, just come down Jean Street, halfway down, and see for yourself!"

Sergeant Jake walked down Jean Street with a big spotlight and he was face to face with the ghost of Ebenezer.

He said, "Hey buddy, you're trespassing in a military construction zone, you have to leave this area immediately!" Ebenezer roared at him and attacked, getting inside of him, and dragged him down the road. He ended up near a row of downed trees screaming for his life.

A policeman came over to help. Joey heard Sergeant Jake screaming and he ran to the end of the road to help him.

"Joey, you're right! Something is here that's not human! I was four or five feet from this monster-like human creature...black all over, and he had red eyes; I swear he was a fuckin Bigfoot! He roared at me like a mean bear and he attacked me, knocking me to the ground, and I was dragged to the end of this street. I did not see him dragging me; I saw him go through me and I felt like it was inside of me, pulling me down the road! I was thrown into the damaged trees! When I started scream-ing I felt like something was coming out of every hole in my body. Like something was coming out of my nose, ears, mouth, bellybutton, my asshole and every hole in my body. It finally released me when I was finished being dragged down the road. I can't explain it. It wasn't Big-foot—it went through my body and out again—it was the most scared I've ever been in my thirty-two years of life!

"I never believed in ghosts but I'm a believer now! And I hope some-thing like this never happens again! I didn't even have a chance to draw my gun it came after me so fast!" said Sergeant Jake

"It was Bigfoot!" one guard said.

"No! It's not a Bigfoot, it's something not of our kind; this fuckin thing went right through me!" said Sergeant Jake.

"I saw this mother fucker too! It was a big black mass of a very big man! It was scary!" said another guard.

"Listen up gentlemen. We have to go through this area shining our flashlights. Have your guns ready in case this motherfucker wants to go to war!!!" shouted Sergeant Jake.

The National Guard, the Mattapoisett Police, and the fire depart-ment went through the tornado damaged area with flashlights and big guns until daylight. An army tank arrived and set up, ready to blast this fuckin Ebenezer away!!!! Helicopters flew over all night with bright floodlights looking for this big black beast! The creature/ghost was not seen again because it knew everyone was after it now. The ghost disap-peared for the rest of the night and vanished from the area for a while!

One month later rebuilding was still ongoing. The Longhorn family arrived with a temporary trailer home until their new home was done being built. They cried when the tornado leveled their home, they lost everything. One month later the two girls who helped the It sisters call in this Ebenezer on their Ouija board were back. The two girls, Kim and Karen, were hanging up Halloween decorations around the trailer home. For a week, two crows landed in the yard looking at the girls then flew off. One morning the girls' mother was sitting in the kitchen eating breakfast and a big black crow landed on the windowsill, looking at her from outside the window.

Karen said, "Mom, how come these black birds are looking at us every day!"

"I don't know honey, just don't feed them!"

The next night the mother went out to throw the trash away in a dumpster down the road in the rain and she was face to face with the ghost of Ebenezer. It was standing between her house and the dumpster. She screamed hysterically! "Ahhhhhhhhhhhhh!!!!!!!!!!!!!!!!!!" Then she ran to the house.

Everyone started turning on their lights, wondering what was going on and coming outside! Ebenezer quickly vanished! "I just saw a big dark figure near the dumpster and he looked like some kind of animal with red eyes!" she cried, then she ran in the house to call police.

"Kim and Karen, don't go outside, someone not nice is out there!"

The police came and they found nothing and the cop said to the neighbors, "Everyone please go back inside, an unknown creature has been reported roaming around this area at night. Stay inside until daylight for your own safety. We're out here looking for it." Then the police left.

More police were driving around Mattapoisett looking for this creature. Several pictures were taken at National Guard sightings, but they were all black screens. No proof of this Ebenezer.

The girls told their mother about the ghost. "We were over Michelle and Marsha It's house and they had a Ouija board calling spirits and they called a powerful spirit from Vermont by the name of Ebenezer. The creature you saw fits the description. It's a ghost, Mom," said Karen and Kim.

Their father was out on a business trip in Dubai, United Arab Emirates; he's a corporate lawyer. He was waiting in a courtyard by himself and the vision of Ebenezer paid him a visit at 1:15 p.m. in broad daylight in the hotel courtyard.

It walked up to him and he said, "Mr. Joseph J. Longhorn. My name is Ebenezer and your daughters, Kim and Karen, called me to Mattapoisett from Vermont with an Ouija board they were playing with. I just want to warn your daughters and your wife Jennifer not to talk about me in Mattapoisett or something is going to happen to them!"

"Who are you!? You know my name and my family. I've never seen you before buddy, how did you get to know my family?" demanded Joseph.

"I was introduced through your daughters, Kim and Karen!" said the Ebenezer ghost.

When Joseph kept asking Ebenezer questions he just stood there, not saying anything. Joseph said, "Ebenezer, I'm asking you questions and I want answers."

Another lawyer came up to him and he said, "Are you coming to the meeting or are you going to keep talking to yourself. You've been having a conversation with yourself for ten minutes!" As soon as Joseph turned to his partner, Ebenezer vanished!

"Did you see that dark ghostly figure threatening me—he had to be seven or eight feet tall! He knows my full name, my wife, and kids back in Massachusetts! I've never seen this person before. I have no idea who he is or where he's from. He's as black as the ace of spades and he has red colored eyes, black skin and black hair, yellow teeth, and he stinks like a dead animal from the swamp!"

"Joseph, are you on drugs!? Did you see a ghost or something! Don't be talking about ghosts in the world convention meeting, especially in Dubai! They'll think you're a mental case! You're one of the biggest lawyers in the world and you're having conversations with yourself in a Dubai hotel courtyard; you must have millions of dollars in the bank or something! Usually when someone has a conversation with themselves, they have millions or billions of dollars; they're talking to their money!" said his partner as he laughed!

"Benson, you didn't see that dark figure?! You can't miss it; it was fuckin huge!" shouted Joseph.

"I have been here for about fifteen or twenty minutes just watching you talking to something that wasn't there!" said Benson, his partner. Then he said, "What is the dark ghostly figure called?"

"He said Ebadima or some fuckin weird name," said Joseph.

Benson laughed hysterically then they went to the meeting. His lawyer friend Benson thought he was nuts, but Joseph believed he was talking to someone.

While Joseph was in Dubai, Ebenezer went back to Mattapoisett for his next attack, because the wife called the police to report the name— "My kids say the man is Ebenezer." Before Joseph gets home he will find more than the horrors of his name.

Jennifer Longhorn was putting the kids in bed one night and the unthinkable happens. At 11:02 p.m. Karen was choking in her bed to the point where she couldn't scream, and she was dead one minute later. 12:02 a.m. Kim was next; she was choked to death. 1:02 a.m. it was Jennifer's turn. She woke up gagging, gasping for breath, and she choked to death! The ghost of Ebenezer killed all three. Then his ghostly vision appeared outside the Longhorn trailer home at 2:02 a.m. and it vanished a minute later.

The next day Joseph was flying home from Dubai and the plane landed at Logan Airport in Boston. He drove back to Mattapoisett and arrived home at 3:02 a.m. two days later. He went in with his passkey and the stink was unbearable! He saw that his whole family was dead in their beds!!! He threw up three times, then he saw the ghost of Ebenezer at 4:02 a.m. It growled at him and knocked him down and he struggled with the growling ghost until it vanished a minute later!

Joseph was hysterical! Then he called the police to report the dead bodies. Several police cars from Mattapoisett and Fairhaven arrived at the scene. The police all arrived at 4:20 a.m.

"Hi, my name is Joseph Longhorn and I just got home from Dubai to find my whole family dead in their beds. I saw this strange man in my house about a half hour ago and I fear it could be a ghost because I saw this same creature looking like a man in the middle of the day while I was in Dubai. He knew my name, my wife and kids' names, and this ghost said if my kids or wife said anything about it something was going to happen. It told me while I was in Dubai, United Arab Emirates.

"My client's lawyer said he saw me talking to myself and he thought I was nuts, but I was talking to something! This person had to be eight feet tall and didn't seem to be something from here; it knew me, my wife and kids! I can't describe it! My client said I was talking to myself. I tried to convince him that I was talking to something. It looked like a big black demon, that's how I can describe it! It was a huge creature with red eyes, black skin as black as the ace of spades, black hair, and it stunk like the dead. I saw this thing a few minutes ago! It was the same ghostly figure I saw when I was in Dubai!" Joseph cried.

"I heard about a strange creature siting by several people, and the National Guard reporting seeing what you're describing. Since this Bigfoot or whatever the fuck it is has been around a lot of people have been dying in mysterious ways, and we need to get to the bottom of this!" said the police. Then Joseph was taken into police custody to see if he had something to do with the killings. He was in the clear and released.

Joseph didn't die because he forgot the name of this ghost!!!!!!!!!!!!!!!! Ebenezer you fuckin dummy!!!!!!!!!!!!!!!!!!!

A few weeks later, voices were heard in the woods on the Marion-Mattapoisett line and Officer Archie Antilli was on call, listening to the chatter at about three o'clock in the morning.

The voices were an argument between the ghost in Mattapoisett/Bridgewater Triangle and Ebenezer: the ghost that's not welcome in Mattapoisett or Bridgewater. Ebenezer has to fight his way into the clan or go back to Bennington, Vermont; he's not welcome here. Now it's getting to be a problem because if Ebenezer does not get released to his own clan more problems are going to happen and more people may die.

For the next three nights Officer Archie Antilli was patrolling this area listening to the ghosts fighting each other. Police officer Archie Antilli recorded the ghost voices he heard the past three nights and a meeting was held at the Mattapoisett police station.

"Good evening. My name is Archie Antilli. I have been hearing voices in the green vine forest on the Mattapoisett/Marion line from two unknown forces fighting one another. We have to separate them before something really bad happens! We have been getting reports of a ghost by the name of Ebenezer brought here from somewhere else. This ghost or spirit was brought here from a game, reports say. We need to find information from the It family, who were killed by Hurricane Bob, and the Longhorn family, who invited this fuckin bastard in!" said Archie Antilli.

The next day the police and fire departments and the National Guard went through the It family's house to find information about this fuckin ghost! And writings on paper were found in the house but nothing was found at the Longhorn's trailer home. Ebenezer was found in the writings in the It family home.

The next day Officer Archie Antilli was parked near the black gate in Marion on the Mattapoisett side of the Marion line. Crosses were burning and a demon demonstration was going on. It's not acceptable and it has to be stopped! The next day, after all the evidence was gathered, a report about the hauntings and how to banish them back where they came from was put together. A meeting was held at the Mattapoisett police station.

"Good evening ladies and gentlemen. My name is Officer Archie Antilli. We found writings at the It residence at 66 6th Street here in

Mattapoisett about a demon called Ebenezer, who was called by an Ouija board. It welcomed Ebenezer, a very strong power, from Bennington/Montpelier, Vermont, to Mattapoisett, Massachusetts. We need to send Ebenezer back to his clan," said police.

A priest from St. Anthony's church in Mattapoisett performed an exorcism to drive Ebenezer back to where he came from and the Indians accepted Ebenezer back to Bennington, Vermont.

# SEVEN

## THE GREY FAMILY HAUNTINGS AT 66 6TH STREET

A family of five. Bob and Maureen are the parents, about fifty years old. Bob is a lawyer; Maureen is a nurse. Brandon, twenty-four, a baseball player for the Buffalo Bison. Michael, a seventeen-year-old high school boy, also a baseball player. Robin, a fifteen-year-old schoolgirl and a cheerleader.

September 1997 is when the Grey family brought the house at 66 6th Street on Route 6. The house, since repaired, has been vacant since Hurricane Bob six years ago.

Bob Grey was waiting for the realtor. "Are you Eric Drome for Arthur's Realtors?"

"Yes sir, you must be Bob Grey!"

"That I am sir!"

"Come in and I'll show you the house. This is the porch, then the kitchen on the right. Continuing, this is the dining room, then the bathroom on the right, then a bedroom straight center, and another bedroom or family room on the left. This door goes down to a finished basement; I will show you that later. The next room is the living room with a corner fireplace and picture window."

"Is it a working fireplace?" asked Bob.

"Yes, it is, use all-natural wood. The door here goes to the front yard and the next door is your coat closet.

"Come upstairs. Straight ahead is another bathroom like the one downstairs. The room on the left is another bedroom and the one on the right is the master bedroom with three windows and a walk-in closet.

Here's another small closet, and this door leads to the attic space from one side of the house to the other. You have a brand-new roof because part of this house was destroyed by Hurricane Bob and Tropical Storm Grace in 1991. These bedrooms were rebuilt up here for the third time, identical to the original. You have gas heat and the electric is from National Grid now instead of Plymouth Power.

"Let's go to the basement. Down here you can rent out if you want. It's a finished basement apartment and you have another working natural wood fireplace. Hook ups for a washer, dryer, and a spot for a deep freezer. You have a stove and refrigerator, a proper kitchen area. Back here is another washroom with a sink, toilet, and stand up shower. This room is where the boiler and water heater are. You have wood storage under the stairs and you have several electrical outlets throughout the house; 111 of them to be exact!

"Outside is the backyard and you have a twenty-foot picnic table out here that can seat forty-two people. You have a flower garden that runs from the front yard to the end of the backyard. You have a doghouse. You have many tall trees and you will own two acres of land. The backyard leads to the farmyard and the woods in back, all the way to the beach. Here on the right is the toolshed and the barn in the back.

"Welcome to 66 6th Street here in Mattapoisett, Massachusetts. The house and the property are worth $500,000. But if you buy today, it's half off, $250,000," said Eric Drome, the realtor.

Bob Grey went for the bait and bought the house. He gave the realtor a lot of money down and was ready to move in. The next day he showed his wife Robin and son Michael the house and they loved it!.

The Greys have a Caravan mobile home parked in the yard where they'll sleep until the furniture comes, because the kids have to get ready for school. Robin is a sophomore and Michael is a senior at Old Rochester Regional High School. Brandon is still playing baseball in Buffalo and he has an apartment there.

An alarm system was being installed and the electric company came. Then the furniture truck arrived and the Greys started moving in the house. While the movers were bringing the furniture in the house, their shadows followed them with the sun shining on them, but other shadows were going the other way! No one noticed.

One of the movers was hooking up the washer and dryer in the basement. Another heard a hissing noise and his hair stood straight up in the air right after hooking up the dryer. He jumped back and he said, "Tell Bob to call the electric company, I almost got electrocuted! It just finished plugging in the dryer to the 250 outlet when I heard a loud noise and my hair stood straight up! It's a good thing I have rubber boots on or I would be a goner!!!!!!!!!!!!!!!!!!!!" He was haunted by an invisible ghost!

The movers reported the incident to Bob and he called National Grid to check it and everything was okay. "You're plugging a unit into a 250 outlet and sometimes there's pressure because the current is so strong. You shouldn't get a shock because it would flip the circuit breaker if there was a defect," said the National Grid worker.

"All the circuit breakers are working properly and you should be alright!" said a second National Grid worker, then they left.

There were four movers moving all the furniture. Bob and Maureen were setting the furniture in place and hanging and putting away clothes (Michael alone had eighteen pairs of shoes and sneakers). Bob and Maureen were giving their kids instructions.

"Robin, you will be sleeping in the bedroom on the left, and Michael's room is on the right. Upstairs is the spare bedroom on the left where Brandon and Lisa will sleep when they come to visit, and our bedroom is on the right upstairs," said Maureen.

October 1997. Bob had a business trip with a group of lawyers and would be away for a week. The kids were at school and Maureen was still trying to get settled, putting things away, home alone for the week before going back to work.

While Dad was away and the kids were at school Maureen had some strange happenings. She was putting things in storage (the attic eaves space in the master bedroom), Christmas decorations and a tree. She saw an orb of light moving in the dark attic storage space, then a second one. They were balls of light, a little bigger than a baseball, and they were moving in circles.

She turned on a light in the storage attic and the orbs disappeared. She turned the light off briefly and she didn't see them again. Later Maureen finished putting things away and she had a second look, turning off the light when she was done, and it was darkness. After getting a good look for a minute or two she didn't see the orbs and she locked the storage door.

A black mist went through the room and out an open window but she did not see it. Then a darkness went through the house and all the lights went dim. A few minutes later the house brightened and the lights brightened as well. The unknown haunting is checking on this family.

She looked outside and it was a rainy day and she saw a very big black bird, some raven-vulture with yellow eyes, sitting on her picnic table. She said, "Oh my God!" Then the giant bird flew away.

Maureen is not aware that she's being haunted big time! She's not scared by the happenings but she's a little uncomfortable!

Then she saw a huge deer with red eyes. Then the phone rang, breaking her eye contact, and the red-eyed deer vanished.

"Maureen, it's Emma from Fall River calling! You need to get to the basement or a shelter a tornado is coming!"

Maureen saw a bright flash of lightning followed by a loud crack of thunder. She went downstairs to the basement and she hid in the wood storage under the stairs. Then she heard three more rumbles of thunder and then it was quiet. She came out a few minutes later and the sun was out and the dark storm was gone and there was no tornado, just a warning. Then she saw a green glowing fog outside in the woods then it went away. Then she saw the two orbs circling around again outside, yellow instead of white.

Later she called her friend back on the phone. "Emma, I'm having a strange day. I see moving lights in my closets and I saw them again out in the backyard. I saw a giant black bird sitting on my picnic table, then I saw a big deer with red eyes, then I saw a green fog. I don't believe in ghosts but something strange is happening here!" said Maureen.

Emma laughed. Then she said, "How big was the ball of light you saw?"

"They were a little bigger than baseballs, like softball size," said Maureen.

"I'm a little puzzled about the light balls being ghosts. I think it's lightning after it strikes, because the energy from the lightning bolt is still electrified and forms these light balls—they're called orbs. Working for the weather department, I study this phenomenon. It's lightning.

Keep your distance when you see this because if it hits you it will burn you just like being struck by lightning and we had a thunderstorm today."

"Emma, I've seen them inside my house! Explain that!"

"Yes, lightning orbs can get inside the house; one has the energy to go through a closed window and dance around in your home until it goes out! When I lived in Tiverton I had a house with a picture window on each side. Lightning struck my TV antenna, hitting the window, and I saw two balls of light travel through my house from a closed window and go out the other closed picture window," said her friend Emma.

"Can it hit something and burn the house down?!"

"Of course it can! If you see it, get away and let it do its thing until it burns out!" said Emma.

"What about the big black bird and the deer with the red eyes I saw?" said Maureen.

"There's a lot of animals out there with red eyes; my pit bull has red eyes! And we have big birds around here. You must have seen an eagle, they're huge! If you saw a bald eagle, America's bird, they're even bigger!" said Emma.

"Can animals appear as ghosts because this is scary, Emma."

"I believe only humans can appear from the dead, not animals. Animals do not have spirits in them, only humans. I doubt you saw a ghost from the things you're explaining. You live in the woods; there's a lot of big animals, birds, etc.... I've seen deer as big as horses," she said over the phone.

Then Maureen put the phone down and she heard a growl and she looked out her window in the kitchen and she saw a big raccoon chasing a rabbit. She said to herself, "I guess it's time to get a big dog!" Then the kids came home from school and Maureen said, "Be careful kids, we have some very big animals running through the yard. I saw a raccoon bigger than a big dog and a deer as big as a horse and a big black bird, big enough to carry people away!"

Michael and Robin laughed! Michael said, "Mom, I'm not worried about the animals we have here as long as we don't have bears; then we have a problem. Let's get a big dog and the animals will go away!"

"I have that in my plans when Dad comes home from his trip. We will get a dog," said Maureen.

The kids did their homework then Michael went out to cut the grass on a riding lawnmower; it was a John Deere. Robin helped her mother with the laundry. Michael finished the lawn and he saw a big bird resting in one tree and a giant raccoon resting in another and some big bees flying around the yard. Then he went in the house before it got dark. He told Robin and his mother what he saw outside.

The next day it was raining and the animals were gone. The kids were at school and mother was home alone once again. She was eating breakfast and she felt like someone was hanging over her, but she kept looking back and nothing was there. Then she heard a chair move and she went to investigate, walking around the house, up and down stairs, and nothing was out of place.

Then she went in to take a shower and a face appeared in the mirror that looked like the devil! She was in the shower she didn't see it. Then she heard a clicking noise when she was in the shower. When she was finished the bathroom door was open. She shut the door and she was drying off with a big towel. She wiped off the mirror and put makeup on, seeing herself in the mirror, not the devil.

Then she heard footsteps walking upstairs. She quickly put on her house robe and ran to the kitchen. She grabbed a big knife and she ran upstairs and nothing was there. Then she checked the closets, pushing the clothes around, then she went in the attic storage and nothing was there. Then she shut the light off, paused, then she turned the light on again in the attic storage and she saw nothing, then she turned the light off and locked the door. She checked both rooms and the bathroom and nothing was there. She rechecked the upstairs rooms and it was quiet. She went through the house and checked the basement about three times, going through every room and closet, and all the doors and windows were locked.

A few minutes later the bell rang and she went to the porch and no one was there. Then she went to the front door. "Who is it?!" she said. She still had the knife in her hands, and she opened the door, and nobody! Then she went down in the basement and no one. She went upstairs to make a phone call. The bell rang again! She put the phone down and she answered the door, entering the porch, and it was her friend.

"Emma, please come in, I was trying to call you."

"Oh, I don't usually just stop by but I forgot your phone number Maureen."

"Here, write it down. 1-758-847-0418 is my cellphone number from LaForge, South Dakota; just call my cell. I had another strange day today. I'm hearing footsteps but I cannot find where it's coming from. Before I was taking a shower and I noticed the bathroom door was open, and I always close the door to keep it warm when I get out of the shower. I thought that was strange.

"Earlier this morning I was having breakfast and I swear I could feel someone was behind me, like I was not alone. I can't describe it! I didn't see anyone. Explain that Emma!"

"It could be a spirit because people died here from Hurricane Bob. Let's go for lunch. Oxford Creamery is closed for the season so we'll go get lunch at Curilli's," said Emma.

Emma and Maureen went out for lunch to get out of the house for a while.

"The realtor didn't tell you about the deaths from Hurricane Bob. You may want to call a priest to come bless your home to get rid of the spirits," said Emma.

"Will they bother me? Are they ghosts!?" said Maureen.

"I wouldn't call them ghosts, but spirits not at rest may make noises and make you feel like you're not alone, like you're describing in your home. They might open and close doors or do something to get your attention, but they will not hurt you. Just call a priest to come and get rid of them!" said Emma.

Later Maureen stopped at a church to get some help. At St. Anthony's church she rang the bell to the rectory and told the receptionist what was happening in the house. A priest went over to bless her house, throwing holy water in each room.

"My name is Father Frank."

"Pleased to meet you, my name is Maureen Grey."

"You have something here; it's not threatening but people have died here and every time someone moves here we come do a brief blessing and then they go away. A girl by the name of Marsha It, fourteen years old, was found dead in this house during Hurricane Bob in 1991. The rest of the family was blown away and the whole family died. The footsteps, opening doors, and feeling you're not alone or thinking someone is in this house could be the dead from the It family letting you know that something happened here. Once I tell these spirits to leave by mentioning their names, they will be at rest and leave you alone. These spirits are not threatening but they can be annoying, making you uncomfortable! And I am here to let them free.

"Now the deer with the red eyes and the giant black bird you saw are something else! It could be something evil the It family invited. I will find out during the blessings. After I am done you should be alright. The only thing that could happen is if the prayers don't work then we need to do a three series exorcism, but I don't think the spirits here are a threat!" said the priest.

"Father, the deer with the red eyes and the big black bird I saw, were they ghosts?" asked Maureen.

"I believe the deer with the red eyes is a ghost, yes, but I don't know about the giant black bird, but I will get rid of all of them!" said the priest.

"Father, I also saw light balls upstairs in the attic storage and again outside. My friend said it's from lightning as we had a thunderstorm that day," said Maureen.

"It could be," said the priest. Then he did the blessings and he left and the house was quiet.

Then the kids came home from school. The kids came home, did their homework then went for a bike ride. Maureen went outside to get some fresh air and she went for a walk through her property, walking in the woods, and the trees looked eerie. The clear sky darkened then brightened. She looked at the tree branches and they were moving without wind, and it looked like the branches were going to come down and grab her.

She picked some blueberries and raspberries and scooped up a big squash grown in the woods. She washed all the fruit then she grabbed a big pan and she went out to pick some more. She got caught in a wishbone tree branch not realizing she was grabbed by it! She wiggled the tree branch to free herself then she found an apple tree and picked a few apples. Finally she went in the house washing all the fruit then she started cooking dinner.

Robin and Michael were on their bikes at Harbour Beach and they saw a green fog working its way to shore. It looked like a genie walking on the water, forming into a person; then it vanished right in front of their eyes!

"Was that a ghost?!" exclaimed Robin.

"I saw it too, let's get out of here and go home," said Michael.

The kids came home, putting the bikes in the shed, and they went in the house.

"Mom, what are we having for dinner?" asked Michael.

"We're having shepherd's pie, and apple pie for dessert."

"Mom, we saw a ghost at Harbour Beach," said Robin.

"I saw it too; it looked like a green fog and it was starting to form a human figure then it vanished in front of our eyes! We got out of there fast!" said Michael.

"Kids, be careful where you go on your new bikes because you're new to the area!" scolded Maureen.

After dinner the kids watched a movie on TV and Maureen watched the news, and later *Cops* on another TV. After the program was over the police arrived and rang the doorbell.

"Hi officers, what's wrong?" asked Maureen.

"Your alarm went off, alerting the police. Is everything alright here?"

"I didn't hear the alarm go off," she said.

"You may have a silent alarm; you have to turn it off when you get home because the police will keep coming."

"Yes sir, officers," she said. Maureen reset the alarm then the police left. A ghost set her alarm off.

Bedtime. Maureen went to bed just before 11:00 p.m. At 11:02 p.m. she heard scratching in the room. She grabbed her husband's gun and she went looking for the animal scratching noises. She checked the closet and the attic eaves, and she found nothing. She put the gun in the nightstand top drawer. Then she went to bed.

The priest's prayers and holy water in every room are not working.

An hour later Michael woke up to a voice, "*Get out!!!!!!!!!!!!!!*" He got up and he turned the lamp on in his room and he saw nothing, then he went back to bed.

An hour later Robin was having a bad dream that a tornado came and took her away. Then she heard a growling noise, waking her up, and the time was 1:02 a.m. Robin got up turning on the light and looking around the room and she found nothing.

The invisible ghost will haunt this family for twenty-four hours; it's an evil spirit.

Brandon went to bed just before 2:00 a.m. and at two minutes after he felt something blowing in his ear at his home in Buffalo, New York. He turned on a light and his cat was lying at the foot of his bed.

3:02 a.m. Bob was at a hotel looking at a computer for his work and the power went out. The power came back on a minute later. He saved his work then he went to bed.

4:02 a.m. Maureen woke up to a loud rumble of thunder. It kept thundering for a minute then it stopped. She looked out the window and it was raining. Then she went back to bed.

An hour later Michael woke up, hearing something growling. He looked at his alarm clock and the time was 5:02 a.m. He got up and he looked out the window and he saw a deer with red eyes looking back at him. He shut the shade and he went back to bed.

An hour later Robin heard a voice calling, "*Get out!!!!!!!!!!!!!!!!!*" She got up and she looked at her alarm clock and the time was 6:02 a.m.

Brandon was getting up just before 7:00 a.m. He was sitting on the bed getting dressed, and he looked at his alarm clock and the time was 7:02 a.m. He saw a flash of lightning in his room at his home in Buffalo.

8:02 a.m. it was Bob's turn. He felt a push and he fell out of bed. He had a funny look on his face then he got up ready to go to court.

Maureen was up and the kids were off to school. Robin said she heard voices she couldn't describe and told them about tornado nightmare and growling dream. Michael heard the same voice Robin heard and he saw a deer with red eyes outside.

"Oh, my God, I saw the same deer the other day. I hope it's not a ghost," said Maureen.

Michael laughed. Then the kids went off to school. Maureen made a cup of coffee and she went to the refrigerator to get the cream and the coffee cup was gone! She turned around to put the cream in her cup and it's not there! She said to herself, "I swear I put my cup of coffee on the counter. That's strange." She found the coffee on the dining room table. At 9:02 a.m. as soon as Maureen turned her back the coffee lifted off the counter by itself, and it settled perfectly on the dining room table while she had her breakfast.

Michael was in history class and the teacher was discussing the Bermuda Triangle. He saw a big black shadow move across the classroom. He looked at the clock on the wall and the time was 10:02 a.m. The dark shadow moved backward then it vanished.

Robin was in math class and she saw the same shadow her brother saw and she looked at the clock on the wall. The bell rang at 11:02 a.m.; time to switch classes.

Brandon was emptying his locker at the Buffalo Bison's baseball stadium and he saw a black shadow move across the locker room. A baseball bat came flying across the locker room, almost hitting Brandon in the head as he ducked to avoid being hit with the flying bat! Then he heard a growl and the time was 12:02 p.m., then he went to lunch at a nearby restaurant.

Bob was in court waiting for the afternoon case to begin. He looked at his watch and the time was 1:02 p.m. He saw a black shadow move slowly across the courtroom then vanish! The next case was canceled. Bob called Brandon on his cellphone.

"Hello!"

"Hi Brandon, it's Dad. How are you doing?"

"I'm doing okay, but I had a strange day. I was cleaning out my locker at the stadium and I saw a black shadow, then a bat comes flying across the locker room, then I heard something growling like a lion! I swear this fuckin place is haunted!"

"Funny that you said that because I had some strange things happen to me too. At 3:00 a.m. I was still working on today's court proceedings and the power went out then my computer went blank. About a minute later the power came back on and all my files were saved. Then at 8:00 a.m., I was woken by a push that knocked me out of bed. I can't understand what it was; at first I thought we were having an earthquake. Then about a half hour ago I saw a big black shadow move across the courtroom. The major case of the day was canceled," said Bob.

Maureen finished lunch and she sat down to write a letter. The chair she was sitting on moved and slipped out from under her so she fell on the floor. It was 2:02 p.m. when she saw the chair move again, by itself, five feet away. The pen she was writing with was resting in the air about two feet above the dining room table. The moving chair tipped over. She felt something holding her down so she couldn't get up as she screamed, utterly hysterical! "Ahhhhhhh!!!!!!!"

Then everything stopped a minute later. The flying pen fell on the dining room table and it rolled off and fell on the floor. Maureen got out of that house as soon as she could, grabbing her cellphone. She was out the door and she called the priest.

"Father this is Maureen Grey from 66 6th Street. Something not right is happening in my house! Chairs are moving, I am falling, and something is holding me down. I need you to come back here and get it out! Please!!!!!!!!!!!!!!!!!!!!" she cried.

The priest came over just after 4:00 p.m. Michael and Robin came home just before 3:00 p.m. and their mother told them what had happened in the house.

"Wait until the priest comes, don't go in there!" Michael went in the house because he had to pee. He saw blood dripping from the wall in the hallway and the time was 3:02 p.m.

"Whoever you are, you better leave because I'm not afraid of you!"

The priest came just before 4:00 p.m. and Robin was outside talking to her mother. 4:02 p.m. a mysterious force picked Robin up off the ground and threw her up against the house, five feet off the ground. It dropped her on the ground and she broke her foot! The priest, Maureen, and Michael watched in shock! Maureen screamed hysterically!

"Ahhhhhh!!!!!!" the priest said. "You have something evil here, the spirit of Ebenezer may be getting angry! You can't stay here; you will need to go to a hotel for about three days because I have to do a three-part exorcism series because my prayers and holy water made things worse!"

"Father, can we sleep here in our mobile Caravan home?" said Maureen.

"Sure, that's a good idea, just don't go in the house and invite the evil in the mobile home," said the priest.

5:02 p.m. Brandon was home with a runny nose. He was blowing it nonstop for about a minute, then all at once it stopped. The house in Buffalo had a pink color during Brandon's runny nose attack!

6:02 p.m. Bob was at a restaurant with a group of lawyers on his trip. A woman walked by, patting him on the back, and she said, "Good job!" She had a nametag on her shirt. Gina was her name and she had black eyes. She faded away and vanished at 6:03 p.m.

Maureen called him at 6:19 p.m. while he was eating and told him what's happening around the house in Mattapoisett.

"You got to be kidding. Our house is haunted; you need to let the priest do his thing. Do the exorcism because we cannot have anything like that! I had some strange things happening to me and so has Brandon, but nothing physical like what happened to Robin. Make sure she goes to the hospital and don't go in the house. Stay in the mobile van until the priest is done with the exorcism and I'll be home by Saturday evening. Call me later and let me know how Robin is doing and I will see you Saturday. Love you," said Bob.

"Love you too! The rescue team is here right now," said Maureen.

They took Robin to the hospital and Michael stayed in the mobile van with Maureen. 7:02 p.m. Maureen had a migraine so bad she had to take a couple of Bufferin pills and lie down, complaining about her headache. A minute later it went away and she was fine. The family doesn't realize they are being haunted at two minutes after every hour for twenty-four hours. Michael was watching TV and the TV shut off by itself and he looked at the alarm clock in the mobile van and the time was 8:02 p.m. The TV came back on a minute later.

"Mom, I think we're being haunted in here too!" Michael joked.

Robin was at the hospital and her foot was wrapped up. The nurse was putting an IV in to help her with her pain. She looked at the clock in the hospital and the time was 9:02 p.m. And Robin saw a face forming in the wall. It looked like the face was trying to break through and she screamed!

"Nurse, look at the wall under the clock! It looks like a face pushing the wall out! We have a ghost in this hospital!" Robin cried.

"I don't see anything Robin, you're seeing things!" said the nurse.

The vision went away a minute later. It was for Robin to see, not the nurse, but the nurse was frightened about Robin being picked up and physically thrown up against her house, and now a ghost face vision in the wall under the clock. She didn't want to go in her room anymore and another nurse took over, but she didn't see anything.

Bob was at the hotel room and he looked at the alarm clock and the time was 10:02 p.m. The lights went out in his room and it was pitch dark. A message came over his computer: a power surge, it said. Then the lights came on a minute later. Then he took a shower and he went to bed. He has one more day on his trip then he goes home to Mattapoisett with no more hauntings.

Brandon was at home stargazing with his telescope, looking at the moon when a bat flew over his lens looking in the same direction. Its mouth was open, showing its teeth. It stayed there flapping its wings—it was a big bat! The time was 11:02 p.m. He was shaken up and he looked up again and the bat was gone. He grabbed a flashlight out of his shed and aimed it up in the air and he saw nothing! Brandon never saw the bat again and his haunting was over.

Maureen drove to the hospital to get Robin and bring her home. Michael was at the mobile van in bed and he looked at the alarm clock and the time was 12:02 a.m. and nothing strange happened. Maureen arrived with Robin five minutes later.

She called Bob just after midnight. "Robin has a fractured right foot and she had a couple of screws put in, she's going to be staying in the mobile van for a while." Maureen went to bed. She looked at the alarm clock and the time was 1:02 a.m. Nothing happened and she slept with Robin.

The priest finished the first exorcism Thursday morning at 2:02 a.m. Later Michael got up, had Captain Crunch cereal, orange juice and a cup of coffee, then he was off to school. Maureen stayed home in the mobile home with Robin.

The priest came over Friday evening to do the second exorcism in the house at 66 6th Street off Route 6 at 8:00 a.m. He was there for three hours and nothing happened for the second day in a row. Maureen, Robin, and Michael went out to dinner at Mike's Steakhouse.

The next day the priest did the last exorcism at the house and nothing happened. He was done at 2:00 p.m. and he had a meeting with Maureen and Michael outside in the yard while Robin rested inside the mobile van.

They sat in the backyard at the picnic table. "Okay. I finished all three phases of the exorcism just after 2:00 p.m. Do not go in the house for twenty-four hours. Stay in the mobile home until after 2:00 p.m.

tomorrow. If I were you, I'd attend 11:00 a.m. Mass at St. Anthony's church tomorrow morning. You should be safe from all the hauntings. I did a lot of work with Father Frank to get rid of all the evil spirits.

"If the exorcisms didn't work then you have to get out because you already have had a physical attack on Robin. If things go wrong the evil energy will be much worse! If the Catholic Church can't move the energy, nothing will! There's no guarantee the exorcisms will work. When Father Frank came to bless your home the energy snowballed, and now physical attacks!

"When I performed the exorcisms all I heard was a few noises, nothing threatening. I didn't see anything and I didn't feel threatened. That's the good news; let's hope it stays that way. You are aware that people have died here on your property. We also did an exorcism on your property all the way to the beach and your shed and barn.

"Later tomorrow afternoon, everybody goes in the house together. You will have a list of prayers to say and you will have crosses or statues in every room. Do not show fear going back into the house. Leave Robin in the mobile home with locked doors and windows. You will say prayers to St. Michael. Just follow instructions. Any questions?" said the priest.

"Yes, Father. If the exorcism doesn't work, how long until the evil spirits come back?" asked Maureen.

"The evil will return in less than a week. It could act up as soon as you enter that house, but if you go a week without incident you're safe. When me and Father Frank were here for three days, we had no problems; hopefully, everything will be fine," said the priest, then he left.

Bob came home from his trip two hours later and they slept in the mobile van. Bob and Maureen were talking about the strange happenings and the attacks before the exorcism with Michael and Robin. Then they had supper and watched TV before going to bed. The next day the family went to church together and then out to eat at the Mattapoisett Inn. Then they went home around 3:00 p.m.

"Robin, you stay in the mobile tonight until it's safe to come back in the house. Me, Mom, and Michael will be sleeping in the house. If any hauntings happen, we're out of here," said Bob.

He went in the house first then Maureen and Michael followed. They went through the house and everything was okay. Around evening,

Maureen was turning on lights and everything was dim. It was not as bright and Michael said, "Mom, the house seems dark even with the lights on!"

"Michael, don't talk negative. The priest said to stay positive!" she said.

"Let's get the paper the priest gave us and say the prayers as we go through every room," said Bob.

When the three of them started reading the prayers on the papers given to them, the lights got brighter and everything was normal in the house. After that they went through the house: in the closets and up and down stairs and through their property, outside and in the shed and barn. Then they went back inside.

Maureen made some soup and she brought some out to Robin staying in the mobile van. Then they watched TV and the lights started getting very dim and then brightened again.

Bob said, "Something's wrong here. I'm going downstairs to check the electrical box." The main power surge switch was between on and off and Bob pushed the switch up to "on" and he put duct tape on it to keep it on and the house was bright again. "The on/off main switch was in between the on-off position, no wonder the house was dark," said Bob.

Later everyone took their showers and went to bed. Maureen is going back to work; Bob goes back to his law office in Marion. And Michael's going to school tomorrow. Robin will be resting all by herself healing from her injury.

Maureen looked at the alarm clock and the time was 10:02 p.m. But no haunting! Bedtime! The night was quiet until Maureen woke up to go to the bathroom and she looked at the alarm clock and the time was 3:15 a.m. She got up and when she got to the top of the stairs a mysterious force threw her headfirst down the stairs, striking the front outside door. She put her hands in front of her to avoid hitting her head. Then she heard a voice, "Get out!!!!!!!!!!!!!!!"

At the same time something was choking Michael in his bed and he was trying to fight the evil

Bob heard Maureen screaming and the evil force pulled him out of bed and bounced him off a couple of walls. Bob wound up hitting his head on the ceiling before the spirit body slammed him to the floor.

It picked him up and threw him back in the bed. He smashed into it, hitting his head, breaking the headboard. Then he heard a loud growling voice! *"Get out!!!!!!!!!!!!!!!!!!!!!!!!"*

Bob was able to get out of the room and he was pushed down the stairs, but he got his balance at the bottom. Maureen and Bob grabbed Michael and ran out of the house. Hearing the voice, *"Get out!!!!!!!!!!!!!!!!!!"* The three ran out to the mobile van and drove away!

Robin cried, "What happened?!"

"Our house is haunted, we almost got killed in there! We can't stay here we have to go!" said Bob, and they drove off!

# EIGHT

## THE PHYSICAL GHOST!

In the last chapter the Grey family was physically thrown out of their house at 66 6th Street by an invisible ghost. Robin broke her foot and Maureen and Bob suffered bruises, getting a little banged up and Michael had choke marks around his throat and neck and scratches all over his body. Bob drove them to the hospital.

Then he called the police to report the incidents. Then the police called the realtor at 5:00 a.m. There was no answer so the police left a message on the answering machine. "Good morning, this is a message for Eric Drome from Arthur's Realtors. Please contact Archie Antilli from the Mattapoisett Police Department! ASAP!"

6:57 a.m. Eric Drome arrived at the office and he found two messages on the answering machine and the first message was the one the police left. Then he listened to the second one.

"Mr. Eric Drome. This is Attorney Michael Bloomberg, please call me! ASAP!"

He called the police first. "Mattapoisett police, Officer Archie Antilli speaking."

"Hi, this is Eric Drome from Arthur's Realtors returning your call."

"Hi Eric, we had a serious issue at 66 6th Street where the Grey family was tortured by an unknown ghost in that house and everyone landed in the hospital with injuries! It's not the first time something happened at that house—how about a number of times! Something has to be done about it!" said the police.

"I will take care of it!" said Eric Drome.

"I hear the same bullshit over and over again! 'I will take care of it.' I don't want to hear that anymore. You better do something about it! You're giving this goddam town a bad name!" said the policeman, then he hung up!

Then Eric called the lawyer. And there was no answer so he left a message. Then the phone rang at the realtors' office and the time was 8:33 a.m. "Good morning, Arthur's Realtors, Eric Drome speaking."

"Hi Eric, this is Attorney Michael Bloomberg for the town of Mattapoisett. Could you meet me at my office about 11:00 a.m. on Wednesday?"

"Yes sir," he said.

11:00 a.m. Officer Antilli met with Eric Drome at the house at 66 6th Street. The realtor had the wrong keys and he had to go get the correct ones to get in the house. As soon as they started walking toward the living room they heard a loud growl, like an animal, and a voice was heard loud and clear! *"Get out!!!!!!!!!!!!!!!!!!!!!!!!!!!!"*

Officer Antilli said, "It's on you buddy. Good luck!" Then he left and he went back to the police station.

Eric said, "No! You get out! You don't belong here! Who the fuck do you think you are, you're on my property now get the fuck out!" Then he started going upstairs and at the top of the stairs he was picked up and thrown back down headfirst, crashing right through the outside door. He broke his neck and was unconscious!

Later a passing driver saw the broken door and a man lying on the ground with blood coming out of his head! He called the police and a rescue crew came to take him to the hospital.

The realtors came to put in a new door the next day. When workers went in the house to reset the front door they kept hearing the voice of the mean ghost. *"Get out!!!!!!!!!!!!!!!!!!!!!!!!!!"*

A priest came to do an exorcism again for three days to get rid of this angry ghost. A paranormal team from Providence College and Georgetown University brought several friars in for a national exorcism to get rid of this fuckin demon ghost! The plan worked!

However the realtors had a bad time selling this house again because of its past history and went out of business from lawsuits. Eric called Arthur's Realtors telling them what happened while he was in the hospital, giving them notice it was his last day, telling them he quit! Then the fear of physical attacks and several exorcisms to get rid of demons put a foreclosure on the house until another realtor picked it up.

11:00 a.m. Wednesday, the lawyer went to Mass General hospital in Boston to see Eric Drome and his busted-up body in his bed! "Hello Mr. Eric Drome. How are you feeling today?" asked the lawyer.

"Very groggy!" he said.

"Eric, I hate to spoil your day, but the Grey family has filed a class action lawsuit against Arthur's Realtors and against you for failing to tell them about moving into a haunted house, and the resulting bodily injuries. I do understand that you were attacked too, I'm sorry to hear what happened to you. But Bob and Maureen Grey were also victims of this same unknown ghost and their son Michael was choked in his bed and their daughter was thrown up against the house, breaking her foot, and they all landed in the hospital.

"The Greys are suing for the cost of the house, the property, and all their belongings left inside. The lawsuit is a total of two million dollars to cover all costs because they do not want to go in the house to collect any belongings. They fear being killed despite a national exorcism scheduled by Georgetown University and the Providence College friars; that's a separate charge that will cost thousands!

"You have two choices: One, we will have a court date set up, or two, we'll set up some kind of agreement with the Grey family and the Friars National Association, or FNA," said the lawyer, Michael Bloomberg. Later the lawyer had paperwork for Eric Drome and Arthur's Realtors and the company made an agreement with the family. All their belongings were left in that house and it was used as a model showroom, a furnished home. The agreement between the Grey family totaled $800,000 and then they left Mattapoisett, leaving everything behind, including their clothes and belongings, and they moved to Vermont.

Meanwhile the Georgetown and PC friars were performing the three-day exorcism with the high power of Jesus Christ to overwhelm the evil from the home, a much stronger exorcism than that of Father Frank from St. Anthony's church. On the first day of the three-day super friar exorcism at 66 6th Street, the devil was winning as several friar priests were being bowled over like bowling pins by an invisible ghost!

The ghosts are frightened, staying out of view because they know they'll be defeated by the end of this exorcism series. The only chance the ghosts have is trying to attack a few friars, throwing them around for a while, hoping to chase the friars away. But it's not going to work because the organization's representatives from Georgetown University and Providence College are way too strong.

The ghost kept throwing things: furniture, glass, anything in that house not bolted down was thrown at the priests and friars, including them being thrown at one another. They were bullied by the ghosts for hours until the spirits gave up from the powerful prayers from the friars and the demonstrations from the paranormal team the second day, along with more priests and friars.

The third day they kept up with the powerful prayers and the ghosts were gone from there for a while! Half of the Greys' furniture and belongings were destroyed because they were used for missiles to throw at the friars. The friars never backed down or showed fear; they dominated the exorcism for the three days.

Arthur's Realtors had to come in the house while the friars were finishing the exorcism to get rid of the broken furniture and clean up the glass and debris. Some windows and light fixtures were broken. The clothes and belongings were moved out of the house and taken to the Salvation Army.

The Grey family skipped town fearing the evil left in their belongings in the house and boy were they right! The friars blessed the family before they left.

About a month later it was mid-November 1997. The new realtors had a meeting with the old realtors.

"Mr. Rex Sax from Bennington Realtors of Vermont. Welcome to Mattapoisett, Massachusetts. My name is Richard Classical taking over for Eric Drome who's in the hospital. I will tell you about that later. Pleased to meet you. Have a seat and I'll get you a cup of coffee, Rex.

"Mattapoisett is a beautiful town and a lot of wealthy people live here. We have lawyers, doctors, famous authors, and movie actors. Movies have been filmed here and we are in Plymouth County. We have a lot of rich history here and we have a dark side as well. Before I talk about the dark side, you will be selling many big homes here, million-dollar palaces and mansions, plus many very nice Cape Cod homes. We have many different homes ranging from royal palaces to cottages. We're going to take a tour through Mattapoisett and I'll show you the nice properties.

"Before we go I want to talk about the dark side of Mattapoisett. We have two haunted houses here. The most dangerous house is located at 66 6th Street and the other is a little cottage at 6 Green Street. People have died in these homes due to the hauntings.

"The main supervisor Eric Drome was called to a haunting about five weeks ago by a family that was thrown physically by an unknown invisible ghost. Everyone living in that home was told to get out. All of them were hospitalized with injuries forcing them out of that home and leaving everything behind. After the hauntings, the police and Eric went in the house and Eric ordered the entity to leave and he went upstairs. He was thrown headfirst down the stairs and through the front door, breaking his neck and splitting his head open. He's in Mass General hospital in Boston in critical condition.

"A Mattapoisett policeman was killed on that property in 1979. Another family was killed in Hurricane Bob in that house. Other families were driven out of that home from the hauntings. People who lived at 66 6th Street off of Route 6 have also seen ghosts of all different kinds.

"We will see that house later and go inside. Five weeks ago a national exorcism from a group of friars and paranormal investigators was done and we were told the house is safe.

"The little house at 6 Green Street has been vacant for thirteen years, but finally someone bought it and moved in on October 1, and so far no hauntings yet. But history shows ghosts were seen in that house. People in town reported seeing a Greenman in Ned's Point, a black mass that smells like death. It and a red-eyed deer are the most dangerous ghosts here. Lately it was an invisible force doing the attacks. One family reported a demon-looking dark ghostly figure in that house and again on their property, identifying itself as Ebenezer, and it looked like the devil. And mysterious unexplained deaths have happened in other areas in Mattapoisett over the last twelve years.

"Regarding the house at 6 Green Street, three people have died there in the last fourteen years. A man had a heart attack in the kitchen. Another man was choked to death in the living room after eating. A woman was struck and killed by lightning in her bed while she was sleeping.

"Let's go for a tour through Mattapoisett. Come with me," said Richard Classical, the co-owner of Arthur's Realtors.

A week later Eric Drome died at the hospital. Realtors, attorneys, doctors, and law enforcement went to Eric Drome's funeral at St. Anthony's church in Mattapoisett. Then Bennington Realtors with Rex Sax took over and Arthur's Realtors went out of business. Later the new realtors went to the house to take pictures in every room, top to bottom, including closets, and cameras were installed. They took pictures of the property around the house and put in lighting and fixed the house.

Later a meeting took place with employees of the new realtor.

"Good morning ladies and gentlemen. We have a couple of homes to sell here in Mattapoisett. One at 66 6th Street and the other at 6 Green Street. These homes will be sold a different way. My name is Rex Sax, the supervisor of Bennington Realtors of Vermont, a national realty company.

"Here I have two catalogs: one for 66 6th Street and the other for 6 Green Street. When people come to see those properties we show them the catalogs then we give them the keys to look at the property then they come here to buy the property. We're no longer going into these homes in case something happens, not unless we have to. These two homes are haunted and people have died at both properties, including Eric Drome from Arthur's Realtors being physically thrown through the house and headfirst through the outside door breaking his neck and splitting his head open. He died at the hospital from an unknown invisible violent force!

"It's similar to the Bennington Estates housing complex in Vermont from the ghost of Ebenezer. The former realty company has been hit by several lawsuits from the attacks and deaths because they failed to tell the families that the property is haunted. We have a problem about that! We can't tell the clients or tenants that the property is haunted or we'll never sell. They have to find out for themselves!

"We had this same problem in Vermont and New Hampshire properties from the Ebenezer ghost! People come; you tell them about the property and show them the catalogs. If they buy the property and something happens we have to give them the remaining money paid and pay their doctor bills to avoid being sued. I don't know what kind of ghosts are here but they must be pretty strong!

"Like the Bennington Ebenezer. I heard reports that the ghost of Ebenezer has been seen here in Mattapoisett. I don't know how true that is, but most realtors wherever you go have some kind of haunted history. I heard that Mattapoisett, Marion, and Rochester, now our region, is part of the Bridgewater Triangle Indian territory and goes through Cape Cod, Martha's Vineyard, and Nantucket. They're the same kind of group as the Vermont Indians from the Bennington Triangle, backing Ebenezer.

"The Bennington Triangle is very powerful. Here's a verse from the powerful Indians of the islands: 'There once was a man from Nantucket, who had a wangadong so long you can suck it, with smiles and grins on my chinny chin chin if my ear was a snake you can fuck it!' The verse comes from a powerful sexual physical ghost; and it's evil!

"If anyone calls in any of these ghosts their employment will be terminated immediately! We do not need another Ebenezer haunting. Let's not bring him back here because he knows who we are!" said Rex Sax.

# NINE

## THE LECTER FAMILY HAUNTINGS

Henry H. Lecter, a new police recruit for the Mattapoisett Police Department, and his wife Helen Lecter, a nurse. She's fifty-two and Henry is fifty-four. Harry Lecter, thirty years old, is a football assistant coach and he got a job at Old Rochester Regional High School. Then Hilary Lecter, twenty, a college student at the University of Vermont. Hilda Lecter a senior-to-be at Old Rochester Regional High School. The family moved to Mattapoisett from Bennington, Vermont, knowing their realtor was moving to Massachusetts, to escape the harsh winters in Vermont and welcome the nice beaches in southeastern New England.

The Lecters were visiting the Mattapoisett Inn for vacation on the Fourth of July and Henry and Helen went to Bennington Realtors looking, for a Cape Codder to buy in town.

July 1, 2003. It had been almost six years since the house at 66 6th Street was abandoned. In late 1997 the Bennington Realtors took over for Arthur's Realtors and the house had several lookers but no buyers, until the Lecters brought the property.

Just great! A new realtor from Bennington, Vermont, where the ghost of Ebenezer is from and a family moving in the house at 66 6th Street familiar with the ghost of Ebenezer called there by the It family! This is a nightmare!!!!!!!!!!!! The Lecter family is also moving from Bennington, Vermont, where the ghost of Ebenezer is from!

"Mr. and Mrs. Lecter! Welcome to Bennington Realtors. My name is Rex Sax, the company manager. You were supposed to meet with Jean Jazzman to take you over and show you the house and property, however things have changed. Here I have a catalog about the house and the land. Look it over and if you like it, I'll give you the keys to look at the house. Grab a cup of coffee and a muffin."

Later... "We like it. How come you don't show the house to us; it's more professional that way," said Henry Lecter.

"Our new policies have catalogs of homes because we do not go in the homes anymore for safety reasons," said Rex Sax.

Bullshit! Henry and Helen Lecter got the directions to the house and they went inside and did their own walk through, like the instructions from the catalog. Then they went through the property and went in the shed and barn. Bees were buzzing around in the barn. Then they went back to the realtor located in Hollywood Beach and they said, "We like it very much but there is one problem. There's a bees' nest in the lower barn," said Henry.

"Don't worry Mr. And Mrs. Lecter, we will take care of that right away. By the way, are you related to Dr. Hannibal Lecter!" Rex Sax joked.

"No sir, I'm Henry and she's Helen, no Dr. Lecter."

July 15, 2003, the Lecter family was all moved into the house at 66 6th Street.

Henry was hired as a police officer at the Mattapoisett Police Department after passing the cadet class, working Wednesday through Sunday from 11:00 p.m. to 7:00 a.m., the graveyard shift. Helen also works nights as a nurse at St. Joseph's Nursing Home in Fairhaven from 11:00 p.m. to 7:00 a.m. Wednesday through Sunday, also working the graveyard shift.

Harry Lecter is working at Old Rochester Regional High School as a football equipment manager and assistant coach during the season, Monday through Friday from 10:00 a.m. to 6:00 p.m. and on Saturdays during football season. He's living in the finished basement he made into his apartment.

Hilda Lecter, seventeen years old, sleeps in the left bedroom, and the room on the right is a spare bedroom. Hilary, twenty-year-old college student, is home for the summer and sleeps across from the parents' master bedroom upstairs.

Then three weeks later the hauntings started all over again at two minutes after every hour, happening to each one of them. They didn't realize they were hauntings right away.

Henry arrived at the police station just before 11:00 p.m. to get instructions from other police officers when suddenly he heard *snap!!!!!!!!* And ashes blew from the bottom of his shoes! The snap was loud enough to blow your eardrum! The time was 11:02 p.m.

"You just got struck by lightning Henry!" said a police officer.

"You're kidding!" he said.

"It's a good thing you have heavy duty police boots on or you'd be a goner!" the policeman joked!

"There's a pretty good lightning storm out there bro!" said another cop.

Then Henry Lecter ran out to his car, running in the rain and flashes of lightning, and he drove to his post.

Helen was working with a patient at the nursing home and a woman was dying and a black cat jumped on the dying woman's bed and laid down. Suddenly the woman died as Helen Lecter watched in shock. The time was 12:02 a.m. when the woman died in the nursing home. The cat was looking at Helen with bright yellow eyes and the cat went *meow!!!!!!!!* very loudly, showing its teeth, standing on its hind legs. It looked like the cat was ready to attack!

Helen ran out of the room screaming, "Nurse Harding, Nurse Harding, Nurse Harding! Elmira died and there's a mean cat in her room, please help! Ahhhhhhh!!!!!!"

Harry was fixing his bed when suddenly he heard a loud noise in the basement fireplace. He looked at the clock on the stove in the kitchen area and the time was 1:02 a.m. The loud noises were heard three times and stopped a minute later. He closed the damper on the fireplace and he locked it shut. Then he put a bunch of books in the fireplace along with other things to cover it up. Then he went to bed.

Hilary was sleeping and she had a dream that a giant black dog with red eyes walked up to her and started growling at her, showing its teeth! She woke up screaming and she turned on the lamp and she looked at the alarm clock and the time was 2:02 a.m. She realized it was only a dream then she got up to go to the bathroom and she looked out the window and she saw a flash of lightning. A black dog ran across the yard but she did not see it. She did her duties then she went back to bed and she shut the bedroom door.

An hour later Hilda had the same dream and the giant black dog jumped at her and she woke up throwing kicks and punches while lying on her bed—Hilda knows karate and she was wrestling with the dog on top of her in the dream. She got up quickly and she turned on the bedroom light and she closed the bedroom door and she went back to bed with the lights on. The time was 3:02 a.m.

Henry was parked on a side street and he saw a car speeding down Route 6 at a high rate of speed then *bang!* —the car hit a pole and caught fire! The time of the accident was 4:02 a.m. The driver went through the windshield and he lay dead, covered in blood, and the victim smashed his head, lying in the middle of Route 6.

Henry Lecter pulled up behind the burning car then he called for help then other policemen saw the dead body in the street. The rescue team came along with fire trucks to put the fire out.

"The dead man was the only one in the car. I know this dude, Eric Bundy from New Bedford. I arrested this dude at least twenty times, crimes ranging from drugs and prostitution, to attempted murder and arson. I guess he got what was coming to him tonight. I told this little dickhead that one day he was going to get himself killed! His head is smashed up like a pumpkin, I assume he's dead!" said a police officer.

The road was closed and Henry Lecter was there for the rest of the night until his shift ended.

Helen was making her rounds just before 5:00 a.m. and she saw a mist floating down the hallway in the nursing home; it looked like someone smoking. The time was 5:02 a.m. when she saw the mist. She said to another nurse, "Claire, did you see that, somebody must be smoking in Room 135."

"No I didn't see nothing. Maybe you saw Elmira's ghost, Helen," she joked!

"Oh my God Claire, don't say things like that." It was break time and Claire and Helen were in the break room talking. "I've been a nurse for twenty-three years and it was the first time someone died on me, it's scary."

"Helen, I had about twenty-three people die on me. I'm used to it!"

Harry felt like someone was sitting on his bed while he was waking up; the time of this haunting was 6:02 a.m. He got up and he looked toward the foot of the bed where he felt it go down and nothing was there. He got up to take a shower and he finished setting up his basement apartment in the house.

Hilary woke up to see the bedroom door open; she knew her door was closed and she was surprised to see it open. She looked at the alarm clock and the time 7:02 a.m. and she got up to greet her mom and dad coming home from their jobs overnight. The four of them sat at the dining room table talking and having breakfast. About 7:30 a.m. the family was talking about the strange evening last night while Hilda was still sleeping.

"When I got to the police station at the start of my shift, I was getting instructions from police officers. Suddenly, a loud snapping noise, and part of the rubber was blown off the bottom of my boot! The officers said I may have been struck by lightning from last night's storm. I didn't know a storm was even going on until I went out to start my shift. The policemen checked me to make sure I was alright. That's not all, it gets worse. Around 4:00 a.m. I clocked a car racing down Route 6 at ninety-eight miles per hour then I heard a crash and found the car on fire after hitting a pole. The victim went through the windshield and he was killed instantly!" said Henry.

"I had someone die at the nursing home about midnight. In all my twenty-three years working in nursing homes it's the first time someone died that I was working on, and a mean black cat was in the room. Then I saw a strange mist coming from the room she was in about 5:00 a.m. just before my break. Another nurse joked that I may have seen her ghost," said Helen.

"Mom, Dad, it could be a ghost. Last night sometime between midnight and 1:00 a.m., I heard a loud strange noise like wind sucking at the basement fireplace, so I closed the damper and I threw a bunch of books and things in there to cover it up. Then I got up about 6:00 a.m. and it felt like someone was sitting on my bed and nothing was there. Maybe it was Grampa," said Harry.

"Oh my God, I guess everyone has a story to tell this morning. I had a dream about a mean big black dog with red eyes coming after me, showing its teeth, ready to attack me!" said Hilary.

8:02 a.m. Hilda was getting up and the bed moved. She fell back on the bed then she got up. She looked around the room and under the bed and she saw nothing! She left the room to join the rest of the family talking at the dining room table. When she left the room the bed moved again by itself up against the chest of drawers. She said, "Hilary, I overheard you talking about your dream. I had the same one about the mean big black dog with red eyes attacking me and I woke up throwing punches and kicks at it."

After a brief breakfast, the parents went to bed because they work nights. Hilary went back to her room to get dressed and she found her bed in a different place up against the chest of drawers. She screamed, "Mom, something's in this room, come and look!"

"What the hell happened here; we must have had an earthquake. We had a lot of them when we were living in Vermont."

"Mom, when I was getting up the bed moved and I almost fell on my ass, so I had to backpedal to avoid falling. Now I come in to get dressed and I find the bed like this and my clothes are scattered all over the room. Something happened!" said Hilary, and she pushed the bed back where it belonged. Then she got dressed.

Helen went upstairs to bed. Henry was in bed and he looked at the digital alarm clock and the time was 9:02 a.m. and he heard a faint voice, *"Get out!!!!!!!!!!!!!!!!"* He sat up on the bed looking around and he said, "Helen, did you hear that? I thought I heard a voice saying, 'bets off,' or maybe I'm hearing things because it's time for shuteye."

"No, I didn't hear nothing!" she said. Then they went to sleep.

An hour later Helen heard a voice whispering in her ear. *"Get out!!!!!!!!!!!!"*

She woke up and she said, "I heard that!"

Henry woke up and Helen said, "I think I just heard what you heard talking in my ear; a voice clearly said, 'Get out!'" They got up checking around the rooms in the upstairs bedrooms and they found nothing. Then they went back to bed. The time of the haunting was 10:02 a.m. The next twelve hours of hauntings will be noticeable and physical for each of them.

Harry was at work in the locker room at Old Rochester High School when suddenly empty lockers started opening and closing by themselves and banging. The time of the haunting was at 11:02 a.m. for Harry. Footballs and equipment fell from the open lockers spreading across the locker room floor. Then it stopped!

Harry said, "Coach Andrew, come look at this! We have a ghost in the locker room. My mother called me earlier this morning saying we may have had an earthquake!" Harry joked.

"Holy shit, what a mess! It looks like we had something here!" said the coach.

"I was tying lacings on footballs about eleven o'clock when suddenly the lockers started opening and closing, throwing footballs and equipment out on the floor, and closing and banging. It seems more like a ghost haunting than an earthquake because I didn't feel any shaking," said Harry.

"That's nonsense, there's no such thing as ghosts! We had a mild earthquake, that's all, but I hope we don't get anymore!" said the coach.

Harry and the coach picked up and straightened the locker room, putting the football equipment back in the lockers and locking them up.

Hilary was packing suitcases and she was getting ready to go back to college. She opened a window to get some fresh air and looked at the alarm clock and the time was 12:02 p.m. Then she heard something buzzing and saw an African baldhead bee the size of a small bird flying around the window, then she saw a second one buzzing over her head. She screamed and she ran out of the room and she shut the door then then she grabbed a towel to put under the door to stop the bees from getting in the house. African baldhead bees are killer bees and if they sting you it kills!

Helen woke up and she said, "What's wrong Hilary!"

"Don't go in my room Mom, there are two giant bees flying around. I had the window open and they came in!" Hilary was hysterical!

"Don't go back in the room until tonight and they will go away," said Helen. Then she went back to bed.

Hilda was outside sitting at the picnic table eating a banana and she saw a deer with red eyes looking at her. She got up and she went in the house. The time of the haunting was 1:02 p.m.

Henry woke up and he looked at the alarm clock and the time was 2:02 p.m. The bed moved back and forth then back; it was over a minute later. He woke up Helen and he told her about the bed moving. He said, "I think we're getting more earthquakes! The bed is moving."

Helen woke up an hour later and she felt something blowing in her ears. She got up and she looked at the alarm clock and the time was 3:02

p.m. Then she looked around and she saw nothing. She heard a hissing sound then it stopped.

Harry was at the school at work answering phones in an office when suddenly papers and pens started falling on the floor and part of the ceiling tiles started falling on top of him. The time of his haunting was 4:02 p.m. Then he got up and he called the coach in to view the mess.

"Well Coach Andrews, is it a ghost or an earthquake!" Harry joked.

Coach Andrew laughed. Then he helped Harry clean up the mess.

Hilary was packing her car and she heard a voice calling, "*Get out!!!!!!!!!!!!! Get out!!!!!!!!!!!!!!! Get out!!!!!!!!!!!!!!!!!*" And she felt like someone was on top of her, she felt like she was not alone! The time was 5:02 p.m. during her haunting. She looked around and she saw nothing, then she slammed the car door and she went in the house.

Hilda was eating dinner and she heard a voice calling. *"Help me! Help me! Help! Help Marsha, please help, help me!"* The time of her haunting was 6:02 p.m. Hilda heard the calls coming from the living room and when she went to investigate she saw nothing. The calling stopped at 6:03 p.m.

Henry was ready to take a shower and the water was red like blood. He let the water run for a while and the water was clear a minute later then he took his shower. The time was 7:02 p.m. during his haunting.

Helen went upstairs to Hilary's room looking for the bees just before 8:00 p.m. and closed the windows. She had a can of bug spray with her and she sprayed the windows before closing them and she didn't see any bees. Then she shut the door again and she put the towel under the door again in case the bees were in the room somewhere. She saw a fog following her down the stairs until she got to the bottom then it vanished! The time of her haunting was at 8:02 p.m. The fog looked like ground fog from outside. Helen thought that was strange.

Hilary went up to her room to finish packing. Harry was downstairs watching TV and he kept hearing a voice. *"Get out!!!!!!!!!!!!! Get!!!!!!!!!!!!!!!!!!!! Out!!!!!!!!!!!!!! Get out!!!!!!!!!!!!!!!!!!"*

Then he saw a black fog coming from the fireplace then it vanished. The time was 9:02 p.m. and he went upstairs and he said, "Mom, something strange is here, I'm going to sleep at my girlfriend's house. I keep hearing something telling me to get out and I saw black soot coming out of the downstairs fireplace. Have a good night because I'm outta here!"

Helen and Henry went down to check it out and they saw nothing. Then they went back upstairs.

An hour later Hilary finished packing and she was ready to leave the room and the bed moved! The shades on both windows flew up, flapping around. The time was 10:02 p.m. for her final haunting and everything stopped a minute later.

Hilary screamed! "Ahhhhhhhhhh!!!!!!!!" Then she grabbed her last two duffel bags and she ran out of that house as fast as possible! She said, "Mom, Dad, I'm going back to college, you can stay here with the ghosts! Love you, goodbye!" She left the house and she went back to college in Vermont.

The parents went to work leaving Hilda home alone. The final haunting before things get physical!

Henry went to work at the police station and Helen went to work at the nursing home.

Meanwhile Hilda was calling friends to come over about ten minutes before 11:00 p.m. and nobody was home. She was alone. She was watching a movie on TV, *Scarface* with Al Pacino, when suddenly the lights went out at 11:02 p.m. She heard a dog barking and she saw red eyes and she heard a roar like nothing before—so loud! Then the smell of death! The poor seventeen-year-old girl used every scream she had until she passed out she was so scared!

Then the lights came back on and the hauntings went away and the TV came back on and *Scarface* was playing, the part when he started shooting up the nightclub. Then the poor seventeen-year-old regained consciousness and she ran out of the house leaving the TV on, and she ran to the police station to find her father.

The hysterical girl knocked on a window at the police station. "Can I help you?" asked a policeman.

"Yes, may I see my dad?!"

"Who are you?" said the cop.

"My name is Hilda Lecter and my dad works here! Tell him there's a ghost dog in our house!" She cried and the policeman buzzed her inside.

"Headquarters to Car #4, Officer Lecter, over."

"This is Car #4, Officer Henry Lecter over."

"Henry, I have your daughter Hilda here and she says there's a ghost dog in her house and she's horrified about it. Headquarters Officer Glenn, over."

"Ten-four, tell her I'll be there in a few minutes, over." Then Henry went back to the station to meet his daughter.

"What happened Hilda?"

"I was watching TV and the lights blew out and a barking dog with red eyes like the one in my dream was in the house. It growled at me really bad and I thought it was going to kill me! The lights came on and I ran out of the house!" she cried.

"Okay. Stay here and I'll go see what's going on! Some strange things have been going on in our house lately," Henry was telling Officer Glenn. Then he went to the house to see what was haunting his daughter Hilda.

The lights were on and the time was 12:02 a.m. and the TV was on. He shut it off and went through the house looking for any strange happenings and there was nothing! He spent forty-five minutes looking around, under beds, searching the whole house, and he found nothing. Then he went back to the police station and he said to his daughter, "You're sleeping here tonight in the nursery; I don't want you to be in the house alone. I did not find a dog in the house but it could be a ghost haunting. I didn't find anything in the house but stay here to be on the safe side and I will wake you up at seven when I leave," said Henry Lecter.

Helen was at work looking at the clock at two minutes after every hour and nothing happened. Henry called Helen telling her what happened with Hilda and that he'd bring her home in the morning.

The following weekend Henry and Helen were at dinner and they met with former officer Billy Wilkins. "I used to live in that house almost twenty years ago and me and my family went through hell. The house at 66 6th Street has been haunted for years by several ghosts. I heard a police officer died on my property before I moved there. We were haunted by the Greenman swamp creature, invisible hauntings and black fog ghosts, a deer with red eyes and hauntings beyond belief. Me and my family never believed in such things, until we moved in that house. The hauntings chased everybody out of that house since it was built. People have died in your house.

"During Hurricane Bob family of five, the It family, was living there and they all perished in that storm. One girl was found dead in the house and the others were found somewhere else. When we were living there we seemed to be haunted in different ways at two minutes after every hour and my daughter Brenda and her kids were horrified being there! I can't explain the horrors in that house, there's been so many," said Billy Wilkins.

"My realtor never told us about a haunted house. When we bought the house they didn't even show it to us; we had to look through a catalog then they gave us the keys to go look at the house! I told them it's more professional if you show the house and they told me it's against their new policy. I thought that was strange and I had on my mind that something was not right. So I went along and followed his instructions, and now I'm beginning to wonder if I should stay or go.

"Me and my family have been experiencing strange noises and voices telling us to get out. My daughters keep seeing a ghost dog with red eyes! Hilary had a dream of this dog, then she saw her bed moving and oversized bees chased her out of the house! She left for college early. Hilda was chased out of the house because she said the big black dog from her dream was in the house barking and growling at her and she witnessed her bed moving. The poor girl was terrified and she slept at the police station for the last three nights while I was at work; I work the 11:00 p.m. to 7:00 a.m. shift.

"My son Harry lived downstairs and he heard voices telling him to get out. He saw a black fog coming from the basement fireplace and now he's sleeping in Hilary's room because he doesn't want to go down there anymore. He told me one day he was at work at Old Rochester High School lacing footballs and putting air in them when all of a sudden, the lockers started opening and closing by themselves and throwing equipment and footballs all over the locker room. He felt it was some kind of a haunting and his coach said it was an earthquake.

"When the beds started moving in our house we thought it was from an earthquake but when we started hearing the voices, me and my wife began to think something is not right here! I was not frightened by it but I believe that something is here that shouldn't be. But when my son and two daughters are threatened I have to do something about it. I have to have a priest come in to find out what's going on in my house because something's not right!" said Henry Lecter.

"Mr. Lecter do you remember me from the police recruiting class,

Officer Archie Antilli?"

"Yes sir, I do."

"Mr. Lecter you were told about the It family that was killed during Hurricane Bob in 1991. Their daughters called in a very powerful ghost with a spirit board by the name of Ebenezer from the same town where your family just moved from: Bennington, Vermont. I hope he didn't follow you here.

"In 1997 the Grey family moved into your house and every one of them were picked up and thrown by mysterious ghosts and ended up hospitalized. The house went through several exorcisms to get it out including bringing in friars from Georgetown University and Providence College to fix the problem!

"We had very few, if any, hauntings since then, until you moved in. Now it's starting over slowly. Before the exorcisms, a realtor was killed just after the Greys moved. He was picked up and thrown through a door, breaking his neck and splitting his head open. He died at the hospital a few days later. The old realtor went out of business because of the hauntings and deaths from the house you're living in.

"Mr. Lecter, it's going to get worse until it gets physical and somebody gets hurt or killed again! My advice to you is when the priest comes tell him to perform another exorcism through your church while the hauntings are light. The two minutes after every hour hauntings are a warning that it's getting stronger and you have to do something about it before it gets physical.

"The two second hauntings on the clock last only a minute then come back every hour for twenty-four hours. If the hauntings come in strong at two minutes after every hour it can last forty-eight hours and it will attack everyone in your house one at a time and then start over, working from the oldest person to the youngest or from the youngest to the oldest. It doesn't matter if you're 110 to an infant! If the exorcism is done and the hauntings get worse, you better pack up and leave if you want to stay alive! But if the evil goes away you're in good shape, but it can come back later on. If it does, listen to what it's telling you: get out!" said Officer Archie Antilli.

The next day was Saturday and the Lecters were at home: Henry, Helen, Harry, and Hilda. Hilary went back to college early because of the hauntings. A priest came over to bless the home and the family had its stories to tell once again.

"Good afternoon, my name is Father Frank from St. Anthony's church. We need to do an exorcism here because every time someone moves into this house something evil happens all over again. Before it gets any stronger we have to get rid of it. The family who lived here before waited too long to do the exorcism when people were getting hurt and hospitalized. Then a real estate person was killed because the late exorcism didn't work, so we had to call in national paranormal investigators and friars from Providence College and Georgetown University to force the evil out, and this house became vacant again. The exorcism worked and things quieted down until this house had a new owner. We're going to do an exorcism again through St. Anthony's church with me, Sister Delores Marie, and the four living here saying the prayers to St. Michael while going through the house and the property. You have some kind of devil still biting around here.

"The hauntings at two minutes after every hour for twenty-four to forty-eight hours are a warning because the evil wants you out! If this exorcism works you should be okay. But if it doesn't you will find out right away! If things go wrong, pack your bags and get out because the hauntings will get worse. Another thing: it may stop for a while and act up later. Do not invite any evil of any kind after the exorcism because if you do it may come back.

"Follow my instructions and repeat my prayers until this exorcism is finished. You will hear voices and you may see apparitions; just ignore them and keep praying! After the prayers, and the exorcism is finished, I will give you crosses, a bottle of holy water, and glowing statues of the Blessed Virgin Mary and you put them in your bedrooms. Put a cross on top of the fireplace and over the one downstairs. We will now perform the exorcism. Let's begin," finished Father Frank.

After the exorcism it was near evening and the house was still kind of dark and dull. Harry went out on a date. And Henry said, "Hilda, I'm going to take you to work with me to be on the safe side. Grab some games to play. You can watch TV and sleep in the nursery tonight because no one is going to be home tonight and I don't want you in the house alone in case something happens!"

She accepted and they were together for a couple of hours at the police station until Henry got a call. He went out just before 1:00 a.m. to Ned's Point because of a loud party. He got there and he looked at the clock in the police car and the time was 1:02 a.m. People were shooting off fireworks and Officer Lecter put on his flashers and the party of about ten people was over as they got in their cars and scrammed.

Officer Lecter got out looking for beer bottles lying around as he was writing down license plate numbers. He stayed in Ned's Point for about an hour and a half in case more partygoers came in.

Meanwhile Hilda had a tracking device on her so she knew where her father was. 2:02 a.m. Hilda was having sex with two police officers in the nursery while Dad was out on calls during the night; she was having a threesome with the two young cops!

Just before 2:30 a.m. Henry was leaving Ned's Point, locking a gate. Suddenly he saw a green shadowy figure in the woods! He pointed his flashlight at it and it vanished! He got a second look flashing his light and he never saw it again! Then driving out of Ned's Point he saw a deer with red eyes looking at him. He beeped the horn and put his police lights on and the red-eyed deer ran off, then he drove away. Before he got to the police station he got another call about a girl, half naked, walking along the beach and crying loudly.

He went to the beach and he saw the girl in a black string bikini. He pulled up in the parking lot of the town beach and put his police lights on before he got out of his car. Flashing his flashlight, he went over to her and he said, "Excuse me miss, the beach is closed."

The girl ran into the water at a high rate of speed and vanished! Then lightning started and Henry went looking for the girl, shining his light out at the water, and she was gone! Henry called the fire department just before 3:00 a.m. Fire trucks, rescue workers, and helicopters went looking for this girl that jumped in the water and nothing was found. "Maybe it was the beach ghost!" a fireman joked.

Henry laughed. He was at the scene for the rest of the night. No body was found.

While Dad was chasing ghosts all night, Hilda was cleaning up from her threesome from the two young cops, then went to bed alone.

Around 3:30 a.m. Helen was at work. Three people died within a half hour and she was horrified. A ninety-eight-year-old woman died in her sleep, and a ninety-four-year-old man and a ninety-two-year-old man in the same room died in their sleep together! Helen Lecter thought it was the end of the world. The bodies were covered and they closed the door until the coroners removed the dead in the morning. Helen's job was to pull the plug when people died in the nursing room. Once that was done, her job was to identify the bodies.

"David Kessler ninety-two, and Robert Shrine, ninety-four, in Room 106. Vivian Roberts, ninety-eight, in Room 118," she said.

Around 4:00 a.m. Harry Lecter came home with his girl and she slept with him. The two stripped butt naked and jumped in the sack and Harry said, "Sharon, I'm going to fuck you good tonight!" Then he heard a scream coming from the kitchen area near the bathroom. The scream was not Sharon, it was not him, and it was not his sister Hilda!

He covered Sharon up and he put a towel around him and he walked around the finished basement apartment looking for where the scream was coming from. He checked the fireplace because he boarded it up earlier when he was home. He checked the outside door and it was locked. He put something heavy against the outside door. Then he checked the bathroom and nothing was there! Then he looked in where the boiler was and there was nothing, and he checked the storage under the stairs and nothing. Then Harry went to bed to finish the job with Sharon.

"What was that Harry!?"

"I think it could be a deer being attacked by a raccoon outside!" Then Harry gave her another stiff one before they got to sleep. Then about 5:30 a.m., Harry woke up with scratches all over him and Sharon woke up too and he said, "Sharon what did you do to me? You animal!!!!!!!!"

"Oh my God, Harry! I didn't do that!"

While Harry was looking at his scratches, a black mass appeared, forming into a figure as Sharon watched in shock! She said, "Harry, what's that!!!!!!!!!!!!!!!!?"

He looked and the figure quickly turned into a jet-black ghostly figure with red eyes and it roared like a mean bear. It charged at both of them, pinning them on the bed, then threw their naked bodies on the floor as Sharon was screaming and crying!

Harry said, "Ebenezer! Leave right now!" Then the apparition vanished! The two of them got dressed quickly and ran out of the house.

"Harry, I didn't believe you when you told me you had a ghost in your house when we went out last night. I never believed in ghosts until now! I will never come here again! What do you have here, the devil!?"

"Sharon, I never believed in ghost either until I saw that! When we lived in Vermont there was an area called the Bennington Triangle, and when we were kids we were told not to go there because the demon Ebenezer may attack. Papers and news reports on TV showed pictures of this Ebenezer, a dark ghostly creature with red eyes and a lot of power. I thought it was a joke. The Bennington Triangle is a place of hauntings and we lived in Bennington all our lives. We just moved to Mattapoisett earlier this summer.

"Now I'm a believer; this Ebenezer must have come for a visit to let us know that he has the power anywhere we go. I told you earlier how when I was at the high school fixing footballs when suddenly the lockers started flinging themselves open and shut, throwing equipment out on the floor. I thought it was some kind of haunting; it only lasted a minute before it stopped. I told Coach Andrew what was happening and he told me it was an earthquake. Then I heard some strange noises, scary noises in our basement apartment. I swear I heard voices telling me to get out. My sister Hilary even left to go to college on August 7 because she was haunted by giant bees she saw in her room and she saw dark shadows and dreamed of attack dogs with red eyes attacking her! We've had strange happenings and weird noises in our house since we moved in here. I was thinking maybe there is a real Ebenezer but I didn't think he'd pay a visit!

"We just had an exorcism with a priest and I thought it was a joke! We all went along with him saying prayers and he said there was a demon in our house and if something happens again we have to get out. Now I don't want to be here alone, because now I have a feeling I never was alone down here and might see something I don't want to see! We'll go to your place and I'll call Mom and Dad when we get there and warn them; they both work nights," finished Harry.

Harry called his parents when he got to his girlfriend's house in Marion.

Back at the police station Henry Lecter arrived at 6:10 a.m. Reporting police and the fire department personnel could not find the body of the girl who jumped in the water and vanished! Officer Glenn was asking Officer Lecter some questions. "Henry, what did this girl look like before she jumped in the water? The rescue team never found anybody."

"She looked like a white girl with a black string bikini and she had black hair," said Officer Lecter.

"When you approached her and told her the beach was closed what did she say?" asked Officer Glenn.

"She didn't say anything. When I got close to her she jumped in the water running pretty fast and I lost sight of her," said Officer Lecter.

"It could be the Mattapoisett Beach ghost because we have had several complaints over the past few years about a girl walking on the beach late at night vanishing or jumping in the water. Her name is Maria Cooper. What time was it when you saw this girl on the beach?" asked Officer Glenn.

"It was around 3:00 a.m.!" he said.

"Mr. Lecter you probably saw a ghost because no body was found in the water or on the beach. Did you see anything else during your routine this evening?" asked Officer Glenn.

"Yes sir, I saw a green mist in the woods in Ned's Point Park that looked unusual and when I went to investigate it vanished! Then I saw a deer with red eyes leaving Ned's Point on my way to the town beach call."

"Mr. Henry Lecter you better go see a priest because you saw three of the Mattapoisett ghosts!" said Officer Glenn.

Officer Lecter told Officer Glenn about the strange things happening in his house. "This is why I have my daughter with me. We just had an exorcism to get a demon out of our house and if it comes back we have to get out of that house," said Officer Lecter.

Henry and his daughter Hilda went home after his shift and waited for Helen to get home. Then she came home and Henry said, "How was your night?"

"It was very frightening. Three more people died last night and I had to take them off the machines. In all my life nursing I never had people dying on me and suddenly we have four in one week!" she said.

"I had a strange night myself. I got a call to a loud party at Ned's Point after 1:00 a.m. and I chased ten people out of there taking down license plate numbers and I closed and locked the gate. Then I saw this green fog in the woods and when I got closer to get a better look, it was gone. Then I left Ned's Point and I saw a deer with red eyes looking at me, similar to the hauntings we have been getting lately here. Then I got a call about a girl with a black bikini hanging around at the town beach. When I got there I questioned her on what she was doing, the beach was closed. I got no response and she jumped into the water so I couldn't find her, so I called a rescue team and no body was found in the water or on the beach and the search went on all night. I reported the girl to the station and Officer Glenn told me that I saw all the Mattapoisett ghosts all evening and he told me to go see a priest. Then I told him what was happening here at the house with the exorcism," said Henry Lecter.

The phone rang a few minutes later in the house and Henry answered, "Hello!"

"Dad, it's Harry. You, Mom, and Hilda, get the hell out of that house! When I got home late last night I was still with Sharon and we were both attacked by the Ebenezer ghost, it must have followed us from Vermont. First I heard screams, but I went looking and found nothing! Then we were sitting on the bed talking, and I felt like something was scratching me and I saw marks all over me. Then we saw a black thick fog form into a demon-like man with pointy straight-up ears, red eyes, and sharp teeth, and it growled at us like a mean bear or wolf. It jumped on us on the bed and it threw me across the floor with one hand, then it picked up Sharon with the other hand and threw her on the other side of the room.. I recognized what I saw and I told Ebenezer to leave. Then it vanished and we were able to get out of the house.

"I'm going to move in with Sharon, I'm not going back to that house. Just throw my things on the lawn in the backyard and I will go pick them up later, and make sure you have a priest with you!" said Harry on the phone.

Helen was upstairs getting ready for bed while Henry was on the phone with Harry. Hilda was out in the backyard drinking a bottle of water looking for something to do. She saw a huge beehive hanging from a tree and she picked up a big rock and hurled it, smacking the beehive, and ran away like a bat out of hell from her backyard and into the woods.

The beehive was full of African killer honeybees and thousands of them flew out and chased Hilda into the woods. They speedily caught up with her, and swarmed all over her, stinging her as she screamed hysterically. She was dead within a few minutes! The bees were still stinging her while she was dead, still swarming all over her.

Henry and Helen never knew what happened, the attack happened so fast!

Helen was getting into bed and she could smell an awful odor. She saw a black mass moving in her room and she screamed! "Aaaahhh-hhhhhhh!!!!!!" Then the black mist lunged at her and growled like a mean bear and knocked her down on the floor. Big hands came out of the black mist and threw her up against the wall  She got up and ran out of the room down the stairs as fast as she could, grabbing Henry, crying hysterically, "We have to get out of the house, a devil attacked me upstairs!!!!!!!!!!!!!"

Bees swarmed all over the windows, trapping them in the house. African honey killer bees three inches long with five-inch wingspans and African baldhead killer bees four inches long with six-inch wingspans! Helen screamed hysterically! "Ahhhhhhhhh!!"

Henry said, "Oh my fuckin God!!!!!!!!!!" Then he said, "Helen call the fire department and I will make sure all the windows are closed and locked. Ebenezer, I know you're here and you need to leave and go back to Bennington, Vermont where you came from!"

Then Henry was saying the prayers the priest told him to say during the exorcism. Then the bees started to lighten up and fly away! All the windows were closed and doors were locked throughout the house and Henry and Helen were trapped there until the fire department arrived.

Meanwhile Henry was calling for Hilda and she was not in the house. The fire department sprayed white foam on the house to chase the bees away until Henry and Helen could run to their car without getting stung. They made it then they drove to the real estate office. Before they left Harry called the police to search for Hilda because she wasn't home.

The bees were still swarming over Hilda's body hours after she was dead.

A policeman was at the beach and he saw a girl that looked like Hilda and he said, "Are you Hilda?"

"Yes Officer, it's my nickname, my real name is Minda. What's up!"

"Your dad just called and he wants you to go home." Then she grabbed her beach stuff and she went home to Marion where she lives. It was the wrong girl.

Henry and Helen went to the real estate office at 11:38 a.m. Henry hadn't been to bed yet and was in a pissy mood. "Good morning, may I speak to the owner, Rex Sax?"

"I'm sorry but he's not here today."

"Oh, that's great! Who are you?"

"My name is Jean Jazzman, the realtor."

"Jean, my name is Henry Holland Lecter and this is my wife Helen. We live at 66 6th Street off of Route 6 and we have a demon in our house that I bought from Mr. Rex Sax and you better get his ass over here right now because I'm pissed! You people have a hell of a lotta nerve selling a haunted house without telling us!"

"I'm sorry sir, but he's in Aruba on vacation!"

"Well when he gets back you have him get in touch with me because he's in a shitload of trouble! Meanwhile you have to put me up in a hotel with my wife, daughter, and son right now until this little prick gets back from vacation!"

"Yes sir, go to the Mattapoisett Inn and I will have a suite for you," said Jean Jazzman.

Henry and Helen left. Henry slammed the door going out then he sped off in his Fifth Avenue Chrysler, peeling out of the parking lot!

"You're welcome!" Jean said to herself.

Nighttime and Hilda was not home. Henry went to the house with the hardware store beekeepers to spray the trees during the night and kill the remaining bees. You have to spray the nests at night to kill all the bees. Then the beekeepers went in to spray the shed and the barn.

Helen took the night off from work, resting at the Mattapoisett Inn. The beekeepers sprayed around the house foundation to keep any bees away.

11:00 p.m. Henry was at the police station and he had no sleep and was in a bad mood! Then he went to the house and he looked at the time in his police car and the time was 12:34 a.m. He searched the house because Hilda's not home and Helen had been calling her all day and she's nowhere to be found.

"Do you think she was attacked by the bees?" a young cop working with Henry said. It was the same young cop that was fucking his daughter all night at the police station last night.

"I didn't think about that Doug. Let's search the yard and the woods and hope for the best!" said Henry.

The two policemen searched the yard and the shed/barn. "We're going to have a lot of dead bees to sweep up tomorrow!" said Henry Lecter.

Officer Doug laughed. Then they went out into the woods and Henry saw a vision in the woods that looked like the Blessed Virgin Mary. Then he looked at his watch and the time was 1:17 a.m. Then he looked on the ground and he was standing over his dead daughter's body. Maggots were eating away at her and snakes were crawling over her body. Flies were all over her, and Henry saw a white mist coming up from the body, rising up into the sky!

He started crying then he threw up seven times and opossums, raccoons, and rats arrived to eat Henry Lecter's puke! Then several cops came and the body was removed. Henry was sick. When he got to his police car he puked again. When he got to the police station and he got out of his car he puked again—twice! When he got inside the station he puked three more times!

Later he called his wife sleeping at the Mattapoisett Inn. The phone at the hotel rang at 2:58 a.m. in Helen's room. "Helen, it's Henry, Hilda is dead! She was attacked by killer bees. I found her body in the woods behind our house!" Henry cried before he puked again at the police station!

Helen cried hysterically! Then she had a series of upchucks, puking for the rest of the night before passing out, and ended up sick in the hospital. The next day Harry came to help Henry sweep all the dead bees out of the shed and the barn and dump them in bags to throw in a dump truck. They raked up piles of dead bees the size of small birds and put them in a wheelbarrow to be loaded into bags. The dump truck carried them away, filled to the top!

Then Henry hired a lawyer to go after the real estate agent in court for failing to tell them they moved into a haunted house. Rex Sax, the owner of Bennington Realtors of Vermont said, "We're a brand-new company and we were not told the house at 66 6th Street was haunted.

That's Arthur's Realtors problem. They're the group who's responsible, they never told us when we took over."

"The rule is the other realtor is responsible. You have to go after them. Arthur's Realtors went out of business. I have dealt with these people before and they have to pay for all the damages. That company owes millions of dollars in damages. You have to give the Lecters a place to stay with nothing coming out of their pockets until this case is final," said the judge.

The next day was Hilda's funeral at St. Anthony's church. The police, fire department, lawyers, doctors and nurses, and family attended. After the burial, September 2003, the Lecters had a meeting with Bennington Realtors with Rex Sax.

"Mr. Henry Lecter, I'm very sorry to hear about your daughter's death and I understand you're very upset because I sold you a haunted house. I did not know that house was haunted but I have another house on Green Street where you can stay for free until a decision in the courts is final. Don't ask me if this house is haunted because I don't know.

"The house is much smaller, it's only a cottage and here's the catalog on the house. It has two bedrooms, a kitchen, dining room, living room with a big brick fireplace. It has a good heating system, wall-to-wall carpeting, and it has central air conditioning. The house is bigger than it looks and you have a separate cottage with a room, bath, and kitchen area. You have a built-in generator and a drive through that can fit four cars. A good-sized yard with a long picnic table like the one you had at the other house, but you do not have two acres of land or a farm. It's a quiet home not far from Harbour Beach. You don't have all the highway noise like you had on Route 6. If you want I can have Gloria Stevens, one of my agents, show you the property," said Rex Sax.

"Please!" said Henry.

"Hi Mr. And Mrs. Lecter, I'm Gloria Stevens, come follow me. The house is at 6 Green Street not far from where you lived before. I'm sorry for your loss," said Gloria, then they met at the property.

She spoke again. "Welcome to 6 Green Street. This little cottage is bigger than it looks. The first room branches off the house. It's a separate room; it used to be a bed and breakfast years ago. In here you have a room you can use as a family room or bedroom and it has a full bath and a small kitchen; it's called the guest room of the cottage. One door and a separate building.

"Back here is the house. You enter a porch that leads to the kitchen and all the appliances and washer and dryer. Next is a rustic style living room with a big rock style fireplace, then you have two bedrooms side by side and a full bath in between. You have gas heat, central air, and built-in generator. You have a good-sized yard and a swimming pool. This is the only house we got left in Mattapoisett," said Gloria Stevens.

## THE LITTLE COTTAGE HAUNTINGS

The Lecter family moved from 66 6th Street to 6 Green Street because of a settlement from a death due to hauntings. But does it do any good? Nope! Unfortunately, they moved into another haunted house on September of 2003.

Henry and Harry helped move their furniture out of the house at 66 6th Street and a priest was in the house saying prayers. And all their furniture fit in the little cottage because Harry moved out of the basement apartment and he moved into his girlfriend Sharon's home. "Don't bring any ghost in here Harry or I'll slap you!" Sharon joked.

At 6 Green Street Hilda's bedroom set went in the separate building and the bathroom fixings from the upstairs bathroom in the other house went in there as well. Henry and Helen slept in the master bedroom across from the living room. The other room belongs to Hilary when she comes home from college, but right now Henry and Helen live alone in this house with two spare bedrooms.

They still work at night and it was the middle of September 2003. Each night between 1:00 a.m. and 3:00 a.m. something is visiting the house at 6 Green Street. Birds' flapping wings sound in the fireplace. Raccoons coming in to visit, squirrels coming in to visit. A fox comes in for a visit; lightning strikes to check out the 6 Green Street chimney! Then a skunk comes once in a great while. Ravens, crows, and hawks come in and fly around for a while—the Lecters better not leave food around or the little elves will get it all! An occasional seagull flies down the chimney to check out the house and one of them left a fish lying in front of the fireplace. And feathers scattered everywhere! All these Santa Claus creatures are activated by the Mattapoisett ghost hauntings from 1:00 a.m. to 3:00 a.m. nightly or at two minutes after every hour!

The hauntings began after the first day of fall, starting on a Wednesday night. Henry got home at 7:11 a.m., heard something flapping on the floor, and saw feathers everywhere from a seagull! Then he saw a pretty good-sized fish flopping in front of the fireplace on the floor. Then he closed the open damper on the fireplace and he picked up the fish. He washed the fish, a bass, and put the live fish in the freezer. He got a good laugh at the mess. Then Helen came home and she said, "Oh my God, what happened here! There are feathers all over the place! Is this house haunted too!?"

"No, the damper was open in the fireplace and a flock of seagulls must have come down the chimney, but besides the mess they left us a treat!" Henry opened the freezer. He said, "When I came home, surprised by the feathers, a seagull must've left a live fish in front of the fireplace! It was flopping on the floor so I picked it up, washed it, and put it in the freezer. I'll cook it later and we'll eat it for dinner tonight!" said Henry.

Henry and Helen cleaned up the feathers and mopped the floors then they went to bed. Around 4:00 p.m. Henry went out to chop some wood to get a fire going in the fireplace. They cooked the fish there because it was big enough to cook in and they had the fish for dinner. Helen said, "The fish is delicious!"

Then they enjoyed a nice warm fire on a cool late September night. They watched a movie on TV before going into work. Henry saw the red-eyed deer while riding in his police car. He turned on his police lights and sounded the siren and the red-eyed deer ran off! Helen was working at the nursing home and it was a quiet night, but during her routine she felt like something was following her, and she kept looking over her shoulder. The invisible ghost from the other house was making Helen's night a little uneasy, following her and making her feel like she's not alone!

Back at 6 Green Street at 1:23 a.m. no one is at home. Henry forgot to close the damper in the fireplace and a hawk flew down the chimney and around the house, leaving black and gray feathers this time. Then a crow got stuck in the chimney an hour later and there were black feathers in the fireplace lying on top of the ashes.

Henry got home just after 7:00 a.m. to see the house covered in bird feathers again. Helen got home and she saw the mess. Henry said, "I forgot to close the damper when we used the fireplace last night." Then they cleaned up the mess and swept all the feathers into a pile in front of the fireplace, enough to fill a wheelbarrow. Then Henry put them in trash bags and placed the bags in the trash bins outside.

Helen vacuumed the house—all the rugs—and swept and washed the floors, with Mr. Clean and Murphy's Oil Soap for the wood floors, making the house smell nice. Henry swept up the ash in the fireplace and he washed the floor in the fireplace. It took two and a half hours to clean the house from last night's mess before they went to bed for the day.

Harry came over to mow the lawn and fix things outside the house. Then he went back to work at the high school. The house was used for a model showing by realtors. The day was quiet after Harry finished mowing the lawn. The Lecter parents got up, straightened up the house, had dinner, and watched TV. Henry went out to get a gate to put in front of the fireplace to keep the birds from coming down the chimney inside.

Nobody has lived in the house at 6 Green Street since 1990, thirteen years ago, because this house is haunted too!

It was Thursday night and Henry and Helen went to work. Around 2:00 a.m. Friday morning a man was standing in the kitchen in front of the stove for about a minute. A man died there years ago who suffered a heart attack; he was a loner at the time. Then, after, he vanished a minute later! Then the fireplace damper flew open and two dead squirrels fell in the fireplace. Henry came home shortly after 7:00 a.m. and the house smelled like death; the stench was terrible!

"Oh my God!" he said to himself and he went over to the fireplace where the smell was strong and he saw two dead squirrels covered with flies in the fireplace. He got some bug spray to kill the flies and they flew up the chimney. He closed and locked the damper then he scooped up the dead squirrels with a dustpan and threw them in the woods behind the house. Then he washed the dustpan off with the outside hose. When he went back into the house the smell of death was gone.

Helen came home. She said, "It smells like bug spray in here!"

"Yes dear, I found two dead squirrels lying in the fireplace covered with flies and the house stunk. I need to put something up against the damper to stop more animals from falling in here." He put a chair inside the fireplace up against the damper, holding it shut.

They went to bed. Then when they got up everything in the house was normal. The only time the hauntings happen in this house is between 1:00 a.m. and 3:00 a.m. Then they stop.

The next night before Henry goes to work he's checking the house and the spare cottage and everything is normal.

Later they go off to work and just after 1:00 a.m. with nobody home once again, a big raccoon made its way down the chimney, pushing the locked fireplace damper open. It made it down in the fireplace, pushing the chair out of the way, and it got into the house. The raccoon tore down drapes, it tore the bed blankets, sheets; even the mattress was torn open and furniture was all scratched up by this fuckin thing! It scratched up the floors, it tore up the rugs in the house and it made scratch marks all over the walls. Not to mention because of the rain the raccoon left muddy footprints all over the house. It got into cabinets and knocked things all over the place, breaking glass and eating all the bread in the house. Then it opened the refrigerator door and the door hit the raccoon in the head, scaring the animal. Shortly after, it ran and hid under the bed because it saw lightning and heard a loud *bang!* of thunder!

Around 6:00 a.m. it got quiet and the raccoon went to the open refrigerator and knocked down a gallon of milk. It splattered all over the floor and the raccoon was licking up some of the milk. Then it grabbed a box of eggs, which fell and broke all over the floor. Then it got some fish out of the refrigerator and ate it. The raccoon threw up then it ate what it threw up and it threw up again while it was slipping and sliding in the mess. Then the raccoon was eating and licking up egg yolk smashed all over the floor. The raccoon kept eating what it could and throwing up again and eating its puke. It kept eating and kept getting sick!

Then the raccoon—as big as a dog! —ran to hide when it heard a car coming. The raccoon puked in Henry's bedroom then it was running in the house. Henry got home just after 7:00 a.m. singing to himself, "Oh what a night!" Then he turned the key and he entered the house and he saw the disaster, then he heard something running around.

He stepped out of the house and he called the station. "Car #4, Officer Henry Lecter to headquarters over."

"This is headquarters, Captain Walker speaking."

"Captain, send some help to 6 Green Street. Someone broke in my house; the house is a big mess! Officer Henry Lecter just getting off shift, over."

Several cops arrived and the fire department and a rescue squad showed up at the house. The raccoon was hiding under Henry's bed and it had shit there! Helen came home and she said, "Oh my God! What happened here?!"

"Helen, don't go in the house! Someone broke in during the night and the house is a mess! They might still be in there. Go to the Mattapoisett Inn and get a room there and get some sleep." She left and got a room.

The police and a S.W.A.T. team with big guns entered the house and they heard something big running around. "Mr. Lecter you may have a bear in here by the looks of this mess!" one cop said.

Other cops were saying, "Come out wherever you are, we know that you're here!"

Henry moved his bed out of the way and this giant raccoon ran out from under his bed into the living room. Then *pop pop bang bang!!!!!!!!!!!!!!!!!!!* The giant raccoon was blown away by police gunfire, lying in the fireplace in a pool of blood! Then the raccoon was taken out of the house and news media were taking pictures of this giant wolf-like raccoon. It was huge!!!!!!!!!!!!!!!!!!!!!

"A raccoon made a mess like this! Even a grizzly bear couldn't do all this. It can't be a normal raccoon to do this kind of damage; it's something else! It ate all my food it threw up all over the house; there's shit and piss everywhere! All the rugs and floors are damaged and all the walls were scratched and damaged. This house will need a complete overhaul to fix it!" said Henry Lecter.

Then he went outside to get a good look at this giant raccoon. It looked like a wolf/raccoon combination. The creature was taken by an animal crew for an autopsy. Henry called the real estate office to tell them what happened then he called his son Harry to come help him clean up the mess.

Henry, Harry, and a wrecking crew came to clean out the house. They had to rip up floors and rugs and take down walls to repair it. The spare room was okay. Henry stayed at the Mattapoisett Inn with his wife until the house was ready to move back in again. Workers wore respirators and masks to get by the stench! All the furniture was scratched and damaged and the bedroom was destroyed. The realtor had to replace the house with all new furniture and a new bedroom set.

"Rex, you need to fix the chimney to stop these creatures from coming in. I had birds flying into my house the past couple of days, leaving me with a mess to clean up and feathers all over the place, and one bird left me a big fish to cook up. I found it alive flopping on the floor in front of the fireplace," said Henry Lecter.

Rex Sax laughed. The next day work was being done on the chimney and a new flue was put in the fireplace and a new damper with a strong lock. The new realtors know that this house is haunted as well.

It was the Sunday before Halloween when the house was ready to move back in. Henry drove around town in his police car and it was a quiet night. Helen also had a quiet night working at the nursing room. Later she was washing clothes in the laundromat. She was all by herself folding clothes and the ghost of Ebenezer—the same Ebenezer that haunted the It family—was standing right behind her for about five minutes as Helen was folding sheets, blankets, and towels, but she never noticed. Then she turned around and it was gone!

Then around 1:00 a.m. a second raccoon crawled up the side of the house at 6 Green Street on the roof and up the chimney. This time there was a chimney cover to keep the creatures from going down the chimney into the fireplace like Santa Claus! Henry stopped by the house around 1:00 a.m. and he looked at the clock in his police car and the time was 1:02 a.m. The raccoon leaped off the chimney then it bounced off the roof, leaping to the ground. It ran in the woods when it saw the car coming in the yard.

Henry walked around the house and he flashed his flashlight in the woods near the house because he heard a noise when he got out of his car. Then he went in the house and he grabbed a beer out of the refrigerator and searched the house to make sure everything was alright. Then he shined his light in the fireplace and the damper was locked nice and tight and the house was nice and clean.

Two orbs were crossing one another in the spare room building, but when Henry checked in there they vanished and he did not see them.

He heard *click!* Then he looked around in the room, kitchenette, and the bathroom. He looked under the bed and moved furniture and he saw nothing. He turned on the lights and he saw nothing, then he left.

Just after Henry left his house a skunk walked around the house, spraying along the foundation, leaving a horrible smell. Then it ran in the woods!

Just after 7:00 a.m. Henry returned to the smell of skunk all over his property. Helen came home and smelled the odor. "Oh my God, it stinks terribly! What are we going to do Henry!? I hope the skunk didn't get in the house!"

"I hope not Helen!"

Before they entered the house Henry called the fire department and they sprayed foam to cut down on the smell, but the aftermath didn't smell like roses! They had to stay somewhere else until the skunk smell went away. Henry built a fence on his property near the woods to keep the wild animals out of his yard; they'll go on someone else's property now!

They stayed at Sharon and Harry's place for the day and slept there. They went out to a restaurant and went bowling later.

The next day was Tuesday, Halloween. Henry spent his day off painting the house and putting up Halloween decorations. Helen was at the stove cooking macaroni and meatballs when two invisible hands grabbed her by the wrist and she was screaming hysterically!

"Henry help me, something is grabbing me in the kitchen! I can't breathe!"

Henry was on a ladder painting the gutters when suddenly he heard Helen screaming. He got down the ladder and he ran in the house to see what's happening! The paint bucket fell from the roof onto the ground. When Henry got in the house the invisible hands released her and she fell on the floor!

"Henry, something grabbed me by the wrist so tight I couldn't catch my breath! We need to get out of here! This house is haunted too!"

"Did you see anything?" he asked.

"No, I was cooking and I felt something grabbing me so tightly it felt like it was going to squeeze me in half! We have to get out of here!"

Henry shut the stove off. Suddenly he was lifted off the ground and thrown headfirst into the living room up against a wall, knocking pictures down. He had his hands in front of his head to break his fall, protecting himself from getting seriously injured! He got up and he said, "Let's get the fuck out of here!"

The Lecters went back to the Mattapoisett Inn. Henry called the realtor to tell them what happened!

"Oh my God, Henry, I'm sorry to hear that! The hauntings followed you from 66 6th Street to the Green Street address. Just stay at the Mattapoisett Inn indefinitely, until further notice!" said Rex Sax of Bennington Realtors of Vermont.

The Lecters stayed in Mattapoisett. Henry still works for the police department and Helen still works at St. Joseph's Nursing Home in Fairhaven. And they stayed at the Mattapoisett Inn and later moved in with Harry and Sharon. They were never haunted again.

The day after the Lecters left 6 Green Street the realtors went in the house. A door was open and a fox, a raccoon, and a turkey vulture were feasting on the macaroni and meatballs, leaving a mess in the kitchen. Rex Sax and Jean Jazzman were in the house and stepped out while the animals were feasting and called the animal control unit.

The animal control unit struggled getting the creatures out of the house. They cornered the raccoon with a device to remove it. The turkey vulture went for an attack and the fox was standing its ground, growling. The fox was shot dead! The turkey vulture was pepper sprayed and tased. Then the animal rescue workers tranquilized the bird with a needle to remove it! Four seagulls were outside in the yard hoping for a piece of the pie, but the animal control workers swatted them away and closed the door to the house.

Later the two went back in to clean the house. Jean heard a voice, "*Get out!*" Rex heard a voice, "*You too! You too! You too! You too!*"

"Jean can you hear that? I keep hearing 'YouTube!'"

"No Rex. but I heard what sounded like 'get it' or 'get out!'" Then Jean Jazzman started choking, coughing, and gagging and she ran out of the house! Rex was picked up and thrown out a window and he landed in the yard with cuts all over him. They both ended up in the hospital.

# ELEVEN

## THE SLATER FAMILY HAUNTINGS

The Slater family is also moving to Mattapoisett. Anthony, fifty-nine, the husband, and Ellen, fifty-six, the wife. Daughter Evelyn, thirty-three, is a writer. Sons Mike Slater, thirty-two, a police officer, and Kenny Slater, thirty, a fireman, both got jobs in Mattapoisett. Mom and Dad work for the Roberts and Slater Law Firm.

They are also moving from Bennington, Vermont. What the fuck!!!!!!!! Are we going to have the ghost of Ebenezer here forever!!!!!!!!!! What the fuck!!!!!!!!!!! The Slaters looked at the model furnished house at 6 Green Street first but they did not like it there.

"We have a house at 66 6th Street with two acres of land and it's a Cape Codder. It's a beautiful home. It's much bigger than the home at 6 Green Street," said Jean Jazzman.

"Let's go look at that property. My name is Anthony Slater, and this is my wife Ellen Slater. We both work for a law firm in Brockton, Massachusetts called Roberts and Slater, Associates at Law at 259 Massasoit Avenue in Brockton, Massachusetts," said Anthony Slater. They liked the house and bought the property on October 1, 2009. This family is Catholic and they do not believe in ghosts, but they'll soon find out.

The family lived in a small family winter village in Bennington, Vermont and they heard about this realtor getting property in southern New England to get away from the hefty snows during the winter. It was a rainy, windy, but mild day when they looked at the home in Mattapoisett.

"This house is perfect for us. It's in a nice neighborhood and we will live near the beach and Cape Cod is beautiful!" exclaimed Ellen Slater.

Evelyn was walking through the house and she felt a little uneasy. "Mom, I swear this house is haunted!" she said.

"Why do you say that?!"

"I don't know, I feel something is not right here; it's dark and I have a strange feeling. I don't know what to tell you, it just doesn't feel right here for some reason."

"Evelyn what do you mean?" asked her mom.

"I feel this house is haunted by a ghost or something could be here. I might be wrong, but the feeling I have doesn't feel right," said Evelyn.

When she was a kid she practiced witchcraft on a spirit board involving the ghost of Ebenezer who's not welcome in Mattapoisett. But he's following the visitors from Vermont moving here. The house at 66 6th Street is where Ebenezer hangs out because the people are buying the house where the ghost of Ebenezer visited in the past.

The truck to move the Slater family in arrived and the family helped move the furniture in the house. Part of the house was furnished from other haunted visitors who lived there before!

Anthony and Ellen slept in the master bedroom upstairs and Evelyn slept in the room across upstairs. Mike and Kenny slept downstairs. Mike was a policeman and Kenny a fireman, both working the nightshift Wednesday through Sunday with Mondays and Tuesdays off. Evelyn was a writer working from home during the day. Anthony and Ellen worked at the law firm in Brockton, Monday through Friday from 9:00 a.m. until 5:00 p.m.

Anthony was at work in his office one day and a fog went across one side of the room to the other and vanished as he watched! Then Ellen was in the basement at the law office looking at some files and she saw a mist moving across the basement room saying, "*Get out!!!!!!!!!!!!!!!!!!!* And it vanished! It reappeared again for a few seconds then it vanished again!

Ellen said to Anthony, "I don't believe in ghosts, but I clearly heard a voice telling me to get out down in the basement. It is not my imagination; I heard it clearly telling me to get out."

Anthony went down the basement where the files are. He was down there for a half hour and he heard nothing or saw nothing. Then he went upstairs and he said, "I heard nothing, there's no such thing as ghosts! Just stay up here and hand me files to go through before tomorrow's court hearings."

Evelyn was at home looking through her computer and she saw the ghost of Ebenezer, a demon-like ghost. She got a good look at the ghost on her computer—it looked like the devil—and she closed the page and she got into a sports page about European soccer! France and Brazil were playing in a 1-1 tie with a few minutes left. She ordered a pizza and she finished watching the game and it ended in a 1-1 tie. She had pizza and beer for lunch watching the game before she started writing on her computer.

She heard a hissing noise in the house. She stopped what she was doing and she went looking where the hissing sounds were coming from. She saw nothing. Then she heard a ball bouncing and being kicked, then a baseball being hit by a bat, then everything went quiet.

Mike works nights at the police station and Kenny works nights at the Mattapoisett fire department. Mike saw the red-eyed deer, the Greenman shadow, and the Mattapoisett Beach ghost. The beach ghost was floating through the air into the woods as he watched from his police car. He called back to police headquarters.

"Officer Slater to headquarters, over, from Car #7."

"Car #7, come in please. Officer Lecter, over."

"I see some strange things in the woods like a deer with red eyes, a girl walking on the beach in a bikini, and a green mist in the woods."

"Officer Slater, just ignore them. They're ghosts looking for attention!"

"Ghosts, are they really true!" said Mike.

"Yes, they are. Let's meet somewhere and I will tell you what happened to me when I lived in your house. We were attacked by an unknown ghost while living in that house and were forced out. I will not go into detail but it was a haunting that was beginning to get physical! When we moved to 6 Green Street my wife was grabbed by the wrist by something invisible and I was thrown against a wall headfirst—that made me believe in ghosts! I could have been killed! I had to get a priest to do an exorcism, that's how bad it was. Good luck living in that house because if you don't believe in ghosts you will soon find out!" said Officer Henry Lecter.

One day Anthony was at work going over some files to get ready for court the next day and he saw a black shadow in his office. It lasted a minute and it vanished. He was shocked at what he saw and he continued to go through his work.

Ellen was going over some work she prepared for the court as she spread the documents out, ready for the next day. She stepped out for lunch and when she returned the documents were gone! She said, "Pandora, did you see where the Davies' case papers were! I had them ready for the court after lunch with Judge Jalen Costantino. I went back there and they're not there! Do you know where they went? They're not here now!" said Ellen.

"No Ellen." Ellen went nuts looking for the files and they were never found.

Later there was a house fire on the Mattapoisett line and Kenny Slater was racing to the fire and Ebenezer was standing in the way. He started hosing down the fire, aiming at the Ebenezer ghost, and it vanished! He looked and waited after the fire was out but didn't see the man again. He went to the fire station to write up a report.

The next day Evelyn was home writing a new book. She heard a voice! "*Get out!*" She paused a minute and she heard a voice, "*Get out!!!!!!!!!!!*" Then she got up to stand her ground. She heard it again, "*Get out!!!!!!!!!!*"

"Who are you!?" Evelyn in the basement heard the voice loud and clear!

"*Get out! Get out!!! Get out!!!!!!!!!!!!!!!!!*" the voice said!

"No, you go fuck yourself Ebenezer, you get the fuck out! Get the fuck out now! You do not belong here! You followed us from Bennington, Vermont. Now you do not belong here, now get the fuck out! You're dealing with Evelyn right now! I'm not afraid of you and you have to leave now! Screw you, you black piece of shit with red eyes, because I'm not afraid of you, now fuck off!" said Evelyn.

A black mist formed then it vanished. Apparently Ebenezer is afraid of Evelyn, but the evil spirit wants to play games with the Slater family at 66 6th Street.

Kenny was putting out a fire in a barn that was hit by lightning and a ghost appeared in the fire. Kenny was hosing the fire down and a white mist formed, but it disappeared by daytime and the fire went out.

Kenny went to the fire department to talk to the chief. "Chief Bentley, I just put out two fires here in town and I have a pretty good idea who's setting them. The first one was a brush fire and I briefly saw a ghostly figure, but I was not sure. I don't believe in ghosts but I did see something. The second fire was a barn hit by lightning and I saw a white mist going by.

"I have heard about the hauntings here since I moved here from Vermont. We lived in an area called the Bennington Triangle. My sister Evelyn knows all about it. It's a place where people mysteriously disappear when they go there looking for ghosts and there's a demon called Ebenezer, a dark ghostly-symbol with red eyes, and it's very powerful. I briefly saw that man while putting out the first fire.

"After tonight I believe that something out there could be settings these fires—was it lightning or something else?! The white mist, I don't know what that was. I told my brother Mike, who's a Mattapoisett policeman," finished Kenny Slater, fireman.

Later the two brothers had their stories to tell before going back to the barn that burned down to finish hosing the area from the fire trucks. The firemen and the police at the scene had their ghost stories, trying to convince Mike and Kenny to believe them.

Evelyn caused a serious problem doing witchcraft from her computer while she was writing her book, a story about the ghost of Ebenezer and the Bennington Vermont Triangle, not knowing that this ghost was in this house before. It took a national exorcism to get it out and now she invited it back and she keeps fighting to get it out again. All that swearing will not do any good and she started saying prayers to get the Ebenezer ghost to leave. She kept hearing *get out* as she continued to fight. Finally she shut the computer off and she went to bed.

The next day Anthony and Ellen were ready to go to work as Mike and Kenny came home from work from their night jobs. Evelyn got up and they all had their stories to tell before Mom and Dad go back to the law firm.

"Good morning Mom, Dad, and Evelyn. Mike and I found out we have an Indian tribe of ghosts from the Bridgewater Triangle here. The town of Mattapoisett was built over an evil Indian burial ground that has several ghosts. I fought two fires during the night. The first one was a brush fire and I saw a dark ghostly figure that looked like the Ebenezer ghost in Vermont. But it was just a vision I saw at the corner of my eyes. I thought it was my mind playing tricks because a man is not going to stand in the flames when I'm trying to put a fire out. But it was there then it was gone! Then I got a call to go to another fire where a barn was struck by lightning near the Fairhaven line, and I saw a white mist trying to form into a figure before it vanished. Policemen there told me about the ghosts hauntings in Mattapoisett and I better believe them," said Kenny.

"Last night I saw some strange things riding around in my police car. I saw a deer with red eyes, the Greenman vision, and the beach ghost sightings; police officers told me I saw ghosts. I was very surprised because I didn't think it was real, but a police and fire department haunted by ghosts is pretty scary!" said Mike.

"Yesterday I was in court waiting to do the next case and I was going over paperwork and I saw a black shadow flying around in the courtroom. I thought that was strange," said Anthony.

"I was in the basement of the court building going over some files and I heard voices and I saw a mist go by. It was cold down there so I went to lunch and when I returned to get the files they were gone! I went to the court clerk and she didn't know where they went and they were never found. I thought I heard some voices in this house. Lawyers at work told me that there is such a thing as ghosts," said Ellen.

"Mom, we do have something here. I was writing my book about the Bennington Triangle spirits and the ghost of Ebenezer appeared on my computer and it would not go away, so I shut my computer off and it came back on showing Ebenezer. I told it to leave because I'm not afraid of this dark bastard with red eyes and then I heard voices telling me to get out several times and I kept fighting him! I hope my novel is not causing a problem here because I will have to take my work to the library. I fear I might have invited Ebenezer from Vermont to our house. I hope not. I kept saying prayers to release it and it slowed down some, but every time I turn the computer off it keeps turning back on showing Ebenezer and freezing up my computer, so I can't change anything. Now I can't even write my book, so I had to pull the plug out to shut the computer off and I gave up and I went to bed. I still heard the voices saying, 'Get out' until I left my bench and went upstairs!" said Evelyn.

"Evelyn, Ebenezer has been here before haunting, the It family eighteen years ago according to records at the police station. Everyone in this house died in Hurricane Bob. A police officer I work with, Officer

Henry Lecter, told me he lived here and some bad things happened while he was. They were also physically injured living at another home that was haunted," said Mike the policeman.

Mike and Kenny went to bed in their bedrooms on the first floor. Evelyn went to her bedroom across from the master bedroom upstairs for a nap while Anthony and Ellen went to work at the law office.

Later Evelyn got up and she went down in the basement. She took her work to the Mattapoisett library and met Ruthy Smith who used to work for Arthur's Realtors. As soon as Evelyn Slater entered the library, Ruthy said, "Excuse me miss but you're not welcome here, go back to where you came from!"

"Go fuck yourself!" said Evelyn, then she went back home to do her work.

She turned on her computer and the screen was blank and then she got to her page on the computer to start writing her book. Ebenezer again appeared on the screen. Then the basement got really dark and a black mass formed over her. Hands and yellow eyes started to appear! Evelyn started waving her hands in the black mass and she said, "You have to leave, it's not your house!"

The hands came out of the black mass and grabbed Evelyn by the throat and choked her until she passed out! Then the apparition vanished. Evelyn was gagging and finally she caught her breath and got up. She heard a loud voice. "*Get out!!!!!!!!!!!!!!!!!!!!!!!!!!*"

Evelyn staggered out of the house and she went over to the bedroom windows, knocking on them and telling everyone to get out of the house.

*Knock, knock*, on Kenny's bedroom window. He woke up and opened the window.

"Kenny, get out of the house! I was just attacked and choked by a ghost, get out of the house now! Wake up Mike and tell him to get out!" said Evelyn.

Evelyn knocked on Mike's window and they got dressed and left the house and met with Evelyn outside. "I saw this black mist with hands and yellow eyes rolling along the basement ceiling. I kept waving my hands through it and telling it to leave and it grabbed me by the throat and choked me until I passed out! I have to call Mom and Dad and tell them what happened. Don't go in the house," said Evelyn.

Ellen was in the basement at the Roberts and Slater law office in Brockton and she found the files she was looking for at the courthouse the other day. Anthony had a client in his office. It was kind of dark in the basement and Ellen was going through the files with a flashlight. Suddenly it smelled like something dead. The smell was getting worse and she turned her back and she saw a black shadow go by. When she turned back around the ghost of Ebenezer was grabbing her by the throat, picking her up, and started shaking her like a ragdoll. It happened so fast she didn't have a chance to scream! She saw this dark ghostly figure with red eyes choking her until she passed out! Then Ebenezer dropped her to the floor then vanished!

Ellen got up, trying to gasp for air. She was gagging then she started screaming and she ran upstairs to Anthony's office with choke marks on her neck. The attack happened at the same time Evelyn was being attacked at the house. "Anthony, help me! Help me! I was attacked by a demon downstairs!"

Anthony looked at Ellen's neck and he saw the choke marks: red and black and blue. He said, "Holy shit Ellen, stay here!" He grabbed his gun and he went down to the basement. He clicked his gun looking around in the dark basement. He said, "Whoever is down here, wherever you are, better come out because you're dealing with Anthony this time." He saw nothing. Then his phone rang.

"Dad, it's Evelyn! Can you come home, there's a ghost in our house! It's black with yellow eyes and gray hands. It grabbed me and choked me! We have to get out of this house!"

"Evelyn, stay out of the house until I get there. Mom was attacked too by some demon in the basement in the law office."

"Oh my God!" Ellen cried.

Anthony looked around in the basement, moving things, and nothing was there. He grabbed the files he was looking for and brought them up to his office. Ellen told him what happened. "It was a dark ghostly figure with red eyes and it looked like the devil and he grabbed me by the throat and started shaking me until I blacked out. I thought I was going to die he came from behind me so fast, and his breath smelled like the dead! It was scarier than being in hell!" Ellen cried.

"Okay, get in the car, we're going home!" Then Anthony went to the receptionist and he said, "Cathy, call a Catholic priest to come bless the law offices and basement. My wife said that she was attacked by a demon in the basement while she was looking at the Davies files. Tell Judge Costantino the lost files at the court turned up here in the basement for some reason. Thank you."

"Was that why all that screaming was going on?" said Cathy.

On the way home from the law office the boys called Anthony about Evelyn's attack. He said, "Stay out of that house. Mom was attacked by a demon at the law office today, something is going on."

Then he told Ellen while driving home, "I have a pretty good idea on what's going on and it may be coming from the book Evelyn is writing in the basement. She's writing a book about the Bennington Triangle ghosts and the story is about the most powerful demon in the world: the ghost of Ebenezer. She may have invited him into our house while writing this book. We caught her so many times using a spirit board calling spirits. I told her it's not a good thing and she said not to worry and nothing happened to us when we lived in Bennington, but Mike told me that another family also from Bennington, Vermont has lived in this house. The two girls living here then used a spirit board to invite this Ebenezer, so this demon was here before and it took years of powerful exorcisms to get rid of it. Now I'm afraid that Evelyn may have invited this thing back writing this book."

Then Anthony called the realtor about the hauntings when they got home. Mike and Kenny were resting on the front lawn with a blanket spread out and Evelyn was sitting with them.

"Bennington Realtors of Vermont. Jean Jazzman speaking."

"Hi Jean, this is Anthony Slater calling. We've been haunted out of our house. My daughter and my wife were attacked by a dark ghost and you have to do something about this."

"Okay. Do not go in the house and get off the property. Meet me at the Mattapoisett military condominiums located in front of the police station and go to Unit #14. I will be there in less than twenty minutes," said Jean Jazzman the realtor.

Mike is the police officer who showed the family where the condo was; because Mike Slater is a police officer the Slater family was able to live there.

Jean arrived with a priest and paranormal investigators. She said,

"Anthony, this is Linda Springer and Larry Legend, they're ghost investigators, along with Father Frank. They're here to bless this new home so the spirits can't follow you. They will go in first and before you enter they will pray with you and ask you questions. The condo is fully furnished and your mortgage will be adjusted from the other home," said Jean Jazzman.

The priest and the paranormal investigators went in the condo with Jean Jazzman to bless the condo. While that was going on the Slaters waited outside sitting on a bench.

Back at the Roberts and Slater law office Judge Jalen Costantino arrived to pick up the Davies files. "Hi Cathy. How are you today? Where's the Davies files?"

"They're down in the basement located on Bench D. Be careful, there's a ghost down there!"

The judge laughed. Then he went downstairs, found the files, and was looking through them. Then he heard a loud voice saying, *"Get out!!!!!!!!!!!!!!!!!!!!!"* Then he was picked up and thrown up against a wall and the files went flying all over the basement, papers everywhere! The judge got up and he saw this big dark ghostly figure with red eyes and it growled at him, saying, *"Get out!!!!!!!!!!!!!!!!!!!!!!!!!!!!!!!"*

The judge ran upstairs faster than he had in his life He grabbed Cathy and he said, "Let's get out of here, there's a demon downstairs!"

Outside the building. "Cathy, you're right, there was something in that basement that I couldn't even imagine! I never believed in ghosts and I thought you were joking because you're a joker. I heard a loud voice telling me to get out then I was hit by an invisible force and thrown up against a wall. Files, papers, and books went flying everywhere then I saw this devilish looking dark ghostly figure with red eyes and big hands with large claws. I can't describe it; it was creature looking like a Bigfoot and the devil. I couldn't believe it. If I didn't get out of there in time I probably would be dead. We need to call a priest to come and get it out because the next time I get a call to pick up paperwork here, I'm sending one of the lawyers, or Mr. or Mrs. Slater can get it for me," said the judge.

Later the judge called Anthony and told him what happened! "Holy shit! Get out of there in a hurry! Ellen was attacked earlier today in the basement. My daughter was attacked in our home earlier this morning.

When I come to the court tomorrow I'll tell you about what's happening to our family. Call a priest to go in to bless the law offices and the courtroom because this ghost may follow you," said Anthony Slater.

After the priest and the paranormal investigators were through in the condo they came out to bless the Slater family of five then the team asked questions.

"Evelyn, my name is Linda Springer from the national paranormal associations, and my partner Larry Legend. We feel that most of the energy is coming off you; you're the main trigger, why your family is being haunted by a very powerful demon. Can you tell me anything paranormal that you have been involved with?"

"Linda I am writing a book about the Bennington Triangle, a story about a ghost by the name of Ebenezer. He was a leader of the triangle because of the death of an Indian tribe in northern Vermont. I had to use a spirit board to locate the death of that tribe through Ebenezer."

"Evelyn, do me a favor, stop writing this book and burn what you have written! You have to tell Ebenezer to go back to Vermont on the spirit board. Then get rid of the spirit board and burn it because you invited a dangerous entity and you have to get rid of it. Take the spirit board out of the house and lead Ebenezer back to where he came from then burn the board and every scrap of this book you have written. If you don't, Ebenezer will kill you!" said Linda.

Evelyn cried. "Evelyn, what happened when you were attacked last night or early this morning?" said Larry Legend the other paranormal investigator.

"I kept hearing a voice telling me to get out and I kept fighting it telling the voice it's my house now get the fuck out! Then I saw a thick black mist with yellow eyes and arms in a dark gray color. It looked like a tornado and hands came out and choked me until I passed out! It was the scariest thing I have ever seen!" said Evelyn.

"It's not Ebenezer, what you're describing. It's another evil entity that may be fighting against Ebenezer. Evelyn, you are in a real mess! You need to see Father Frank and get an exorcism because you're fighting two against one!" said Linda.

"Evelyn here's an itinerary on what we were talking about. Follow the instructions. First see Father Frank and do an exorcism, then follow the itinerary then a second exorcism with Father Frank. This is your only way out! You have to do this!" said Larry Legend.

Anthony told the priest and paranormal investigators about the ghost sightings he saw. The priest said, "Ellen, what happened to you today?"

"I was working at the office at the law firm with my husband. He had clients in his office and my job was to go downstairs in the basement and go through files for court the next day. I found the files from the courthouse that were missing in the basement at the law office and I was going through them. Then I heard a blaring voice saying, 'Get out.' Then I looked around and I saw a black shadow go by. I turned around to finish what I was doing and out of nowhere two hands were grabbing me by the throat; it picked me up and shook me! I saw a devil in front of me with red eyes and it stank like the dead, worse than a skunk ever could be, and it choked me until I passed out after throwing me down. When I got up I saw this big black demon and I ran upstairs. I had choke marks on me and I felt like I just visited hell on earth in my law office! It was the scariest thing I have ever seen! I have been a lawyer for thirteen years and I have never seen anything like this!" said Ellen Slater.

"Okay. We need to do an exorcism at your home before anything can be moved out of there. Also your property and your vehicles and we have to do one in the workplace. This demon has been here before brought here by another family living in that house that moved here from the same town you people lived in. Your daughter writing her book about this demon brought it back," said the priest.

The priest later explained what was happening to the Slater family then Jean Jazzman showed them the condo.

"Welcome to the Mattapoisett condominiums, serviced by military personal, police, and fire. Our first room is the entrance hall with a washer and dryer and a walk-in coat closet. The next is a big kitchen with microwave and conventional oven and built-in refrigerator-freezer combo. Dishwasher, garbage disposal. A table that sits eight people. This condo is all furnished. The living room has couches, recliners, TV, and a gas operated fireplace. You have a full bath with a jacuzzi. Two bedrooms, a twin bedroom and the master bedroom with a king size bed, a separate bath with a jacuzzi Also, there's a gas heated fireplace, entertainment center, and bar, in the living room. Upstairs has two bedrooms with queen size beds, walk-in closets, and built-in drawers. There's storage space in each of the four bedrooms, and you have another bath with a built-in bar set up over the tub. There's ceiling and wall lighting in every room. I hope you enjoy your new condo because it's beautiful!" said Jean Jazzman.

Ellen stayed in the condo to rest while Anthony, Evelyn, Mike, and Kenny went to the other house to get what they could to bring to the new condo, and a U-Haul truck came to get the furniture at 66 6th Street.

The priest and the paranormal investigators went in first before the Slater family got there. All the furniture was busted up into pieces! It looked like a tornado struck! The priest said prayers and the paranormal team did their work to avoid being attacked. A mist was floating across the ceiling while they were in there and the priest was throwing holy water on it and the paranormal team was chasing it out with sage and prayers. Dishes and glass was smashed and broken everywhere! The sage cleansing was working and the prayers and holy water removed whatever ghost was in this house so the Slaters could get what they could.

"Before you enter get ahold of yourselves! The house is a mess. A powerful entity was here that wants to kill. Luckily, everyone was out of this house before this demon went off! All your furniture was damaged and there is glass all over the house! Get whatever clothes you have and leave this house before it gets dark. It's 4:14 p.m. and time is running out it; will be getting dark in another hour," said Linda Springer, paranormal investigator.

Larry Legend and the priest went downstairs with Evelyn and she saw her desk computer smashed all over the floor and her work bench damaged. Overall, the basement was a mess! She was shocked! Most of the furniture was not theirs; it came with the house because they moved into a furnished home and they were not fully moved in. Yet the ghosts attacked right away because of Evelyn's work. When it got dark the Slaters went back to the new condo—they will have to wait until tomorrow to get the rest of their belongings.

After Evelyn was attacked and the rest of the family left the house the evil ghost struck again, hours later. The black mass's hands came out of the mist, picking things up and dropping them on the floor, smashing things into pieces. Cupboards opened in the kitchen and plates and glasses flew out striking the walls and the floor; some went through windows. The dining room table was picked up and dropped on the chairs, smashing them to matchsticks. Beds were tipped over, smashing other bedroom furniture as the black mass kept flying around the house breaking things!

Hands came out of the ghost, throwing small things against the walls including lamps and lights, smashing them into pieces. Late at night pipes broke, causing a water main break that flooded the house, causing severe damage. The gas was shut off by the gas company when the damage was reported. Mike called the gas company to shut the gas off two minutes later, just before 11:00 p.m. Pipes broke around 5:00 a.m. and Kenny went over with the fire department because it was setting off alarms.

Before that happened, Anthony and Ellen were sleeping, until his cellphone rang just after 3:00 a.m. "Hi, Anthony, it's Judge Costantino. I have bad news. Your law office is burning to the ground right now, there's nothing left! The fire department is here putting out the fire and right now it's a roaring inferno!"

"Oh my God, you've got to be kidding. Stay there until I get there! I should be there within the hour."

"Anthony, what happened!?" said Ellen.

"Our law office is burning to the ground right now. Just stay in bed while I go to see what happened, I'll see you in the morning." Then he drove to the law office in Brockton and there was nothing left. He met with the judge and the judge was talking to Anthony about what happened.

"That fucking Ebenezer burned down my law firm!" The time was 3:02 a.m. when the fire began and by 4:02 a.m. nothing was left. 5:02 a.m. Anthony got another phone call.

"Dad, it's Kenny, sorry to bother you at five o'clock in the morning. I'm at the house and all the water pipes broke, flooding the whole house, and a gas line ruptured. It's a good thing Mike called the gas company last night to shut the gas off before this happened, but the house is a real mess."

The next day Mike and Kenny got the rest of their clothes out of the house in six inches of water. Once they left that house they were never haunted again. It took Bennington Realtors of Vermont a year and a half to clean up the mess at 66 6th Street and the house was not sold for a long time after. Anthony and Ellen opened a new law office in Marion a year later. Mike still works for the police department and Kenny still works for the fire department. Evelyn is now a clerk at the law office.

# TWELVE

## The Second Coming of the Ebenezer Demon

December 12, 2009. A town meeting was held at the Old Rochester High School gym. Father Frank and the paranormal team of Linda Springer and Larry Legend, the Slater family, and police officer Archie Antilli were the speakers.

"Good evening, it's a cold and snowy night outside tonight. Welcome to the Mattapoisett, Marion, and Rochester town meeting here at OR. My name is Archie Antilli from the Mattapoisett Police Department. We have Father Avery Frank from St. Anthony's church, a group of friars from PC and Georgetown Universities, and several paranormal investigators here tonight because of a powerful demon interfering with residents in Mattapoisett.

"There have been issues in Marion, Rochester, and Fairhaven as well. This demon has been here before and the National Friars Association from Georgetown University and Providence College was called to remove it with a series of powerful exorcisms! The name of this demon is Ebenezer, an evil spirit with very strong powers from the devil. Witnesses reported seeing a big dark ghostly figure about seven feet tall with red eyes, straight up pointy ears, sharp teeth, and bad breath like the smell of death. Without the horns this entity looks like the devil. This demon has attacked people, killed people!

"Mrs. Ellen Slater who is here tonight was grabbed by the throat and thrown on the floor at the law office where she works. The next day Judge Jalen Costantino went to the same law office to pick up files and paperwork in the basement and he was attacked by this Ebenezer demon. Evelyn Slater claims she wrote a book about the Bennington Triangle. She had to ask a spirit board to use the Ebenezer ghost to get information on the findings of the Bennington Triangle to write this novel. In doing that she invited Ebenezer back in.

"The Bennington Triangle believes that the ghost of Ebenezer may have come from a UFO from another planet and they believe he may have come from the following possibilities: the moon; Venus; Mars; one of Mars' moons; Europa or Helios, two of Jupiter's moons; or one Saturn's moons. Indian believers say it could be a Bigfoot creature or a deformed demonic monkey! Others believe Ebenezer was a deformed humanoid!

"Some also believe in giant birds known as mothmen creatures, condor hawks with a thirty-foot wingspan; others believe they're thunderbirds. Others site encounters with things such as orbs of light, giant snakes, and humanoids half human and half animal. Balls of light from space, space bugs, creatures from other planets; they believe in poltergeists and anything paranormal!

"We have a triangle here in Massachusetts. The Bridgewater Triangle, two hundred square miles where they claim UFOs were seen landing and taking off. Also, there's a swamp monster called, the Greenman, coming out of the Hockomock Swamp believed to have come from another planet, a humanoid that's not from here! The Bridgewater Triangle is located in the following areas: Bridgewater, East and West Freetown, Fall River, Rehoboth, Dighton, Brockton, Abington, Whitman, Middleboro, Halifax, Kingston, and Plymouth. All these towns and cities have their hauntings as part of the Bridgewater Triangle. Here in Mattapoisett, Marion and Rochester and parts of Wareham, we have been haunted by the same hauntings in the Bridgewater Triangle.

"The most deadly ghost here is the Hockomock Wave. It's a black mass with red eyes, yellow or green, with black arms and gray hands. The methane devil is an invisible ghost that will kill you! The Greenman ghost is part of the Hockomock swamp monster; it's not as aggressive but if you challenge it or if it becomes active, it can kill you. Then we have the red-eyed deer. It's not aggressive if you keep your distance but if you stare at it, it will cause you problems! Then we have the beach ghost. She walks the town beach around 3:00 a.m. or three o'clock in the afternoon. Her name is Maria Cooper and she's known as the town wanderer also. She's a girl that appears in a black bikini and comes to people and gives them a warning that a haunting may happen or danger is coming. When she comes to you, listen to her because she knows the future. She's the Nostradamus of Mattapoisett.

"I'm an environmental adviser for the Mattapoisett Police department, a very sophisticated man talking about ghosts. They're real!

"Let's get back to the second coming of the Ebenezer demon, about eighteen years ago maybe. The It family moved into the house at 66 6th Street. They were from Montpelier, Vermont, and two girls in that family practiced witchcraft or devil worship! The two teens Michelle and Marsha It, invited this demon to take their lives! They invited the Ebenezer ghost into their home, already haunted by a ghost from the Bridgewater Triangle, and it was not welcome here and made it worse for the It family! They all died in Hurricane Bob being blown away. Only one body was found in the house as the roof was blown off, taking the rest of the family away!

"Several families had to leave because of these hauntings. The Grey family was also affected by this demon and the Longhorn family was killed. The Grey family was forced out of their home and that's when the friars were called to release Ebenezer back to Bennington, Vermont where it belongs.

"The Lecter family was haunted out of their home when Bennington Realtors of Vermont took over. They moved to Green Street to get away from it and the hauntings followed them there. Sorry to hear Hilda Lecter was killed by a ghost! Now when the Slater family moved from Vermont to here, their house was destroyed. Evelyn, being attacked by the Hockomock Wave, and Ellen, being attacked by the Ebenezer demon, were forced to move into a condo near the police station. The Slaters lost their law firm in Brockton. Judge Costantino was attacked by Ebenezer as well from his connection to the Slaters.

"Something has to be done with this Ebenezer demon because he's capable of killing people. Kenny Slater saw this Ebenezer ghost while fighting a fire the other night and we have to find out where he is now. We have to start at the ruins of the Roberts and Slater Law Office that burned down in Brockton. Another thing is the Hockomock Wave and Greenman swamp monster, the two strong ghosts of the Bridgewater

Triangle, tangling with the Bennington Ebenezer. We don't know what's going to happen. We have attacks in Brockton in the Bridgewater Triangle where it's not welcome.

"It is the second time we have dealt with this demon. The paranormal investigating teams will have to start where Ebenezer last attacked. We need to go to Brockton where the law firm burned down and do an exorcism and sage ceremony to get rid of this demon. Bennington Realtors of Vermont will no longer sell the properties at 66 6th Street and 6 Green Street for the safety of the town of Mattapoisett because they're from the town of this beast. It's not because they're a bad company, it's because they're from the area of the Bennington Triangle. For anyone who wants to share their stories the floor is yours," said Officer Archie Antilli.

Others shared their stories about the Ebenezer ghost. The next day an exorcism ceremony was performed over the ashes of the Robert and Slater Law Offices with the Catholic priest and the paranormal investigating team in Brockton. The Brockton police were asking questions.

"During last week's fire a neighbor reported seeing a big dark ghostly fiigure standing in the flames while the building was burning down. I find that kind of strange. Judge Jalen Costantino reported being attacked by a dark figure with red eyes earlier that day and a woman who reported seeing and being attacked by the same man claims it was a ghost. She said she was attacked then she saw it vanish! What is this, some kind of game!?" said the officer.

"Officer, I'm Larry Legend, a paranormal investigator, and this is my partner Linda Springer. We are dealing with a ghost here! A very powerful demon may be causing these fires. Look here, I have a picture here in my phone. This is the ghost of Ebenezer, a powerful demon from Vermont, and we are here to remove it. If we do not get rid of this demon and it tangles with the Bridgewater tribe you will have some serious problems. The lawyers and the judge never believed in ghosts until witnessing them for real. Let us do our job and you go after the last attack. Thank you Officer."

The paranormal investigators and priests and all local church pastors were doing the exorcism along with the National Friars Association to remove the ghost of Ebenezer from the site of the fire.

One year later. The Slater couple has a new law office in Marion, and Judge Costantino brought a house in Hollywood Beach overlooking the water. He was home one night, looking over files, and a book came flying across the floor as his dog came in the room.

"What are you doing Sparky, are you throwing the book at me!" Then he let the dog outside to do his thing. Then the fire lit in the gas fireplace all by itself. He got up to shut it off then a black shadow went by but he didn't see it. Then a chair moved. He said, "Sparky!" Then he realized Sparky was outside and he let the dog in. Then he sat down to work on his files.

The judge was home all alone with his dog Sparky. Then he heard a *thump!* and something hitting the sliding glass door. He got up and he went outside and he saw nothing. He went back inside and the fireplace was on again. "What the hell is going on here," he said to himself. Then he shut the fireplace off, put his files in a box, and left them on the table. He went for his shower and, of course, the lights went out and the water shut off while he was there, then the power and the shower came back on a minute later. He heard thunder when he got out of the shower. Then he went to bed. The files were a case about the Ebenezer ghost. He will close the case tomorrow morning when he goes to the court, but he might have invited the ghost into his house on Hollywood Beach.

His wife was at a bowling league at Wonder Bowl. She got up to bowl and her teammates said, "Beth you only need eight pins to win," because she is the anchor on her team. As she saw a black shadow go across the bowling lanes she threw the ball right down the middle and she got the 4-6-7-10 split and her team ended up losing. She went to the bar for a drink with her teammates.

She came home from bowling and it was raining. She heard a crow calling but she couldn't see it then she went in the house.

The next day Judge Jalen Costantino got up, grabbed the files, and went to work. His wife Beth stayed home with the dog. She let the dog out and it was running around in the yard barking.

"Sparky, what are you barking at!" she said then the dog wanted to go inside. Then the phone rang and Beth picked it up and there was static in the phone receiver. Then she hung up. Then the house smelled like a dead animal and Beth looked under baseboards and opened cupboards but couldn't find the source. She turned around and the ghost of Ebenezer's hands were on her throat, choking her in the kitchen. It threw her up against a wall and she saw the big black Ebenezer with red eyes in the kitchen in her house. Her dog Sparky leaped at Ebenezer's balls and went right through him. He didn't feel the dog attack because he's a ghost then charged at Beth again, growling at her like a mean bear!

But Beth was able to get away and she said, "Ebenezer!!!!!!!!! Go away!!!!!!!!!!" Then it vanished. Sparky was barking and growling at the ghost!

Then Beth grabbed the dog, ran out of the house, and she drove to the law office in Marion. She said to the receptionist, "Where's Judge Costantino?"

"He's in court," said the receptionist.

"Could you get in touch with him and tell him his wife Beth is at the office because I have a ghost in our house and he has to come home."

The judge finished the case about the Ebenezer ghost hauntings and a lawyer took the files of the case home with him; he also lives in Mattapoisett. "Allen, lock those files up in case we have to look through them again when you get home," said Judge Jalen Costantino. The judge met his wife at the Robert and Slater law office in Marion.

"Jalen, we have a ghost in our house! It was Ebenezer, the same black ghost with red eyes that attacked you in Brockton last year! It grabbed me right by the throat and threw me up against a wall in the kitchen. When I got up I sicced the dog on him then I recognized him and I called his name and told him to leave. He vanished right in front of me and I grabbed the dog and ran out of the house!"

"Okay. We have to call Father Frank to come here and then go to our house!" said the judge. "Ebenezer knows he's being overtaken through exorcisms from the Catholic Church and from paranormal investigators and when someone calls his name he loses power and latches on to someone weak or someone that's not religious." The priest and the church monsignor came to do prayers with them at the law office and their home. After the blessings, Judge Jalen Costantino and Beth were never haunted by Ebenezer again!

The judge handed the finished files to Allen Gemini, another lawyer at the court. He brought the files to his house and he locked them in filing cabinets in the basement. It was a few days before Thanksgiving a year later when Allen Gemini was going over the closed files of the Ebenezer ghost hauntings, deaths, and sightings, not to mention millions of dollars paid out from real estate companies selling haunted properties, with another lawyer. Then he put the files away again. He had the files stored in his basement for about a year.

Thanksgiving week 2010: Strange things began to happen to the Gemini family starting with Allen, living on 47 Marion Street near the town beach. The Sunday before Thanksgiving he was going for a walk by the town beach on a sunny but cold windy day and he saw this girl wearing a black bikini walking on the beach about 3:00 p.m.

Allen said, "Excuse me miss, but it's kind of cold out here to be walking around like that!"

"Mister, just be prepared for what's to come! My name is Maria Cooper!" Then she turned toward the water and vanished in front of Allen's eyes!

He said, "Maria, don't go in the water, it's too cold!" Then he saw a white as snow mist and she disappeared! Allen watched, then he ran to the water's edge and he saw nothing! "I guess there are such things as ghosts after all!" he said to himself.

Another person was walking along the beach and he said, "Excuse me miss, but did you see that lady walking on the beach in a bikini?"

The lady walking looked at him funny and she said, "No sir, I haven't seen her."

The next day Allen met the lawyer he had in the basement looking over the Ebenezer ghost files at a coffee shop early Monday morning. "Good morning Edward."

"Good morning Allen, we meet again!"

"Edward. The other day at my house we were looking over the Ebenezer ghost files. People believe they were haunted by this ghost and that it has killed people and the case required several exorcisms to remove it! I believe in spirits that warn people or come to someone who's dead! I never believed they would attack people who're alive because a spirit, ghost, etc., is something that comes from the dead. When something is dead, it's dead! That's why this case settled fifty-fifty! I was brought up Catholic and we always believed that spirits were from the dead. I never saw a spirit or ghost personally Edward but yesterday that may have changed!

"I was going for my Sunday afternoon walk and I saw this girl wearing a bikini and it's thirty-three degrees! I said to her 'why are you dressed like that' and she told me to be prepared for something and she identified herself as Maria Cooper and she ran toward the water and vanished. It was a white mist—*poof!* and she's gone! Making me believe I saw a ghost!" said Attorney Allen Gemini.

"You did, Allen. Maria Cooper is the Mattapoisett Beach ghost! She gives warnings that something is going to happen, such as an earthquake, a big storm, or something just to you. Good or bad, she's a psychic ghost and she's known to be the friendliest ghost in town.

"Well, we had better get to the office because we have several case files to get ready for the court on Tuesday," said Edward, the other lawyer.

While Allen was at the office around 3:00 p.m. Tuesday afternoon, Allen's wife was down in the basement and she heard something growling. She does not have a dog, but it sounded like a loud dog growling. She picked up a baseball bat and she went looking for the barking dog or animal in the basement and she found nothing. She went upstairs as quickly as she could and she grabbed a shotgun out of a closet. She closed the basement door and called the police.

"Hi, this is Mary Gemini from 47 Marion Street. Something is in my house. I heard the growling of a big dog or wild animal in my basement. I don't have a dog. I was downstairs ready to put a load of laundry in the washer and I heard the growling somewhere near the file cabinets."

"Okay Mary, don't go downstairs until we get there and get something to protect yourself," said the police. The police arrived and searched the house and they found nothing. "It could be a raccoon or a fox. Keep your house closed and locked because it's cold outside and wild animals are looking for a warm place. They will hide under your deck on cold days like today," said the police.

A little while later Allen came home and his wife told him about the animal growling. He went downstairs and he started pulling out filing cabinets but found nothing. He went outside looking around the house. He looked in the eaves and checked under the deck and a rabbit was under there and it ran away. He checked the gutters and he looked for holes in the house where animals could get inside. Nothing! Then he went through the house itself, looking in closets, opening cabinets, and he found no animal, even in the basement.

"It could be a raccoon or fox like the policeman said," Allen said to his wife.

The next day the family will be arriving for Thanksgiving 2010. Tuesday night and all day Wednesday strange things started to happen at two minutes after every hour. All the Mattapoisett ghosts play along, haunting the Gemini family before Ebenezer makes his last appearance before his name is called on.

Nighttime on the Tuesday before Thanksgiving at 11:02 p.m., Allen saw a flash of lightning outside and it was snowing when he looked out the window. Mary was in bed and she heard a buzzing noise and she looked at the time on her alarm clock and the time was 12:02 a.m. The buzzing sound went away a minute later. Allen woke up hearing a thumping noise, like something hitting the house, and he looked at the alarm clock and the time was 1:02 a.m. He got up and he looked out the window, saw the trees blowing in the wind, and went back to bed.

Mary had a dream of a ghost watching her and it looked like the devil and she woke up screaming! The time was 2:02 a.m.

Allen woke up and he said, "What's the matter Mary!?"

"I had this terrible dream about a monster in our room staring at me and it looked like the devil!" Then she lay back down and went back to sleep.

Then Allen had a dream about a big black dog with red eyes chasing him and it leaped at him to bite him and he woke up! He looked at the time and it was 3:02 a.m.

Mary woke up and she said," Allen, are you okay!"

"Yes, it was my turn to have a nightmare about a junkyard dog with red eyes coming after me and trying to bite me!" He laughed.

4:02 a.m. Mary was still awake and she heard water running in the bathroom. She got up to turn off the water on the sink then went back to bed. The face of the Ebenezer ghost appeared in the bathroom mirror but Mary did not see it; the vision went away at 4:03 a.m.

Allen woke up with a bad headache and the time was 5:02 a.m. and he was feeling dizzy so he got up to take a couple of Advil and went back to bed. The headache went away a minute later and he was fine.

Mary woke up and she couldn't move or speak and she felt paralyzed. The time was 6:02 a.m. She tried to move and speak but she couldn't! A minute later it went away and she got up like nothing happened! She got up to take a shower before Allen gets up to go to work and make breakfast for him.

Allen heard a man's voice calling him. *"Allen, Allen, Allen get up!" Echo echo!* He woke up and the time was 7:02 a.m. The alarm sounded at 7:05 a.m. He shut the alarm off and he got up for his shower and he got dressed, putting his suit on, ready to go to work.

He was eating breakfast and he said, "I heard a voice calling me to get up but it wasn't yours, it was some man's voice. I guess I was still dreaming while I was waking up. Good morning Mary!"

"Allen I woke up about six and I couldn't move or speak, I thought I was paralyzed! I really thought it was over, wondering how this can happen waking up! Then I was able to get up; I was so stiff and then I got up and I was okay. It was scary! I never felt like this before!"

"Something's going on Mary. Last night I woke up with the worst headache ever! It was so bad I felt like I was going to die. I got up to take some Advil and it went away; it didn't last long but it was bad! I have sinus attacks when the weather changes. It's sixty-seven one day and it was down to eighteen degrees yesterday and makes your body stiff and you can't move sometimes," said Allen.

The lawyer and his wife don't realize that they're being haunted by the ghosts in Mattapoisett.

Allen left for work on his way to the office on a cold, raw, rainy dark morning and saw a deer with red eyes in the middle of the road, but he turned off before getting closer. The time was 8:02 a.m. when he saw the red-eyed deer.

9:02 a.m. Mary heard an alarm going off and she went to the bedroom and she shut it off.

Allen was looking at his computer and a bunch of numbers appeared on the computer screen, then his computer went off and the lights went out at the Roberts and Slater Law Offices. It was 10:02 a.m. The power came back a minute later. A ghost appeared in Allen Gemini's office as soon as he stepped out to get a cup of coffee. No one saw it.

Mary was making the bed and she heard a big *bang!* like a loud gunshot about three times around 11:02 a.m. She was shaken up! The gunshot sounds stopped at 11:03 a.m.

The next twelve hours of hauntings are going to get interesting!

12:02 p.m. Allen was warming up a sandwich in the microwave oven in the break room. Suddenly the microwave blew up and the door flew open. His sandwich flew out and landed on the floor and it looked like a burnt piece of charcoal. Others saw what happened waiting to warm up their food.

Anthony Slater joked, "Oh my God Allen, what are you eating for lunch! A rat!?"

Everyone including Allen got a good laugh at the burnt sandwich. "It was a ham and cheese but I don't know what it is now!" Allen joked.

Just after 12:30 p.m. Mary was at home just finishing her lunch and the ground shook. Faucets came on in the kitchen and the bathrooms all through the house; the time was 1:02 p.m. She turned them all off and she called Allen at the office.

"Did you hear that earthquake?!"

"No I didn't hear anything, but I lost my sandwich today because the office microwave blew up and my sandwich burned like a piece of charcoal!" Allen joked.

2:02 p.m. Allen was in his office. It was getting dark in there and a rocking chair was rocking back and forth. Allen saw what was happening while he was on the phone. The rocking chair stopped rocking and Allen's office brightened back to normal.

Anthony Slater came into the office and Allen told him what he saw. "Maybe it's Ebenezer coming back for a visit," he said.

Mary was at home and her company arrived just before 3:00 p.m. Family members and kids arrived when suddenly the lights went out at 3:02 p.m. "Oh my God, not again. We lost power! We might have had an earthquake earlier today. The ground shook and all the water faucets turned on in the house. Pam, Manny, have a seat. Hi kids. Jose, Patrick, Rose, Dennis, and Danny have a seat and I'll get some snacks and drinks. The Penny family is here, yeah! Paula, Dick, Paul, and Bobby Bowton will be here soon and we will have everyone for Thanksgiving," said Mary. The lights came back on a minute later at 4:02 p.m.

Allen was in the office break room and he slipped on some water on the floor and he fell down but he was alright. He got up and the lights went out in the break room and came back on a minute later. The custodian came in with a mop to dry the wet floor and the floor was bone dry. The wet floor dried up by itself after Allen fell.

The Bowton family arrived with Dick, Paula, Paul, and Bobby just before 5:00 p.m. At 5:02 p.m. Mary was cooking and Pam and Paula were helping out. Mary heard a loud snapping noise in the kitchen while she was cooking and she saw a light floating around in circles, which disappeared a minute later. She went looking to find out where the noise was coming from. Chicken soup and bread were served for supper as the girls were doing the cooking, getting ready for Thanksgiving tomorrow.

The lights blinked on and off at 6:02 p.m. Allen went down to the basement to check the fuse box. One of them was off so he put it back and went upstairs. All thirteen people in the house sat down to eat a super pre-Thanksgiving meal. Apple and squash pie and tea were served after.

7:02 p.m. Allen heard a growling noise coming from the basement. He said, "Did anybody hear that!" No one heard the growling. Allen went downstairs to see what it was; it was pretty loud. He heard the growls two times and it stopped a minute later. "Mary, you're right, there is an animal in this house somewhere!"

Allen called animal control and they came to search the house with Allen and found nothing. Animal control had a device to check the walls, attic, and along the foundation of the house and they found nothing.

8:02 p.m. Mary, Pam, and Paula were still in the kitchen still cooking and cleaning up after supper and Mary saw a bat flying in the kitchen. It landed in the sink full of pots and pans and she screamed! "Ahhhh-hhhhhhhh!!!!!!!!!!!!! Allen there's a bat flying in the house it landed in the sink!"

Allen pulled everything out of the sink and there was no bat. The animal control workers were still there looking for the bat and found nothing! The worker joked, "Maybe you saw a ghost! Animals are all clear, there's nothing here!" Then they left.

Allen put the fireplace on in the living room and he sat down to watch TV. He looked at his watch and the time was 9:02 p.m. Then the fire went out in the fireplace and he went over to check it out and the fire came back a minute later. Pam, Paula, and the kids were wondering what was going on in this house.

"I don't know, things are going crazy. I have to call the electric company after Thanksgiving because the lights have been acting strange lately, going on and off. Now the animal control can't find the raccoon or fox growling near the house," said Allen.

Mary was cleaning up the dining room and she saw a small white tornado spinning across the tile floor, dissipating when it went into the living room over the rug. Paula saw it too! They both screamed! The time of the mist twister was 10:02 p.m. "Allen something is here! Paula and I saw a white twister spinning on the floor in the dining room."

"It's probably steam from all the cooking you're doing in the kitchen because it's so hot and you have the sliding glass door open in the dining room. The wind from the cold air outside mixing with the warm air causes a spinning effect. Maybe some snow blew in from the wind," said Allen.

"Do you want me to close the sliding glass door so we don't get a bigger tornado!?" Paula joked.

11:02 p.m. there was a flash of lightning and the lights went out in the whole house followed by a big *boom!* of thunder as the lightning flashed again. The lights came back on a minute later. Then the fire burning in the gas fireplace formed a face that looked like the devil, then it burned into a regular flame but no one noticed. The twenty-four-hour hauntings at two minutes after every hour went pretty much unnoticed by the Gemini family, and all the hauntings stopped for the rest of the night.

The Geminis have four bedrooms in their home with two queen beds in three of the rooms while the master bedroom has one king. Pam and Manny slept in one room, Paula and Dick in another room. Pam's kids, Jose and Patrick, slept in one bed, while Dennis and Danny were in the second bed in the fourth room. Rose slept in a sleeping bag in Pam and Manny's room. Paula and Dick's kids, Paul and Bob, slept in sleeping bags in the living room. All the kids' ages range from ten to fifteen years old.

The next day was Thanksgiving Day 2010. The family is staying for the weekend and everyone is helping out getting the dinner ready for the big day. Manny and Dick took some of the boys to a high school football game while others prepared the turkey and the rest of the food. Dinner was served after the rest of them came back from the football game. The turkey was put on the table, two of them feeding thirteen people sitting around the table. Then stuffing, mashed potatoes, sweet potatoes, squash, butternut squash, string beans, carrots, broccoli, turnips, cranberry sauce, red and white wine, and juice for the kids.

Allen sat at the head of the table and he was cutting the turkey. Mary sat at the other end. Pam, Manny, Dick, Paula, and Rose sat on one side and Jose, Danny, Patrick, Dennis, and Bob sat on the other. Allen lit the fireplace and everyone was ready for the Thanksgiving dinner.

Mary said grace, "Dear God we have a wonderful meal for our wonderful family to enjoy for Thanksgiving. I thank you Lord for bringing our family safe together for today's big day in Jesus' name, Amen." Then everyone helped serve each other until everyone's plates were filled before eating.

A few minutes later it was quiet and everyone started eating! A black mass formed crawling up the wall behind where Allen was sitting.

Paula said, "Oh my goodness Allen, what's that behind you!?"

The black mass formed into a man. Mary saw it and she was having a heart attack! Then it roared and growled leaving the smell of death, it stank worse than ten skunks' shit! It was the ghost of Ebenezer ruining the Gemini family Thanksgiving! Everyone started screaming! Then it blew wind out of its ghostly mouth, blowing all the food and drinks off the table, and it farted too! Then it lifted the table and turned it upside down so it landed on top of people. Food was thrown everywhere, splattered all over the walls and on top of people then it smashed the table in half!

Allen kept yelling, "Ebenezer leave!!!!!!!!!! Leave this house right now!!!!!!!" The ghost figure downgraded into a black mass and it went up the wall where Allen was sitting and crawled on the ceiling. It vanished and the chandelier fell and smashed over the broken table. Everyone ran out of the dining room screaming in fright, but Paula was killed when the table landed on her head, splitting her head open, and she was carried out covered in blood!

Mary was taken to the hospital with a few kids from injuries. Several rescue workers, police, and the fire department arrived because a fire started. It was put out by Kenny Slater spraying the flame with a fire hydrant. Rescue workers were removing the injured and firemen and policemen were removing the broken table when a black mass appeared, coming out of the ceiling, trying to grab someone.

Kenny Slater yelled, "Ebenezer!!!!!!!!!!!! You have to leave!!!!!!!" Then the ghost vanished. Once again a paranormal team and priests had to come and get rid of Ebenezer!

# THIRTEEN

## THE ROGERS FAMILY HAUNTINGS

The 66 6th Street house has been vacant since 2009 when the Slater family was chased out by the local ghosts and the second coming of Ebenezer! Sadly, it did not stay that way. The house was sold six years later to the Rogers family from California. Robert Rogers, fifty-five, Katrina Rogers, fifty-three, daughter Debby Rogers, twenty-seven, sons Dobbie, nineteen, and Dennis, seventeen. It was August 2015.

Robert is a contractor; his wife Katrina works as a dental assistant. Debby is a patio and brick designer. Dobbie is in college helping his dad during the summer and Dennis Rogers is getting ready to finish his senior year at Old Rochester. The family works days.

It was August 2, 2015 and Robert and Katrina met with the realtor during a thunderstorm. They pulled up in a 2012 Toyota Camry.

"Are you Mrs. Jean Jazzman from Daily Dot Realtors?" asked Robert.

"Yes, I am. Let's go in the house, there's lightning outside." The realtor showed them the house. The same bullshit from all the other years and different realtors showing the house at 66 6th Street, the porch first, the kitchen, the dining room, the bathroom, the two bedrooms on the first floor, the finished basement, the living room with the corner fireplace. The two bedrooms and the bath upstairs, closets and storage spaces and the shed, the barn, and the property out back and the doghouse.

"This house is all furnished just like I told you over the phone. What's here stays here just like in Vegas! The mortgage is $2,500 a month for ten years. The property is $375,000, but if you sign today, it's $250,000. $25,000 down and a set mortgage, or $2,500 a month," said Jean Jazzman.

"What is your best way?" asked Robert.

"Your best bet is to pay monthly $2,500 for ten years and the house is yours after that; that's the quickest way to pay your mortgage! Twenty-five grand down then $2,500 a month!" said Jean Jazzman the realtor.

Robert made the arrangements and they moved in. Dobbie and Dennis came later looking at the house and Debby looked around and she said, "Mom, Dad, this house is nice, we have two fireplaces and a fire pit out in the backyard and the property and the trees and flowers are nice. But I have a feeling that this house may be haunted just like Uncle Jack's house in Oakland when he was haunted by the Deopolo demon ghost three years ago. I feel that something like that is here or it has been here; not Deopolo, but something like it!"

"What makes you think that Debby?" asked her mom, Katrina.

"I don't know for sure but I feel that something's here. I can't see it or feel it but I think something happened here over the years. You know how I sense things Mom, but I feel something's wrong here!"

"Debby, don't think that way, let's enjoy our new beautiful home. There's no ghost here!" said Katrina.

Nighttime. Robert and Katrina slept in the master bedroom. Debby slept in the other bedroom upstairs. The two boys slept in the two bedrooms downstairs. The next day everyone went to work.

Robert and his son Dobbie were at a construction site and a cement truck was pouring cement and Dobbie yelled, "Dad, something black jumped in the pouring cement!"

Robert stopped the cement mixer from dumping cement and construction workers were digging through the freshly poured cement with shovels looking for what jumped in there. "Dobbie, what did you see jumping in the cement?"

"It looked like a small dog or cat Dad!" Nothing was found and the construction site was clear.

Debby was working and a truck arrived to load bricks and slate slabs. She was writing up a bill and as soon as she got out of his office the truck lost control of its brakes and crashed into her office, smashing everything! Debby was terrified! What a first day on the job!

Katrina was working at a dental office in Marion and lightning struck a window. She jumped out of the way and the lightning bolt blew her window in, passing through the dental office and out another window. All the workers in the office screamed in fright! A small fire started from the lightning strike and it was put out with a fire extinguisher by Katrina.

A dump truck was dumping gravel and Robert Rogers was directing the truck backing up near a foundation to dump the gravel. The ground gave way and the truck smashed the foundation. It was stuck in a rut and tow trucks had to come with cranes and chains to get the truck out of the hole. Worse, Dobbie ran in back of the truck minutes before the ground gave way. Robert said, "Dobbie get out of there!" It was "Oh shit!" a few minutes later! It's a bad day at the construction site.

Dennis was at the high school registering for the coming school year, the 2015-16 season. He was given books and he went home, ate lunch, then he felt a gust of wind go by him. The windows were open. Then he locked up and he went to the beach for the afternoon, meeting friends there. He went for a swim and went to get some ice cream from a truck before going back to his beach towel.

An older lady wearing a black bikini walked up to him looking at him; she has black eyes. She came up to Dennis and she said, "Hi, my name is Maria Cooper, the town beach drifter. What's your name honey?!"

"My name is Dennis Rogers; you're a little too old for me. What do you want?"

"I want to tell you that danger is coming to you soon and be ready to be risen to the Lord!"

"Lady, you're fucked up! Go away!" said Dennis.

The lady took three steps walking toward the water and she vanished! Dennis was shocked as he watched! He said to some other lady sitting on the beach, "Excuse me miss, did you see that lady talking to me? She had black eyes!"

The other lady said in a stuck-up way, "I didn't see nothing! I heard you talking to yourself! Maybe you saw a ghost!"

Dennis laughed. Then he grabbed his belongings and he left the beach.

Suppertime, the Rogers family had their stories to tell of their first full day living in Mattapoisett while eating pizza.

"Today me and Dobbie had a rough day at the construction site near Marion. There was a dump truck accident. When I was directing the truck to back up Dobbie ran in back of the truck. I saved his ass by telling him to get out of the way so he didn't get run over! Then the ground gave way and the truck fell into the freshly made foundation and damaged the whole area! Not only that, but Dobbie saw a cat or dog jump into freshly poured cement and the workers worked frantically to dig the animal out and nothing was found," said Robert.

"My office in Marion was struck by lightning, blowing out the window and damaging my office, setting a fire! The lightning traveled across the dentist office and out another window! It was scary! I grabbed a fire extinguisher to put out the fire. The lightning bolt just missed hitting me in yesterday's storm," said Katrina.

"I almost got killed today! I was in my office writing up a bill for a truck brick and slate delivery and when I left my office the truck crashed into the building, right through my office! Everything was destroyed," said Debby.

"Oh my God! It seems like something is after us!" Katrina joked.

"Wait until you hear my story today. After the thunderstorm I went to the beach. This weird old lady came talking to me and she introduced herself to me. She said her name was Maria Hooper or something like that! She asked me who I was and I told her my name. She was a tall lady with a black skinny bikini and she had black eyes! She reminded me of a ghost! She said to me, 'Danger is coming to you soon be ready to be risen to the Lord.' I told he that she was f'd up and to get lost. The lady went in for a swim and she vanished! It was like she disappeared! I wasn't thinking she could be a ghost but she looked like one to me. She was weird.

"I asked a lady sitting next to me if she saw that lady. She said she saw nothing and I was talking to myself in a snotty way. She said maybe I saw a ghost. I picked up my stuff and left the beach," said Dennis.

Nighttime, everything was normal and the next day was normal for the family.

The weekend. Robert and Katrina went out for breakfast and they met a lady there and some friends.

"Hi, are you the new family that moved in the house at 66 6th Street about a week ago?"

"Yes, my name is Katrina Rogers and this is my husband Robert."

"Welcome to Mattapoisett. My name is Gloria Stevens, an air traffic controller at Logan Airport. I used to work for Bennington Realtors of

Vermont and I was fired from that company because they told me not to tell people that some of the homes are haunted. People have been dying in these homes and we were getting sued; actually, I quit before the lawsuits.

"Your house is haunted and people have died there and priests and paranormal investigators have been there several times. The last time someone lived there was five or six years ago. Ghosts in that house and property have chased everyone out and it's the most haunted house in Mattapoisett.

"I just want to let you know. No realtor is going to tell you that you're buying a haunted house because the house will not sell. Tell your realtor that you found out that your house is haunted and they have to do something about it! Don't tell them who told you about it; just say you heard it from a friend. For your safety, get a priest to bless your home right now before you go to the realtor," said Gloria Stevens.

The Rogers told Gloria about the freak accidents the first day living at the house during breakfast.

"It's a death warning; it tells you to get out before something bad happens! If it tells you to get out listen because you better leave. Get a priest! Good luck," said Gloria Stevens.

After breakfast, the Rogers went to the church and told them that the house they just moved into was haunted.

"Okay. Stay here until one of our priests gets back. His name is Father Jay Gray. Do not go to the house until he comes," said one of the priests at St. Anthony's church.

The two boys and the daughter were at home when two priests arrived with Robert and Katrina.

"What's going on!?" asked Debby.

"I heard our house is haunted and the priests are here to bless our home in case something bad could be here."

"Mom, I suspected something was wrong when we moved in here and I still feel there's a ghost here!" said Debby.

The priest got the family together saying prayers, going through the house, the shed, barn, and the property. After, they called the realtor to report.

"Daily Dot Realtors, Jean Jazzman speaking."

"Hi Jean, this is Robert Rogers from 66 6th Street. I have a bone to pick with you! I found out our house is haunted through a friend. What are you going to do about it!?"

"We are unaware of your house being haunted. Nobody has told us about it! Did you hire a priest?" asked Jean.

"Yes we did. But if something happens, what are you going to do?" demanded Robert.

"We will move you somewhere else!" said Jean Jazzman. For the next three months there were no hauntings then mid-December 2015 the gas boiler quit working and the gas company came to replace it. Then the house was nice and warm with both fireplaces going while the gas company was replacing the old boiler. About an hour later the lights in the house started to go dim then brightened to normal.

Katrina said, "I'm going to bed I have an awful headache!" She took a couple of aspirin and she went to bed. Robert went down to check the boiler and it was working. Then he went to bed. His eyes were burning as he was rubbing them, and he took a couple of aspirins and he went to bed. Debby was watching a women's basketball game on TV and she fell asleep. Dobbie fell asleep in front of the warm fireplace. Dennis felt dizzy and yawned a couple of times. He drank a cold glass of milk from the refrigerator and he went to bed. Everyone was in bed sleeping before 11:00 p.m.

11:02 p.m. Robert took his last breath and he died in his sleep. An hour later it was Katrina's turn. 1:02 a.m. Debby was next! 2:02 a.m. Dobbie woke up coughing and he suffocated and dropped dead in front of the fireplace, then Dennis stopped breathing and he died in his sleep at 3:02 a.m. At 4:02 a.m. a black mass hovered, crawling on the ceiling and up and down the walls and vanished an hour later. A worker hooked up the new gas boiler the wrong way and everyone in the house, a family of five, all died from carbon dioxide poisoning.

The next day there was a snowstorm and a foot of snow had fallen when suddenly the alarm went off in the house, alerting the police. Officer Lecter arrived and he saw all the cars in the yard and rang the doorbell, but no one answered. It was 5:02 a.m. when the alarm in the house sounded.

Officer Lecter rang the bell and knocked on the door several times and no one answered. The policeman went in with a pass key to reset the alarm and he heard a soft voice, *"Get out!"*

The policeman said, "I'm just resetting the alarm, it's the police." Then he left. It was 6:02 a.m. when he turned it off.

7:02 a.m. the alarms at 66 6th Street went off again. The police had to come again, ringing the doorbell and knocking on the door, and no one answered for more than a half hour. The police went in again with a pass key to reset the alarm and an invisible force picked the policeman up, threw him up against a wall, and dropped him on the floor. It was 8:02 a.m. when the mysterious ghost attacked the cop! He got out of there fast and sped out of the driveway in his police car in the snow, back to the police station. He had a story to tell when he got back!

"Lieutenant Green, I went to 66 6th Street to turn off an alarm and there must be a ghost there. After I reset the alarm on the porch I was picked up and thrown up against a wall and it threw me down on the ground! I didn't see anything; it came out of nowhere! I wasn't about to wait to see something, I got out of there as fast as I could!" said the cop.

Lieutenant Green laughed, "That's why I sent you over there! No one else wants to go there because that house is haunted!"

"Holy shit! No kidding! I saw cars in the yard and I kept ringing the doorbell and banging on the doors to wake people up and either they couldn't hear me or no one is home!" said the cop.

"Maybe they're all dead!" Lieutenant Green joked. The other cop laughed.

Green guessed right! 9:02 a.m. the alarms went off again at 66 6th Street alerting the police again. "There's more than a foot of snow on the ground, we're not going over there again!" said Lieutenant Green. Then he called Bennington Realtors of Vermont and the phone was disconnected so he called the fire department.

10:02 a.m. the alarm at 66 6th Street went off and reset itself. The fire department arrived over an hour later, ringing the doorbell. Nobody answered the door so they left.

11:02 a.m. The alarms sounded again and police called the fire department to go there again. The alarm was blaring away this time and *ring ring, knock knock, bang bang!* No one answered so they forced their way into the house and it was full of smoke and it smelled like a fire was starting. More fire trucks were called to go to work and police and a rescue team arrived in a snowstorm. The first fireman went in to shut down the alarm. A second one started spraying the smoke with a fire extinguisher and the rest of the police and the paramedics went in the house opening windows. The ghostly smoke went out of the house at a high rate of speed and the smell of smoke disappeared and the house was clear.

12:02 p.m. they saw the trail of death. "Oh my fucking God! Fellas, we may have several dead bodies here!" one fireman said to another.

Debby's dead body was in front of the fireplace. Dobbie and Dennis's dead bodies were found in their beds by police.

"There's two more dead bodies in the end bedrooms. We need to shut the boiler off downstairs and call National Grid to shut the power off. We may have carbon dioxide poisoning here," said the police. The bodies of Robert and Katrina were found dead in their beds. A black mass appeared at 1:02 p.m. crawling along the ceiling. Firemen sprayed it with a fire extinguisher and it vanished.

2:02 p.m. Rescue vehicles all got stuck spinning tires on Route 6 during the snowstorm. They had to bring stretchers on foot through the snow to get the dead bodies out of the house. Police closed both sides of Route 6 for the rest of the day and evening.

3:02 p.m. National Grid gas found the problem. "The God damn boiler and water heater were hooked up wrong! Who in the hell would set up a heating system like this? It was hooked up backwards and all these people died of $CO_2$ poisoning! Jesus fucking Christ, we have a serious problem here!"

National Grid workers were telling the police, paramedics, and firemen about what happened. The firemen opened the windows and the heating system was disconnected. Then the National Grid workers left.

4:02 p.m. A news helicopter landed in the farmyard near the barn and news reporters and media crew had to walk through snowdrifts to get in the house from the basement entrance.

5:02 p.m. Firemen heard a big *bang!* in the fireplace and they looked to see what it was. "Maybe Santa Claus is stuck in the chimney!" one fireman joked.

The firemen looked up the chimney and nothing was there! They closed the damper and the glass doors. "A bird may have flown in there," said one of the firemen. The electricity in the house was turned back on but the heaters would not be replaced until after the snowstorm.

6:02 p.m. Snowplows arrived to clear the streets so emergency vehicles could keep moving. News reporters and media were taking down reports for tonight's late news.

7:02 p.m. It was thundering and lightning and the snow was really coming down.

8:02 p.m. The lights in the house went out with news reporters still there and the lights came back on a minute later.

All the roads were clear before 9:00 p.m. 9:02 p.m. News reporters and media heard a voice, *"Get out!!!!!!!!!!!!!!!!"* Everyone left the house just after 9:00 p.m. and the helicopter lifted off and flew to New Bedford.

10:02 p.m. The house had ghostly figures of the dead walking around. It all stopped an hour later. The firemen cut the alarm in the house so the fucking thing didn't keep going off all night! Then the news came on TV about the 66 6th Street nightmare.

"Good evening, we have breaking news on Channel 6 in New Bedford. Five people died from carbon dioxide poisoning in Mattapoisett last night. National Grid reported a wrong hookup to a heating system at 66 6th Street and a family of five was found dead in that house. Mattapoisett police said there have been several hauntings reported in that house for a long time, but this issue has nothing to do with the hauntings. Police did report an officer being attacked by a strange force after getting several calls about a faulty alarm system in the house. He was picked up and thrown down police say but he's okay. Lisa Johnston, Channel 6 News."

The next day was Sunday. The sky cleared, but it was a cold day. The storm left about fifteen inches of snow on the ground. Priests went in the home at 66 6th Street to perform another exorcism and put crosses and glowing statues of the Blessed Virgin Mary in every room to keep the ghosts away after the Sunday Mass. The police kept calling real estate offices to find out which real estate company sold this house.

7:02 a.m. Monday morning police got a call from the new realtor Daily Dot, the company that sold the house. Jean Jazzman heard the news, she was sick! Later the realtor moved all of the Rogers' belongings out of the house and put them in storage until they could contact relatives in Oakland, California. The house was sprayed with disinfectant and cleaned. Another new boiler and water heater were replaced and hooked up right. The worker that screwed up got fired and National Grid got sued! The house was shut down for the rest of the winter.

St. Anthony's church had a funeral Mass that followed cremation for the Rogers family. Relatives came from California to attend the funeral services and get the Rogers' belongings to bring back to Oakland, California. Posters were placed outside the house: Golden State Warriors NBA champions 2015, and another poster of the Oakland A's baseball team.

A meeting took place with real estate owners. The meeting was held at the Old Rochester Regional High School gym just before Christmas 2015.

"Good evening. My name is Joseph Johnson, the manager of Daily Dot Realtors. Merry Christmas to everyone. Unfortunately, we lost a family of five a week and a half ago to $CO_2$ poisoning due to a National Grid error: hooking up a heating system the wrong way. I'm from Livingston, Vermont and I drove down here to have this short meeting. I was told the house at 66 6th Street has had a series of hauntings for years according to the Mattapoisett police and fire and St. Anthony's church.

"Does the carbon dioxide poisoning error have anything to do with the hauntings? I don't know. I did hear bad things have happened there and people have died there before, due to reported hauntings. When we sell homes or properties we cannot tell them it's haunted or people died there because it will not sell! But starting January 1, 2016, if someone asks about the history of the home and property and if it's haunted or if there were deaths there, we have to tell them. The Mattapoisett police will finish the meeting. Thank you," finished the Daily Dot manager.

# FOURTEEN

## THE BROWN FAMILY HAUNTINGS

It was July 15, 2021 when the Brown family from California bought the house at 66 6th Street through Daily Dot Realtors. Finally, the company sold the house six years, later all furnished. The Brown family has six members: John Brown, forty-eight; Claudette Brown, forty-six; Ronny Brown, fifteen; Turner Brown, thirteen; Franky Brown, twelve; and Dorothy Brown, ten.

John and Claudette are schoolteachers at Old Rochester Middle School and their son Ronny is going to the high school. Turner and Franky will be in the middle school this fall, and Dorothy will attend the fifth grade in school this fall. The family was at the house waiting for the realtor.

The Brown family was burned out of their home in California and stayed in a shelter for a year because of the loss and the corona virus in 2020. When they got insurance money from their losses they moved to the East Coast not knowing what's waiting for them!

"Good afternoon. Are you Mrs. Jean Jazzman from Daily Dot?"

"Yes."

"My name is John Brown and my wife Claudette and our four kids. This is Ronny, then Turner, and Franky, and my daughter Dorothy."

"Pleased to meet you. Let's go inside, it's 101 degrees outside. Before we look at the house I'm sorry about your loss from the fire in Santa Monica and the corona virus restrictions last year. It was a bad year for you people and for all of us. This house is a classic Cape Codder here in beautiful Mattapoisett. You have two floors, a finished basement—all furnished—and two acres of land, a toolshed, and a barn. You will see that later. Let's go see the house," said Jean Jazzman.

The same routine, it's the same haunted house being shown all over again six years after the Rogers massacre in 2015 when they all died from $CO_2$ poisoning. The Brown family never asked questions about the house; they loved it, needing a nice place to live!!! The house was remodeled and it looked brighter inside.

"Why are there so many crosses and statues of the Virgin Mary?" asked Dorothy.

"The family who lived here before were very strong devoted Catholics! You will be blessed living in this wonderful home. The home and property go for $400,000 but if you sign a ten-year lease the rate goes down to $250,000. Then you can resell after the ten years for double or more, it's worth the gamble!" said Jean Jazzman.

The Browns went for the bait and moved in. John said, "Dorothy, you will be sleeping in the bedroom upstairs on the left-hand side and we will be in the master bedroom on the right. Ronny, you will sleep in the basement bedroom, and Turner, you sleep on the ground floor left side and Franky, you're on the right. When the truck comes with our stuff we will put things away together before we go out on the town."

Dorothy was putting clothes away in her room and she heard a bird flapping. It sounded like it was in her room. She looked out the window and she saw a crow sitting on a tree branch flapping its wings as another crow landed near the first one, looking at her from outside. She closed the shade. It was getting dark and a thunderstorm was coming with flashes of lightning.

Ronny was outside sitting at the picnic table when a bolt of lightning struck a tree nearby stripping the bark off. A small fire started, but the rain came down hard it put the fire out! Ronny screamed and he ran into the house.

John was outside getting things from the truck in the rain when there was a bright flash and the loudest *bang!* shaking the ground! He ran in the house fast! The flash was the same lightning bolt that struck the tree!

Claudette was in the kitchen cooking when suddenly another bright flash came, followed by a big loud *bang!* of thunder. She saw a bright lightning ball come in the house through a closed window. It moved slowly into the dining room and went out another closed window then vanished! Claudette was shocked!

"John, a lightning ball came in the kitchen through a window and went out the dining room window and they were closed!"

"You're kidding; how can that happen!? We're getting a bad storm out there!"

"Dad, I saw a tree get struck by lightning, frying the tree, and it caught fire before the rain put it out!"

"Ronny, stay in the house!"

Turner was in his room closing the window and the lightning flashed. He got a shock from the lightning and he screamed! "I just got hit by lightning closing the window!"

"Turner get away from the windows!" said John.

Claudette looked him over and she said, "You got a shock from the lightning but you will be okay! If you were hit by lightning you would know it! You just got a little shock, you'll be alright. Don't go near the windows." Claudette and John checked Turner out and he was okay.

Bedtime. Everyone was in bed and the storm came again. A bright flash followed by a big *bang!* picked Franky up from his bed and dropped him on the floor! He screamed hysterically! Franky ran upstairs to his parents' room and he slept in a chair there for the rest of the night. It rained for the rest of the night as the storm came and went until it was over.

The next day was clear but another hot day. The kids went to the beach for the day and John and Claudette went for a boat ride and did some fishing. Ronny, Turner, Franky, and Dorothy all sat together on a big beach blanket with their towels, beach bags, and water bottles.

A few minutes later a lady in a black bikini came over to them and stopped and she just started staring at them.

"She has black eyes!" shouted Ronny. "What do you want lady? Do you want to get laid?" said Ronny. The rest of the brothers and his sister laughed!

"My name is Maria Cooper, the town drifter. I just want to warn you that the Deopolo ghost followed you here from the West Coast. The Deopolo ghost is a demon from the Alaskan Triangle, haunting California all the way to Mexico. However, this demon does not mix with the East Coast."

Ronny said, "Lady how do you know that we're from California?"

"The Deopolo ghost told me!" she said. Then she walked away and vanished!

Dorothy said, "Did you see that! She vanished in thin air! Did we see a ghost?!"

"I don't know but she was strange," said Ronny.

Turner Brown said to a group of people sitting near them at the beach, "Excuse me, did you just see that weird lady with a black bathing suit and black eyes?"

"No, we never saw her," they said.

After the beach, the four of them went home. Later John and Claudette came home. Franky said, "Mom, Dad, we saw this strange lady at the beach and she looked like a ghost. She knows we're from California because some ghost from Alaska followed us from California and it was a demon!"

"You've got to be kidding! Where did you see this lady?"

"We saw her at the town beach around three o'clock. She was a tall old lady with a black bathing suit and she had black eyes and she knows who we are!" said Franky.

"She vanished right in front of my eyes," said Dorothy.

"There's a powerful demon known in California as the Deopolo ghost! We have to find this lady because this is very strange. Maybe you did see a ghost at the beach, but if she knows who you are and where we live we need to find her," said Claudette.

"Mom, this lady said to me that some kind of a demon ghost followed us from California and she said her name was Maria or Mary Hooper the town drifter. She said the ghost came from Alaska, haunting California all the way to Mexico, and this demon doesn't mix on the East Coast. Then she walked down by the water and disappeared!" said Ronny.

"Ronny, let's take a ride to the beach and find out who this lady is," said Mom.

Claudette, Ronny, and Mom walked along the beach asking questions about the Mary Hooper ghost and came up empty handed. Everyone shook their heads no and most people had never heard of her, then they went back home. Claudette and Ronny were saying her name wrong. It's Maria Cooper.

Later after dinner, the Brown family went to a music concert at the Shipyard Park gazebo. They spread blankets down on the grass and watched the band in the gazebo, and food was served with fireworks after.

During intermission between bands, the Brown family was socializing with people waiting in line for food. The parents met a cop at the food line. "Excuse me Officer, may I ask you a question? My kids saw this strange lady at the beach wearing a black bathing suit and they said she had black eyes," said Claudette.

"The beach ghost! Her name is Maria Cooper. She appears at the town beach around 3:00 p.m. or 3:00 a.m. once in a while and she goes to people to warn them that something may happen to them or to be prepared for something to happen. She's a spirit that protects others from evil. Sometimes she comes into view or you'll hear her voice.

"Here's a card for Julie Antilli, the wife of one of our police officers. She's a psychiatrist and psychic. You can call her and she will tell you all about the Maria Cooper hauntings," said Officer Henry Lecter.

Later after the fireworks, the concert was over and everyone went home. Claudette said, "Well kids we found out that you did see something on the beach, now we have to find out about her."

The next day was Sunday and everyone went to church. A black cloud was over the heads of the Brown family while they were in church but they could not see it.

A nun saw the black cloud and she held up a cross and it went away. It looked like a thin black fog you can see through, though the church was dark. The nun said prayers holding the cross, and the fog went away. Nobody in the church noticed the church brightened then.

When she walked by the Brown family she said, "Is anybody smoking here, there's no smoking in the church." Claudette looked at her kind of funny.

After Mass, the family went to the beach but they got no leads about the beach ghost. A lady at the beach said to John Brown, "Are you people new here?"

"Yes, we just moved here from Oakland, California."

"Welcome to Mattapoisett," she said.

"Do you know anything about the Mattapoisett beach ghost?" asked Claudette.

"No, I never heard of her," the lady said.

The kids told her what they saw. "Wow! That's strange!" she said.

At bedtime there were noises that sounded like cracks and something hitting the house and silent roaring sounds; it was a very windy night. The roaring sounds were something different but the Browns believe it's only the wind. It's the invisible ghost passing through the house at 66 6th Street waiting to strike at the right time. The black cloud in the church was another evil entity following the Brown family from the house.

The next day Claudette and John called the psychic on the card Officer Lecter game them Saturday night at the concert. Then they went to see her.

"Good afternoon, my name is Julie Antilli."

"It's a pleasure to meet you. My name is Claudette Brown and this is my husband John and my son Ronny.

"Please sit down. How can I help you?" asked Julie.

"My kids were at the town beach Saturday afternoon and a lady ghost came up to Ronny, giving him a warning because a demon ghost followed us from California. The lady said it's a ghost that haunts Alaska, California, and Mexico, and it followed us from the West Coast.

"Ronny asked her, 'How do you know we're from California?' The lady told him the ghost told her! Then she walked toward the water and Dorothy said she vanished into thin air. Officer Lecter told me to contact you. When we lived in Oakland, California we heard stories about people missing in the Alaskan Triangle due to a powerful demon called the Deopolo ghost. It always crossed the earthquake zones and weak areas in California, living in the mountains, and haunted certain areas in Mexico, crossing another demon named Mega there. Ronny said he heard something like the Deopolo ghost the lady was threatening him about and it has me quite worried!" said Claudette.

"The beach ghost—Maria Cooper is her name—was raped at 3:00 a.m. on the Mattapoisett town beach and staggered on the beach until she died twelve hours later at 3:00 p.m. She's been haunting this beach for a long time, contacting several spirits along the way. She appears as a tall middle-aged woman in a black bikini with black eyes. She is scary looking, but she's a ghost! She's not dangerous but she will give you a warning when something bad is going to happen," said Julie Antilli.

"Julie, how does this ghost know where we are from and call us by name? Something from the dead! How is this possible?" said Claudette.

"Ghosts can feed off of people! Have you ever heard the term, 'ashes to ashes, dust to dust?' Maria Cooper is from ashes and she feeds through the dust. We are dust until we die. Ghosts feed off energy. If you had contact with this ghost she finds out. Somehow it followed your family here from the West Coast. That does not mean the Deopolo is going to get you, but in the area where you lived or somewhere you traveled to it hooked on to you and it follows its mate from behind the grave. It's a hard topic to understand.

"I don't mean to scare you, but the energy I am feeling from you reflects the Deopolo ghost following you here. I know about the Deopolo ghost from Alaska, called the Deopolo, or Debra. It's a female demon similar to Maria Cooper and the two look alike! Maria Cooper is looking for answers and the Deopolo is a female devil also looking for answers. She was lost in the mountains in part of the Alaska Triangle and later died from the Oakland, California great fires. The Deopolo is a spirit that follows people as they travel. Don't ask me why! That's the way ghosts work. The Deopolo is not a ghost that will haunt you even though it followed you here, unless you provoke her or call for her. This demon is looking for another source of power.

"We had a ghost by the name of Ebenezer from the Bennington Triangle in Vermont and another powerful demon right here in Massachusetts called the Hockomock Swamp monster that gave birth to another powerful demon called the Greenman of Mattapoisett, once again not aggressive unless threatened. These demons are ghosts of the Bridgewater Triangle. Several areas, not only Mattapoisett, are affected by these ghosts.

"In Mattapoisett the Greenman is a ghost covered in leaves with a straw face and he makes himself visible sometimes, and if you see it keep your distance. Then we have the red-eyed deer; it's not a normal deer, it's a ghost. Don't stare at it, look the other and it will go away. Then we have the beach ghost, the one you saw, Maria Cooper. Then we have the invisible ghost and the black mist ghost; both are dangerous. If you don't contact them they will not bother you, and if you see them just keep your distance because they will find a way to play games with you.

"When the Vermont ghost was invited here he did not mix with the

Bridgewater Triangle spirits. Paranormal investigators believe there are Bigfoot creatures, big snakes, thunderbirds, mothmen creatures, poltergeists, ghosts, orbs of light and fireballs, UFO sightings. It is believed by the Indians of the Bridgewater Triangle that these ghosts could be from another planet. It's a dangerous area.

"When you go to Abington, Brockton, Bridgewater, or Whitman, be careful who you talk to and do not bring up anything to do with the Triangle. If you do witchcraft in these areas their ghost will get you. The spectral area of Vermont's Bennington Triangle is two hundred square miles, ruled by the Ebenezer.

"The Ebenezer ghost was called to Mattapoisett from a family inviting him in by a spirit board and challenging him. The Ebenezer killed people here and it took several exorcisms by powerful Catholic friars to get rid of him. He was called or brought back years later and went on the attack again. The Ebenezer followed people from here all the way to Dubai, that's how powerful this ghost was. It was a big demonic figure with red eyes and big hands and it choked people to death.

"Brown family, I haven't told you the bad news yet! The Deopolo is just as strong as the Ebenezer from Vermont. She will not bother you if you don't provoke her. Don't talk about or challenge her. Just because she followed you here doesn't mean she will attack you. She came with you because another family from Oakland moved to Mattapoisett and invited her, but she followed you instead.

"It's hard to understand. I wouldn't lose sleep over it. She will not bother you unless you invite her through a spirit board. She was introduced by Maria Cooper just warn you that the Deopolo followed you here. The Deopolo will latch on to Maria Cooper to contact other ghosts.

"Go to the church and tell the priest that you talked to me and you want the Deopolo spirit to be removed from your family. I have a prayer book and I'll say some prayers and ask the Deopolo to be removed from your souls and to be let free in a nice way. I have another person coming in fifteen minutes. Any questions?" finished Julie Antilli.

"Yes, suppose she's already in our house because we have been hearing strange things lately," said Claudette.

"It could be checking you out but it will not last; she probably wants to know what's there, what you people are about, and she will go. She's from the afterlife; she might make a little noise but she will leave she will not bother you," said Julie.

"What does she look like!?" Ronny joked.

"She looks like Maria Cooper but she wears a black button-down dress. She has black hair and black eyes. One more thing; here's a computer readout on the conversations we had. Take this to the church," said Julie Antilli.

The Brown family went to the church to see the priest. The priest said prayers to try to get this demon off their backs. They went home and threw holy water in every room but strange things continued to happen.

Mid-August things started happening a little at a time. The counselor Julie Antilli can't tell them they live in a haunted house because she'll lose her job!

John and Claudette were at the Twin River Casino in Lincoln, Rhode Island one Saturday night and they were getting drinks at the Lighthouse Bar. Claudette was looking at the Lighthouse Bar band stage and she saw a vision of the Deopolo ghost the way Julie Antilli described her, standing on the stage and shown on the big TV screen above, then it wasn't there.

Then they went gambling and the vision of the Deopolo ghost appeared in the distance on the gambling floor between slot machines. Then they went to eat dinner at Fred and Steve's Steakhouse upstairs at Twin River. They were eating at the restaurant and she saw the vision again at the far end of the restaurant then it walked into another room and it was gone!

She said, "John I keep seeing this lady that looks like the Deopolo ghost from California. I just saw her at the other end of this restaurant. I saw her again downstairs when we were gambling, then I saw her at the bar earlier on the TV screen. It can't be, it must be a special lady for the casino but she looks like the Deopolo ghost! Did you see the lady?"

"No Claudette, I never noticed," said John.

While John and Claudette were at the casino the kids also saw a vision of this lady walking through the yard. Ronny said, "Excuse me miss, you're on private property." Then the lady ran into the woods and Ronny chased her and she was gone. Turner, Franky, and Dorothy saw her as well before Ronny challenged her.

The rest of the evening went well at Twin River for John and Claudette. On the ride home coming off the highway, taking the Mattapoisett exit, she saw the same lady at the casino crossing the road and John ran her over.

Claudette said, "John, watch out!!!!! But it was too late. John slammed on his brakes after hitting the lady and there was no sound of a strike noise or anything! John got out of the car and he ran to the front of impact and nothing was there! He looked under the car and looked around the area and he saw nothing.

"I saw the woman and I ran her over but I can't find her, she's nowhere to be found!"

"John it's the same lady I saw at the casino! I wonder if she's the Deopolo ghost!"

"Claudette we have to go to the police!" John tried to drive off and the car would not go! He put on his hazard lights and he tried again and the car wasn't going anywhere! A police car drove up on the exit and stopped behind him.

He got out and he said, "You have trouble here!"

"Yes sir, double trouble, you just came at a good time! I hit a lady coming off the exit; she ran right in front of my car coming out of nowhere and it was too late, I couldn't stop in time. I got out and looked in front of my car, under my car, and she was gone! Now I'm stuck here!" said John.

"Maybe you struck a ghost!" the policeman said.

"My wife said she saw this lady at Twin River Casino earlier this evening," said John.

"What did this lady look like?" said the policeman.

"She looked like a lady in a black button-down dress and she was white with black hair, dark eyes, and black high-heeled shoes. I was coming off the exit and the next thing I knew she was in front of my car and I slammed on the brakes. I didn't hear anything and I got out to check on her and nothing was there!" said John.

The police examined the accident site and he found nothing. He shook his head and he said, "You must have hit a ghost because there's nothing here!" Then John drove off and went home. Claudette was shocked!

They got home around midnight and the kids were watching a movie on TV. "Hi kids, did everyone behave this evening?"

"Yes Mom. We were watching movies on TV. We watched *Top Gun,* *Good Fellas,* and *Fast Times at Ridgemont High* on HBO. Mom, someone was in our yard walking around. I told her she was on private property then she left," said Ronny.

"What did this lady look like Ronny?"

"She looked like the beach ghost! She had a long button-down dress and she was a white lady with black hair. She was walking slowly through our yard," he said.

"John, she's the same lady we ran over on Exit 19 and the one I saw at the casino. She's the Deopolo ghost. We need to talk to the priest after church tomorrow," said Claudette.

"Okay kids, no more movies. Let's go to bed, we have to go to church tomorrow," said John.

Bedtime. John was getting ready for bed and he heard a whisper calling his name, *"John."* He looked around and he saw nothing.

When Claudette came in the room ready for bed he said, "Were you calling me?"

"No!" she said.

"Good night!" Dorothy said and went to bed.

John looked at the alarm clock and the time was 12:34 a.m. and he went to bed. He shut the lamp off then the lamp turned on by itself on Claudette's side of the bed. She said, "Okay Deopolo, stop playing games!" She shut the light off.

Dorothy was sleeping and something was blowing in her ears and she woke up. The windows were open in her room and there was lightning outside so she closed the windows and went back to bed. The blowing in the ears stopped.

An hour later the Deopolo ghost was standing at the top of the stairs while everyone was sleeping then it went into John and Claudette's room and vanished! No one saw it but it's in the house!

Turner was in bed and the bedspread started slipping away from him. He woke up and he grabbed the bedspread to cover himself up. Then he slept with a light on.

A few minutes later Franky woke up and he saw a black spot on the wall from the light on in the hallway. He got up to touch the black mark and it was still there. He turned the lamp on in his room and the black spot was not there! He turned the lamp off and the black spot reappeared. He turned the lamp on again and the black spot was gone. He slept with the lamp on.

Later Ronny was sleeping downstairs in the finished basement and felt like he wasn't alone. Lying on his side he felt like someone was standing over him and the hairs stood up on his arms, legs, and head. He turned over quickly and he put the lamp on and jumped out of bed but saw nothing! He looked around the room, under the bed, and he put lights on. He looked at his alarm clock and the time was 6:30 a.m. He heard owls and crows outside.

Later everyone got up, had breakfast, and they went to church. After church, the Brown family went to the rectory to see a priest. "Hi Father Pedroia. Remember us, when you came to our house to remove any spirits at 66 6th Street?" asked Claudette.

"Yes I do. Have you seen anything?"

"Yes, Father, I have been seeing the Deopolo ghost, the one from California, at the casino in Rhode Island. Coming home I saw her again and John ran her over. A policeman came and he told us that we may have hit a ghost because he couldn't find her! My kids saw the lady out in the backyard trespassing through our property," said Claudette.

"She came to you to let you know she followed you, and she wants you to know she's here! That is why she showed herself to you and when John ran her over it was a sign that she was released from your lives. Then she will latch on to another spirit. She just wanted to hitch a ride from the West Coast on your back to make other connections," said the priest.

"Father, why did I see her at Twin River, not at my house?"

"First of all John was not a true believer or he has no fear. She didn't want to show herself to your kids until she reached you first, and it was you the spirit was attracted to so the visions came to you first at a neutral site. It can be anywhere and it happens when you least expect it. Second, you're not going to be thinking about ghosts in a casino, bar, restaurant, etc. Deopolo wanted to catch you off guard! Go home and say the prayers from the instructions I gave you and you should be okay," said the priest.

Two weeks later there's no hauntings and Deopolo was asked to move on, but what about the others? September 2021 everyone is in school and

John and Claudette are teaching at the Old Rochester Middle School. Everyone in the Brown family is normal but the ghosts have other ideas in their home when nobody's there.

When the kids in walking distance came home from the high school and middle school, Ronny, Turner, Franky, and Dorothy walked into the house and the dining room table was lying on its side with two chairs tipped over. Franky's bed was standing up against the wall over the window and the bedclothes were stripped and hanging on the door. The kids ran out of the house and waited for their parents to come. Ronny had a big stick waiting for the intruder to come out of the house.

The parents came home with a bunch of books in their hands. Ronny said, "Mom, Dad someone broke into our house!"

John called the police and they went in the house and saw the mess. The policeman pulled out his gun, saying, "Anyone here!"

John put the dining room table down and he put the chairs under it. Then he went into Franky's bedroom and he moved the bed. Ronny helped him set it up and Claudette made the bed up and cleaned the room.

Ronny went downstairs with the policeman to check the basement and everything was normal and the outside door was locked. John grabbed his shotgun and he went through the house and he went upstairs and he checked the bedrooms, bath, closets, and attic storages and everything was normal.

The policeman said, "There's no sign of a break in, the alarm was still on before it was shut off. The only thing I can think of is someone may have broken in through a window, not setting off the alarm. Make sure all your windows are closed and locked on the ground floor when you're not home." Then the policeman left.

Claudette started cooking and the kids were doing their homework. John was outside raking leaves and he saw the tree branches moving without wind. He finished what he was doing and he looked out into the woods and the branches were not moving. Then he saw a bunch of jumbo honeybees flying around a big nest in a tree. The leaves were covering the nest. The nest was as big as a couch and thousands of these jumbo bees were flying around the nest, protecting it.

John was raking leaves from under that tree when he noticed the bees. He stopped what he was doing and he slowly walked away until he was able to get in the house. He saw the queen jumbo honeybee and it was the size of a small bird flying up above, following him, flying lower and lower. Luckily he made it in the house before the giant killer bee caught him.

John went in through the basement entrance and he saw Ronny and he said, "Ronny don't go outside there's a big bees' nest in the tree near the shed." Then he went upstairs to warn the rest of the kids before he called the police.

The police said, "Call your local hardware store or hire a beekeeper to come and remove the nest."

John looked in his computer to find a hardware store. Mahoney's was in Mattapoisett but they were closed, so he called and he left a message.

Bedtime, everyone was in bed and it was a cool mid-September night. All the windows were closed and locked and the night was normal. Dorothy was sleeping and a ghostly shadow went across her room over her head and vanished. No one saw it, and it was gone.

The next day everyone was in school and John and Claudette Brown were teaching. Claudette teaches history and John teaches math and physical education.

While no one was at home a deer broke into the barn in back of the house at 66 6th Street and it was attacked by a swarm of killer African jumbo honeybees. A raccoon was attacked, and a bunny rabbit outside in back of the barn was killed by the bees. Crows were also attacked and died, lying on top of the barn and shed; about eight birds were killed by the jumbo bees.

After the kids came home from school and went to do their homework, John went to Mahoney's Hardware, now known as Ace Hardware. He pulled up near a handicapped parking area and he went inside. He said to the store clerk, "Good afternoon sir. I have a big problem outside in my backyard. I have a bees' nest as big as Arizona! How can I get a beekeeper to remove a nest of killer honeybees!?"

"Very easy sir, I have a spray that will kill them all! UAE Dubai Finisher is the name of the product. You spray the nest in the middle of the night when the bees are sleeping and it will kill them on contact! Do not spray the substance right now or during daylight or you'll be a dead man! The spray is forty-eight dollars. Only use it when it's dark. If you hire a beekeeper to remove African killer bees it will cost you a couple of grand," said the clerk, Bob, according to the nametag on his shirt. John bought the solution and he waited for the right time to spray the bees.

Bedtime, everyone was in bed sleeping and John went outside to spray the nest and he soaked the fuckin thing! And he heard *buzzzzzzzzzzzzz!* And he left the solution there and he ran in the house as quickly as he could!

Ronny said, "Dad, did you kill them!?"

"We will find out tomorrow!" Then he went to bed. Ronny looked out the window and he saw the dead bees falling out of the tree like snow falling. He laughed.

The next morning, Claudette said, "John what's all that yellow and brown stuff outside in the yard?"

"Those are all the bees I killed last night! We have one hell of a mess to clean up when we get out of school this afternoon." The kids laughed!

The school day went normally and opossums, raccoons, and giant field rats as big as small dogs came to feast on the dead bees, spreading them all over the yard, making more of a mess to clean up! Raccoons were eating the honeycombs from the nest, making it easier for the nest to fall out of the tree so the animals could finish it off! The honeybee buffet was no match for the animals. Eat the honeycomb and nest, fill up on dead bees, and go back in the woods and move on!

After school was over John and Ronny Brown had a big mess to clean up in the backyard; there's so many dead bees, enough to fill up a dump truck. John and Ronny went to the barn to get rakes, shovels, and equipment to clean up the dead bees. John saw the barn door was broken into and a dead deer was lying inside, covered with giant bees. There's another nest of African baldhead killer bees inside the barn and shed; these bees are the size of small birds with eight-inch wingspans.

"Oh my fuckin God! Ronny, get in the house!" said John. Then they left the area and went in the house so they didn't disturb the bees. Today's job was put on hold. The kids were stuck in the house because there were more killer bees, even bigger than the other ones, and it's raining outside anyway! A day to eat dinner, watch TV, and play games, cards, etc.

Bedtime. John went out in the yard in the pouring rain and he shuffled the dead bees off the spray bottle to use it on the rest of the bees. He went to the barn and he sprayed the UAE Dubai Finisher spray all over the inside of the barn and on the dead deer, soaking the place.

Then he went in the shed and he sprayed all over the walls, soaking the shed from ceiling to floor, even through the cracks. He decided to finish off the spray bottle, spraying the outside of the shed and barn and on top of the roofs. Dead birds slid off the roof of the barn and he saw more dead animals in the back of it. He sprayed on the dead animals and the ground around the barn and shed then he put the bottle in the barn and went in the house.

John said to Claudette, "We had another nest in the barn and shed with bees the size of birds, and several dead animals were behind the barn. I'm going to stay home tomorrow to get this mess cleaned up. Then I'll call Jack Bronson, a friend, to help, then call in Channel 6 to identify what kind of king bees I have here!"

The next day the kids went to school and Claudette went to work. John called Channel 6 News to identify the bees then he called his friend to come over. John put a large trash bag into a trash bin and he shoveled all the dead bees into the trash bin. He filled three big trash bags before his friend arrived.

"Good morning John." They shook hands and John showed him the terror in his yard.

"Jack, come look at this! There're dead animals everywhere! A dead rabbit, several dead crows, a deer and a raccoon. Look at the size of these bees. These are African killer bees. I used this spray on the nests at night.

"The other night I sprayed a nest bigger than my dining room table and filled three big bags with dead bees from the nest in that tree. These bees are African killer honeybees and the bigger ones are regular African killer bees. Channel 6 News is coming here in a while to identify these bees in the barn. Look at the size of them!" said John.

"They look like murder hornets!" said Jack.

"Jack, I would like you to grab the rake and rake the dead bees in the yard up into a pile and load them into these bags while I move the dead animals in the wheelbarrow," said John.

Channel 6 News arrived and went to the barn to see the huge dead bees. "Oh my God, are they murder hornets?!" one newsman said to another.

The other news reporter said, "These are African baldhead hornets but could go by the name of murder hornets! If one of these stung you, you'd be dead in less than ten minutes! Look what they did to these dead animals!"

John told the news reporters about all the killer bees he killed the last three days; there were so many of them. He showed them the honeybees in the trashcan. The news reporters took pictures and video on TV cameras and interviewed John and told him it would be on the news later. Jack helped John lift the dead deer into the wheelbarrow and scooped up some dead birds to go dump in the woods. Then he scooped up the rest of the dead animals— the raccoon, the rabbit, an opossum, and some rats—to dump into the woods.

The workers had work gloves on and they were wearing facemasks. John put all the dead animals in an open field in the woods all together then he went to the barn to get a can of gasoline to pour on the dead animals. "In fact, let's bring the bags of the dead bees in the trash and burn those motherfuckers too!" said John.

They brought four full bags of dead honeybees to the pile of dead animals after the yard was raked up. They put some downed dead trees on top of the pile then John poured gasoline all over the pile and set it ablaze and it was one big bonfire!

"John, what's all this yellow grass around the barn, and that tree...is it rotted away?"

"I think I killed the grass spraying these fuckin creatures! Let's go in the house and have some lunch. My wife made chicken salad sandwiches, tuna salad, and egg salad."

While the fire was burning in the open field near the woods, John and Jack were feasting on the sandwiches Claudette made and drinking down a few Buds.

"After lunch we'll go out and sweep the hornets out of the barn and shed and throw them into the inferno!" said John.

The sun was shining on a piece of broken glass in the yard near the barn. It started a small flame and the barn caught on fire and was ablaze into an inferno in seconds! The Deopolo ghost was standing between the two fires in the middle of the open field between the set bonfire and the second fire that was started by the sun. John and Jack were too fuckin busy downing beers in the front yard and now two bonfires are burning!

"Well buddy, let's get this job done before my kids get home from school," said John. They went to the backyard and they were in shock! The barn and shed were burning to the ground! "There's goes that job!" said Jack.

"Oh my God, I lost a lot of good stuff! I never should have started a bonfire! The fire must have burned underground somewhere for this to happen. Maybe the Deopolo ghost did it! I lost my brand-new John Deere sit down lawnmower," John cried.

"The Deopolo ghost, what's that!?" said Jack.

"We had a ghost follow us from California when we moved here!"

"John, be real, a ghost?" said Jack.

John called the fire department then he told Jack about the ghost stories! The firemen said, "What happened here! Are we burning the forest down!?"

"No sir, one fire was set and the other was an accident! The first fire was me burning a bunch of dead bees and animals from my yard, and I believe the chemical I was using may have set the barn on fire."

The fire department put the fires out. The kids came home to see that the barn and shed burned to the ground. Everyone was hysterical! The Deopolo ghost burned the barn and shed down.

Suppertime. "Good evening, this is Channel 6 News in New Bedford. We have breaking news: Two forms of killer bees and murder hornets were found at a residence in Mattapoisett. Here is John Brown reporting."

"I had a nest of killer African honeybees in a tree in my backyard the size of my dining room table and I sprayed the nest and killed thousands of bees. The next day I noticed my barn was broken into and I found a dead deer with giant bees on it and flying around in the barn."

"The bees may have come from a boat from Africa because bees like this are unheard of on the East Coast. Here's a scene of killer hornets the size of a small bird. The bug is three and a half inches in diameter with an eight-inch wingspan. Stings from these bees can kill in minutes! There were no injuries and John Brown did a good job spraying them. If you see these kinds of deadly wasps please contact Channel 6 News. Janet Brown, not related, reporting."

Before dark John was raking up the ashes; the shed and the barn were gone! He cleaned up the yard, scooped up the charred bones from the dead animals, filling trash bags, and cleaned the area. It was a twelve-hour day to clean up the mess from the bees and the dead animals.

"Dad, what happened?" asked Ronny.

"I think the spray I was using to kill the bees ignited from the sunlight and set the barn on fire. The spray killed the grass around the barn, shed, and tree, turning it yellow and the spray is highly flammable!" yelled John.

The next day John borrowed a lawnmower from his neighbor down the road to cut the grass around the yard, the day after that there was a rainstorm. Then on the weekend, John went to La Salette shrine to buy a giant statue of the Blessed Virgin Mary and lights. He planted the statue in a round slate structure where the barn and shed burned down, and he put colorful lights and a water pool inside. It was beautiful at night with the colorful changing lights rotating and lighting up the Virgin Mary in different colors to keep the God damn fuckin ghosts away!

He also built a fire pit outside to hold parties outside or for cooking. Then John bought a steel shed, and he bought a new lawnmower, a snow blower, and new tools, shovels, and rakes, and replaced what he lost, spending thousands of dollars to rebuild his beautiful yard.

From late September to mid-November 2021 there were a lot of nice evenings to enjoy the fire pit. They had Thanksgiving dinner outdoors, roasting a big turkey in the fire pit, sitting twenty people at the picnic table. It was a nice fifty-degree day and sunny. Most nights the family toasted marshmallows over the new fire pit until the snows came.

December 2021 was a snowy month and the colorful Virgin Mary was pretty with the snow falling, reflecting the lights and making her glow. It was beautiful. The ghosts even got a good look at the colorful Virgin Mary in the wee hours of the night as it was getting close to Christmas.

The first week of December there was a big snowstorm. The Greenman appeared at 3:00 a.m. one night then vanished. Then the beach ghost Maria Cooper and the Deopolo ghost came to visit at 3:00 a.m. another evening. Then the Ebenezer appeared another night at 3:00 a.m. Then the black mist arrived with yellow eyes and hands trying to grab the statue, and finally the red-eyed deer came for a visit, all at 3:00 a.m. when everyone is sleeping!

The Brown family never saw the action outside late into the night. The Virgin Mary statue slowed down the strange happenings for three months at 66 6th Street until the ghosts visited the shrine during the December snowstorms. John decorated two trees in the front yard and one pine tree in the backyard near the fire pit with Christmas lights and a Christmas tree in the living room.

The ghosts are no match for the powerful Virgin Mary statue lighting up the night, but all the ghosts put a curse on the family. The night before Christmas was very cold and there was no heat in the house because the pilot went out in the boiler. John went down to check the boiler and he relit the pilot. The boiler came on and the house was getting warm. Then the Brown family went to midnight Mass for Christmas. At midnight the house blew up! There was a gas explosion!

# FIFTEEN

## The Deopolo Ghost

12:06 a.m. Christmas morning, sirens were heard from everywhere! Mattapoisett, Rochester, and Marion fire trucks arrived at the fire at 66 6th Street. The home was blown to pieces, there was nothing there!

12:14 a.m. during midnight Mass Jack Bronson was also in church and he got a text message on his phone about the explosion! He was sitting six pews in front of the Brown family and he went over to them. "John I have bad news; your house blew up!"

"Oh my God!" Claudette cried. Then the police came in the church to get the Brown family. They went to the house and the fire trucks were putting out the flames. "Oh my God!!!!!!!!!!!!!!!!!!!!!!!" Claudette cried.

Then the police asked questions. "Mr. John Brown, do you remember the last thing before you left the house?" asked the police.

"About 10:00 p.m. I noticed there was no heat in the house so I went down to check the boiler and the pilot was out. I relit the pilot and the heat came on. The house was warm before we went to church."

"It could be a gas explosion because the fire department smelled gas while fighting the fire; we'll find out soon. I hope you have insurance on the home!" said the police.

"Yes, of course! I have Liberty Mutual!" said John.

"The statue of the Virgin Mary is very pretty, maybe she saved everyone tonight," said the police.

"Thank you," said John. The Brown family watched in horror after the fire was put out. All you could see was the lit Virgin Mary statue and a Christmas tree on the other side of the yard, then suddenly the Deopolo ghost appeared standing between them with her arms spread out!

Claudette and Dorothy screamed hysterically! "I just saw the Deopolo ghost standing between the Christmas tree and the Virgin Mary statue! Dorothy saw it too!" Claudette cried.

"You've got to be kidding! Maybe she has something to do with this!" said John.

"We lost all our Christmas gifts!" Dorothy cried.

"This is the worst Christmas we'll ever have," said Ronny.

"What are we going to do?" groaned Turner Brown.

"We have to go to a hotel for the rest of the night and deal with this after Christmas," said John.

"Dad, can we go for a walk through the yard and in the woods? Maybe our Christmas gifts may have been blown there!"

"No Franky, if the house disintegrated so did the Christmas gifts!"

The police escorted the Brown family to the Mattapoisett Inn until further notice.

7:02 a.m. the lights on the Virgin Mary and the Christmas tree shut off from a timer. The Mattapoisett, Marion, and Rochester police and fire departments bought Christmas presents for the Brown family with drug money. Later the police found a girl's bike lying near the tin shed in the yard and brought it to the Mattapoisett Inn.

John said, "Oh my God, we should have listened to Franky. Here's your Christmas present Dorothy, police found it near the shed. It's amazing it's in one piece from that explosion, it was blown out of the box!" said John.

Later in the day before dark John and Ronny went to the backyard looking for more Christmas gifts. They searched where the house burned down, in the yard, and out in the woods and came up emptyhanded! It was snowing and it was icy. Then they went back to the Mattapoisett Inn for a nice Christmas dinner. Claudette called the church and a meeting will be held in a couple of days when Christmas is over. The Brown family got Christmas gifts from the police and fire departments and donations from the church.

Later, they went to the realtor to make other arrangements to find another place to live. The Browns moved to the condos near the police station.

December 28th, 2021 an exorcism ceremony at St. Anthony's church.

"Good afternoon, welcome to St. Anthony's church. My name is Father Jonathan and this is Sister Mary Dolores Maria, the head nun here. We are here to get rid of any evil spirits that may be attacking you. Give me a brief description of the ghost you saw on Christmas morning after your home burned down."

"I saw this ghost called the Deopolo that followed us from California when we moved here in July. The ghost is also known as the Debra poltergeist. When the house exploded I had a lit Christmas tree in the backyard and a new statue of the Blessed Virgin Mary. Me and my daughter Dorothy saw the ghost standing between the Christmas tree and the statue," said Claudette Brown.

"What did this ghost look like?" asked Father Jonathan.

"It's a lady in a black button-down dress or coat with white buttons. She has a white face, black eyes, and black hair, and she wears a pulled down hat. She's from the Alaskan Triangle and she lived in the mountains. She's a female demon that haunts the San Andreas Fault all the way to Mexico," said Claudette.

"You people were protected by the Virgin Mary statue. That was the best thing you did, planting that statue of Mary, because without that all six of you could have been killed. John, you were not feeling well and almost decided not to go to midnight Mass that night, but it's a good thing you did because the Blessed Mary was with you," said Sister Mary Dolores Maria.

"Have you people experienced anything else since you've been living there in that house?" asked Father Jonathan.

"Yes, we had nests of killer bees, African honeybees and African bald-head bees or murder hornets the size of small birds, and dead animals in my yard being attacked by these bees. I saw the tree branches move when the wind was not blowing and trees being struck by lightning. Fog in the yard at times too; sometimes the fog is a regular color and sometimes the fog turns black when thunderstorms are coming.

"We came home to find our house ransacked and police told us there was no forced entry. We heard strange noises in the house and some of them sounded scary. One day I had a bonfire burning the dead animals when suddenly the barn and shed mysteriously went up in flames. It was a warm September day and the spray I was using to kill the bees may have ignited from the hot sun or something from hell burned it down!" said John Brown.

"Claudette, did you have any kind of contact with this Deopolo ghost, such as using a spirit board or witchcraft, to make this entity get into your life?" asked the nun, Sister Mary Dolores Maria.

"When I was sixteen in high school we had to write an essay about the history of the Deopolo or the Debra poltergeist. She appeared to me one day in an open field at the high school when I was playing soccer. Then about a year after I saw the Deopolo ghost a few times when I was alone, living in an apartment in Oakland, California. I had nightmares and sleepless nights until I had to hire a paranormal investigator to get rid of it. It took seeing a Catholic priest and an exorcism to get it out of my life."

"Then when we moved here my kids saw this strange woman on the beach and she told them that this ghost followed us from the West Coast and mentioned its name. That freaked me out!" said Claudette.

"This ghost found your weak spot and since you kept contacting it, it never left you despite your moving from one area to another. When you moved here to Mattapoisett the ghost found another ghost to get back to you. Then your kids met this woman ghost. Her name is Maria Cooper, the so-called town drifter. She drew energy from your kids to contact the Deopolo ghost and she gives people a warning on what this ghost is going to do. Somewhere or somehow you must have made this ghost angry for her to come back to you and do what she did. We will find out during the exorcism," said the nun.

"Mr. and Mrs. Brown! Did you realize you were living in a haunted house?" asked the priest.

"No I didn't, but my wife feared something happened here and she felt like it was something bad," said John.

"What did the realtor tell you when you bought the house? Did he say anything about the house being haunted?" asked the priest.

"He told us it was a dream house for our family and told us about the quiet town of Mattapoisett. He showed us the property and gave us choices about buying the house or leasing it. He didn't say anything about a haunted house."

"John, your home has been haunted for years by several demonic spirits. People have been killed there, and the strong Catholic faith that your family has saved you! It could have taken six more lives! This is a wonderful town of beauty but we also have a dark side. We have a lot of ghosts here in Mattapoisett: the Greenman, the red-eyed deer, Maria Cooper the beach ghost, the black mist creature, and the invisible ghost. These five are evil spirits from the native Indians of the Bridgewater Triangle that haunt Plymouth County and settled in Rochester, Marion, and Mattapoisett.

"The swamp monster is a Bigfoot creature, leader of the Bridgewater Triangle, mistakenly of the Greenman. The Greenman ghost rules the land here in Mattapoisett.

"We had another powerful demonic ghost called the Ebenezer, leader of the Bennington Triangle in Vermont. Now when you people moved here something even stronger than the Ebenezer arrived, and we had a bad enough time getting rid of the Ebenezer ghost from Vermont. It has killed people here and it has taken over your home. It attached to other people and we had to call paranormal investigators and strong priests such as the friars of Providence College and Georgetown University out of Washington D.C. The Ebenezer came back six years later following another family from Vermont and we had to do the same process all over again.

"The Bermuda Triangle also has a female demon by the name of Emma Grace. The Emma Grace spirit of the Bermuda Triangle is the most deadly demon on earth due to sinking ships, airplanes falling out of the sky, and hurricanes. Emma Grace is the world's biggest killer!

"The Connecticut Devil is also a female. The native Moodus Indians in Connecticut believe that the creature came from the planet Venus. They think it came from a meteor and it was a dragon creature that sprays fire like Godzilla!

"I don't know what we are in store for, but the Deopolo ghost haunts Alaska all the way to Mexico, a powerful demon covering a wide area. We do not know much about the Deopolo ghost on the West Coast but what we do know is that she's a double-edged sword and she's also known as the Debra poltergeist. We do not know if she is part of a series of demons or she's two in one; we have to find out!

"If you read the Bible it says that there'll be a time the devil will take over the world and we must be prepared. Are these demonic spirits coming from another planet like the native Indians believe? We don't know. They are here and we need to pray to keep them away!

"This exorcism is going to be a three-day series starting here at the church then we go to your property. After that we go to where you're staying now. When that's done your last address in California will need an exorcism.

"We will begin the exorcism ceremony here in the church saying prayers with all six of your family with Sister Mary Dolores Maria. Tomorrow friars from Providence College will meet us where the house burned down. Then we go to the condo where you're living now for the third day. On that same day friars from Georgetown University will perform the exorcism on your last residence in California. Daily Dot realtors will cover all costs of the exorcisms. We are dealing with something much stronger than the Ebenezer ghost. I hope we can help you.

"To summarize, day one is here at St. Anthony's church. Day two will be at the 66 6th Street burned out property. Third day is the military police condos and at same time your previous California residence with the Georgetown friars. Before we begin, are there any questions?" said the priest.

"Yes, if the new owners at the California address do not want the exorcism or if they're not religious, what happens?" asked Claudette.

"The spirit will get them because we're going to send the Deopolo Debra back to where she came from and when she leaves the first place she's going to visit is where you used to live. Whatever it did to you people, it's going to happen to them! If nobody is there the exorcism will still take place. If buyers are there they will not refuse the exorcism, trust me!" said the priest. Everyone laughed.

"We will begin by saying prayers from the book of St. Michael the archangel to release the devil. We need to send the Deopolo Debra back to the Alaskan Triangle where she came from. Paranormal investigators and demonic psychics will be at the 66 6th Street burn site and that's when we will find the energy from the Deopolo Debra. Let's get started by saying prayers to St. Michael," said the priest.

After the church exorcism they went to the property the next day, December 29, 2021 saying prayers during a snowstorm and it was ten degrees outside with a strong wind and blowing snow. The priest and the nun and friars from Providence College and Jean Jazzman from the real estate office were there. The day's exorcism took place beginning on the burn site. Jean Jazzman started getting sick and she threw up on the burned ashes and collapsed. She was taken to the hospital in a rescue van. The Brown family of six stood on the ashes wearing thick winter coats, hats, gloves, and warm winter boots. Claudette was hysterical when Jean got sick.

The priest said, "Don't worry, she will be okay. The exorcism may make you sick and you could see spirits. The ceremony may get scary but we're here to protect you because the evil spirits are no match for God's people and we have them outnumbered! If you see something or get sick just ignore it and keep praying, they cannot hurt you during an exorcism. They can knock you down or make you fall but they can't hurt you while we are here. It's like a big crowd overtaking a few people! Same thing here, we will hurt every evil spirit in Mattapoisett by the time this powerful exorcism is over!"

The priest started saying the prayers as everyone followed. Then more prayers were said around the lit Christmas tree and finished in front of the Virgin Mary statue. There were no ghostly visions and nobody got sick and day two went smoothly after Jean Jazzman got sick.

Unfortunately, the Deopolo ghost went into Jean Jazzman because she's not protected. She was attacked before the exorcism began because the Deopolo Debra knows she's in for a big fight against powerful priests, nuns, and friars! So she picks on someone weak to strike to stay alive and attack the other spirits in Mattapoisett to see if she's welcome to the evil clique. The powerful Ebenezer from Vermont was not welcome and the powerful priest did a good job getting rid of him after two strikes and a third strike can't happen unless he's invited in from witchcraft, but the Deopolo Debra is much stronger! The priest said just a few prayers to protect Jean Jazzman before she went to the hospital but it's not going to be enough, the fuckin thing is inside her!

Toby Hospital, Wareham, Massachusetts. A doctor came in to ask Jean Jazzman some questions. "Hi Jean, how are you feeling?"

"I'm fine Doctor."

"So tell me, what happened to you that landed you in the hospital?"

"I was at an exorcism ceremony when suddenly I felt like something hit me in the stomach so hard it made me sick! I started throwing up and then I passed out and I woke up in the hospital."

"Well Jean you're okay and you can go home now. We found no injuries or anything wrong with you and you're okay," said the doctor.

Jean called one of her friends to come pick her up at the hospital and bring her to her car located at the burn site at 66 6th Street and she drove home.

The next day, December 30, 2021, was the third day of the exorcism located at the military police condos where the Browns are staying. The PC friars, Father Jonathan, and Sister Mary Dolores Maria finished the exorcism there.

"When we finish the exorcism we will go back to the church and finish the ceremony and answer questions. We will begin at 2:00 p.m. The residents on the West Coast must start at 11:00 a.m. Pacific time. The exorcisms must start at the same time to make it work. We will be in contact with the new residents at the same time with prayers," said the priest.

13435 Firestorm Way, Oakland, California is where the Brown family from Mattapoisett used to live. About 10:15 a.m. Pacific time, Catholic priests and Georgetown friars and nuns arrived.

"Good morning, are you Mrs. Pauline Colchester?"

"Yes!"

"My name is Father Frank from St. Anthony's church in Mattapoisett, Massachusetts and I am with Sister Cindy Sledge and Father Richard McKenny from St. John's parish here in Oakland, along with friars from Georgetown University. We are here to perform an exorcism because the Brown family who lived here before was involved with a very powerful demon ghost called the Deopolo Debra from the Alaskan Triangle.

"Their home blew up in a gas explosion on Christmas Eve while they were attending midnight Mass. Claudette Brown and her daughter Dorothy saw the Deopolo ghost apparition after the fire sparking a national Catholic exorcism to remove this ghost during a three-day ceremony, and today they are in their third session at their new home. The exorcism will begin at 2:00 p.m. eastern time. We have to begin here at 11:00 a.m. and communicate with them to clear the Deopolo Debra. You have two choices: accept the exorcism and we will say prayers together to remove this entity from both addresses, or reject the offer and the Deopolo Debra will come here and haunt your residence and it will get physical—look what happened to them!" said the priest.

The Colchesters accepted. The two families followed prayers from a computer with Skype. Later in Mattapoisett the Brown family went back to St. Anthony's church.

"Mr. and Mrs. Brown, according to the pictures shown here from the killer bees and murder hornets, wasps this size don't exist! This is work from the devil! We released several demons you were trapped with living at 66 6th Street. The Virgin Mary statue you installed there saved you because the Deopolo ghost wanted you dead along with the other evil spirit trying to get your souls.

"My name is Crystal St. Catherine, a nun psychic from Providence College. Keep saying your prayers and stay away from Ouija boards. Do not practice witchcraft because if you do you may lose your life next time."

Later final prayers were heard then the Brown family went home to their new condo and they were never haunted by any ghosts again! The Colchester family in Oakland living in the Brown's former residence, was also saved from the Deopolo Debra.

December 31, 2021, a Friday. Jean Jazzman will not be so lucky. She was trying to sell a home in Marion then she went to the real estate office and had a meeting with other realtors there.

"Good morning. As you know, we lost a home at 66 6th Street that blew up on Christmas morning from a gas explosion. The Brown family was at midnight Mass at St. Anthony's church, thank God no one died there! That house has been haunted since the 1970s and it has gone through several real estate agents trying to sell this home. Every time the home is sold something happens there; people have died there. The property is haunted by ghosts.

"We have another home on Green Street that's haunted. It was vacant for thirteen years through different realtors. Me being the manager of Daily Dot Realtors, I don't want to put another house there. I will sell the land and the new owners will decide what they want to do with the property. I will tell them what happened because I do not want another house on that property!" said Jean Jazzman.

Lunchtime, Jean was warming a sandwich up in the microwave and she took a coffee mug out of the cabinet and put it on the counter. She went to get her sandwich out of the microwave and the coffee mug flew off the counter, crashing into a wall and smashing in tiny pieces as Jean watched in shock!

She screamed! "Aaaaahhhhhhhhhhh!!!!!! Gloria we have a ghost here or something! I was getting my sandwich from the microwave and the coffee mug I put down flew off the counter and smashed up against that wall. I could not believe what I just saw!"

They cleaned up the broken glass with a dustpan and broom then Gloria Stevens and Jean Jazzman had lunch together with no further incidents. Jean said, "A few days ago I was called to an exorcist performance where the home exploded at 66 6th Street. Something hit me in the stomach and it felt like something was going inside me, I can't explain! Then I got sick throwing up and I passed out and I ended up in the hospital. When I got there I was feeling better and the doctor said that I was okay, so I went home.

"I was never a believer in ghosts, demons, or whatever! The people who lived there said they saw ghosts. I have heard many stories about haunted houses but I always believed they were hoaxes! I thought it was their imaginations but when I saw that coffee mug fly off the counter by itself and crash into the wall I believed there was something supernatural! I don't believe something from the dead is going to pick something up and throw it at you! I do believe the Earth's magnetic field and solar energy may have something to do with it!" said Jean Jazzman.

"One day I was showing the house at 6 Green Street and I saw a table move and a chair slide across the floor and a chandelier swing back and forth!" said Gloria Stevens, a real estate worker.

"It's magnetic solar activity! Let's stop talking about ghost stories and I'll see you at my New Year's Eve party. I hope 2022 will be better than 2021 because 2020 sucked too! See you tonight," said Jean Jazzman.

She went out to get food and booze and she went home to start cooking. She lives alone in a small mansion in Hollywood Beach and she's expecting about fifty people tonight: policemen, firemen, military personnel, doctors, nurses, lawyers, and real estate brokers. All rich people and sophisticated professionals attend this party. Jean Jazzman is a rich bitch but the ghosts don't care!!!

Jean left the office around 2:00 p.m. Then she and some of her friends were doing the cooking. A brief shadow of the Deopolo ghost appeared near the fireplace around 5:00 p.m. when it was getting dark, but no one noticed.

It was zero degrees when people were showing up. Hors d'oeuvres were passed around and Jell-O shots of Yukon Jack, and people were smoking pot, hash, and cocaine. There were gin drinks, Jack Daniels, Absolut vodka, brandy, whisky, bourbon, beer, wine of all kinds. Everyone had good food and they all were drunk before the disc-jockey showed up.

The DJ started playing about 9:30 p.m. and the crowd was dancing by 10:00 p.m. The DJ had two big speakers, a computer and a large video screen, a disco ball, and lights, and the party went all night long! "Ladies and gentlemen, welcome to Jean Jazzman's New Year's Eve party, my name is DJ Big Dick playing your favorite tunes tonight!"

Food, snacks, booze, and drugs were being passed around all night into the early dawn with people partying, dancing, and some sex along the way! 11:00 p.m. the DJ released the fog machine filling the room with lights and lasers shining in it. 11:02 p.m. a black mist appeared above the DJ and hands and arms came out of it briefly. The crowd thought it was part of the show and it disappeared a minute later. It was the evil black mist ghost! Then the countdown for the New Year showing the Times Square celebration in New York. Then Happy New Year!!!!!!!!!!!!! 2022!

A short time later the power went out! Everyone was screaming, "Oh no!!!!!!!!!!!!!!!!!!" The time was 12:02 a.m. Then the lights and the music came back on a minute later and the party resumed. The DJ played "Celebration" by Kool and the Gang and the party was going wild! A mysterious force was pushing people down on the crowded wood dancefloor area in front of the DJ during a song, "Get a little bit funky now, lower and lower." The time was 1:02 a.m. when the dancing crowd kept getting pushed down to the floor. People standing around drinking were also being forced to the ground or fell. People having sex or doing drugs were sterile! The force stopped a minute later while the song was still playing.

2:02 a.m. the DJ was playing a slow song and a loud roar came through the speakers sounding like a bear. It continued roaring like a wild animal for a minute, then stopped. The DJ was checking his equipment to find out where this noise was coming from and everything went back to normal.

3:02 a.m. a voice came through the DJ's speakers again, *"Get out! Get out! Get out!!!!"* The song the DJ was playing didn't make sense and it went back to normal a minute later.

At 3:30 a.m. the party was still in full force and the DJ was playing fast dance music and the crowd was going wild, not knowing ghosts are haunting the New Year's Eve party!

4:02 a.m. a growling noise started coming through the DJ's speakers and it started soft, got louder, then it went to normal a minute later. The DJ knows growls from animals or a wild dog don't come from this song. He was checking his equipment again then he mixed in another song and everything went back to normal.

At 4:30 a.m. the party was breaking up and a few stags and couples remain.

At 5:00 a.m. the DJ was still playing. 5:02 a.m. the DJ was mixing another song and the stereo shut down and everything went quiet! A minute later the DJ's stereo came back on, mixing in the song by itself.

The DJ joked, "I had plenty to drink tonight and I'm having a great time playing music but a lot of strange things are happening here. Animals don't roar or cry through my speakers and the equipment keeps shutting down and playing by itself; this never happened to me before! Do you have a dog, big cat, or a lion in here!??"

Jean Jazzman laughed! She said, "Here's six hundred dollars, you did a great job tonight Big Dick," and she kissed the DJ, sticking her tongue in Big Dick's mouth! Then the DJ took down his equipment with some help and he heard a growl going to his van, the time was 6:02 a.m. Jean heard it too! The DJ called her on his cellphone.

"Jean there is something out here, it sounds like a bear or a big animal so be careful!"

"I heard it too, it's something outside," said Jean.

A few people slept over for the night. It was starting to get light and it was snowing outside and Jean saw a deer in her yard with red eyes. Jean closed the blinds and she went to bed with a man from the party. It was 7:02 a.m. when she saw the deer. She fell asleep with the man after having sex with him.

Then the door in the bedroom burst open at 8:02 a.m. and she saw a woman standing there with a white face, black hair, black eyes, big tits, a button-down black dress with white buttons, and black shoes.

Jean said, "Excuse me, but you're in the wrong room, I thought you left already." Then she turned around and she walked away. The woman closed the bedroom door going out and she vanished in the hallway. She was the Deopolo Debra ghost!

Jean said to her partner, "I don't remember seeing that lady before! She must be a party crasher, not something I haven't seen before!"

"Maybe she was a ghost!" the man joked! Jean laughed. Then Jean woke up to something pushing her down on the bed and she couldn't move until it released her a minute later. The time was 9:02 a.m. when the invisible force held her down.

She sat up on the bed for a minute and the room was going around because she had a big headache. Then she woke up an hour later and she ran to the bathroom, puking her brains out. The time was 10:02 a.m. when she threw up. It went for a full minute then stopped, after which she crawled back to bed.

She woke up hearing a crow outside her bedroom window and it was 11:02 a.m. When she heard the crow acting up she looked out the window and the black bird was on the window ledge looking at her. Then the crow flew away and she closed the window shade and she went back to bed.

At 12:02 p.m. she had a dream the Ebenezer ghost was on top of her ready to choke her with his big hands and his red eyes lit up like Rudolph the Red-Nosed Reindeer. She woke up out of a sound sleep heavy breathing!

"Are you okay?" asked her partner.

"I just had a bad dream about a ghost I heard about when I was living in Vermont!" she said.

Jean Jazzman doesn't realize that she's being haunted by ghosts at two minutes after every hour in her mansion home in Hollywood Beach.

She woke up again around 1:02 p.m. to go get a bottle of water out of the refrigerator and she saw a green colored mist moving across the snow along the beach outside her window.

Then she got up to start cleaning up from last night's party. People staying over were still in bed and some started leaving. "Bye Fred, Happy New Year! Bye Donald, Happy New Year! Bye Jeff and Jenn, Happy New Year! Bye Kevin and Nate, Happy New Year! Bye Linda, Happy New Year! Bye Gordon and Brenda, Happy New Year! Bye Alison and Happy New Year! Bye Bobby, Happy New Year!" said Jean Jazzman.

2:02 p.m. a glass fell off a counter in the kitchen and broke on the floor. She cleaned it up. She was bringing black trash bags filled with beer and liquor bottles out to the trash bins behind her garage and she saw a big black shadow go by.

The time was 3:02 p.m. and she said, "Ebenezer, if that's you; you better get lost because you do not belong here!" Then she went in the house and she attacked her partner in the bedroom with a violent sexual aggression, growling and roaring at her friend like a wild animal. The time of the attack was 4:02 p.m. and she didn't stop until a minute later.

The man said, "Jean, are you crazy! What the hell are you doing!" He had a hell of a fight trying to get her off of him! Then she was normal. The man said, "What animal got into you! You were not like this last night, you were gentle like a lamb and now you attack me like a lion! Look what you did to me, I'm covered with blood and I have scratches all over me, and bite marks!"

"Oh my God! How did this happen!?"

"You attacked me and you were growling like a lion and roaring like a bear. You jumped on top of me scratching me and biting my face, arms, and body until I was bleeding. I had to push you off of me before you kill me!" said the man.

"Oh Louie, I'm so sorry I don't remember anything! There have been some strange things happening in this house since last night and I fear I might have a ghost in here! I was taking out some trash and I saw a black shadow go by and before that a glass fell off the counter and broke on the floor and before *that* I saw a deer with red eyes glowing outside. I thought that was strange, then there were black crows looking at me from outside my windows. Come in the bathroom and I'll wash the blood off of you and put some bandages on you," said Jean.

The man took a shower and Jean fixed him up from her attack. The man said, "I never believed in ghosts until I came to this party, and only because I heard a lot of strange noises from the DJ. He must have invited something in here then something got inside of you because I've known you for at least five years and nothing like this has ever happened. You were like...the devil was inside of you," said the man.

"Again, I'm sorry about the attack because I don't remember doing this to you. Get dressed and I'll fix you something to eat," said Jean.

The man was looking in the mirror and he saw a black demonic face that definitely wasn't his! Jean saw something black running into her dining room at the same time the man saw the ghost vision in the bathroom mirror. He screamed and he ran out of the bathroom. The time of the visions happened at 5:02 p.m.!

The man said, "I'm out of here! I'll see you at the office because I just saw the devil's head in the bathroom mirror!" The man grabbed his coat and he was out the door and he drove to the hospital to get more treatments for Jean Jazzman's sexual attack!

6:02 p.m. her cellphone rang with a voice saying, "*Get out!*" three times, then stopped. She put some wood in the fireplace and she got a fire going and she grabbed a glass of wine. She sat crying in front of the fireplace and suddenly the fire went out at 7:02 p.m. and came back a minute later.

She said to herself, "Something's strange in this house!" Now Jean Jazzman is by herself in her house.

She finished cleaning up after last night's party then she had a sandwich and a salad sitting by the fire with a glass of wine. Then she saw a flash of lightning outside and the time was 8:02 p.m. She got up and she looked out the window, turning a flashlight on, and it was snowing hard so she's not going anywhere tonight! Then she heard thunder. Then she put the dishes in the sink after eating, then she grabbed another glass of wine and she sat in front of the fireplace. Then she fell asleep.

Then something was blowing in her ears waking her up. The time was 9:02 p.m. and she got up looking around and she saw nothing. Then she called her friend on her cellphone when suddenly the lights went out at 10:02 p.m. "My lights went out and I'm in my own home being haunted from strange things happening since last night's party!"

While Jean was talking on her phone the lights came back on. Then she took a shower and she put her PJs on and she was getting ready for bed.

She closed all the shades in the house and she made sure the doors and windows were locked.

"Nobody's coming in now unless they break a window to get in!" Jean said to herself. Then she finished washing the dishes and putting them away and sat down in front of the fireplace with her glass of wine to keep warm. Then she fell asleep.

Then she heard someone in the kitchen and she got up to investigate, and she saw the Ebenezer demonic ghost, a big dark figure as black as the ace of spades with red eyes and big hands, scarier than the devil!

Jean screamed hysterically! "Aaaaaaaaaaaaaaaahhhhhhhhhh!!!!!!!!!" Then she picked up a vase and threw it at the Ebenezer ghost's head and it went right through the big dark ghostly figure. Ebenezer reached out his long arms and big hands and he grabbed Jean Jazzman by the throat and picked her up and shook her like a ragdoll, choking her to death. He dropped her to the floor and he vanished! The time of the attack was 11:02 p.m. finishing the twenty-four-hour hauntings in Jean Jazzman's house and now she's dead!

A few minutes later the Deopolo Debra was standing over her to make sure she's dead! A strong gust of wind blew down the chimney the still-burning fire in the fireplace was blown in the house. The burning wood set the house on fire and the house quickly burned to the ground with Jean Jazzman's dead body in it! The Deopolo Debra ghost was standing in the flames while the house was burning down! Just like the Christmas day fire at 66 6th Street. Fire trucks, police cars, and a rescue team raced to the Hollywood Beach fire in eight inches of snow and when they got there the vision of the Deopolo Debra disappeared!

The Ebenezer had always been in Jean Jazzman's soul from Vermont to when she moved to Mattapoisett, all while working for Bennington Realtors of Vermont, now Daily Dot Realtors. What happened when she was called to the St. Anthony's exorcism performance was the Deopolo Debra got into her soul unprotected because the priest did little to pray for her and she got sick, ending up in the hospital. The connection with two super powered ghosts had them attacking one another, leading to Jean Jazzman's death.

The Deopolo Debra is much more powerful than the Ebenezer. One is a male and the other a female demon but it doesn't matter for strength and power. The Ebenezer was only able to attack Jean Jazzman because she had no protection. The Ebenezer was forced out of Mattapoisett twice by strong Catholic exorcisms and now the Deopolo Debra was pushed out and forced to return to Alaska where she's from. However, she found a weak link in Jean Jazzman before she returned back home to the West Coast.

The Ebenezer killed Jean Jazzman, choking her to death, because he was pissed that another much more powerful ghost entered her soul. The Deopolo Debra overtook the Ebenezer after he killed Jean Jazzman, forcing him to flee back to Vermont to be with his contacts. The only strength the Ebenezer had left in Mattapoisett was his return with Jean Jazzman. The Ebenezer was forced to kill Jean Jazzman and move on or be overtaken by the Deopolo Debra.

The Deopolo Debra finished the job, burning Jean Jazzman's house down. She is also not welcome in the Bridgewater Triangle clique or on the southeastern Massachusetts paranormal scene. The Deopolo Debra went back to the West Coast to her clan because she no longer has power in Mattapoisett because of the Catholic power.

Back to the January 2nd fire in Hollywood Beach. The firemen put the fire out in a couple of hours and Jean Jazzman's body was discovered. No ghosts were seen. Then the evening news.

"Good evening and Happy New Year to everyone, but the news is not good in Mattapoisett where there was another fire, this time in Hollywood Beach, and a woman was found dead there! The fire was believed to be caused by a faulty chimney. The dead woman is not yet identified.

"Early Christmas day, a fire from a gas explosion burned down a house at 66 6th Street. Luckily the six people living there were all at midnight Mass and there were no injuries at this fire. This is Lisa Canotch reporting from Channel 6 Sunday Evening News on January 2, 2022."

The next day police and firemen believe they know what might have caused the fire at Jean Jazzman's house: ghosts!!!!!! The firemen and police know about all the hauntings and ghosts in Mattapoisett. They were told about the new powerful ghost in town along with the Ebenezer. Plows were moving the snow and the police were writing up reports while the firemen were going through the burned down home to find out the cause.

"Officer Lecter, we have the report of a chimney fire here," said a fireman.

Jean Jazzman's body was taken to the Fairhaven morgue and the coroners were working on the cause. The phone rang at the Mattapoisett police station. "Mattapoisett police, Archie Antilli speaking."

"Hi, this is Newman Springs from the coroner's office in Fairhaven, Massachusetts. I have the report on the death of Miss Jean Jazzman at

877 Hollywood Road. She was strangled to death by an unknown force and the marks on her neck were not from a human. It was from some kind of animal, a very strong animal like a possible bear attack!"

The police called the paranormal investigating team to identify the official death of Jean Jazzman. "She was killed by a ghost! Not one, but two of them!"

# SIXTEEN

## The Never-Ending Terror in Mattapoisett

*Tuesday January 4, 2022 at the Daily Dot real estate office in Marion*

"Good morning, my name is Gloria Stevens, the new manager of Daily Dot, and I have two paranormal investigators here, Mrs. Linda Springer and Mr. Larry Legend. Happy New Year! The year is not starting off the way we would like it. As you know Miss Jean Jazzman was found dead in her home on Sunday morning. Her home burned down due to a chimney fire, but the autopsy on her body showed strangulation from a wild animal or bear. According to Larry Legend's report she was strangled by the Ebenezer ghost and the Deopolo Debra finished her. Here's Mr. Larry Legend."

"Thank you Gloria. Miss Jazzman had marks consistent with the strangulation of the Ebenezer ghost. The Ebenezer was a demon from Vermont called to Mattapoisett through a spirit board from a family that moved to Mattapoisett from Vermont, inviting Ebenezer in. The spirit clique from here did not accept the powerful demon and it went on the attack. Catholic exorcisms forced the Ebenezer out and it went back to Vermont. Then a few years later the Bennington Realtors of Vermont arrived in Mattapoisett, now called Daily Dot. Miss Jean Jazzman, who is not religious, was into witchcraft in her younger days and practiced with the Ebenezer and brought the demon back here and it started killing people!

"The Ebenezer demon was an evil killer! The Catholics had to get rid of it again with national exorcisms with friars from PC and Georgetown University after it left a trail of death and destruction! But his soul was still with Miss Jazzman because she's not religious and she was not protected during the Catholic performances.

"When a more powerful ghost takes over a soul it takes about forty-eight hours to make its move because the Ebenezer has no power here anymore, only enough to pick on someone weak like Miss Jazzman. When the Deopolo Debra demon took over her soul, the Ebenezer killed her to get released. The Deopolo Debra took over after she was dead and she has something to do with the house burning down.

"Beyond the dead is a hard thing to understand! The Deopolo Debra was also removed from the Catholic Church and she had to finish the job of overruling the Ebenezer before she could go back to the West Coast to keep her power."

"Thank you Larry."

"My name is Linda Springer. When the Catholic Church moves these demons, don't call them back because they will come back as deadly as ever! We have other ghosts here that come and go and they have been here a lot longer than the Ebenezer or the Deopolo. Those two demons can be moved because they're not from here or in our clan and both are not welcomed in the Bridgewater Triangle or the Hockomock swamplands. They have their place to stay and we have ours.

"The Greenman, the red-eyed deer, the Mattapoisett Beach ghost, the black mist, and the invisible ghost will always be here. The Catholic Church can move these ghosts from haunted properties but they will return as soon as someone else moves into the property; that's how ghosts work. The house at 66 6th Street has been haunted for years; that's why all the ghosts go there, they all follow one another."

"Thank you Linda. One: We need to get the Catholic Church to do an exorcism on Jean Jazzman's property so these powerful ghosts don't come again. Two: We will not build homes on those properties. For now 6 Green Street is on its own. However, if that house goes down we will not rebuild," said Gloria Stevens.

Six months later, July 2022, the home at 6 Green Street was sold and the Lang family moved in. Larry Lang, fifty-eight; Lucy Lang, fifty-six; Cindy Lang, twenty-two; and Victoria Lang, eighteen.

Larry and Lucy are schoolteachers at Old Rochester Regional High School and Cindy works at a craft store now located at 66 6th Street.

Victoria will be going to college but for now she works at Dunkin' Donuts.

Gloria Stevens met the family at the house. A turkey vulture landed on the chimney of the house then two more landed on the roof, flapping their wings.

"You must be Mrs. Gloria Stevens showing the house," said Larry.

"Yes, please come in. It looks like you have company up there, some big birds to watch your house when you're not home."

"This is a small house with two bedrooms and the house is furnished. You have a pullout bed in the living room. Let me push that back in, it shouldn't be out right now. You have the kitchen, dining room, and living room with a big stone fireplace; this is a warm house during the winter. We had a bad winter this past season. I forgot to show you the separate building to this house and it has a third bedroom. It used to be a garage but it was renovated and converted into a third bedroom with a bath. This house is bigger than it looks. This property has a small yard but you have no basement.

"The retail price is $275,000, but if you buy today it's $175,000. That's a great bargain for Mattapoisett!" said Gloria.

Larry bought the house. They slept in the separate building. Cindy slept in one room and Victoria slept in the other room. Cindy said, "This house is spooky and scary looking."

"I like it; this home is completely renovated and furnished and it's all new. We will be here forever!" said Lucy.

The family had a little black dog by the name of Mookie, it's a male dog named after Mookie Betts, a former Boston Red Sox player. The family put posters and pictures of Boston sports teams, the Red Sox, Patriots, Celtics, and Bruins all over the house. The dog kept looking around in the house, walking from one room to another, and his dog bed was in the kitchen.

7:02 p.m. After dinner Victoria took the dog for a walk and she looked on top of the roof and the three turkey vultures were still there. Then she went for a walk with the dog, and when she got back a fourth vulture landed on the roof. The dog was barking at them and two of them flew off! Then she went in the house.

Bedtime, the house was dark and quiet but the dog was still walking around keeping the house in check. Larry and Lucy were in bed and they heard the turkey vultures making noise until midnight. Larry went out with a whistle and five of them were up there. He blew the whistle and finally the birds flew off!

The black birds are the devil bringing in the ghosts. 6 Green Street is also haunted and the Lang family will find out soon. The rest of the night was quiet.

The next day Cindy got a job at a new craft store and met Gloria Stevens again, as she also owns the store. The store has arts and crafts, dolls, and crystals.

Cindy comes in. She says, "You look like the lady who sold us the house at 6 Green Street."

"Yes, I'm Gloria Stevens, how can I help you?"

"I'm looking for a job, are you hiring?"

"Yes, I need someone at least three days a week six hours a day. Tuesdays, Thursdays, and Saturdays from 10:00 a.m. until 4:00 p.m.," said Gloria.

The next day was Saturday and Cindy showed up and opened the store. She set things up and then she sat and waited for customers. Dolls in the store started dancing by themselves and singing. Things started moving around in the store. Then everything went quiet. Then a turkey vulture landed outside looking in at her and she shoved the bird off with a broom. A few minutes later the dolls started dancing again and singing, then stopped, and it was quiet. She picked up one of the dolls and she couldn't find out why they were singing and dancing.

Then she heard a noise when she was in the restroom. A glass figure of the Virgin Mary flew across the store up against a wall and smashed into pieces; it made a loud noise! When Cindy Lang came out of the restroom the outside door entering the store closed and locked! She saw the mess from the flying glass and she called Gloria on the phone.

"Someone broke into the store, broke a glass, and ran out and shut the door. I couldn't find the person!"

"Cindy stay put! Don't touch anything, don't clean anything up, and wait until I get there. I should be there in ten or fifteen minutes!" said Gloria Stevens.

Then another glass piece fell on the floor and slid over to Cindy's feet lying flat down. Cindy Lang was shocked! Then a black shadow whipped by her and her hair blew straight up like the wind was blowing her hair, but there was no wind.

Then Gloria arrived. Cindy was sitting outside the store on the steps.

"What's the matter Cindy, did the ghost chase you out!?" Gloria laughed.

"You have something paranormal here! First I thought someone broke in when I heard glass breaking, then I saw a glass vase or something fall off the counter and slide across the floor to my feet as I watched in shock! Then I saw a black shadow blow by me and a gust of wind blew my hair straight up in the air and there's no wind. It was the longest fifteen minutes of my life waiting for you. I can't work in this kind of environment, there's a ghost here or something," Cindy said.

"There was a house here about seven months ago that burned down from a gas explosion. The six people living there were not home when it happened, thank God. But the home and the property here have been haunted for years. There were two fires at that house. First the barn and shed burned down and then the house last Christmas morning.

"The Daily Dot Real Estate decided to build something else other than a house and a Virgin Mary statue was placed where the barn used to be before it burned down. The construction for this little craft store called Gloria's Arts here started in March and finished in mid-June. This store has been open only three weeks and you're the second person who reported strange happenings with things moving around and breaking!" said Gloria Stevens.

Gloria started picking up things and moving items around while Cindy was sweeping up the broken glass with a dustpan and broom and dumping it into a wastebasket. Then an antique grandfather clock started rocking back and forth and fell, smashing the glass door and clock. Then it slid across the floor from one side of the store to the other, smashing into a table, and several priceless artwork vases, glasses, and pictures broke into pieces. The crash totally destroyed the six-thousand-dollar grandfather clock and the mahogany wood frame structure broke apart!

Cindy and Gloria screamed hysterically together! "Aaaaaahhhhh!!!!!!"

Then Gloria said, "Cindy get out quickly! Something's evil here!"

While Cindy and the owner of the craft store at 66 6th Street off Route 6 were being haunted, the other sister had issues at home at 6 Green Street. The parents were out shopping and Victoria was home alone. Victoria was at home looking for work on her computer and a voice came over her computer, *"Get out!!!!!! Get out!!!!! Get out!!!!!!!!!!!!!!!!"* She was on Indeed.com looking for work when the screen changed on her computer telling her to get out! Then her computer shut off all by itself and she couldn't turn it back on, so she closed the lid and she put the computer away.

Then she went outside with a blanket to lie in the sun and she saw a big black dog or wolf with red eyes growling and coming at her. She started screaming and running to get in the house then three big black turkey vultures attacked her, biting her ears, her neck, face, and legs. She kept fighting the birds off of her as they kept biting her and she ran up Green Street covered in blood. The birds were still attacking Victoria as she kept fighting with them, pulling them off of her and punching and kicking the giant black birds with red eyes!

Victoria knows karate but it didn't do any good; the vultures attacked her until she ran to another house to get help. The people there fought the birds off her and got her safely in the house before they called for help. She was covered in blood with bite marks and cuts all over her. Then a rescue team came to take her to Toby Hospital in Wareham.

Cindy came home and she saw a trail of blood and she was shocked! Later Victoria called the house and she told Cindy what happened. "Don't go outside, there're devil birds and a devil wolf outside, they almost killed me!"

Then Larry and Lucy came home with bundles of food and clothes and Cindy cried, "It's a bad day today! Victoria's in the hospital, she was attacked by the birds on the roof and a wolf in the yard with red eyes! There's blood all over the yard!!!!!!!!!!!!!!"

Larry Lang grabbed his shotgun and he went out three times, looking up on the roof for the birds but they were gone. He went looking in the woods and around the property and he found nothing. He put the gun in his car and he and Lucy went to the hospital to see her.

Cindy was in a coma—she was just about eaten alive! Her ears were practically bitten off just like Evander Holyfield when Mike Tyson bit his ears off in a boxing match; she looked just like him! Her titty nipples were bitten off! Her nose was gone! Her lips were chopped up like spareribs on a bone! Her eyes were plucked out! Her legs looked like she was attacked by a lion or bear! She looks like she's going die!!!!!!!!!!!!!!!!!!

Lucy threw up on the floor at the hospital and Larry puked in a toilet. When they got back home at 8:02 p.m. the killer vultures on the roof were not there! They were having dinner, spareribs on a bone, and there was thunder and lightning outside.

"Mom and Dad, how is Victoria?" Cindy cried.

"She's in a coma because she was bitten up pretty good, but I think she will be okay. She just needs to heal for a while," said her mom, Lucy Lang.

"I can't wait to see those birds again because I'll blow them away like a fuckin squash pumpkin!!!!!!!!!!!!!!!!!!!!!!!!!!!!!" said Larry.

"Dad, I was haunted on my new job today at Gloria's Arts and Crafts store at 66 6th Street. I was having a shit in the restroom when suddenly I heard glass breaking and a door closing and locking. I thought someone had broken in. I called Gloria and she told me not to do anything until she got there in ten or fifteen minutes. Then I saw this glass vase or something fly off the shelf and slide all the way to my feet; that freaked me out. Then she came to help me clean up the mess. Then a big antique grandfather clock worth thousands of dollars was rocking back and forth and it fell over, sliding across the floor, smashing into a table full of arts and crafts. It broke everything and the wood frames on the clock broke into pieces! Gloria told me to leave because the store on the property was haunted!"

Larry was shocked! After dinner Cindy went bowling with a friend at Wonder Bowl in New Bedford and she bowled a 199 game, her best game ever. Her friend bowled a 179 game; he did good too and it was a good night out.

Bedtime. Cindy didn't come home she stayed at her boyfriend's home after bowling. No hauntings there!

Back at 6 Green Street, Larry and Lucy were in bed and they heard the turkey vultures knocking on the roof, making a noise and being a nuisance! Larry went out to his car and he got the gun out of the trunk. He saw two turkey vultures on the roof of the house and three more on the roof of the separate building where he sleeps. There were five black birds in total, some with red eyes and some with yellow eyes.

He cocked his shotgun and he started shooting at the birds. He blew the first two off of the roof of the spare room and the third one got away. He started shooting at the other three machinegun style and he got two more; only one fucker got away! The birds he shot were lying on the ground still alive flapping their wings and Larry fired more than 150 rounds to finish the mother fuckers!

Then a mean big black wolf with red eyes charged at Larry, leaping for its attack. Larry fired over fifty more rounds to finish off the hauntings!!!!!!!!!!!!!!!! The wolf still charged at Larry as he was shooting it and the charging wolf roared worse than a bear, still managing to knock Larry down, knocking his gun away! He was able to get to his gun and he got into the house.

Just then the police drove up because of all the noise from the gunshots; it sounded like a fuckin warzone. The police arrived at 6 Green Street and they saw the dead turkey vultures lying on the ground blown into pieces and blood splattered everywhere!

The policemen got a good laugh! They said, "Jesus Christ, what the fuck happened here!?"

"Attack birds sir. There were five or six of them and they attacked my daughters and they were ready to attack me and my wife. I went to war with them and finish those motherfuckers! And the red-eyed wolf!!!!!!!!!!"

The police officers laughed, and they said, "Larry! Please keep the noise down!"

Then Larry went to bed. He'll clean up the dead bird mess in the morning!

3:02 a.m. lightning struck the house and the spare room and began burning, forcing them out! The police came, then the fire department as the house at 6 Green Street was burning to the ground.

After the fire was put out, there was still thunder and lightning. A Greenman ghost appeared! Larry and Lucy Lang watched this vision standing over the ashes! It was a green man covered in leaves and he had a straw face like the scarecrow in the Wizard of Oz and a glowing green veil covering his appearance! The Greenman rules the land in Mattapoisett.

*The End*

# ABOUT THE AUTHOR

*A Haunting in Mattapoisett*: A terrifying horror novel written by Richard Rezendes, his third horror novel.

Book one: *Ground of the Devil*
Book two: *The Revelation of Emma Grace*

Made in the USA
Middletown, DE
14 September 2020